S0-BDL-564

PRAISE FOR EVE K. SANDSTROM AND
The Violence Beat

"Fascinating. Nell Matthews shines through as
a strong and unique character. I found myself
looking forward to the next in the series."
—Sue Henry

"Sandstrom writes with confidence.
An impressive debut for a wonderfully
conflicted heroine."
—Margaret Maron

"A good book with great characters, and a
twisting plot. I look forward to further
adventures of Nell Matthews."
—*I Love A Mystery*

"Sandstrom . . . spins a good story."
—*Houston Post*

"Sandstrom unravels an intriguing plot
with an exciting climax."
—*Publishers Weekly*

THE
HOMICIDE
REPORT

Eve K. Sandstrom

AN ONYX BOOK

ONYX
Published by the Penguin Group
Penguin Putnam Inc., 375 Hudson Street,
New York, New York 10014, U.S.A.
Penguin Books Ltd, 27 Wrights Lane,
London W8 5TZ, England
Penguin Books Australia Ltd,
Ringwood, Victoria, Australia
Penguin Books Canada Ltd, 10 Alcorn Avenue,
Toronto, Ontario, Canada M4V 3B2
Penguin Books (N.Z.) Ltd, 182–190 Wairau Road,
Auckland 10, New Zealand

Penguin Books Ltd, Registered Offices:
Harmondsworth, Middlesex, England

First published by Onyx, an imprint of Dutton NAL,
a member of Penguin Putnam Inc.

First Printing, September, 1998
10 9 8 7 6 5 4 3 2 1

Copyright © Eve K. Sandstrom, 1998
All rights reserved

 REGISTERED TRADEMARK—MARCA REGISTRADA

Printed in the United States of America

Without limiting the rights under copyright reserved above, no part of this
publication may be reproduced, stored in or introduced into a retrieval system, or
transmitted, in any form, or by any means (electronic, mechanical, photocopying,
recording, or otherwise), without the prior written permission of both the copyright
owner and the above publisher of this book.

PUBLISHER'S NOTE
This is a work of fiction. Names, characters, places, and incidents either are the
product of the author's imagination or are used fictitiously, and any resemblance to
actual persons, living or dead, events, or locales is entirely coincidental.

BOOKS ARE AVAILABLE AT QUANTITY DISCOUNTS WHEN USED TO PROMOTE PRODUCTS OR
SERVICES. FOR INFORMATION PLEASE WRITE TO PREMIUM MARKETING DIVISION, PENGUIN
PUTNAM INC., 375 HUDSON STREET, NEW YORK, NY 10014.

If you purchased this book without a cover you should be aware that this book is
stolen property. It was reported as "unsold and destroyed" to the publisher and
neither the author nor the publisher has received any payment for this "stripped
book."

For Ruth, John, and Betsy
Who patiently put up with a journalist mom

ACKNOWLEDGMENTS

In writing fiction I often use the research technique of a reporter meeting a daily deadline. I find a "source"—somebody who can explain what I need to know and who can provide good quotes while they do it. For this book I relied on the advice and expertise of Inspector Jim Avance of the Oklahoma State Bureau of Investigation, who not only tells me what my detectives do wrong, but also how they can do it right and still make the plot work. I also relied on the skills and help of the pressroom crew at the *Lawton Constitution*—Michael, Benny, Rusty, Paul, Ron, Monte, Bill, Pat, and Mike—true-life characters more colorful than any fictional creations could ever be.

Chapter 1

Mike and I were standing on a metal grille, hanging twenty feet in the air. Beyond a spidery-looking railing, duct work snaked around the ceiling, only a few feet above our heads. Heavy electrical cables hung down, looped and tangled like tropical vines. Beneath us, rows of giant cylinders extended into infinity, blasted by glaring lights that cast harsh black shadows between them. Most of the cylinders were standing on end, but some were lying on their sides, looking like a building set abandoned by some mammoth child. A flimsy-looking circular iron stairway twisted from our perch down to the concrete floor.

"I call it the Hellhole," I said.

"Not a bad name." Mike's voice was tense. "There, way at the back—that's where we fall off the edge of the earth and the dragons eat us up, right?"

I laughed. "You've got it. You're seeing the secret dungeons of the *Grantham Gazette*. All those offices, computers, and meeting rooms upstairs—that's just a facade. The real story is down here."

I leaned close and whispered. It wasn't hard to put an ominous note in my voice. "Newsprint. Paper storage. Printing presses. Ink by the barrel. All that dangerous stuff."

"Scary as hell," Mike said. His shoulders were rigid, and his knuckles were turning white from clutching the iron railing. "My God, Nell! I'd hate to have to come out here all the time."

"Reporters don't have much business in the storage areas, but when I was covering the violence beat I came this way a lot. This landing is a shortcut from the break room to the Fifth Street loading dock. It's the quickest way from the newsroom to the fire department and the courthouse."

"It looks like a quick way to Hades."

I realized Mike wasn't kidding about his reaction to the Hellhole and to our unsubstantial-looking roost above it.

Mike is six foot two, redheaded and athletic. He's a cop who's earned medals for wrestling armed bad guys into submission with his bare hands. But I realized that he was scared stiff by the see-through flooring and fragile-looking railing of the little iron balcony we were standing on.

"It's perfectly solid," I said. "See." I jumped up and down.

"Quit that!"

I grinned. "I didn't know you had a problem with heights, Mike. You go up that climbing rope at the gym like a monkey."

"Yeah, and I look at the ceiling all the way up. I'm not good at looking down. Particularly when I can see through"—he repeated the word—"*through* the floor I'm standing on. Not when there's concrete down there."

I moved close to him and rolled my eyes. "What? We're finally alone, and you're not going to take me in your arms?"

"Not unless I can do it without letting go of this pipe."

I ducked under his arm and came up between him and the railing. "How's this?"

"Probably pretty interesting to whoever that is down there in the Hellhole."

"Somebody's down here?" I ducked back under his arm and moved away. I'm sure everybody I work with has figured out that Mike and I sleep together. But we try to restrain ourselves from handholding in public.

"Nobody should be down here this time of the evening,"

I said. "Nobody except Martina, and she wouldn't be out in the Hellhole."

"I couldn't see who—or what—it was. Just movement." Mike stared into the bowels of the block-long basement.

"I hope it wasn't a rat." I shivered. "I've been told they call in the exterminator once a month to keep the creepy crawlies out down here."

"Maybe it was my imagination," Mike said. "The Hell-hole could make you imagine anything."

I shivered again. I might have teased Mike about his re-action to the Hellhole, but that was because I didn't want to admit the big basement storage area had always given me the willies, too.

"I guess I'd better do my errand," I said. "City editors must be obeyed. Especially by junior copy eds."

Three months before, I'd been moved from a reporter's slot to the night copy desk at the *Grantham Gazette*, work-ing hours two p.m. to ten p.m. A week later Mike had started an eleven p.m. to seven a.m. rotation with the Grantham Po-lice Department. These hours made it hard for us to see each other. So we had developed the habit of eating dinner in the *Gazette* break room, snatching a few minutes together over pizza, hamburgers, or carry-out Chinese.

As a result, the city editor had known where I was when she needed a message delivered. We had barely picked a table for our submarine sandwiches when she called down to the break room and asked me to find Martina Gilroy, the *Gazette*'s chief copy editor and head busybody.

Martina was another creature of habit. She always took a nap during her dinner break. She did this in the only ladies' lounge in the Grantham Gazette Building which contained a couch—a facility that happened to be in the basement. There was no phone there, and the operator couldn't page in that particular lounge.

Martina's lounge was just down the stairs from the classi-fied and circulation departments, an area that in the daytime was more populated than the Hellhole. But the quickest way from the break room to that lounge led through the big storage area and skirted the pressroom. That was the route Mike and I were using.

"Just where did Martina go?" Mike asked.

"The lounge is at the opposite end of the basement, near the stairs to the side door—the one that leads to the parking garage."

Mike pointed at the winding, flimsy-looking stairway leading down from our perch. "Martina went down those stairs?"

"Yeah. She does it every night."

"She has more guts than I do."

"Maybe she floats down. I've always thought she looks like a helium balloon bobbing around on a string. One of those funny character balloons with acrylic hair on top and accordion-pleated legs and arms dangling down."

Mike laughed. "Pretty good description. Why does everybody dislike her so much?"

"She's professionally officious and personally snoopy. But I guess I'd better find her. Do you want to wait in the break room?"

"Anything to be with you. I'll brave the Hellhole and come along."

I moved toward the stairs. "You're the guy with the medals. Pretend there's a bad guy to be arrested down there. Come on. I'll hold your hand."

"Thanks, but I'll use both hands to hang onto this railing. It feels firmer than it looks."

Mike followed me, and we edged down the winding black metal stairs, each with a strip of industrial yellow painted along its edge.

"Whew!" Mike said when we were standing on the concrete floor. He looked back up the stairs. "What a place to take a header!"

"Martina goes down it in high heels."

"She must be part acrobat."

"Yeah, and the rest is witch with a capital B. I'm not looking forward to disturbing her rest. She'll pay me back with snide remarks for a week."

We started down a pathway outlined with yellow paint. It wandered through an underground Stonehenge formed by giant rolls of paper.

And a noise came from behind the rolls.

It was a crumpling noise, as if someone had stepped on a piece of paper.

Both our heads snapped toward the sound, and we both stopped in mid-step. I couldn't see anything except solid walls formed by rolls of newsprint.

"You said nobody's down here this time of the night," Mike said.

"The pressmen are the only ones who work in the basement during the evening, and we just left the whole crew upstairs on dinner break."

"Maybe one of them wasn't hungry."

"That could be," I said. "I don't know how many are on the crew, so I guess somebody could have stayed behind. That might explain the movement you saw."

Having assured ourselves that the noise hadn't been anything important, we walked on down our yellow-edged path.

"This paint always makes me think of the road to Oz," I said. "But it winds up at the witch's castle, not the Emerald City. I guess the yellow is an OSHA requirement. The forklift zips back and forth through here during the day."

The Gazette Building covers a square block, and the Hellhole is a block long and half a block wide. It's filled with rolls of paper in a variety of sizes—from full rolls, which are nearly as tall as I am and are a whole lot bigger around, down to quarter rolls, the ones the pressmen call "dinks," which are about the size of coffee tables.

An ax murderer could squat down and hide behind one of the half rolls. A dozen full rolls, lined up, could hide a band of terrorists. And twenty rolls, stacked ten on top of ten, could hide a band of terrorists riding in an armored personnel carrier. Even a dink could hide a rattlesnake or a rabid rat.

Quit being silly, I ordered myself. I didn't want Mike to see that the Hellhole made me jumpy, so I began to talk.

"Martina is simply the nosiest person I've ever known," I said. "Once she cornered me in the break room and told me she wanted to know all about you and about our 'hopes, plans, and dreams.'"

Mike laughed. "I'd like to know about those, too."

"Or, like that first time you and I went to Dallas. I didn't tell a lot of people we were going, but Martina got wind of it. She followed me into the ladies' room and quizzed me like the D.A. going after a third-strike-and-you're-out criminal. Had you gone on the trip, too? Where had we stayed? Did we have a suite or a double? Did the room have a king-size bed? She wanted to know all the details—and I don't mean about the Dallas Museum of Art."

"What made her so curious?"

"She wanted me to know that she knew that we were sleeping together. It gives her some perverted sense of power to know other people's private business."

Mike's voice sounded suspicious. "Just what did you tell her?"

"Oh, I was sweet as sweet. And I told her all about the Treasures of the Tsars exhibit. Believe me, I didn't tell her about the hotel, or the suite, or exactly what happened to the chocolates on the pillow."

Mike leaned close and whispered in my ear. "I'll never forget those chocolates."

"You nut!" I laughed, but I could hear a tremble in the sound. I had heard another unidentifiable noise.

I walked on quickly, tugging Mike's hand. When he flexed his fingers, I realized I was clutching him the way he had clutched the metal railing at the top of the stairs. I tried to relax my grip before I sprained his fist.

No one was there, I told myself. No ax murderer, no band of terrorists. Not even a rabid dog. Only a noise. Noises happen. Buildings shift. Or they do get mice. Mice are more afraid of people than people are of mice. The noise had been nothing. It had no importance. It was my imagination. And we had nearly reached the other end of the Hellhole without meeting disaster.

The path among the monoliths turned, and we neared the back hall. "The press is around this next corner," I said. "You'll have to come down here sometime when it's rolling. It's an interesting sight."

But as we turned, sight was not the sense that we used. Smell came into play. We both gasped and covered our noses.

"Dang!" I said. "What is that odor?"

"Paint thinner?" Mike said. "Kerosene?"

"Ooh!" I said. "I've smelled it before. It's some chemical they use on the press, but it's never been that strong."

"Why did it hit us as we came around that corner?"

"I don't know. But let's get out of here before we suffocate!"

Mike ignored my remark. He pointed ahead, down a short passageway, toward a box lying on its side in the middle of the floor, beside a pile of red industrial rags.

"Those rags must be where the fumes are coming from," he said. "What's back there?"

The rags were heaped up in front of a door.

I gasped, and this time it wasn't the fumes. "That's the door to the ladies' lounge!" I said. "Martina's in there!"

Chapter 2

I kicked some of the rags out of the way and opened the door to the ladies' lounge. The fumes were fierce inside, and Martina was laid out on the couch. All she needed was a satin pillow and a blanket of roses.

She was flat on her back. Skinny ankles and legs stuck out from under the floral dress that covered her broad hips and round stomach. Her white linen jacket had fallen open, and her left arm trailed onto the floor. Her fake blond hair was teased into a bush around her wrinkled face. Her eyes were closed, and she wasn't moving.

I was sure she was dead.

Then she snored. The snore sounded better than anything I'd heard on the Top Ten recently.

"Martina!" She didn't respond. I shook her arm. "Martina!"

This time her eyes flickered open. But they didn't focus. They rolled around, each one independent of the other, like one of those games where you try to roll BBs into a clown's eyes. Her expression was as goofy as the clown's. She giggled.

"Mike! She's high as a kite!"

He came in then—I wondered if he'd been waiting to make sure she wasn't sitting on the pot—and knelt beside her. She did the eye-rolling bit again.

"It's as if she's been sniffing gasoline," he said. "We'll have to get her out of here."

"And get ourselves out, too!" The fumes were awful. I was beginning to feel light-headed and giggly myself.

Mike picked up Martina's arm. It was as limp as the jacket she wore. She opened her eyes and rolled them in different directions again. Mike pulled her to a sitting position. Her head flopped back, and she giggled. One eye must have focused on Mike then, because she said his name. "Mike Svenson! Big, handsome cop!"

"See if we can stand her up," Mike said. He took one arm, I took the other, and we hoisted.

Martina was no help at all. "Big, handsome cop," she repeated. "Boo'ful couple. Both redheads. Screwing." She pulled her arm away from me, and her knees collapsed. She nearly went back down flat on the couch.

"Whoops!" she said. "Need boo-ty sleep."

"Damn right," Mike said. "But you need to take it someplace else today." We hoisted again. This time Mike got her left arm over his left shoulder. "Help me get her on my back," he said. "I can lift her that way."

I caught on, finally. "Would that stool help?"

I kicked a large footstool over, and Mike sat on it. We draped Martina over his back, with her armpits over his shoulders. Mike grasped her arms. He stood up, I boosted, and he had her aboard.

Martina crowed with delight. "Piggy-back!" She sounded like a three-year-old. "Piggy-back!" She paddled her feet back and forth, kicking Mike in the back of the knees with her high-heeled shoes.

"Quit kicking!" I said.

I held the door open, noticing that Mike had shoved the red industrial rags aside and covered them with the cardboard box. The fumes were less potent already. Mike carried his awkward burden out of the lounge, along the yellow-edged pathway, toward the circular stairway and the entrance to the break room. I trotted alongside.

Martina's head bounced sideways, and she almost focused one eye on me. "Big, handsome cop. Fun guy." She grimaced, and I realized she was trying to wink. "Going to make an honest man out of him?"

I didn't reply. Damn the woman! Even when she was out of her head she was poking in where she had no business.

We reached the foot of the circular iron stairway, and Mike went over to a line of newsprint rolls, all resting on their ends. They were three-quarter rolls—five or six inches more than a yard high.

I guided Martina's fanny onto one of them, and Mike let go of her arms and turned to face her. She sagged limply, and we held her upright.

"You go call an ambulance," he said. "I'll keep her from falling off these things."

I raced up the iron stairs toward the break room. I could hear Martina talking. "Now, Officer. She's a nice girl, she really is. Good reporter. Never any troubles with the five w's and h." She went into gales of laughter. As I looked back, I saw her trying to take off her white linen jacket. "Don't hold family against her."

I stopped dead on the top step and stared back at Martina. "Don't hold family against her"? What was Martina talking about?

Martina sagged against Mike's shoulder, and he looked up at me with a pleading expression. I ran on into the break room, grabbed up the phone, and punched 9 for an outside line, then 911. I'd figure Martina out later.

I told the dispatcher to send an ambulance to the Fifth Street loading dock, then called Ruth Borah, the city editor, to tell her what was going on. I stationed one of the press-room guys on the dock to show the crew how to reach the basement by elevator.

When the pressmen had heard me calling 911 and using the words "nearly asphyxiated," several had gone down-stairs. So when I went back down the stairs, Mike and Martina were no longer alone. Martina was lying down, curled across two rolls of newsprint, with her jacket tucked over her like a shawl and her knees pulled up under the skirt of her flowered dress. The pressroom guys were excitedly asking what had happened. When Mike told them about the chemical-soaked rags, the shortest one, a bulky man named Bob Johnson, rushed back toward the ladies' lounge.

I stood beside Martina and took her hand. She opened one eye and looked at me. "Fugitive," she said.

"What is she talking about?" I asked.

"Apparently I need to run your name by the National Crime Information Center," Mike said.

"Not Nell!" Martina tried to sit up and nearly fell off the rolls of paper. Mike and I grabbed her. She clutched Mike's shirt front in a death grip and pulled his face close to her. "Not Nell! Alan!" she said. Then she whispered. "A-L-A-N."

Her eyes rolled again, and Mike laid her down on the paper roll. She snored gently.

Mike looked puzzled. "What was all that about?"

I didn't answer. I felt as if a dart had just hit my balloon. One minute I was a whole person. The next I was a hollow and formless piece of scrap rubber. And it was all Martina's fault. I glared at her. If I'd had muscles like Mike's, I'd have hoisted her up and taken her back to face the fumes.

"Alan?" Mike said. "Who's Alan?"

I had to try twice before I could croak out an answer. Choke, gag, swallow. I cleared my throat and forced my voice to sound normal.

"I don't know what she's talking about," I said. "It's probably a coincidence."

Ruth Borah came running down the spiral steps then, so I couldn't say any more. She would go to the hospital with Martina, she said. Jack Hardy, her assistant, would take over city desk.

"You," she said, pointing at me. "Nell, you'll have to han-

dle the copy desk by yourself for the rest of the evening.
Jack will need help, too. But eat first."

Eat? Wasn't my dinner hour over?

The ambulance crew came then, and I stepped away from
Martina and checked my watch. It had been only fifteen
minutes since Mike and I left the newsroom. Only thirteen
minutes since Ruth asked me to find Martina before I ate
dinner. Only ten minutes since Mike and I had left our submarine sandwiches and chips on the table in the break room
to make what we thought would be a quick run into the basement before we ate them.

We went back up the circular stairs—going up didn't
seem to bother Mike—and found our food undisturbed, still
in its sack in the middle of the Formica-topped table against
the back wall.

I looked at Mike. "Are you still hungry?"

"Sure," he said. "It takes more than asphyxiation to spoil
my appetite. Adrenaline makes me hungry. Sit down, and
I'll buy you a Coke."

"I'm not sure salami will be good for the knot in my stomach."

"The Italian dressing on that sandwich will dissolve any
knot known to medical science," he said. Then he displayed
his people-handling background. "Sit down and assimilate
this experience for a few minutes."

"You've had too much psychology," I said. But I knew he
was right. I needed to think about Martina's accident—and
about her drugged maunderings—for a few minutes. And
Mike couldn't make me talk if I didn't want to.

And I knew I didn't want to talk to Mike about one thing
Martina had said. "Alan," she'd said. "A-L-A-N."

A true copy editor. Even half-conscious, she'd spelled the
name.

But what did the name mean?

Probably nothing, I thought. After all, Alan is a common
name. There were dozens, hundreds, thousands of Alans—

spelled A-L-A-N—in the United States. It was unlikely that
Martina was talking about the same one I had thought of.

No, it couldn't have been the same Alan. For one thing,
Martina would have been sure to mention it earlier. Rub it
in. I opened my corn chips and offered one to Mike. He gave
me a potato chip in exchange. We ate silently. He moved so
that his knee nudged mine. But he didn't talk, and he didn't
seem to expect me to say anything.

The members of the staff of the *Grantham Gazette* were
not so considerate. People began to rush in, each of them ex-
claiming, "What happened?" Mike and I had a hard time
taking more than one bite at a time.

In about five minutes, Ed Brown came trotting up with
his constant companion, his clipboard. Ed's title is plant
manager, and his job description covers a lot. He hires and
supervises the two dozen people in the maintenance department—the carpenters, electricians, plumbers, and janitors
who keep the Gazette Building clean and repaired. He buys
most routine supplies—from paper clips to those giant rolls
of paper in the Hellhole—and sees that they are delivered,
stored, and retrieved when needed. He sees that we have
warehousemen on duty to move the rolls of paper around,
that their forklifts beep properly when they back up, and that
the company's trucks and cars are maintained and fueled.
He's a busy guy.

Ed looks much better from a distance than he does close
up. He's slim and has well-formed features, and from across
a room he looks great. But closer to him, you can see the
lines, the network of furrows that bracket his eyes and ridge
his cheeks. Far off he looks thirty-five. Up close he looks
seventy. It's disconcerting, as if he aged forty years in ten
feet.

One of Ed's jobs is dealing with the Occupational Safety
and Health Administration, the dreaded OSHA. So I wasn't
too surprised to see him looking doleful as he approached

us. Martina's accident was going to mean he had to fill out a bunch of forms.

He opened the conversation with a deep sigh. "I guess Martina Gilroy has already hired a lawyer," he said.

I tried to smile encouragingly. "Not that I know of, Mr. Brown. If the company gives her a couple of days off and makes sure our health insurance covers her hospital bill, maybe she won't file a lawsuit."

Ed Brown shook his head. "I doubt it. Ms. Gilroy usually seems to enjoy making trouble." He asked me to tell him my version of the incident, and I did.

He frowned and sighed again. "There would be no reason to have a box of rags soaked in blanket wash back in that hallway," he said.

"Blanket wash? Is that what that chemical is?"

"Yes. It's a solvent. It's used to clean the blankets—the parts of the press that actually print—and all the other parts that carry ink. There would be no reason to soak rags in blanket wash at all. The rags would normally be used one at a time. The used rags are placed in a metal drum with only a small opening. The rags are stuffed in there, and then the industrial laundry comes and takes them away, barrel and all, according to safety regulations. Used rags certainly wouldn't be placed in a cardboard box."

"All I know is what we saw. And what we smelled."

"I almost hope Ms. Gilroy does sue," Ed Brown said. "I'd rather fight her on the legal front than put up with the snide remarks she usually specializes in."

He nodded glumly and left.

Mike frowned and gulped down a bite. I thought he was going to comment on Ed Brown, but our next visitor arrived before he could speak.

J.J. Jones is a hybrid between an ad man and an editor. He edits special advertising sections—Christmas Gifts, Health Care, Summer Fun, Used Car Buying Guide, and a couple of dozen others the *Gazette* publishes every year. The supplements are put out by the ad department, but J.J. assigns a few local articles for each, then uses canned copy to fill up the rest. Since they look like news pages, J.J. writes and edits them on the newsroom computer system, but he's an advertising employee.

J.J. came to Grantham from Texas. He has bushy white Colonel Sanders hair, and his accent is more Southern than a big plate of grits and gravy. I'm not sure how much of his language is an act. I'm also not sure if he just likes bright sports jackets or if he thinks they go with the ad man's image, but you can always see J.J. coming a block away. That night he had on a Kelly green blazer, a plaid shirt, and a yellow tie.

"Hi, y'all," he said, stopping beside our table. "Jes' what happened to Miz Gilroy? The pressmen says it's a-gonna make my section run a mite late."

Since I had just taken a big bite of my sub, Mike answered, giving a brief description of Martina's accident.

J.J. shook his head. "How bad off is she?"

"We haven't heard," I said. "Ruth went to the hospital with her. I'm sure she'll call as soon as they know something."

"Martina will probably be okay," Mike said, "since she's away from those fumes. But if it's like sniffing gasoline, it may take a while for the effects to wear off."

"It's plumb peculiar—" J.J. began.

Right at that moment a noise came from the doorway which leads out onto the metal grille. J.J. looked around, then gave a little jump.

"Oh, migawd," he said. "Time's passin' faster than salts through a widder woman. That press is gonna be rollin' before I can git down the stairs." He swung around and sped off down the hall, toward the other end of the building and the east stairs to the pressroom.

I watched him go. "He must be afraid of those iron stairs,

too," I said. "It's quicker to get to the pressroom the way we came up, through that door."

The door to the metal grille and the Hellhole swung all the way open then, and Arnie Ashe came through it.

Arnie was our new night-side police reporter. He was a thin man, maybe fifty years old, a little taller than average. He had sandy eyelashes and light brown brows, and he shaved his head. The effect was extremely bald. He looked like an extraterrestrial, but he wasn't unattractive. He had a well-shaped skull, and his ears lay flat. He could get away with bald.

"What's been going on?" he asked. "I was over at the fire department, and I heard an ambulance call for the Gazette Building."

Once again I explained about Martina's accident. "She's gone to the hospital," I concluded, "and Ruth went with her. So your copy's at my mercy tonight."

"I'll chance it." Arnie shrugged. "This isn't one of those papers where they'll want a story about this sort of an accident, is it?"

"I doubt it," I said. "We wouldn't do one if it happened at the gas company. Somebody would have to be killed or the whole neighborhood evacuated to make an industrial accident newsworthy. But it's up to Jack. He's filling in for Ruth."

Arnie stopped two tables over, just inside the smoking section. He hung a gray suit jacket on a chair, then reached into the pocket of his white dress shirt and pulled out a pack of cigarettes and a deck of cards.

"Guess I'll smoke before I go upstairs," he said. "Will it bother you two?"

"Not over there," I said. "Arnie, you ought to meet Mike Svenson, anyway. You need to know every cop you can. Mike, this is Arnie Ashe, our new police reporter."

Mike waved a potato chip, and Arnie nodded, then sat

down and lit a cigarette. He shook the cards out of their little box and began to shuffle them.

"I'm new to the *Gazette*, but old in the newspaper business," he said. "Another weird old news type like Martina."

"You'd have to go some to be as weird as she is," I said.

"Just what is so strange about Martina?" Mike asked. "All I've ever gotten out of you is that she's nosy. Isn't that a good quality in a newspaper editor? What's wrong with her?"

Arnie and I looked at each other.

"Of course, copy editors and reporters are natural enemies," I said.

"But she takes it to extremes," Arnie said. "We all want to get our copy right. We appreciate the copy editor finding errors. What we don't appreciate is a copy editor who takes pleasure in finding errors."

"That's it!" I said. "If she finds something wrong, she never assumes it's a typo or a momentary lapse or being in a hurry—just an ordinary human error. She acts as if the reporter either didn't care or was ignorant or was doing it wrong deliberately. And it delights her!"

"She's damn obnoxious," Arnie said. He laughed shortly. "It's the way she smirks and preens when she tells you how she saved the paper from having the word *avenue* spelled out when it should have been abbreviated. And she's far from perfect herself. In one of my stories last night she got all bogged down in the right way to punctuate a series, then missed a mistake that libeled a defense attorney I've already figured out is Grantham's most aggressive. Luckily, I reread the story and found the error myself."

"Plus," I said, "she doesn't have a life outside the office, so she takes a strong interest in everyone else's. When Jack Hardy and his wife got a divorce—well, it's a wonder Jack didn't karate-chop her with his pica pole. She quizzed him for days. Where was he living? Was his ex-wife seeing anyone else? Was he seeing anyone else? All stuff that was none of her business."

"It's hard to believe something bad happened to Martina by accident," Arnie said. "So many people would love to do her in."

The smoke from his cigarette drifted into his eyes, and he squinted and threw his head back. He shuffled his cards one more time before he spoke again. "Mike, I hear you're the chief hostage negotiator for Grantham P.D."

Mike nodded and kept chewing his sub.

"Might be a good feature in that."

Mike shook his head, gulped, and reached for his can of Coke. "Whatever the PIO wants," he said. "But I'd rather not. If I have to go up against some guy in a hostage situation, I'd just as soon he hadn't read a lot about exactly what I do."

"That makes sense. But how about a backgrounder?"

Mike's eyes flickered at me, so I interpreted. "An interview for background only. General information Arnie would have, so he could understand what's going on if the occasion ever arises."

"Maybe so," Mike said. "But, like I say, it's up to the public information officer to set up."

"Good enough."

I was glad Arnie hadn't pushed Mike any harder with his interview request. Mike's probably the only publicity-shy policeman in the United States. Maybe the world.

He's publicity-shy because he's ambitious. That may sound odd, but Mike's background and career are odd. For starters, Mike's dad—the locally famous Irish Svenson—was Grantham's police chief. A building has been named after him, and a picture of his open, freckled face hangs in the main hall at the central police station.

When his dad was chief, the nepotism laws of our state made it impossible for Mike to be hired by the Grantham Police Department—even though he had the right college

degree and passed the aptitude test with flying colors. So at
twenty-two Mike had joined the Chicago Police Department. He'd compiled a terrific record, according to his su-
periors there. (I once had to interview him, so I called and
asked.) He spent eight years in Chicago and was trained as
a detective and as a hostage negotiator.

Then, two and a half years before, Mike's dad had been
killed. And six months later Mike left the Chicago force as
a sergeant of detectives and joined the Grantham P.D. as a
rookie patrolman.

In Grantham, as in most police forces, everybody has to
start as a rookie. So Mike gave up eight years of rank and
benefits to come back to his hometown. He said it was because he got tired of the weather "up north." But everybody
in Grantham was sure it was because he wanted to be chief
someday, and he thought he'd have a better chance in
Grantham, where he was a hometown boy, than in a city
with the population and politics of Chicago.

This belief may be right. Mike's never told me it's true,
but he doesn't deny it, either.

This belief made a lot of Grantham police officers regard
Mike suspiciously. They either saw him as competition for
promotion or as a guy who was able to pull strings for his
personal benefit—after all, lots of the higher-ups in the department had been his father's friends and protégés. Mike
could easily have been the most hated guy in the department.

Mike had dealt with this natural suspicion by hanging out
with cops, by supporting department blood drives and sports
teams and picnics, and by not asking or accepting special favors from the higher-ups. And never, never, not ever did he
mention how things were done in Chicago.

Part of his plan seemed to be keeping his name out of the
news. I kidded him that he dated me only so he'd have an in-
sider who was willing to cut any reference to him out of the

Gazette. Not that I did. We treated him just like any other officer.

Mike's efforts to keep a low profile seemed to be working. Most of his fellow officers now considered him a regular guy, not a creep trying to ride his father's coattails to success. Nobody but me and a few GPD officers who had worked closely with Mike seemed to have caught on that this image wasn't exactly true.

Mike wasn't a "regular" guy. He was definitely special—self-confident, energetic, ambitious—and so intelligent he knew he'd attain his ambitions faster if he hid them. I knew Arnie would have to twist Mike's arm to get him to sit still for an interview.

Arnie dealt out the first cards of a solitaire hand, but something beeped. He stopped in mid-gesture, pulled his beeper from his belt, and looked at the number it displayed. He pushed the button that stopped the noise. "City desk," he said. "Guess I'd better go on up." He stubbed out his cigarette, told Mike it had been nice meeting him, and left.

By now, despite interruptions and discussions, Mike and I had finished our sandwiches, and I began to gather up the debris. "Guess I'd better get back," I said.

Mike finished the final bite of his sub, then stared at me, frowning.

"Is something wrong?" I asked.

"I've been sitting here gathering data," he said.

"The five w's and an h?"

"What do you mean by that? Martina referred to them, too."

"Who, what, why, when, where and sometimes how. It's the reporter's litany. The elements each news story must contain. It's the first thing you learn in your first journalism class."

"Oh. I'd like to concentrate on why."

"Yes, Officer?"

"Martina gathered up a lot of information about her fellow employees, right?"

"Right. She asked a lot of questions and she actually did research—looked into public records and dug things out of the library!"

"What did she do with that information? Was she a black-mailer?"

"You mean, for money? No, I'm sure she didn't do that. Nobody around here has any money. I think she just liked to let you know she knew it. Like the way she rode me about our weekend in Dallas."

"Okay. Now let's go on to how. Would anybody object if I took another look at the Hellhole?"

Chapter 3

I must have stared. Mike hadn't acted as if he enjoyed the Hellhole any more than I did.

"What are you up to?" I asked.

"Just want to check the layout," he said. "Will anybody mind?"

"No. They give guided tours of the building all the time, and they include the basement. Of course, they don't want anybody down there unaccompanied, because of the machinery. Poke the wrong button, and something could hurt you, or you could hurt it."

"I won't touch a thing. Just look."

"I know you're smart enough to keep your arms out of the press. But there's no secret about anything down there. In fact, you haven't really seen the point of a newspaper until you've seen the press run. And according to J.J. Jones, it's about to start. I'll see if I can take you down."

I called the city desk, and Jack didn't sound too nervous, even though it was the first time he'd put out the paper on his own. Things weren't too far out of control. He said I could take another ten or fifteen minutes of dinner break.

"Do you want to go down from the other end of the building?" I asked. "Use the normal stairs?"

"I think I can manage the scary ones."

As we went down the circular iron stairs Mike held the railing again, but he didn't trip or have a nervous breakdown. We once again walked among the monolithic rolls of paper. But this time there were other people present. The pressmen had finished their dinner break, and a half dozen or so were working in the Hellhole.

Maybe it was their presence—the knowledge that we weren't alone—that made me wish we were alone. Anyway, when Mike brushed my shoulder, I had to battle the temptation to shove him into one of the niches between the rolls of newsprint and rip his clothes off. Of course, Mike never had to do much to make me feel that way.

Mike was thirty-two and I was twenty-eight, and we'd both been around the block a couple of times before we met each other. We were both a little cynical, so we'd been stunned when we found ourselves involved in an adolescent love affair.

In other words, we couldn't keep our hands off each other.

At first this had been no problem. We were consenting adults, after all, who knew all the rules about birth control. We both took part in blood drives, Mike at the Grantham P.D. and me at the *Gazette*, so we had up-to-date blood tests and weren't worried about AIDS. Mike lived alone, in a house with a king-size bed and a terrific walk-in shower. I had roommates, but they didn't worry if I didn't come home. We had all the seclusion and sex we wanted. It had been a lot of fun.

Then, two months earlier, we'd both shifted to night work, and Mike had begun the final push on the research and writing of his master's thesis.

The scheduling did not work out at all well for our personal lives. Mike went to work just after I got off. I was asleep when he got off. He was asleep by the time I got up. By the time he got up, I was ready to leave for work. To add to the confusion, I was working Tuesday through Saturday, with Sunday and Monday off, and he was working Sunday through Thursday, with Friday and Saturday off.

A little handholding on my forty-five-minute dinner break had become a major romantic interlude for us. And after two months of this schedule I was in the mood for a lot more than an hour snatched here and there.

Besides, our personal deadline was staring me in the face.

When we first fell for each other, Mike and I had agreed to give our relationship six months to grow. Six months in which we wouldn't worry about the future, we'd simply enjoy the now. At the time it seemed to be a good plan. I had never fallen for anybody as violently as I'd fallen for Mike. Making this emotional turmoil into something that would last—sometimes it hadn't seemed likely.

But Christmas had come and gone, trees had leafed out and the spring storm season was starting. We were still seeing each other, and both of us still seemed to be in an almost continual state of sexual excitement. We'd become good friends as well as lovers.

And in two weeks our six-month trial would be up.

During the past five and a half months, I'd discovered that Mike was organized. I knew he'd probably written our six-month anniversary on his calendar. "Talk to Nell about hopes, plans, and dreams." And he'd bring it up on the appointed date.

The thought gave me a thrill, half hope and half fear. Mike had already told me that he was ready to settle down. Maybe have kids. He'd been brought up by loving parents in a strong family. He wanted to have a family like it.

But my earliest memories were of the bitter quarrels between my parents. My father had left my mother and me. She had died, and I'd gone to live with her parents. They'd been kind and loving, but I'd had trouble dealing with my father's desertion. Even after twenty years I worried about why he left me.

Was I capable of being a partner in a solid, functional family? The kind Mike wanted and deserved? I wasn't sure.

But now, walking through the basement, just touching Mike's arm, feeling him beside me—it was wonderful. Also frustrating, since we couldn't act on our feelings. As we walked through the Hellhole, I compensated by talking brightly.

"I'm always amazed to see how the pressmen can move these rolls around," I said. "The full rolls weigh nearly a ton."

"Three quarters of a ton," said a gruff voice behind us. "It's like pushing a car. Once you get them going, it's not that hard to move them."

I turned to find that a square-jawed man with bulky shoulders and a brush of crew-cut gray hair had come up behind us. It was Wes McLaird, the pressroom foreman.

"Oh, Mr. McLaird," I said. "You're the expert on all this." I introduced him to Mike. "Mike would like to see the press run. Will we be in the way?"

"No, it's all right," Wes said. "Of course, this Used Car section is only twenty-four pages. Eight-four, eight-four. It's not as impressive as a big Sunday paper. But we like to show off our press. And we'd sure like to change the impression Mike probably got when we nearly asphyxiated Mrs. Gilroy."

"You obviously have an operation that's extremely careful about safety," Mike said. "What do you think happened to her?"

Wes frowned and shook his head. "We haven't figured it out. Especially since you say there was a box of rags in that back hall when you found her."

"There was," I said. "We both saw them. In fact, Mike scooped them into a heap and covered them up before he carried Martina out."

Wes shook his head. "Well, Bob Johnson says they weren't there when he ran back to check after the accident. But Mrs. Gilroy sure did act like she'd been breathing those fumes."

We walked on, and Wes answered the questions Mike asked. Wes is one of the key employees of the *Gazette*, of course. The press is the single most expensive piece of equipment owned by a daily newspaper. And the most important piece of equipment. If the press is down, we can all go home.

The typical reader probably doesn't stop to think that a newspaper is a manufacturing plant. We're not a public service or an entertainment medium or a bulletin board. We make something, something we hope the public will want to purchase, just like General Mills makes cereals or Ford automobiles. All the advertising and all the news stories in the world are useless unless Wes and his crew get that press rolling. And it wouldn't roll if Wes and the other pressmen weren't real experts on highly sophisticated pieces of machinery.

We followed Wes back to the pressroom, and he led us down another set of metal stairs—these didn't corkscrew—to the sub-basement, the bottom level of the press. He showed us the elevator that brought the giant rolls of paper from the floor above, the main storage area, to the level where they are actually loaded onto the press. I was concentrating on what Wes was saying when Bob Johnson came sailing by.

Bob is short and bulky. He hardly has the physique of a figure skater. But he literally glided across the basement, coasting without moving his legs.

"How'd he do that?" Mike asked.

"Paper cart," Wes said.

"It's like a skateboard for newsprint," I said.

Wes showed Mike the tracks for the paper carts. The tracks are embedded in the concrete floor of the basement. They serve as a roadbed for steel scooters that are for all the world like wide skateboards with concave tops. These are used to move the giant rolls of paper into position before they're loaded onto the press. And they also give pressmen a quick ride across the basement.

Of course, the paper carts and their rails serve only limited parts of the basement. Wes explained that the forklift is used to get the rolls into the correct area. Then the pressmen move the rolls by pushing them around.

Bob Johnson rode the cart back and jumped off it. He glared at Mike and me. I wondered what was eating him, but I didn't ask.

Then Bob and Wes pulled out their paper knives—wicked-looking pocket knives with vicious curved blades. They slit the heavy brown paper that covered one roll of newsprint, and stripped the covering off. They rolled the giant cylinder toward a little ramp beside the track. Wes stepped back and let Bob push the roll.

"See," Wes said. "Once you get it going, it's not hard to move."

"I can start it by myself," Bob said angrily. He glared at us again, and I once more wondered why he was so mad.

Wes's lips tightened, and he glanced at Bob narrowly, then turned back to us. "The press is going to roll any minute," he said.

Mike nodded. "Do you mind if I take a look at the press? And at that back hall?"

Wes escorted us to the metal stairway beside the press, and we went up a level, into the main pressroom. Wes pointed out the parts that would be cleaned with blanket wash. Then he showed us where the blanket wash was stored, where the bags of red commercial rags were kept, where the exhaust fan was installed, and where the drum for the used rags was placed.

We sniffed and nodded. "That's what we smelled," I said.

"I don't doubt it," Wes said. "But I don't understand it, either. You see that this drum has just this little opening." He pointed at a small opening in the top. "The rags go in there, and they aren't taken out again. The whole drum goes to the laundry."

J.J. Jones, green sports jacket and all, came from the other end of the pressroom then, and he, Mike and I—the pressroom outsiders—stood in a little clump near the door to the paper-storage area.

All the time we'd been talking to Wes, men had been moving around, and a bell had been giving short blasts. These indicated that the huge rollers on the rotary press were being moved so that plates could be placed on them.

Now the bell gave a longer blast, and a humming sound began.

"They're starting up," Wes said. He went to the nearest wall and reached down three sets of ear protectors. He held them out to Mike and me. "Have some earmuffs."

I shook my head. "I can't stay but a minute," I said.

"I have to leave, too," Mike said. He shook Wes's hand and thanked him for the tour.

Then Wes stepped over to a control panel that would have been right at home on the bridge of the starship *Enterprise*. He punched buttons, and with a rumble that grew in intensity, the press started. The rollers of the press began to move, and the paper began to fly by, speeding along in an intricate maze that shot up high, then down low, ran under cutters, folded itself and refolded itself in an astonishing pattern.

The noise was incredible. The clicking, clacking, rumbling and roaring made it plain why the *Gazette*, as well as OSHA, required the pressmen to use ear protectors.

In less than thirty seconds neatly folded newspapers began to move along a conveyor belt. The first ones were blank, and a pressman grabbed them off and tossed them into a giant wastebasket. But within a minute the papers spewing out were covered with a colorful design. Six-inch letters reading USED CARS almost jumped off the page.

J.J. grabbed one off the conveyer belt and rapidly began to look through it. I knew he was checking that nothing obvious was wrong—no pages out of order, no datelines with the wrong date. It was too late to make editing changes, but they'd stop the press for a serious error.

Wes and the other pressmen also snatched up samples

from the conveyer belt. They looked through them rapidly. One man checked nothing but page numbers. They were checking for technical quality as well as the order of pages. The noise kept them from communicating by talking, of course, but they punched pages with their fingers and held them up for Wes to see. Wes made adjustments at his space-age control panel.

After a few minutes I looked at Mike questioningly. He nodded, and we waved at Wes and mouthed our thanks again. I took one of the Used Car sections, and we moved back into the paper-storage area. I turned down the hall where we'd found the rags, the hall that led to Martina's hideaway and, beyond it, to the stairs that ended at the alley door.

The door between the Hellhole and that hall had been open earlier, but now I closed it. The noise was cut dramatically.

"Whew," I said. "Wes gave you the full tour. Impressed?"

"Mystified."

"Mystified? What do you mean?"

"The pressroom supervisor and the building manager have both told us they don't see how Martina's accident could be accidental. And if the system works the way they say it does, I don't see how it could be, either."

I stared at Mike. Then I laughed.

"You're joking, Mike!"

He shook his head.

I laughed again. "But who would want to harm Martina?"

"According to you, everybody who knew her."

"That's silly! True, any one of the reporters or editors might yell at her—she's absolutely maddening—but none of the pressmen even know her. And they're the only ones who would know how to pull this particular stunt."

"You know a lot about the press. I'll bet people who've been in the newspaper business longer than you have know even more."

"Probably so. But, Mike, it's out of character. None of us likes her, true. I suppose someone might go berserk and hit her with a—a dictionary or something. But laying a trap for her—it just doesn't seem possible."

Mike was still frowning. "I guess she's safe at the hospital," he said.

I took his hand. I led him to the stairs, and I stepped up one, then turned to face him. Since Mike is ten inches taller than I am, this position brought us almost nose to nose.

"I've got to go upstairs," I said. "May I have a good-bye kiss?"

"If you'll promise to be careful," Mike said. "Stay out of that basement ladies' room and other lonely spots. Let's make sure the *Gazette* doesn't harbor a mad maniac with a yen for smothering copy editors."

"The Phantom of the Hellhole? Do you suppose he wears a mask?"

Mike moved against me and wiggled his eyebrows suggestively. "As long as he doesn't play the organ."

Then he got down to the business of saying good-bye. After a few minutes, Mike looked at his watch over my shoulder. "I don't do my best work under a deadline," he said. "And you've got to get back."

"I know." We held each other. "Listen," I said. "I forgot to make my bed this morning. Mind if I use yours tonight?"

"If you won't be lonesome. I won't get home until sometime after seven."

"You could nudge me when you come in, and I could fix you some scrambled eggs. If I'm still sleepy, I could go back to bed. Or something."

I could tell Mike was responding positively to that idea. "Do you have your garage door opener?"

I nodded.

"Then it's a date." He peeked at his watch again. "I guess I'd better leave."

I leaned forward for one more kiss, but then I jumped back.

Over Mike's shoulder I could see that the door at the other end of the hall—the door to the Hellhole—was swinging open.

I managed to be several steps up by the time J.J. Jones came through it.

Mike and I nodded to him, then walked sedately on up the stairs. I opened the door to the hall, crossed the back landing and let Mike out into the alley. I could see Mike's black pickup on the ground level of the parking garage.

We said another good-bye—one appropriate for viewing on the security camera over our heads. Then the door closed behind Mike, and I turned to go back upstairs.

But J.J. Jones was coming out onto the landing, and he spoke. "Miz Matthews? Can I consult you about a problem?"

I glanced at my watch. "If it's not a serious problem. I was due in the newsroom ten minutes ago."

He frowned. "Well, it might take a few minutes. Will you be takin' another break this evenin'?"

"If I find time. Why?"

"Well"—he turned it into two syllables—"Miz Nell, I jes' wanted to ask you a coupla questions about the Grantham po-lice."

"I've been off that beat since November. Just what did you want to know?"

He cleared his throat with a sound like molasses pouring over magnolias. "Jes' some background information I told an advertiser I'd dig out. It's a mite complicated. If you take a break, when would it be?"

"I often don't get around to taking one, J.J. If we're busy."

"I know, and they keep y'all as busy as three windmills in a tornado."

I laughed, even though I was beginning to feel as if I was getting the treatment J.J. gave his ad clients. "Well, as my old granny used to say, I'd better get back to my rat killing," I said. "If I get a break, it'll be in a couple of hours."

"I'll be in the break room, hopeful as a young boy on his first date, Miz Nell."

He almost bowed as I turned and walked rapidly away. I shoved him out of my mind. And I pushed down the strange remarks Martina had made under the influence of blanket wash. I simply didn't have time to think about Martina or J.J. Jones right then. I knew Jack Hardy would be wondering where his copy editor was.

Back up in the newsroom, a couple of reporters wanted a firsthand account of what had happened to Martina. But Jack shooed them away. The "proof" file, the computer category for local stories, was full. I worked pretty hard for the next hour and a half.

The only break came when Ruth called Jack from the hospital. As Mike had predicted, Martina was improving rapidly.

"Ruth says they may let her out in an hour or so," Jack said. "Ruth's going to hang around to take her home. So I'm in charge until the presses roll tonight."

"You're doing fine," I said. "I'm nearly caught up. I'd hate for Ruth and Martina to find out we can manage without them."

Then the next bombshell hit.

I saw it coming as soon as the door to the back stairs opened. Bob Johnson—the short, broad pressman who'd been glaring at Mike and me—shot into the newsroom, aimed toward the copy desk.

Chapter 4

I watched Bob come. He was short but hulking, with broad, muscular shoulders and forearms like Popeye.

The pressmen rarely come into the newsroom. It's not off limits or anything, but it's three flights up from their basement hideaway, and they usually don't have anything to do up there. If the newsroom and the press room interact, the interaction is usually down in the break room and takes the form of a casual nod. Or else it's by phone and takes the form of editors yelling about color quality or pressmen screaming about missed deadlines.

However, I knew Bob Johnson, because I'd once interviewed him. Bob Johnson was president of a middle-aged motorcycle touring group, and the members had gotten all bent out of shape over something we'd run about motorcycle gangs and crime. To soothe them I was given the assignment of writing their organization up and explaining to the public that not everybody on a Harley was a hoodlum. I guess I'd done all right, because since that time Bob Johnson had thought we were friends.

He was about as tall and about as big around as a full-sized roll of newsprint. I didn't know if he lifted weights or hoisted his Harley with one hand or what, but Bob was a mass of muscle, topped off with a round head and black hair. He had always gone out of his way to speak to me and tell me jokes. That's why I had been so astonished earlier that

evening when he glared and snarled at Mike and me when
we toured the pressroom.

I remembered that one of the original atomic bombs had
been nicknamed "Little Man." As I watched Bob come toward me, he looked like five feet, four inches of nuclear de-
struction headed in my direction. Crew cut bristling, he
marched toward my desk, face grim as death, brows beetled,
and anger in every swing of his arms. He stopped in front of
my terminal.

"What's this crap about negligence?" he said.

"What are you talking about?"

"Your detective boyfriend claimed that a box of rags had
been left in that back hall. Ed Brown thinks that was the
cause of Martina Gilroy's accident."

"Bob, I don't know what happened. I do know that when
Mike and I smelled the fumes, we looked back there, and
there was a heap of rags—those red industrial rags—right in
front of the door to the lounge. They looked as if they'd
fallen out of a box that was lying on its side."

"Well, where have those rags gone? Where did that box
go?"

"I don't know. Mike covered the rags up with the box, but
we left them. We concentrated on getting Martina and ourselves out of there. The fumes were about to overpower us,
too."

"There are always fumes in that part of the basement
when they're using blanket wash!"

"I know. So maybe Martina lay down in her cubby hole,
thinking, 'Gee, the blanket wash smells strong tonight.' She
could easily have drifted off to sleep and not realized the
smell was getting stronger and stronger."

"I was in charge of cleaning the press, and there was no
box of rags left out in that hall!"

I was beginning to get really mad. "If it wasn't there, Bob,
how come I saw it?"

"Are you sure—"

I cut him off before he could finish the question. "Yes, I'm sure of what I saw! And of what I smelled! And, yes, Mike saw and smelled it, too."

Bob glared. "The rags weren't there by the time I ran back to check. And that wasn't more than five minutes after this rescue the big hero claims to have made!"

"Mike sure didn't haul Martina out of there on his back just to show off his muscles!"

"You and your boyfriend made up that part about the rags to get me in trouble!"

"Bob!" Now I was getting loud. "What conceivable reason would Mike and I have to want to get you in trouble?"

"That's what I want to know!"

That's when Arnie entered the fray.

He popped up suddenly, almost between Bob and me, and he looked so mad I thought he was going to punch one of us out.

"Listen, you!" He stabbed a finger at Bob. "What the hell do you mean, coming up here and yelling at Nell? Hit the road, buster!"

I was absolutely astonished. I hadn't seen Arnie coming, and I wasn't very happy to see him arrive.

I jumped up, sending my chair rolling, and yelled.

"Cut it out! Both of you. Bob, lay off! Arnie, butt out!"

I don't know if I was loud and authoritative, or if Arnie had surprised Bob into silence. But neither of them said anything. We all stood there and looked at each other.

The police scanner crackled, and I realized that the newsroom had become completely silent. The few people there that late were staring at us, craning their necks around partitions and rolling their chairs into the aisles for a better view.

"We're acting like some stupid situation comedy," I said. I sat down and stared at my VDT's screen. "I have to get back to work."

From the corner of my eye I saw that Arnie had turned red, clear to the top of his bald head. But he didn't move.

Bob Johnson ignored Arnie. He leaned over the top of my
VDT and spoke ominously. "If you and your cop boyfriend
found a box of rags in that hall—and they disappeared by
the time I went to look for them—then somebody put them
there on purpose and then took them away. That would
mean what happened to Martina Gilroy wasn't an accident."

He pivoted like a robot and marched stiffly out of the
newsroom, leaving inky footprints.

Arnie muttered a few words. The only one I caught was
"Sorry." Then he went away, still red from shirt collar to
crown.

I stared at the VDT and pretended I was reading copy. I
felt completely humiliated, and I wasn't sure why. I hadn't
started the fracas, but I thought I had been holding up my
end. I didn't know if I was madder at Bob Johnson for coming up there and yelling at me or at Arnie for interfering.

What gave him the idea that I needed help fighting with a
pressman?

I heard Jack Hardy giggle. Despite his recent promotion
to assistant city ed, Jack's one of our goofier staff members—outwardly. When it comes to noticing what's missing
from a story, he's tack-sharp, but he has a nervous snicker
that sounds as if he's just heard a dirty joke. He used it now.

"What's eating Bob? Does he think he'll be blamed for
Martina's accident?"

"I don't know what's going on. And I don't really care.
One of the names in this United Way story looks crazy. Do
we have a list of Grantham social services?"

"Look in Martina's files." Jack dug through a rack of
manuals, directories, and loose sheets on Martina's desk and
pulled out a red-backed book. "Here's the Grantham Community Directory. That's as close as we come."

The reporter had spelled an agency director's name almost right, the equivalent of being a little bit pregnant. Just
as I found the correct version, Jack spoke again. "Have you
read the story about the homicide in Audleyville?"

"No." I turned back to the proof file.

"Give it a look-see. I'm not sure what Arnie made of it."

I opened the file and read the story. "Well, it's okay," I said. "Of course, Arnie's new around here. He didn't know to call the Highway Patrol."

"Get him to rewrite."

I buzzed Arnie's phone, in the police reporters' pod of desks. No answer. So I punched the extension for the break room and asked for him. He came to the phone immediately.

"Arnie Ashe."

"Arnie, this is Nell. You need a little more background on this Audleyville homicide."

"Be right up." The phone went dead. Arnie hadn't argued or asked to finish his cigarette. Good. And he hadn't acted huffy because of our argument. Good again. Arguing or getting hurt feelings—that's one mark of an amateur to me.

When Arnie came in the door from the stairwell two minutes later, he walked straight to my desk. "What's the problem?"

"Your story's fine, Arnie, but you don't know the trash on Audleyville."

"Tell me about it."

"Audleyville's traditionally the spot where Grantham gangs bury the bodies. So if they find a body down there— and it seems like they're always finding one—you need to ask about gang connections."

He nodded. "I'll call the sheriff's office back."

"Don't bother. They'll never tell you anything. Or they wouldn't ever tell me anything. They're very touchy down at Audleyville. But the Highway Patrol supervisor for that district is one of the good guys. He's usually ready to talk. His name is Doc Blaney, and you can find him through the troop office."

"Got it."

"Tell him I sent you. And tell him I want to know how his son's getting along in college."

Arnie grinned widely and went away chuckling. I didn't know just what I'd said that was so funny. But at least Arnie seemed to be over his fit of poking into my business. I was relieved. We had to work together whether we annoyed each other or not. Bob Johnson I could ignore. Arnie I couldn't.

In twenty minutes, Arnie had an improved story that hinted at gangland connections and cited previous killings with similar M.O.'s in the Audleyville area. I deduced that he'd not only called Doc Blaney, but had also gone to the *Gazette* library for background. He stood at my left shoulder while I read the story.

"Good job!" I said.

Arnie chuckled.

"What's so funny?" I said.

"Oh, nothing." But he was still grinning. "Doc Blaney says his son made the dean's list."

"Glad to hear it."

"Nell, I owe you an apology. And I have a few questions about the cop beat. When you take a break, let me buy you a Coke and pick your brain."

"Sure. In fact— Jack, would this be a good time for me to take a break?"

Jack was on the phone again, but he checked the proof file with one eye and nodded. So I followed Arnie down the back stairs.

"I don't know why we don't take the elevator," I said.

"This is the only exercise I get," Arnie said. "That and shuffling cards."

"At least you should have nimble fingers. And knees."

As we entered the break room, I saw J.J. Jones. He was sitting near the back door. I'd forgotten all about him.

"Rats," I said.

"What's the matter?" Arnie asked.

"I'm so popular tonight that I forgot I already promised to talk to somebody on my coffee break." I waved at J.J. "One of the ad guys. I'll see what he wants. In fact, he wanted to talk about the Grantham P.D. We can sit with him."

"He's in the non-smoking section." Arnie's voice had an annoyed edge. He pulled change from his pocket. "Diet Coke? Is that what you were having earlier?"

"Sure."

I filled a styrofoam cup with ice and turned toward J.J. Or rather, I turned toward where J.J. had been. He was no longer there.

"What is the deal?" I could tell that my voice sounded annoyed. "The guy says he needs background on the Grantham P.D. for some advertiser. Then, when I'm ready to talk to him, he runs out."

In fact, to do his disappearing act J.J. would have had to run out the back door, out the door that led to the Hellhole. The door I was now thinking of as Martina's door. The door he had avoided earlier in the evening.

"Did you particularly want to talk to him?" Arnie asked.

"No. He wanted to talk to me. And now he's gone."

"Strange." Arnie shrugged indifferently, then handed me the Diet Coke can and put money in the coffee machine. "Do you mind sitting in the smoking section?"

We sat, drank our drinks, and talked about the Grantham P.D. I gave him a brief rundown on the recent scandal in the Amalgamated Police Brotherhood, the local police union, which had resulted in the suicide of a member of the force and other excitement. Then we discussed the department's recently appointed public information officer, who—so far—didn't know from up. The cop reporters were trying to get him trained.

While we talked, Arnie kept fingering the deck of cards in his shirt pocket.

After about ten minutes I pointed at the deck. "I don't mind if you play sol while we're talking."

"It's a dumb habit," he said. "But it keeps me to two cigarettes per break. And sometimes it helps me think."

"If it would help me think, maybe I ought to take it up. But I haven't played cards since I was a kid. I was a mean Dirty Eight player."

He laughed. "Dirty Eight, huh?" He pulled out the cards, shook them from their box, and shuffled. As he dealt eight to each of us, he spoke. "I'm sorry I got into the act with you and that pressman. You didn't need my help."

"Forget it. Bob's a hothead. We all know that." I picked up the eight cards Arnie had dealt me and arranged them by suits. I didn't have any eights. Arnie put the rest of the deck in the center of the table and turned over the top card. Queen of spades.

I tossed the queen of clubs on.

Arnie frowned at his hand. "But he sure does seem convinced that Martina's accident couldn't have happened the way it did. I don't suppose anybody could have really wanted to get rid of Martina." He discarded the two of clubs.

"Everybody would like to get rid of Martina." I pulled out my two of spades, then put it back and played the ten of clubs. "I heard the two of you trade angry words yesterday."

"She can really be annoying." Arnie played the ten of hearts.

"Dad gum! Now I've got to draw!" I said. I drew three cards before I got a heart. "What were you and Martina mad about?"

"Oh, she was dragging up a nickname I'd had back in Tennessee. One I thought was buried long since." Arnie played the eight of hearts. "Diamonds," he said.

"Ha! Little did you know that I'm loaded with diamonds." I proved it by tossing the king. "Nobody gets along with Martina. She can't read an obit without alienating the obit kid."

Arnie dropped the jack of diamonds on the pile. "The kid could learn a lot from Martina, obnoxious as she is."

"Oh, I admit she's a good copy editor." I played the six of diamonds.

"More than that." Arnie knocked ashes off his cigarette, then played the five of diamonds. "Back when I knew her in Tennessee, she was winning prizes as an investigative reporter."

"Wonder what happened?" I played the five of spades.

"A spade! You little sneak!" Arnie drew. "Ha! Lucky at cards, unlucky at love." He tossed the nine of spades he had drawn onto the stack, then took a drag on his cigarette. "What happened to Martina? That's an interesting question."

"Inquiring minds want to know. Why did a star investigative reporter turn into a nitpicking copy editor?" I played the two of spades.

"The two qualities are related, of course," Arnie said. He played the two of diamonds.

"I guess so. Both require digging." I played the nine of diamonds.

"Yeah. Martina was never a very brilliant writer. But she sure could dig out the facts." He played the four of diamonds, then held his remaining card close to his chest.

"You can't hide that card from me," I said. "I can see you're about to go out. But I'm not through yet." I played the four of clubs.

"Played right into my hands," Arnie said. He laid down the four of hearts.

"Hell's bells! You won." I checked the time. "Just as well. I've got to get back."

As I stood up, Arnie spoke. "Is Mike going to investigate Martina's accident?"

I stared at him. His voice sounded different. Much too casual. What was he getting at?

"Mike isn't a detective," I said. "He's in an odd position at the Grantham P.D. He's just a patrolman. The 'chief hostage negotiator' business doesn't bring him any rank. Any sort of investigation would be handled by the detectives. Why?"

Arnie was frowning at the ashtray. "It was just such an odd accident, that's all."

"The *Gazette*—or the *Gazette*'s insurance company— might want to investigate."

Arnie shrugged and stood up.

And the phone rang. I was closest, so I picked it up. "Break room."

"Nell, this is Jack. There's somebody up here—maybe you'd better talk to him."

"Who is it?"

"Some friend of Martina's."

I snorted. "Martina has a friend? I'll be right up."

Arnie and I tossed out our cans and cups and walked back up the two flights to the newsroom. Arnie disappeared somewhere in the vicinity of the men's room, and I went by the city desk.

"This guy's a salesman," Jack said. "He hangs around here quite a bit. I didn't realize he had any connection with Martina. But it seems he wanted to invite her out for a hot date."

Chapter 5

I looked toward the elevator, which doubles as the night entrance to the *Grantham Gazette*.

The security guard was standing in the little reception area between the newsroom proper and the elevator, scowling at a large man of sixty or so. Like Jack, I remembered seeing this man before, roaming around the building with Ed Brown.

His hair was his most distinctive feature. It was funny hair—funny ha-ha and funny peculiar. He would have been very ordinary-looking if he hadn't had this fuzzy gray hair and if he didn't part it low over the right ear and comb it over the top. It covered his bald head like an angora shawl.

As I approached, I heard his voice. It was high-pitched, as if his vocal cords weren't as large as the rest of him. "Listen," he told the security guard. "I'm a friend of Martina Gilroy's, and I want to know what hospital she's in."

"I'm not allowed to give out personal information, sir," the guard said. "I repeat, you'll have to call back tomorrow."

The angora-haired guy frowned forlornly. I tried to look sympathetic as I leaned across the railing that separated the newsroom from the reception area.

"I'm Nell Matthews, one of the copy editors," I said. "We got a phone call from the hospital, and apparently Martina's doing much better."

"Thank God!" The man looked at me as if I were the last rowboat off the island. "What hospital is she in?"

I exchanged glances with the guard. I wasn't a fool. There are good reasons for the rule about not handing out personal information about staff members. You never knew when the harmless stranger at the front desk might turn out to be an angry ex-husband with a pistol in his hip pocket. Or a furious politician who claims he's been slandered and has a subpoena to serve.

"Actually, nobody told me what hospital they took her to," I said. That was true, but I knew. Our company insurance gives preference to St. Luke's, and it's closest to our office, so I was sure she'd gone there. "The city editor went to the hospital with her. I could take a message and make sure Martina gets it tomorrow."

"That would be wonderful." He reached into the inside pocket of his gray suit and pulled out a card case. "I'm at the Downtown Holiday Inn. Martina and I have known each other for years—she was in college with my wife. I always look her up when I'm in town. I just got in this evening, and I hoped she could go for a late supper after she got off work. So I came by, and then I hear about this accident."

He wrote "Downtown Holiday Inn, Room 305" on the back of a card and handed it to me. "I'm Dan Smith," he said. "I'm with Foster and Company."

I took the card. "Foster and Company. Printing Supplies. From Pica Poles to Presses." His address was Denver. The firm meant nothing to me, since I have nothing to do with the mechanical side of the newspaper. All I do is requisition pencils from the newsroom supply closet.

"I'll see that Martina gets this," I said.

Dan Smith mopped his forehead. "This is a real shock," he said. "Martina and I go way back. I find it hard to believe something like this could happen to her."

"It was certainly a freak accident," I said. "How long will you be in town?"

"Oh, several days. I make Grantham my headquarters while I call around this part of the state."

Dan Smith thanked me again and went down the elevator. I walked back to the city desk.

"Mike called," Jack said. He tossed a scrap of paper in my direction. "He left a number."

I recognized the number as the one for the Grantham Central Division squad room. "He's already gone to work," I said. I punched in the number, and Mike answered.

"Standing there waiting for my call, huh?" I said.

"I wanted to be sure our appointment is still on," he said.

My internal organs had a conniption fit. "I'm counting on it," I said.

Mike paused. "Yeah," he said, as if he were answering a question. "I'm over here at the squad room."

"Can't say too much?"

"That about sums it up. Any more excitement over there tonight?"

"No. One guy is defensive about the rags in the hall."

Mike didn't laugh. "He may have a point. I'm going to talk to Jim Hammond about it tomorrow."

"What in the world for?"

"It's pretty strange." He paused, then he used our code. "What's new?"

"What's new with you?" I answered.

"What's new?" means, "I love you," in the code we use when other people are around. My heart pounded, and a few other body parts throbbed, and I hung up in a much better mood. A little more than eight hours and I'd be in bed with Mike. Yahoo!

I calmed myself enough to read the three short stories that had appeared in the proof file. That should be the end, since ten o'clock, deadline for local copy, had passed. Then I checked the advance-copy file. Nothing pressing there. My mind strayed back to Mike and our highly satisfactory, if hard to arrange, romantic life.

Then I wondered about Martina and her friend Dan

Smith. Were they more than friends? Did Martina have a boyfriend?

She knew all about everybody else's life, but she was secretive about her own. I thought she was divorced. Martina didn't strike me as the type of woman who'd be particularly attractive to men, but I supposed it was possible that she dated. It was hard to visualize.

I recalled the story I'd heard about Mike and his reaction when his widowed mother had started going out with a long-time family friend. Mike had thought it was fine until he walked in his mother's house early one morning and met the old family friend wandering down the hall in his undershorts. When he realized that middle-aged people still like companionship in the bedroom as well as at the country club buffet, he'd been shocked.

But Mike's mom was an extremely attractive woman, even if she was old enough to have a thirty-two-year-old son. And her boyfriend, Mickey, was a macho grandpa. They were energetic and intelligent, and they acted mature. They weren't weird, like Martina—trying to hold on to youth with hair dye and spike heels—or like Dan Smith— trying to hide his bald head with a swirl of angora.

Come to think of it, Martina and Dan might make a good couple. I pictured Martina's teased blond hair entangled on a pillow with Dan Smith's fuzzy gray shawl, and I giggled.

"If you're just going to sit there and laugh," Jack said, "you might as well go home."

I didn't argue. I collected my shoulder bag and headed down the back stairs. I waved at the guard via the security camera's lens, and went out the side door into the alley that separated the Gazette Building from its three stories of parking garage.

Immediately a car's headlights flashed on, and a voice called my name. "Nell! Miz Matthews!"

The accent was unmistakable. "Mr. Jones? J.J.?"

"Yes, ma'am! Can you talk a minute? I promise to be quick as a flash a' Texas lightnin'."

The headlights went out, and I could see a vague shape standing beside a sporty car of some sort. The driver's-side door was open, and the interior lights were shining on the flashy green blazer and yellow tie of J.J. Jones. I walked toward the car.

I didn't know J.J. Jones all that well, even though he does a lot of his work in the newsroom. The *Gazette*, a daily paper in a city of around 350,000, has several hundred employees, and we're organized by departments. Advertising and newsside meet at the Christmas party, the annual picnic, and in the break room. J.J. was well known around the *Gazette* because he was a colorful character—a reputation he worked hard to maintain—but we'd never really exchanged more conversation than a "Good Morning." Until he'd sought me out that evening.

"It's this client a' mine. Needs to know somethin'," he said.

"What does your client need?" I said.

"Jes' a little information on police policy."

"I'll tell you anything I know."

"Well, it's like this. It's a financial institution. And they suspect someone's been dippin' into the company funds." J.J. scratched his head. "In fact—"

I finished his sentence. "In fact, they're sure of it."

"Sure as sunrise tomorrow. But—"

I continued his thought again. "But they don't want any publicity about it because they don't want their customers to get the idea that their deposits aren't perfectly safe."

J.J. chuckled. "I see you've run into this situation before."

"That attitude's probably responsible for three-quarters of America's white-collar crime. People know they can steal and get off without any jail time, because the company doesn't want the word to get out."

"Got it first guess. I knew you weren't raised under a tub."

"Your client had better talk to a lawyer. If the D.A. hears about a major theft, he can't pretend he doesn't know about it. Are they sure they've got the right person?"

"That might be the problem."

"Oh, then they want a detective to investigate."

J.J. nodded. "Right. But if they bring in the police, would they have to file charges?"

"Maybe not. Tell 'em to talk to Jim Hammond. He's a senior detective. He may be able to work it out."

"What about the police reporters?"

"If the company doesn't file a complaint, there won't be any paperwork for them to find. So they won't write anything. But if the cops make an arrest or the D.A. files charges, then it becomes public record. We won't be able to keep it out."

J.J. frowned. "If they talk to Jake Edwards—?"

"Nope. The managing editor won't break that particular rule. I've been around when people tried it. I suppose the publisher could—it's his newspaper—but it never happened in the nearly two years I was on the violence beat."

My eyes had adjusted to the strange lighting of the parking garage—half glare and half dead black—and I could see that J.J. was grinning.

"My dear, you're a most helpful young lady," he said. "I'd be highly honored to buy you a cup of coffee and a piece of cheesecake around the corner."

"No, thanks, J.J. I'm ready to head home." I didn't need to tell him I wasn't going to stay there.

"You've had a busy night," he said, his voice oozing kindness. "I 'magine you feel like you've been drug through a knothole."

"Why?"

"Well, with Ms. Gilroy's problems and all."

"That was more exciting than tiring. Mike's the one who had to carry her out."

I saw J.J.'s teeth flash. "I won't ask why you and your fella happened to be in the basement."

"Ruth Borah sent me down with a message for Martina. And Mike's curious. He wondered what was down there, so he came along to see."

"Jes' a tour?"

I nodded. Near enough the truth. "But when we found Martina, I was sure glad to have someone along who knew how to do the fireman's carry without breaking his back."

"Well, Ms. Gilroy was lucky as a whole fistful of four-leaf clovers. From what the pressmen were sayin', I guess she could really have smothered to death in there. There wasn't anybody else around, was there?"

"Not then. Not while the pressmen were at dinner. And even when they're working, they don't go into that back hall." I moved toward the second row, where my car sat alone.

"Will the Grantham police be investigatin'?"

I decided not to bring up Mike's suspicions. "Not so far as I know," I said. I kept walking away.

"I do thank you for your advice," J.J. said.

I got in my car, and he got in his. He waited politely until I'd started my engine. By the time he drove out of the parking lot, I had forgotten he existed. Because when I had reached into my purse for my car keys, I had pulled out Dan Smith's business card.

Martina might want to know that a friend had come by looking for her, I realized. It might buck her up. If she had family, none of them lived in Grantham. I decided to see if she was still at St. Luke's. I drove to the hospital and went in the emergency door.

It was packed, of course, but a question at the desk led me to a cubicle where Martina was lying on a narrow, hard examining table and Ruth was sitting in a chair. Martina looked miserable, and Ruth looked delighted to see me.

"We're just waiting for paperwork," Ruth said. "Martina still feels pretty lousy, but the doctor says she can do that in her own bed. As soon as the insurance forms are filled out."

Martina held out a hand to me. "Nell, I'm so grateful to you and your nice boyfriend for pulling me out of that basement."

"I'm glad we were on the spot, Martina. It was a pure accident."

"I have only the vaguest memory of the whole thing. I don't think I was very cooperative—and here you were trying to help me."

"Mike says that breathing in those fumes—the blanket wash—must have been a lot like sniffing gasoline. He'd handled high teenagers before."

"I'm afraid I talked a lot of nonsense."

"I don't recall that any two words you said went with each other."

"I hope I wasn't too silly."

"It was silly enough that I don't remember any of it." I reached into my purse. "Someone asked about you. . . ." Dan Smith's card had disappeared into the depths, and I groped. "He said you'd known his wife in college."

"Not J.J. Jones?" Martina broke off in the middle of her sentence and frowned. "I can't imagine him bringing up his wife. She's done everything to keep him down since the divorce. He's had a rough time."

I found the card and handed it over, and Martina gave a secretive little smile. "Oh, Dan! I didn't know he was going to be in town," she said. "Yes, Dan's wife and I were in college together—along with some really important people, such as Margaret Gordon Jones. I'll call him when my head doesn't feel quite so rotten."

Ruth's husband was in the waiting room, ready to take

Martina to her house and Ruth on home, so I said good-bye. As I left the cubicle, Martina spoke again.

"Please forgive me if I was too silly, Nell."

I waved casually and went to my car. But as I started it, I wondered about her concern. Was Martina afraid she'd made embarrassing revelations while under the influence of blanket wash? Actually, she hadn't said anything about herself. She'd been talking about Mike and me.

She probably had some memory of telling us that we were "screwing." Well, we were. There was no particular secret about it. Mike and I were both legally unattached; neither of us thought sleeping with another single person was a hellfire offense. Of course, it wasn't anybody else's business—certainly not Martina's.

And Martina hadn't seemed shocked. She had assured Mike I was "a nice girl." Even if I did have trouble with my hyphenation.

My family problems, she'd said, were not my fault.

What the heck had she meant by that? True, I didn't come from an all-American, mom-and-apple-pie family, but having divorced parents doesn't usually make you an outcast in today's world.

And then she'd said that name. And spelled it.

I shoved the name deep into my brain and thought about something more pleasant. Mike Svenson. The guy I was in love with. The guy with the king-size bed and the walk-in shower. The guy who had given me the opener to his garage and the key to his back door. I drove out of the hospital parking lot in a hurry.

I swung by my house and picked up some clean clothes, then went to Mike's. I punched the automatic opener, drove into the garage, and discreetly closed the door. Mike had a neighbor who was so nosy she probably knew more about our love life than we did, and we both preferred not to leave my car sitting in the drive. My key let me through the kitchen door.

Other people who had worked nights had warned me of something I was finding out was true. You can't go straight to sleep when you get off work. It may be after midnight, and it might be past your normal bedtime, but coming straight in from work and hitting the sheets is useless. You have to unwind.

So I hung the outfit I'd brought to wear to the office the next day in the walk-in closet. I took off my clothes, washed my face, brushed my teeth, put on one of Mike's old T-shirts, then climbed into the king-size bed with the latest chapter of Mike's master's thesis.

Almost immediately the house began to groan and creak threateningly.

I've noticed this about every house I've ever been in alone. Day or night, spring or fall—as soon as it's quiet and there's nobody else around, the house begins to taunt you with groanings and creakings. They're meaningless, but they're spooky.

I read two pages of Mike's thesis, but the groanings and creakings continued. I couldn't get the thesis to make sense.

So I tossed back the covers and took action. I knew there was no one there, but I also knew I'd never get to sleep until I checked. I went from room to room, and I checked all the doors and windows. I didn't look under either of the beds— the double in the guest room or the king-size I planned to share with Mike—but I checked the closets and looked behind the shower curtain in the back bathroom.

I was definitely alone. Still, I left the light on in the living room. I got back in bed confident that I'd settled the spooks, and I sighed with satisfaction as I picked up Mike's thesis again. This particular chapter was all statistics. It had me nodding in five minutes. I turned out the bedside lamp and scrunched down under the covers, already half asleep.

"Alan."

My eyes popped open. I looked around the room, startled from my first doze and wondering who had said the word.

My heart was pounding, and my stomach turned over. Had it been Martina's voice?

But no one was there. It had been a whisper from my own past.

"Stupid." I said it aloud. "Forget it. Go to sleep."

But I was wide awake again. Awakened by a stupid name dredged up from the depths of my own subconscious.

Oh, I'd read all the books. I'd taken psychology. I'd talked to a counselor about it. And every time I thought I had this particular problem whipped, here it came again.

"Damn!" I said. I turned on the bedside lamp and began to read Mike's thesis again. No good. Statistics didn't interest me enough to bury the memory. All I could think of was Alan. I got up and went into the living room, looking at the bookshelves until I found something soothing. Aha, a shelf of boys' books, left from Mike's childhood. Mike's mom had been the ultimate conscientious mother. He'd had all the classic boys' books. Should I pick *Huckleberry Finn* or *Treasure Island*?

When Mike came in at seven-thirty the next morning, I turned over and realized *Treasure Island* was open on my chest. The bedside lamp was still on, and sunlight was oozing in around the edges of the room-darkening shades.

Mike was locking his pistol in the box on the closet shelf. He kicked his shoes off, then walked over and sat on the edge of the bed, unbuttoning his uniform shirt. "You okay?" he said.

"Now I am," I said. I sat up and helped him with the buttons. Then I helped him with his zipper.

"I ought to take a shower," he said.

"Later," I said.

Later we took a shower together—I've kidded Mike about exactly why he installed an ultra large walk-in shower with a built-in bench, but he swears I'm the only person he's ever shared it with. Then Mike made coffee while I dried my hair. Then I scrambled eggs, and he buttered toast.

"We make a good team," Mike said as we sat down at his kitchen table. "Pass the salt."

It was comforting there with Mike, doing simple domestic chores, sitting around in no makeup, wearing his robe. Food, drink, sex—privacy and no-strings companionship. It was safe.

But it was threatening, too. Our deadline was approaching. I knew Mike wasn't going to be satisfied with the situation forever. He'd told me that. We'd agreed not to talk about firm commitments for six months, but the six months were nearly over. Unless we had a major fight within the next two weeks, Mike was probably going to ask me to marry him.

I loved him, I enjoyed being with him, we were compatible in and out of bed, and we didn't even argue about money. I couldn't think of any logical reason to refuse to marry him.

Did that mean I'd have to come up with an illogical reason?

That had been my pattern in the past. I'd thought I was in love before. One guy had even given me a nice diamond ring. But when things got too serious, when he began to press me to set a date, I picked a silly quarrel and gave the ring back.

I didn't want that to happen with Mike. But I was terrified that it would.

Mike spoke. "More toast?"

"No, thanks."

"More coffee?"

"All that caffeine is going to keep you awake," I said. "It's about time for you to go to sleep and for me to get dressed and think about leaving."

"Let's drink one more cup and communicate for a few minutes." Mike filled both our cups, then clicked the coffeepot's warmer off. He sat down, pulled an empty chair out from under the table, and propped his feet on it. "Are you ready?"

"Ready?"

"To communicate."

"Oh." I sipped my coffee. "Ready as I ever am, I guess. Do we have a topic for communication?"

"Yeah." Mike pulled one knee up against his chest, rested his elbow on it, and drank coffee. When he put the cup back on the table, his gaze became level, and I knew he was ready to say something serious.

"Who is Alan?" he said. "And why did you run away when Martina said his name?"

Chapter 6

The big build-up Mike had given the question had let me guard myself against it. It wasn't the question I'd expected—I'd been afraid he was scrapping our deadline and talking about marriage—but I had immobilized my face before he spoke. So I hoped he didn't see how shaken I was.

I sipped coffee, concentrating on keeping my hand steady. "Alan is a common name," I said. "I don't know who Martina was talking about."

"Why did she upset you?"

"Rescuing a fellow copy editor from death by asphyxiation—barely—tends to be upsetting."

"You didn't act upset until she began to talk about Alan."

I shrugged.

"Okay." Mike drank coffee, then rested his mug on the knee that was against his chest. "Let me guess. Since the only time you and Martina get together is at the *Gazette*, Alan has got to be somebody related to the newspaper. I'll bet Alan was another copy editor. He tried to rape you on those circular stairs."

"No!"

"Then he was one of your news sources. Offered you a big story—but to get it you had to put out."

"Mike!"

"Wrong again? Then he was the twelve-year-old paper boy who fathered your illegitimate child."

"That's it!" I glared at him. "You've discovered my secret. I have a perverted passion for little boys. Immaturity turns me on! Now you understand why I'm nutso about you."

Mike looked at me steadily. "Oh. A passion for little boys. That explains why you fell asleep reading the ultimate boy's story, *Treasure Island*. And why you had to have a night light."

I forced out a laugh. I couldn't stay mad at Mike. And we were both aware that he knew how to manipulate me.

"Okay, okay," I said. "You've made your point. The things you can imagine about Alan are worse than the truth could be. And, yes, bringing up the name did give me a bad night. But the Alan who's my personal *bête noire* is not the one Martina was talking about. That couldn't be true."

"So who was he?"

I still had to gulp a little coffee before I could answer. "My father's name was Alan," I said. "Alan Matthews. Spelled A-L-A-N."

Mike didn't say anything.

"If you're such a great detective, you should have figured that out," I said. "You already knew I have all kinds of hang-ups about my father."

"I know you won't talk about him. But you won't talk about anybody in your family except your grandmother."

"There's not much family to talk about. Just my aunt and uncle and one cousin. I don't like my aunt much, and she keeps my uncle under her thumb. My cousin, Carrie, and I were close when we were growing up, but she got married and had three kids—bing, bing, bing—in less than five years. All she can talk about now is diaper rash and Dr. Seuss. They all live in Amity, where I went to high school and where I worked before I got on at the *Gazette*. I used to go down there to see Carrie—until I got so involved with you I didn't want to leave town on the weekends."

"So what about your dad?"

"I haven't seen him since I was eight. I don't know if he's dead or alive. And, frankly, I don't much care."

Mike drank coffee. He didn't say anything. So I had to speak.

"Well, obviously I do care. If I didn't care, the sound of his name wouldn't give me a sleepless night. But he knew where I was all those years. If he didn't care enough about me to look me up, then I'm not going to try to track him down."

Mike remained carefully deadpan. "It's a natural phenomenon for kids to blame themselves for problems between their parents."

"No, it's more than that. He left my mother, true. I could accept that—they fought all the time. But, Mike, my mother was killed just a couple of weeks after they separated. My mother was gone! But my father didn't come back for me. He just wrote a note to my grandmother and grandfather, naming them my guardians. He gave me away!"

"Maybe he didn't have a lot of choice, Nell. He may have felt that he couldn't take care of a little girl. He may not have had much money—"

"That's true! He must have been practically poverty-stricken. He was a newspaper man!"

That information hung over the breakfast table like poison gas. I could see Mike's brain processing it. After thirty seconds of silence, he put his foot back on the floor, put his coffee cup on the table, and turned to face me directly.

"Nell, if that's true, Martina might have known your father. Didn't you say she'd worked for several newspapers in different parts of the country?"

I shook my head. "Martina had been around the newspaper world, true. But if she'd known my father, she would have mentioned it. Rubbed it in."

We both drank coffee, thinking. Mike broke the silence. "Whoever Martina's Alan was, she said he was a fugitive."

"That's one reason I don't think Martina was talking

about my father. My aunt hates him so much that I feel sure she would have told me about it if he'd been in trouble with the law."

"That's probably right. But you need to find out who Martina was talking about. Ask her."

I shook my head. "Not Martina. I couldn't ask her."

"I know you don't like her, but—"

"Mike, it's too humiliating! It's dreadful to tell you, and I know you love me. I simply couldn't face asking Martina if she knows anything about my father—admitting to that bitch that I don't!"

I got up and began to clear the table. Mike sat frowning while I made two trips back and forth to the sink. On the third trip he reached out and caught my hand. "I'll do the dishes," he said.

"I have to leave, and you need to go to bed. If you leave the dishes sitting around dirty, you'll get bugs."

He pulled me onto his lap. "I love you, and I'll do the dishes," he said. "Later."

He kissed me then, under my jaw, and I put my arms around his neck. "I'm not sure I feel romantic," I said. "But I sure do need a hug."

"I have an ample supply of hugs," Mike said. "And they're distributed without any romantic requirements." Then he demonstrated his non-romantic hugging technique, and I demonstrated mine.

One of the reasons I like to wear Mike's robe is that if I tie the belt in the proper knot, a tweak opens it. I think that's also one of the reasons Mike likes me to wear it. So after a few minutes of non-romantic hugging, I tweaked the belt. He ran his hands around my rib cage, inside the robe, and demonstrated a different hugging technique. We clutched each other, bare skin to bare skin, and we nuzzled each other's necks.

And I realized I was crying. In a minute Mike realized it, too.

He didn't say anything. He just held me tight against his chest, with my head buried in his neck.

"Mike," I told his shoulder. "I sent my father away."

"Don't be silly."

"It's true. The night he and my mother split up, he came to my room to say good-bye. I was so unhappy. I was so frightened. I finally yelled at him. I said, 'Just go away! Just go away and leave me alone.' I never saw him again."

Neither of us moved. Mike finally spoke. "You were just a little kid, Nell. Your dad wouldn't have taken that as a permanent rejection."

"I've told myself that for years," I said. "I didn't really mean it. But I've kept on doing that same thing all my life. The people I love best—I get afraid, and I send them away."

"You'd better not try that with me," Mike said. "I'm not going, no matter what you tell me to do." He hugged again.

Later, back in the king-size bed, Mike seemed to be soundly asleep. I got up, took my clothes into the bathroom, and dressed as quietly as I could. As I tiptoed past the bed, Mike opened one eye. "If you want, I'll call Martina and ask about Alan for you."

I leaned over and kissed the eye closed. "No, I'll ask her myself. As soon as she's back at work."

I figured that would give me a couple of days to gather my courage, but Martina was back at work that afternoon. She looked haggard, but her blond hair had been teased until it was cranky, and she was wearing her highest heels and her brightest print dress. Naturally, her white air-conditioning jacket topped the outfit.

I was sorry to see her. I knew it was no good putting our interview off. Mike would nag me until I talked to her, until I found out who Alan was. And I knew he was right. I needed to ask what she'd been talking about.

Martina and I worked slightly different hours. I came at two p.m. and usually left at ten. Martina came at four and stayed until midnight, or until all the copy was read for the street edition. I'd stayed late the night before, when Martina was taken to the hospital, so Jack wouldn't be facing the local copy without a copy ed.

I decided to let Martina get her work under way before I tackled her about Alan. She had, of course, read the morning paper thoroughly before she came in. Naturally, she had found some errors I should have caught. And naturally she pointed them out smugly. She was the most maddening woman. It wasn't that I minded her finding the errors—I like to do good work—but I hated the pleasure she took in finding them. Her corrections turned into insults.

No wonder she was the most unpopular person at the *Gazette*. Maybe somebody really had tried to do her in.

If I hadn't told Mike I'd talk to her about Alan, I would have shied off. But I had told him I'd do it, and I knew I should. So after she'd been there about an hour, I walked the six feet around to her desk—the four editors who handle local copy sit in a pod of four desks, but I didn't want Ruth or Jack to overhear. I leaned over the top of her VDT.

Martina looked up and gave her usual saccharine smile. "Yes, Nell?"

"Martina, when you were under the influence of blanket wash yesterday, you did say one rather odd thing."

"Oh, my! I hope it wasn't too embarrassing!"

"Not embarrassing at all. It was just odd. You talked about someone named Alan."

Martina's eyes dropped to her VDT screen, and she hit a couple of keys. "Well, Alan's a common enough name—"

"You spelled it. A-L-A-N. And you linked it with some comment about me. About my family. It made me wonder—"

Martina made a low gurgling sound, but I took a deep breath and forced out the words I'd been avoiding for a lot of years. "My father's name was Alan Matthews, Martina. He was a newspaper man. I wondered if you had ever worked with him."

Martina looked as if a load had been lifted from her shoulders. "No, Nell, I never worked with anyone whose name was Alan Matthews," she said.

I was relieved. Or maybe I wasn't. Either way, I turned and moved toward my own desk.

"Nell." Martina's voice was sharp. "You referred to your father in the past tense. Does that mean he's no longer living?"

I concentrated on keeping my voice steady. "We lost contact after he and my mother split up, Martina. I was raised by my grandparents. I don't know anything about my father's current life—or even if he's still living or not."

Martina frowned. I would have expected her to go into one of her gushes of sweetness—"Oh, you poor thing," and all that crap. But she didn't. She simply frowned at her keyboard. When she spoke, her voice was very quiet, and for once she sounded sincere. "I'm sorry to hear that, Nell. If your father was a newspaper man, I know he would be very proud of your professional accomplishments."

I shrugged. "He could find me if he took the trouble to look. If he's alive. About yesterday—I didn't mean to pry, but the things you said—under the influence of blanket wash—had raised my curiosity."

"Sorry. I don't know what I was raving about."

We both went back to work, and the newsroom had a period of calm for about an hour. Then Martina's salesman friend Dan Smith, the one with the mohair shawl on his head, came by with Ed Brown and his clipboard. Dan stopped at Martina's desk. She got all fluttery, and they took a twenty-minute coffee break. She slipped the white jacket off before they went downstairs, and she put it back on as soon as she got back. It seemed to have replaced the old-fashioned eyeshade and sleeve protectors as Martina's idea of an editor's uniform.

Martina worked steadily, but I was aware that now and then she looked at me with troubled eyes. I'd apparently given her something to think about. Maybe she was now the one trying to figure out who Alan was.

When the time for her dinner break came, she stood up and told Ruth she was leaving. Then she came around to my desk.

"Is Mike bringing your dinner?"

"No, he has a conference with his thesis adviser tonight. I was going to run down to Goldman's. Do you want me to get you something?"

"Oh, no! I brought my lunch." Martina frowned. "It's just . . ." Her voice trailed off. Then she took a deep breath and went on firmly. "Nell, maybe we do need to talk."

"Sure. Now?"

"No, no! Not in the newsroom."

"Whatever you say."

"Are you going to dinner in thirty minutes?"

I nodded.

"Well, meet me in the basement lounge as soon as you go down."

I laughed. "I thought you might want to avoid that lounge."

"It's still the best place in the building for a quiet nap." Martina leaned forward and whispered. "Or a quiet chat."

I stared at her, but she turned and walked away, headed toward the back stairway.

I broke for dinner in exactly thirty minutes, and I practically ran down the stairs. I wasn't sure Martina was going to tell me something I wanted to hear, but—I'm a real reporter, I guess, or maybe just humanly curious. I couldn't wait to hear whatever it was.

In fact, I was going down the back stairs so fast that on the first floor I nearly knocked J.J. Jones flat. He was coming out of the door to the basement stairs, and I swung the door open fast and right in his face. Then I nearly ran over him.

"Careful, young lady!"

"Sorry, J.J."

We dodged back and forth in the hall, dancing over a set of inky footprints some pressman had left on the tile. I felt as if I were learning to dance by following the painted feet— the way my teen magazines offered to teach the Hustle. If I stepped to my left, J.J. stepped to his right. Then we did it the other way around, with me going right and him going left. His brilliant green jacket swirled. I almost expected him to pirouette, but he didn't. The inky footprints seemed to grow in number, as if we were being invited to dance harder.

Finally J.J. gave an exasperated sigh and stopped dead, with his back to the wall. He waved me by, and I went past him and on toward the break room. I was surprised that J.J. hadn't come up with some folksy saying. Something about "dance with the one that brung you" maybe.

Martina wasn't among the dozen or so people in the break room—most of them pressmen—so I knew she'd gone on down to the lounge. I bought some cheese crackers from the junk food machine, and I started toward the back door, headed for the basement and for the downstairs lounge by way of the spiral stairs Mike found so scary.

Someone said my name. "Nell."

It was Arnie, sitting alone at a table in the smoking section, shuffling his cards. He beckoned, and I went over.

"Got time for a game of Dirty Eight?"

"Sorry, I promised I'd meet Martina. She probably wants to lecture me about something."

"Editorial problems?"

"Thank God I'm not a real editor!"

Arnie nodded, and I knew he understood. Jake, our managing editor, believes that no reporter really understands how a newspaper works until he or she has had to deal with editorial problems. So, after you've been a reporter two years, you have to do six months on the copy desk. With Martina as your supervisor. If you live through that, Jake feels, you might make a real news hound. This policy is explained to all new reporters.

"You're getting there," Arnie said. "Listen, before you go to meet Martina, let me pass one idea along."

"What's that?"

"I know most of the stuff that pressman—Bob Johnson—was raving about last night was junk."

"Right. Mike and I are not trying to frame Bob for causing Martina's accident."

"Yeah, you can ignore that part. But you might pay attention to the last thing he said."

I tried to remember. I must have looked blank, because Arnie went on. "He said that if it happened the way we said it did, it was no accident."

"You mean, somebody tried to asphyxiate Martina on purpose? That's hard to believe."

"True. But the more I think about it, the more I think it was a really strange mishap."

"Martina's hard to get along with, but surely no one would really try to gas her!"

Arnie frowned. "Just be careful, Nell."

"Always," I said. I gave him a casual wave, then went out the back door. I stopped on the metal grid, scanning the expanse of giant paper rolls, taking in the glaring light on the pathways and the dark and shadowy niches between the rolls and behind the equipment. As soon as my eyes had adjusted, I grabbed the handrail and started down the circular iron stairway.

I had rounded the first curve before I saw the vivid colors of Martina's dress, heaped up on the basement floor.

Chapter 7

I guess I vaulted down the rest of those stairs. One second I saw Martina beneath me, and the next I was kneeling beside her.

And I was yelling. "Help! Call an ambulance! Help!"

But my screams brought no reaction. No one could hear me. I was alone in the basement, and solid, soundproof metal doors were between me and the rest of humankind—the people I'd seen in the break room and any stray souls in the warehouse.

Should I run for help, or should I try to help Martina myself? She was lying flat on her face, with knees drawn up, lifting her rump into the air. Her arms stuck out to the sides, and the bright flowers of her dress formed a grotesque design where they met a puddle of blood under her head and shoulders.

I was afraid to move her, but I forced myself to feel her wrist. I couldn't find a pulse, but that didn't mean anything. I can never find my own pulse, much less anybody else's. I put my head down on the floor beside her head, and I tried to see what was under here.

There was nothing under there. Martina's head lay flat on the concrete floor.

Her face was gone.

I probably screamed again. Then I was racing back up the stairs. I struggled with the heavy metal door to the break room and rushed inside. The pressroom crew was still arguing about the baseball season, and Arnie was dealing out a sol hand.

"Arnie!" My shriek stopped all conversation. "Call an ambulance! Martina's fallen down the stairs! I think she's dead!"

And I rushed back. I was still afraid to touch her, and I didn't know anything I could do for her, but the thought of leaving her down there alone was worse than being down there with her.

I was kneeling beside her again by the time the press crew rushed onto the metal grid and leaned over the iron railing. One or two even started down the stairs.

"Stay up there!" I was still screaming. "Don't come down unless you know first-aid!"

Bob Johnson came down. "I'm the official first-aider on this shift," he said.

He knelt beside her, and he touched her wrist with more authority than I had used. He used his other hand to gesture toward her head and a puddle of blood.

"I can't feel a pulse, and she's quit bleeding," he said. He moved his hand to her rib cage. "No breathing. I think she's gone." He put his head flat on the floor and looked. "Ummm!" He sat up quickly, looking white. "There's sure no way for an amateur to try mouth-to-mouth," he said.

I nodded. Martina had no mouth.

The two of us knelt beside her in silence. The press crew was quiet, and Arnie came out and jostled his way through the group. He came down the stairs.

"There's nothing you can do," I said. "It's probably best to stay away."

He nodded, but he came down anyway. He looked at me, not Martina. "Are you okay?"

"Not exactly."

"Go upstairs."

I shook my head. "No. If Martina and I weren't friends, at least we were co-workers. I'll stay with her."

He touched my shoulder, then stood behind me. In less

than five minutes the ambulance crew from St. Luke's got there. The cops came, too. When the emergency people began to work, I went upstairs. Arnie came behind me, his hand on my elbow. I should have resented it, but I didn't.

As I reached the landing, the door from the warehouse opened, and Mike came in. That's when I nearly collapsed. I took his hand, and I gulped furiously, but I made it without breaking into hysterical sobs, even when he put his arms around me.

Mike and Arnie and I went into the break room and sat down. Arnie nervously lit a cigarette, even though we were in the non-smoking end of the room.

"How'd you know what happened?" I asked Mike.

"We're an item at the cop shop," he said. "The dispatcher tracked me down at home as soon as she heard you'd found a body."

"You've got to get out to Grantham State, meet with your adviser."

"I'll call him." Mike went to the phone, looked up a number in the book, and called to cancel his appointment with his thesis adviser. Ruth Borah came in, spoke to us, and ran out onto the metal grille. She came back in and said the ambulance was taking Martina away.

Then the four of us waited. A young woman police officer came up and took a preliminary statement from Arnie and me, and told me a detective would call the next day.

"It's probably an accident," she said, "but we have a routine for all unattended deaths—accidents, suicide, homicide. We fill out the same reports."

"I know," I told her.

She smiled. "Yeah, I've read your stories. You've gone over plenty of those suckers."

Ruth told me I could go home, but I said I thought I'd rather go back to work. I was beginning to feel like a little kid— Arnie, Mike, and Ruth were all trying to take care of me.

"Come on, folks, I've seen bodies before," I said. "Three

years on the violence beat in Amity and two years here. Remember? I've been out on a lot of ten-sevens."

Ten-seven is radio code for "out of service." Cops use it to refer to their dinner breaks—or to dead bodies.

I did walk Mike to his truck, parked on a side street, and I even climbed inside for a good-bye snuggle. Then he drove me around the block and let me out at the Gazette Building's main entrance. I went up the elevator and into the newsroom, trying to be calm as I spoke to the security guard and the night switchboard operator and receptionist.

I'm not sure how good my copy editing was. The whole staff was rattled—the few who were working that evening—and there were plenty of errors to find. I did take a moment to call the Downtown Holiday Inn and leave a message for Dan Smith. He seemed to be Martina's only friend. I hated for him to learn about her death in the morning paper. The managing editor showed up, looking serious, to call Martina's family. He stopped by the city desk and told Ruth he'd gotten the number of a brother in California from his files.

Arnie, as nightside police reporter, drew the job of writing up Martina's accident.

"A veteran employee of the *Grantham Gazette* was killed Tuesday evening in what appears to be an accident in the Gazette Building," he wrote.

Martina Gilroy, 60, chief copy editor for eight of the ten years she'd been at the *Gazette*, apparently fell down an iron staircase leading from the employee break room to a basement area used for paper storage. She suffered massive head injuries and was declared dead on arrival at St. Luke's Hospital.

An investigation, described by a Grantham Police Department spokesman as routine, is now under way.

The stairway where the fall occurred was frequently used by Gilroy as a shortcut from the employee break room to a women's lounge in the basement. Gilroy was found within a few minutes of her fall by a second copy editor, Nell Matthews, who immediately summoned help.

Gilroy's death was described by *Gazette* managing editor Jake Edwards as a serious loss to the newspaper.

"Martina was a key staff member, although her duties meant that she had little contact with the public," Edwards said. "Copy editors are the first level of supervision for reporters, and Martina herself had many years of experience as an investigative reporter. She understood the importance of detail and routine in producing accurate news stories. The *Gazette* newsroom won't be the same without her."

No, the *Gazette* newsroom wouldn't be the same. It might be better. Or at least more pleasant.

I kept that sentiment to myself. I hadn't liked Martina at all, and I wasn't going to pretend otherwise. But I'd wished her an early retirement, not a terrible accident. I wanted her out of my hair, not dead.

"She was a pain in the rear, but nobody deserves something like that."

The words echoed my thoughts so clearly that I jumped. Looking up, I realized that Arnie had been standing behind me, watching as I read his article.

"Well, I'm afraid I'll miss her expertise," I said. "Jake described her perfectly, of course. 'Detail and routine.' Picky, picky, picky. She nearly drove me crazy. From her fetish about 'whether' instead of 'whether or not,' to the way she could pull up the middle initials of thousands of people from some mental encyclopedia, to her absolute insistence that we never use the word 'Methodist' without 'United' in front—well, I hate to admit it, but she taught me a lot. But even her office routine—dinner from six-thirty to seven-fifteen exactly, sharpening three pencils before she sat down—even that white jacket . . ."

I quit talking and gulped in amazement. I thought about what I'd said, and I pictured Martina's body lying at the foot of the stairs. Then I turned to Arnie.

"Arnie! Martina wasn't wearing that jacket!"

He frowned. "Wasn't she?"

"I'm sure she wasn't," I said. "I remember what a pattern the puddle of blood under her shoulders made, and how it seemed to merge with her dress. You were in the break room when she was eating. Did she have the jacket on then?"

"Nell, I don't remember. I didn't look at her any more than I had to, even when she was alive."

He shrugged and turned to Ruth Borah. "I'm trying to get hold of the medical examiner on that Audleyville body," he said. "Maybe they'll have a cause of death. On the record. So that's yet to come." He went back to his desk.

I ran the spell checker on Arnie's story, then shipped it over to Ruth's working file. Poor Martina. She'd probably be doing good to make Page 5A, the Metro News page. The only people who were going to notice she was gone were her co-workers. And we weren't exactly going to miss her. Or her jacket.

I copyedited a couple of stories, but my curiosity bump was itching. What had happened to Martina's white jacket? Would she have taken that jacket off when she went down to dinner?

If she ever took it off, she draped it over the back of her chair. It hung there all day before she came to work. I knew that because I'd seen it there. Plenty of times, when I was still a reporter, at times when Martina wasn't on duty, I'd sat down at that desk to use her terminal—usually because the dayside city editor and I were talking about some story, and I wanted to access the article and talk at the same time.

Once or twice I'd even knocked that white jacket onto the floor. When that happened, I was always careful to pick it up and brush it off, by golly. Martina and I had enough problems over copy. I wasn't going to start more trouble by treating that jacket with disrespect.

Each weekend, when Martina had her days off, she took the jacket home. And each Monday she brought it in, freshly washed and even ironed.

Martina usually wore it the entire time she was in the building. She'd had it on the evening before, when she was gassed in the downstairs ladies' lounge, that's for sure. I remembered that she had struggled out of it after Mike hauled her back to fresher air. She had curled up and gone to sleep on top of the paper roll, with the jacket wrapped around her like a baby blanket.

But this evening, when Martina took her fatal fall, she had not been wearing it.

Why would she have taken it off? And where?

Did it matter? I decided to ask Mike, so I picked up the phone and dialed his number.

He wasn't home.

Well, that made sense. He'd probably gone on out to Grantham State for his appointment with his thesis adviser, even if he had to be late.

I left a message on his answering machine and got back to work. With Martina out, I had to copyedit the obits, and they have to be checked against the originals faxed in by the funeral homes. Every date of birth, every spouse name, every funeral time and place, every name of every son and daughter, every total number of grandchildren. All had to be checked against the original copy.

Or so Martina had told me. I realized that she'd be haunting me for the rest of my journalistic career.

It took me forty-five minutes to get caught up. Then Dan Smith called, answering the message I'd left at the Downtown Holiday Inn, and I got to be the one who told him Martina was dead.

He didn't say anything right away. Then he grunted like a gorilla. "Huh! Huh!"

I began to talk nervously. "I wondered if she was still feeling bad, Dan. Weak from the effects of that blanket wash yesterday. It could be she fainted. You probably know how awful those stairs are."

Dan sniffed. "Seems like everything you've got over there is dangerous," he said. He asked a couple of questions about her next of kin, but I told him he'd have to ask Jake.

"I'll find out from the funeral home," he said. "Thanks for letting me know." I heard another sniff as he hung up. Maybe one person was sincerely mourning Martina's death.

I was finishing up the last of Arnie's violence-run copy when my phone rang. It was the front desk's security guard, calling from fifty feet away. When I looked at him, I saw why. Mike was standing at the front desk. He was dressed for duty, in dark navy pants and shirt, with gear hung all over him—pistol, radio, nightstick. I went to meet him.

"You called," he said.

"Yes, but you didn't have to rush right over."

He grinned. "It's on my way to work."

I checked my watch. He had about thirty minutes before roll call, and the Grantham Central Station was about five minutes away. I went through the swinging gate that serves as a psychological barrier when strangers come to the newsroom, and we sat on the waiting room couch.

"I'm probably being silly," I said. Then I sketched my concerns about Martina's jacket. They sounded pretty dumb when I verbalized them to a guy wearing a police uniform.

"So you see, there's very likely nothing to it. I've made you go to work early for nothing but a good laugh."

"It doesn't sound laughable to me," Mike said.

"But I don't want to stir up a bunch of trouble over an accident."

"You won't be stirring up anything. I assure you Martina's death is on the case list for the detectives. They've been tied up tonight, or you'd already have had somebody over here asking questions."

"Why?"

"Because when the same woman has a near-fatal accident

on one night and a fatal one the next, it's just a little too co-incidental."

"You don't think she was still feeling weak or something? That she got dizzy and fell down the stairs?"

"Maybe. It's possible. But like I say, it's just too coincidental. So this jacket may be important."

"Then you think I should tell the detectives about it?"

Mike nodded. "Unless the jacket turns up between then and now."

"I haven't looked for it."

"Where could you put a jacket around here?"

"She always hung it on the back of her chair, unless she was wearing it."

"You don't have a coat closet?"

This time I grunted like a gorilla. "Uhhh! Of course we do! Hell's bells! I didn't even think of that."

Mike stood up. "Let's go look in it."

We threaded our way through the cubicles and pods of desks that dotted the newsroom toward the back stairs.

"Actually, there are three closets, close to the back stairs, so they'll be handy as people come and go from the parking garage in bad weather," I said. "And that's why I didn't think of them. I don't know anybody who uses them for anything but raincoats or heavy coats. It's a long way back there. If we have sweaters or blazers—indoor-type jackets—most of us just keep them at our desks. Lifestyles even has a hall tree they share."

The closets are down a short hall from the door to the stairway, opposite the third-floor rest rooms. They're strictly utilitarian and usually have muddy floors. In the Southwest at this time of the year—mid-April—rain is common, but hardly anyone still wears a winter jacket.

The first closet was empty, except for somebody's lunch bucket on the shelf and a ripped plastic raincoat hanging crooked on a wire hanger.

The second closet held a windbreaker I recognized as belonging to Jack Hardy, and a trench coat that had RUTH B. in the back of the neck. They'd probably want coats when they left after midnight. I was leaving late, too, but I was wearing a sweater I'd kept on in the office. Martina had been right about needing an "air-conditioning jacket" because of the vent over the copy desk.

The third closet seemed to hold a few leftovers from a garage sale. An umbrella with a drooping rib was propped in one corner. Two old sweaters on wire hangers were shoved against the left-hand wall.

"Looks as if nothing's here," I said. But I moved the sweaters out, sliding their hangers along the metal pole.

And there, crammed behind a sky blue cardigan, were the lapels of a white linen jacket.

"There it is!" I reached for the jacket.

"Don't touch it!" Mike's voice was sharp.

But he was too late. I'd already grabbed the jacket by the shoulder and pulled it out of the closet, hanger and all.

I held the jacket at arm's length, slowly taking in the reddish, brownish stains that spotted its front.

"What's that?" I could barely hear my own voice.

"I don't know," Mike said. "But we'd better get the lab to check it out."

I pivoted the hanger in my hand, turning the jacket around.

There was another stain on the back, square in the middle of the back. But this stain wasn't reddish or brownish.

This stain was black. It was shaped something like a figure eight. A black figure eight about a foot long.

"It's ink," I said. "Mike, it's ink. And it's in the shape of a footprint."

"Put the jacket back," Mike said. "Just put it back where it was."

But I was frozen. "My God, Mike," I said. "Somebody kicked Martina down those awful stairs."

I went back to my desk, and Mike used one of the reporters' phones to call in. I guess he called the detective bureau, and pretty soon a detective showed up. Mike showed him the jacket, and they put it in a paper sack and labeled it. The detective came by and told me I'd have to include this in my statement the next day. I agreed to go by his office before I went to work.

Ruth and Jack wanted to know what was going on. I would have told them, but Mike brushed the question off, so I followed his lead.

Mike left—he'd called his sergeant to say he might be late for roll call—and the detective left. I read a final story. Then Ruth told me all the copy was in, so I could go home. I headed for the parking garage, via the back stairs.

As I came out of the stairwell on the first floor, I had my head down, looking for my car keys, which always hide in the bottom of my purse. So I almost bumped into someone who was coming the other direction.

"Whoops!" We both jumped back, and I was reminded of the little dance I'd done with J.J. Jones just before I discovered Martina's body.

But this time my partner didn't dance. He simply stood back and held the door for me. It was Ed Brown, our building manager.

Ed looked more like a dissipated matinee idol than usual. His face was extremely sour. For once he was not holding a clipboard.

"What are you doing here this time of night?" I said.

"Always problems," Ed said. "Now somebody's been prowling in the pressmen's locker room."

"Oh, my gosh! Didn't they lock up their billfolds?"

"Sure, that's not the problem. It's shoes."

"Shoes?"

Ed nodded. "When the eleven p.m. shift came on, one of the guys couldn't find his shoes. Swears they're gone from his locker."

Chapter 8

First an inky footprint. Then missing shoes. There had to be a connection.

I tried to call the detective who had just left with Martina's jacket, but he wasn't in. I left a message, but I was almost glad I didn't have to talk about Martina anymore. I was so tired of the whole thing I just went home and went to bed.

My own home. My own bed. It would have been nice to be with Mike, but my own bed was pretty good, too.

My two girl roommates were already asleep, apparently, and the guy who lives downstairs, Rocky, was on duty at the gay bar he owns. His hours run even later than newspaper copy editors' hours. So I saw no one, talked to no one until I tried to call the detective bureau when I woke up at nine-thirty the next morning.

After the detective bureau clerk, Peaches Atkinson, hollered out my name, I heard the voice of Jim Hammond, a senior detective, in the background. "Let me talk to her," he said. "I've got something to say to that young woman."

Jim and I have worked together a lot, naturally, since I covered his office for nearly two years. Grantham P.D. policy is that the public information officer issues statements to the press, but both the former and the current PIO's were good about linking up reporters with the detectives who really knew the low-down on important cases. If the case was at all touchy, or was merely dramatic, Jim Hammond usually got the job of handling the press.

In addition, he and Mike had a rather low-key friendship going, a friendship strongly affected by Mike's strange position in the Grantham P.D. It was a position that could be described as between a rock—his father's position as an honored former chief—and a hard place—Mike's awareness that he'd get further faster if he didn't take advantage of his family connections.

Mike was careful not to get too chummy with the higher-ups in the department. The chief, Wolfe Jameson, and Jim Hammond had been his father's protégés. Mike made sure he never socialized with them, never seemed to be seeking their favor or friendship. When they showed up at the Christmas buffet his mother gave, Mike stayed at the other end of the room.

But Jim Hammond was a problem for Mike. He wasn't willing to be snubbed. He'd worked with Mike on a couple of cases, with Mike as a uniformed officer temporarily attached. Jim was already pressuring the promotions board to shift Mike to the detective bureau, even though policy said Mike needed another year on the street before he was eligible. Jim's request left Mike torn. He coveted the job, but he didn't want special consideration. So far Mike hadn't endorsed Hammond's request, and the promotions board hadn't acted.

Whenever Mike and I ran into Hammond, an odd little maneuver came into play. I called Hammond "Jim" and punched him in the arm. Mike called him "Captain Hammond" and saluted respectfully.

Jim looked at our romantic relationship with an avuncular eye, but he looked at my status as a reporter suspiciously. So when he told Peaches he wanted to talk to me, I didn't know who was coming to the phone—Uncle Jim, who pictured himself as a father figure for my boyfriend and me, or Tough Jim, detective who claims he eats reporters for breakfast.

"What's going on over there at the *Gazette*?" His voice was a growl. Must be Tough Jim.

"Darned if I know. Y'all are the detectives."

"Because of you we had to get a judge out of bed, get a search warrant, call in off-duty officers, and search a four-story building with more hidey-holes than a Baptist Easter egg hunt. All over a missing pair of work shoes."

"What!"

"Haven't you been searched?"

"No! I didn't get off until midnight. If you want to know the truth, I'm still in my pajamas even as we speak. I don't go to the office until two o'clock."

"Well, as soon as you get there, we're gonna search your desk."

"If there's anything embarrassing in my desk, I don't want to be there when you find it. Go ahead and search it now."

"No, you've got to sign a waiver. We're making sure every little thing is legal."

I thought about that one. "The *Gazette* has a couple of hundred employees, Jim. You mean you're searching every desk?"

"Yep. Every desk. Every locker. Every credenza, file drawer, and storage closet."

It boggled the mind. The *Gazette* has rooms full of old newspapers, offices that are packed solid with desks, work-shops stuffed with tools and with the bits and pieces that ac-cumulate in workshops. The *Gazette* employs two full-time electricians and a carpenter, for heaven's sake, and more than a hundred printers. It has a garage full of trucks, fork-lifts, and company cars. It has entire rooms of telephone equipment. Satellite dishes and a miniature weather station hold down the roof. There are banks of filing cabinets, rows of computers, acres of drawing boards, copying machines of all sizes, several kinds of darkrooms, giant cupboards that hold advertising art. The number of—well, wastebaskets, for example—was staggering.

And a pair of work shoes could be hidden anywhere in this accumulation.

"What a job!" I said. "I guess you started in the alley, checked the dumpsters first."

"Oh, yeah. That was a fun job. Do you know how much fast food you *Gazette* employees eat? Nasty stuff, catsup."

"I believe it. But whoever kicked Martina had several hours between the time she went down the stairs and the time Mike and I found that jacket. And another hour before the shoes were missed from the pressmen's locker room. It would have been pretty easy to just take the shoes out of there and throw them in the trash at—well, at McDonald's or someplace."

"Do tell! Gee, I hadn't thought of that!" Jim's voice was its most sarcastic.

"Okay! Okay! I won't make any more suggestions."

"Peaches says be here at one o'clock to give your statement," he said. "She'll have a detective free to take it."

I had barely put the phone down when it rang again. This time it was Mike.

"What are you doing awake?" I asked. "You're supposed to be asleep at nine-thirty in the morning."

"I wanted to talk to you. How about lunch?"

"Sure. Do you want to come over here?"

He paused. "How about Goldman's? Maybe neutral territory would be better."

"Neutral territory? What is this?"

"Just something we need to talk about. See you then."

And he hung up.

I drank some coffee, read the paper, took a shower, got dressed in brown plaid pants with a linen shirt and jacket. But I did it without the usual zing in my step and song in my heart—the zing and the song I usually got when I knew I was going to see Mike soon.

"Neutral territory," he'd specified. Somehow I was afraid I wasn't going to enjoy this interview.

Despite having little or no sleep, Mike looked great when we met. He was wearing khakis and a cotton sweater that wasn't quite maroon and wasn't quite rust and wasn't quite brown. I'd bought it for him for Christmas because it nearly matched his eyes, and his eyes nearly matched his hair.

We picked up our food at the counter—Goldman's doesn't offer table service—and took Mike's Reuben and my bowl of chili to the back room. I crumbled some crackers into the bowl before I spoke.

"Okay," I said. "Why did we need neutral territory?"

Mike stuffed strands of escaping sauerkraut into the side of his sandwich. "I wanted to know if you talked to Martina yesterday before she took her tumble."

"Well, there was no point in talking to her afterward."

"Come on, Nell. Get serious."

"You mean, did I talk to her about my dad?"

"Right."

"Yes. I asked her if she'd ever worked with an Alan Matthews, and she said no."

Mike shrugged. "Okay. Then—"

I cut him off. "Then she seemed to have second thoughts. She asked me to meet her in the basement ladies' room when I started my dinner break." I ate a spoonful of chili. "That's where I was headed when I found her."

"I see." Mike mulled that over while he ate a hunk of his sandwich. "Then you never got to find out about Alan."

"No. But she'd denied knowing my dad. I have no idea what else she might have wanted to tell me. The name of a good private eye? The phone number of the Salvation Army missing persons service? I'll never know."

"What are you going to do next?"

"What do you mean?"

"About finding your father."

"Finding my father! Who said anything about finding my father?"

Mike ate silently.

"Look, Mike, I'm not at all sure I want to find my father. If I were to find him, it would probably be in a drunk tank someplace."

"Did he have a drinking problem?"

"No! I just mean—well, he didn't go away because he just loved me to pieces, obviously. Something was wrong. He didn't want me."

"Do you remember him?"

"Of course. I was eight the last time I saw him."

"Was he abusive?"

"No. He never even spanked me. In fact, I remember at least one time that he should have, and he didn't. And he and my mom yelled a lot, but if they ever hit each other, I didn't know about it. He was . . ." I paused. "Mike, he was just Daddy. What does an eight-year-old know? I used to run out to meet him when he came home from work. He took me to the school carnival. He taught me to play Old Maid and Dirty Eight and how to ride a bicycle. He mowed the lawn. Turned football games on TV, then fell asleep on the couch."

"Is that what he and your mother quarreled about?"

"No." I thought about it. "I don't know what they fought about. They kept quiet in front of me— of course, I could tell something was wrong. It was kind of polite tension. The arguments began after I was in bed."

"And you have no idea what the problem was?"

"I doubt there was only one problem. I can remember my mother pleading, 'Please, please, I've got to get out of here,' and my dad yelling, 'No! I'm not giving up this chance.' But surely my mother wasn't upset by the move we'd made."

"Move?"

"Yes. We'd lived in Amity, which was my mom's home-town, until around six months before the big break-up. Then we moved to Michigan. Maybe my mom was homesick? But that's hard to believe. She'd first said she was looking forward to getting away from her family. But, Mike, what is the point of this? Why are you bringing it up?"

"Because it's something you need to settle."

"It seems pretty well settled to me. I don't know where my dad is, and I don't much care."

"Then why did you lie awake all night after hearing someone say his name? Why did you tell me, 'I sent him away. I send everybody I love away'?"

I laid down my spoon. Goldman's peel-your-lips-hot chili had become completely tasteless.

Mike reached across the table and took my hand. "Listen, Nell. I took Psych 101. So did you. Something like this has to be resolved. You can't let it hang around in your subconscious, making you afraid you'll do something to blow up any serious relationships. If you don't get this settled, the time will come when it affects us!"

I pulled my hand out of his. "I see that it already has."

Our table had become a war camp, and we stared at each other through barbed wire.

Mike broke the silence. "I love you, Nell. I don't want you to send me away."

"You said you wouldn't go."

"I won't go willingly. But you're pretty ingenious. You could push me out of your thoughts. Starve me out of your emotional life." He grinned suddenly. "Cut me out of your hopes, plans, and dreams."

I laughed, but I could hear the tremble in the tee-hee. "What are you saying? I don't get sex until I go to a shrink? I've already had counseling."

"Before you need counseling, maybe you need facts."

"Facts? The reporter's litany? Who, what, where, when, and sometimes why? Sometimes how?"

"Yeah. Those little boogers."

"Okay. I'll repeat one of them. Why?"

"Because Martina wanted to tell you something, and she was murdered before she could."

Talk about stopping the conversation. Mike's answer stunned me. It opened up possibilities that were truly frightening. I stared at him while they tumbled around in my imagination.

"Mike, you can't possibly mean what you're saying. Any-body—anybody—might have had a reason to kill Martina. She was the most disliked person on the *Gazette* staff."

"True. And why was she disliked?"

"Because she was obnoxious!"

"What was obnoxious about her?"

"She was so nosy—"

I quit talking and stared at my chili bowl. The crackers were soggy. I forced myself to eat a bite. If I dug to the bottom of the bowl, it was still hot with fire. It was hot with pepper clear through. I shoved it away.

"Okay," I said. "You've made your point. Martina was nosy. She didn't seem to have any life of her own. No friends, no family that I ever heard of. No hobbies, pets, or interests outside the office. She just sucked up vitality from other people, poking around in their lives."

Mike nodded. "And, yes, if she poked too deep, if she found out something that wasn't healthy to know—"

"You think that's the reason she was killed."

"What else could there be, Nell? Hammond had me in as soon as I got off duty this morning. Wanted to know all about the relationships down there. Of course, I didn't know much to tell him."

"Did you tell him I was going to ask her about my father?"

"No, I thought I'd let you tell him that."

"So you're warning me."

Another long silence.

"Is Jim Hammond handling this case?" I asked.

"Yes. I think the publisher called the chief, and the chief decided it required a senior detective named Jim."

I guess I frowned, because Mike went on. "Look, Nell, Jim would have to mother-hen it. He might as well be up front. It's bound to be a high-profile case."

"That's true."

If a news-media figure gets in trouble—at least in a city the size of Grantham—the case is going to get lots of attention. We're all afraid the public will think the accused person is getting special attention, so we bend over backward to show that he's not."

Look at the Collins case. Joe Collins was an Oklahoma City newsman who shot his wife five years ago. Probably thirty-five Oklahoma men shot their wives that year. They mostly pled out—made plea bargains—for varying degrees of manslaughter. In a town the size of Oklahoma City, this would be worthy of two or three stories on inside pages. It would get very little attention elsewhere in the state. But Joe Collins was splashed all over the front pages of Oklahoma's newspapers for months. The legislature even passed a domestic-abuse bill called the "Marsha Collins" law.

Joe was a rotten guy, true, and I'm glad they locked him up. But he got a lot more attention than the other thirty-four wife killers that year combined. Because he was in the news business, and we all wanted to make sure no one thought we were sweeping anything under the press.

I poked at my chili bowl with my spoon. "You've ruined my appetite," I said.

"Sorry, but there's no ducking it."

"I know. And I'll certainly answer anything Jim or his detectives ask me." I glanced at my watch. "I've got to be over there at one o'clock. If you don't mind, I'll leave. Then I can go by the office and sign the release so they can search my desk while I'm giving my statement."

"Okay." Mike's plate was nearly empty. His appetite hadn't been affected.

I stood up, and he reached out and took my hand. "Think about what I said about your dad, Nell."

"I'm sure a psychologist would say you're right, Mike. But you suggested getting facts. Where would I start?"

"Family?"

"My dad didn't really have any family. His parents died rather young. I vaguely remember going to my grand-mother's funeral. I guess I was about three. And he didn't have any brothers or sisters."

"How about your mother's family? How about this aunt?"

"I'm sure she doesn't know where he is!"

"Maybe not. But she may know where he went when he left."

"Mike, Aunt Billie and I don't get along. I can't face talk-ing to her."

He squeezed my hand. "She may be your best lead."

"Forget it! I'm happy as an orphan. I'm not asking Aunt Billie any kind of a favor!"

I yanked my hand away. Mike set his jaw. We glared at each other.

Then I turned my back on Mike and left. I walked the two blocks to the *Gazette* office with a knot in my stomach.

My Aunt Billie and I kept our relations on a superficial level. How've you been, Aunt Billie? Just fine, Nell. And you?

The thought of asking her anything important was terrify-ing. I stuffed the thought back below the surface of my mind and thought about the next few minutes. The first thing I had to do was see if I could sign my release and let the detectives search my desk while I was gone to the P.D.

The newsroom was not crowded—it was still lunchtime. I saw Arnie's bald head sticking up over the partition that marked off the territory of the violence reporters. As I walked by the entrance to their pod, I saw that Arnie was standing behind a young detective, Boone Thompson, who was sitting in Arnie's desk chair. Boone had just pulled the top left-hand drawer open.

"Hi, Boone," I said. "Are you the guy with the releases?"

Boone looked up. He'd be no good for undercover work—too odd-looking. He had cotton white hair and light lashes and a bright red complexion—skin darker than his hair.

"Yeah. I'm the guy," he said. "I'll get you one as soon as I get through with Mr. Ashe's desk."

"It's close to empty," Arnie said. "I haven't been here long enough to rat-pack it."

Boone looked in the drawer he'd pulled out, then shoved it closed.

"Aren't you going to count the pencils?" Arnie said.

"Nope. Since we're looking for a pair of men's work shoes, we can't look at anything smaller," Boone said.

He pulled out the bottom left-hand drawer. It was full of books, hardbacks marked GRANTHAM PUBLIC LIBRARY. Boone picked them up. "A science fiction fan," he said. "Do you like C.J. Cherryh?"

"One of my favorites," Arnie said.

Boone looked through the titles. Was he going to read them all?

I checked my watch. Twelve fifty-five. "Boone, I don't like to hurry you," I said, "but Peaches has a slot for me to make a statement at one o'clock sharp."

"Okay! Okay!" Boone gave a cursory look at the back of the drawer—which was empty—and turned to open the right-hand drawer, the double-deep one under the computer terminal. Arnie had an old desk. Most of the desks don't have a drawer there anymore. It's too hard to get to. Nobody uses them. I expected the drawer to be empty.

But it had file folders in it.

"Old stuff," Arnie said. "I've barely looked at it."

Boone riffled through the folders, and the drawer started to fall shut of its own weight. But Boone grabbed it and pulled it all the way open. He ducked his head until it was nearly between his knees, and he peered into the deep recesses of the drawer.

He gave a soft whistle. Then he pulled a pair of plastic

gloves out of his pocket and slowly put them on, holding the drawer open with his knee.

Then he reached into the drawer, into the pocket behind the file folders, and he pulled out a black work shoe. He put it down on Arnie's desk, and he reached in again and pulled out another.

"My God!" I said. "Arnie! How did those get there?"

But when I turned around for Arnie's reply, he was gone. He had disappeared from the newsroom.

Chapter 9

With Arnie's disappearance stated that baldly, it would seem that Grantham Police Department would have issued an all-points bulletin for him immediately. That didn't happen.

I merely said, "Gee, where'd Arnie go?" and Boone said, "He sure disappeared fast, didn't he? I'll look in the men's room." Then I said, "Do you still need to search my desk?" And Boone said, "Maybe not. Go on over to the P.D. and make your statement, and we'll catch you later."

Many of life's significant moments seem undramatic at the moment they're happening, I guess. Anyway, I went to the P.D., made my statement, came back to the office, and copyedited three of the dullest stories on record. Then Arnie called in.

He called the city desk number, and Ruth Borah wasn't at her phone. So I answered. "City desk," I said.

There was a long silence before Arnie spoke. "Nell?" His voice sounded angry, but I recognized it.

"Hey, Arnie. Where'd you go?"

Again I got a long silence. So I spoke. "Arnie? Are you there?"

"Listen, I've had an emergency come up," he said. "Somebody will have to cover the cop beat for me tonight. Maybe for a couple of days."

"What! Arnie, where are you?"

"I'm on my way out of town."

"Wait a minute! Have you talked to the cops about those shoes?"

"I don't know how those shoes got there."

"I didn't think you did, Arnie. But you need to tell the cops that."

He didn't reply to that remark. "I've got to go," he said. "I just wanted Ruth to know I'm not coming in."

"Arnie!" I started to argue, but he'd already hung up.

I sat there with the phone in my hand. Ruth Borah came back to her desk, and she said, "You look puzzled, Nell."

"Ruth," I said. "I think maybe Arnie is going to fly the coop."

"Don't be silly," she said. "He's doing fine. So why would he leave this job? He called in a lot of favors to get it, or so I hear."

"What do you mean?"

Ruth leaned close to me. "I hear that Arnie had done Jake some good turn years ago, and Arnie used it as an in to get the job."

I frowned. "Jake? As in our managing editor? The guy who does the hiring and firing around here?"

"Right."

"What could Arnie have on Jake?"

"Oh, I don't think it was blackmail! I think he and Arnie met at some regional press meeting, and Arnie kept him from getting into some sort of difficulties—professional difficulties. Slipped him the word on a false news tip. Something like that.

"Anyway, Jake said Arnie was a smart reporter, and we were lucky to get him. And so far he's been great. So I'm surprised if he just doesn't show up."

"At least he called in."

That was the first hint we had that Arnie was on the lam. It wasn't yet a topic for office gossip. Mike and I were to claim that distinction before the evening was over.

I had reported for work at two o'clock. At six-thirty, Mike

got off the elevator that serves as an after-hours entrance to the *Gazette* newsroom. He still wore his khakis and the sweater that matched his hair and eyes. I waved, but Kimmie, the night switchboard operator and receptionist, rang my phone anyway.

"Mike's here and says he needs to talk to you," Kimmie said.

"Send him in."

"He says he'll wait out here until you can come over," Kimmie said.

I kept an eye on the newsroom reception area while I finished the story I was working on. Mike sat on the plain and uncomfortable plastic-covered couch that's out there, and I could see Kimmie giving him the full treatment. She's a junior at Grantham State, and she's a sort of live Barbie doll, blond and curvy. The night switchboard and receptionist job is perfect for students, because it gives them some time to study. But Kimmie put her books away as soon as Mike sat down.

I laughed to myself, maybe to hide a pang of jealousy. But I didn't seriously think that Mike would be enticed by Kimmie/Barbie. If I were going to be jealous, my feelings would focus on Mike's former girlfriend, Annie. They'd lived together in Chicago for two years. Annie hurt Mike badly when she broke up with him. Something about the way he never mentioned her name tended to make me uneasy.

No, I wasn't worried about Kimmie. I was a little worried about what Mike was going to say when he found out I had left something out of my statement for the Grantham P.D. I hadn't mentioned the reason why I'd gone down the stairs to the *Gazette* paper-storage warehouse, the reason I had been on the spot to find Martina's body.

I hadn't told them Martina wanted to tell me something.

And I was a little worried about the way Mike and I had parted company at lunch. It hadn't been friendly.

He'd been urging me to call my aunt. But Mike had never

met Aunt Billie, I reminded myself. He hadn't known what he was asking. I made a determined effort not to hold his request against him. I made sure I was wearing a pleasant expression as I went to the front and leaned over the narrow railing.

"Hi." Maybe I said it a little too brightly. "Are the detectives looking for Arnie?"

"I'm not here about Arnie." Mike's words came out with surprising force. "I wanted to tell you a couple of things."

He beckoned me out into the waiting area. That was odd. But I went through the swinging gate and sat beside him on the couch. He spoke very quietly.

"I've got to go out of town," he said.

I was completely amazed. "Out of town!" I probably gaped. Mike glanced at Kimmie, who wasn't even pretending not to listen. When I spoke again, I followed his lead and dropped my voice. "This is sudden. Where are you going?"

"A little personal business."

"Well, that's a noncommittal reply."

Mike propped his left tennis shoe on his right knee, then frowned at the arrangement of feet and legs. "It shouldn't take more than a couple of days."

"Is there any point in my asking you where you're going?"

He was still staring at his tennis shoe. "I was able to get some emergency leave."

"That answer wasn't responsive to my question," I said.

"I know." He looked at me. "Listen, Nell, before I go I need to know something. Did you tell Hammond that you'd talked to Martina about your dad?"

I steeled myself for a fight. "No, Mike, I didn't. I can't believe that has anything to do with anything. She said she hadn't worked with him. Whatever she wanted to see me about—well, there's very little chance it had anything to do with my father."

I was surprised to see a relieved look cross Mike's face.

"It's probably just as well," he said. "But I'm still worried about you. You've got a killer loose in this building."

"Maybe. But we've also got a couple of hundred people who are not killers. I'll try to hang around with the right crowd."

"Try more than that. Try to act real dumb, okay?"

"Dumb?"

"Yeah, dumb. You're just as nosy as Martina was, you know."

"Thanks a lot!" I drew myself back. Then I realized that my body language alone was giving Kimmie a juicy item for her coffee break, and I leaned toward Mike and spoke in a low voice. "They pay reporters to be nosy."

"True. And you're a good reporter. But this is not a good situation for using those valuable news-gathering skills. Pretend you don't want to know anything about it. Okay?"

"Butt out of police business?"

"More than that. I even take back what I told you at noon. This is not a good time to look into what happened to your father."

I probably stiffened up again. "What are you doing? Using reverse psychology? Trying to get me to call Aunt Billie by telling me not to call Aunt Billie?"

Mike rolled his eyes and gave a disgusted shrug. "Your mind is too tricky for any psychology I could use, forward or reverse. I just want you to keep from stirring up anything while I'm out of town."

"Stirring up anything?"

"About Martina's death." He made an impatient gesture. "I can't get out of this trip. Will you promise me you'll be careful?"

"I'm always careful."

He shook his head. "You're never careful. At least get the security guard to walk you out to your car tonight. Okay?"

"If I feel like it."

"And one other thing." He was looking at his tennis shoe again, staring anywhere but at me.

I wondered what else was coming. "What is it?"

"I've got a repairman coming over to the house while I'm gone," he said. "I need your garage door opener."

I felt as if I'd been slapped. Mike's neighbor had a front door key so she could let repairmen in and out. He didn't need my garage door opener for a repairman. If he needed my garage door opener, it was for some other reason.

Such as, he didn't want me in his house any longer.

Talk about throwing cold water on a relationship. I'd just been told to stay away from Mike's house. Not to use the garage door opener. Well, I wasn't going to make a scene, not in front of Kimmie. Or anywhere else. Not ever, not no way, not at all.

"Of course," I said. "I'll get it."

"Nell—"

I didn't wait to hear what he was going to say. I jumped to my feet and walked back to the copy desk as quickly as possible. I opened the bottom drawer of my desk and took the garage door opener out of my purse. I also got out my key, the one that opened the door between the garage and the utility room.

I smiled sweetly as I walked back across the office, leaned across the railing, and handed Mike the key and the opener.

"I don't need the key," he said.

"Neither do I," I said. "Have a good trip."

I went back to my desk without looking back, but I felt sure Kimmie got an eyeful of the whole episode. She took a break right after that, at the same time Alicia Hess, our arts editor, went downstairs. Those two were Martina's closest rivals in gathering and spreading news. My fight with Mike would be an item, even if it didn't show up in the morning *Gazette*.

I didn't leave the building for my dinner break. Why buy

food when your stomach is in such a knot you can't possibly eat it? I went down to the break room and got a Diet Coke and some snack crackers out of the machines, then opened a copy of the *Gazette* to the crossword puzzle and stared at it. I'd forgotten to bring a pencil, but maybe the puzzle would keep people from talking to me.

My plan didn't work. As usual, the early pressroom crew was taking their boisterous break, and Bob Johnson snarled at me as he walked by the table. I ignored him.

Ed Brown came through, still looking handsome from across the room and haggard close up. He was with Dan Smith, who was still wearing an angora shawl on his head.

Dan had to come over and make sad sounds about Martina. I didn't want to hear it. As shocked as I had been by Martina's death, I was realizing that—for me—trouble with Mike was worse. I'm sure I made sympathetic noises at Dan, but I was too sunk in my own misery to worry much about his.

I even had trouble being polite to J.J. Jones when he stopped to thank me for the advice I'd given him the night before.

"My client really appreciated it," he said. "You're nice as a cotton hat, li'l missy. Cute as a bird dog pup under a red wagon."

I went back upstairs before I puked on his gaudy plaid sports jacket.

Things didn't go well on the desk, either. We were all realizing how much we'd depended on Martina, even if we hadn't enjoyed her company. I spent thirty minutes digging through stories from the *Gazette* library so I could figure out that a young Grantham businessman was "Judd G. Bowen II," not "Jr." and not "III." Martina would have needed only thirty seconds to explain that he had been named for his grandfather, Judd Gerrard Bowen, not his father, Judd Geoffrey Bowen. So his grandfather, who had founded a local oil field-equipment firm, had been "Judd G. Bowen" and his father, current president of the firm, was "J.G. Bowen" and the younger man, who had just joined the firm, was "Judd G. Bowen II." The whole thing gave me a picture of the Bowen family—twenty-five-years ago—sitting around the cradle of Judd G. II, plotting the best way to confuse the newspaper. Seemed as if they'd have better things to do with their time.

To make it worse, I was the only copy editor, so I had to stay late. It didn't matter. I had no place to go and no one to see. And I could use the overtime.

But eleven finally arrived, the police reporter who was filling in for Arnie turned in his last story—just an hour late—and Ruth told me I could leave. I would have ignored Mike's directive about getting the security guard to walk me to my car, but Ruth insisted I call the guard.

"I'm nervous as a cat myself," she said. "I want everybody to be extra cautious."

"The parking lot's full of circulation trucks," I said. "Those guys are tougher than the security guard."

"Humor me," Ruth said.

So the guard accompanied me out into the covered garage, checked out my little Dodge with his giant flashlight, and stood there while I made sure the motor started, the doors locked, and the lights worked. I drove off, thinking how ironic it would be if the guard got mugged on his way back into the building.

I live in central Grantham, about a mile north of the downtown area, in an area called College Hills. It's near the Grantham State campus, and it's an area a real estate professional would call "historic" maybe. Or maybe the word is "spotty."

In other words, the neighborhood has lots of nice new apartment houses, ratty old houses turned into apartments, old fraternity houses remodeled into unconventional homes for professors with big families, houses remodeled into businesses, strip shopping centers, trendy restaurants, and silkscreen shops. It also has lots of big trees and bushes. And narrow streets with cars parked on both sides.

My two girl roommates, Brenda and Martha, were both graduate students, and the three of us had the second floor of an old house. We each had a bedroom but shared a bath, and we'd improvised a tiny sitting room on the landing.

Downstairs was Rocky, who called himself our landlady. Rocky owned the house. He had his own bedroom and sitting room, and all four of us shared the kitchen and downstairs living room. It was a temporary arrangement. Martha and Brenda were both due to receive their master's degrees in June, and Rocky planned to bounce us all then and remodel the house into two flats. I'd thought about moving in with Mike when Rocky evicted us, but if I didn't have a key to his house, that obviously wasn't going to happen.

Rocky was part owner of the Blue Flamingo, Grantham's most respectable gay bar. Our house was only a few blocks from the Flamingo, so Rocky usually walked to work. The Flamingo was in the Campus Corner shopping area, and it had an odd little alley but no parking.

Anyway, "spotty" is probably a good word for our neighborhood. And "bushy" and "wooded." In fact, it was silly to worry about danger in the *Gazette* parking lot. My backyard was the place where anybody smart would hide for a surprise attack.

Why the guy in the great big car didn't do that is beyond me. But, no, he came up beside me on Mississippi Avenue and tried to run me into the curb.

When you get off work close to midnight, you get used to having the street to yourself on the way home. I keep my doors locked, and I ignore the few other vehicles on the road. That's the safest way. So I didn't notice the big car for a while. I don't know if he'd followed me from the *Gazette*, or if he picked me up later. I wasn't aware that he even existed until he came up behind me fast, cut out to the left, almost passed me, then moved over into my lane on top of my left front fender.

I yelled, and I blasted the horn, and I hit the brakes. My Dodge slowed enough that the big car could slide in front of me. He skidded to a stop. Luckily, my brakes worked better than his, so I got stopped without running over his back bumper. In fact, I had around four feet to spare, so I swung the steering wheel left as hard as I could, and I gunned the motor. I shot into the left-hand lane and passed him, nearly taking off his driver's-side door, which seemed to be opening. I floorboarded the Dodge and headed on up Mississippi.

I'm not a complete idiot. I knew that carjackers cause accidents, then rob or kill or rape or maim the drivers who stop. I wasn't stopping.

Neither was the big car. As I passed it, I'd mentally placed it as an old Cadillac—white. I hadn't gotten the tag number, and I hoped it wouldn't get close enough for me to get it. But when I checked the rearview mirror, I saw it was coming after me.

I drove several blocks at top speed. This isn't exactly a record-breaking pace in a compact Dodge, and I could see that speed alone wasn't going to get me away from the Caddy. It was gaining on me. I was going to have to use guile.

So I braked sharply and turned at the next corner. This put me in my own neighborhood, on residential streets I was familiar with. Of course, it also put me at great danger of killing some innocent bystander, because these particular residential streets were crowded with parked cars. In my neighborhood the Dodge has to hold in its stomach to pass a car going the other way, and pedestrians tend to pop out from between parked cars at the least expected moments. I took the middle of the street and hoped no one else wanted to use it.

I shoved the gas pedal all the way down again. I glanced at the speedometer and nearly panicked. A safe speed in this neighborhood was around twenty. I was going fifty. And be-hind me I saw the behemoth turn off Mississippi. It seemed I could hear it roar, but maybe that was the Dodge. I was pushing it.

I turned right at the next corner. Then right again. Then left. And every time, just before I could turn, I'd see those horrible headlights behind me. The blocks were too long for me to disappear before the Cadillac was on my tail.

"Why don't you quit!" I yelled. "My car's worth nothing! I've got nothing to steal!"

A driveway, I thought. Maybe a driveway was the answer. I turn a corner, pull into a driveway, cut the headlights. Maybe the Cadillac wouldn't figure it out.

But if the beast did figure it out. I'd be boxed in. Trapped. No, I didn't dare turn into a driveway. Unless it was a police station drive. But that wouldn't work. The Central Station was the closest one, and it was clear back near the *Gazette* office. I had to do something faster than that.

God! I was doing things fast enough. The cars along the curb were whizzing by. Some people were standing on a lighted porch, saying good-bye. One of them pointed, and they all turned to look as I flew by. I heard faint yells.

I turned around another corner, teetering on two wheels because I didn't dare slow down. Where could I hide? Could I get back to Mississippi? To a main street? No, the Cadillac could outrun me there. And here, with houses all around, at least there were people who might hear me yell. Mississippi was deserted after midnight.

If I didn't dare pull into a driveway, maybe I could sim-ply hide among the cars along the curb. They were bumper to bumper in the whole neighborhood. We'd turned our backyard into a four-slot parking lot, and sometimes we had to chase the neighbors out of it. College Hills has a contin-uous parking problem.

I had a mad impulse to laugh. Even if I wanted to leave the Dodge, I'd never find a parking spot.

But maybe that was the best idea I'd had. I began to scan the curbs, looking for an opening. I could go on past it, swing around the block, maybe come back and nab it before the Cadillac caught up. But the likelihood of finding such a spot was practically nil.

Then I saw it. It wasn't a parallel spot. It was an angle. It was the middle spot of the four used by the Campus Dry Cleaners for their delivery vans. Usually they had four vans parked abreast there. But tonight there were only three.

Every night the Campus Cleaners drivers pulled the vans into the driveway that led to the drive-through windows. Usually customers from a tavern on the corner parked behind them, blocking them in. Nobody objected as long as the cars were gone by the six a.m. opening hour of the Campus Cleaners.

But somebody was just pulling out of one of those spots behind the vans. I blasted my horn, and the car stopped and rocked back on its springs. It was a red sports car of some type, with a canvas top. A hand gestured out the window, not too politely. I kept the horn going until I was past, then swung around the next corner. That put me on University Boulevard, one of the streets that border the college, headed north. I gunned the motor, then skidded around the next corner. Sure enough, the Caddy came out onto University before I could get out of sight. I sped east on that street for a block, then whipped a right at the next corner, heading south. Before I'd covered a block, the giant Cadillac once again appeared in my mirror. I took the next corner at fifty, the Dodge teetering. Now I was headed west.

As soon as I got around that corner, I cut my lights. The streetlights and porch lights and the security light at the Campus Cleaners gave me enough vision to see the delivery vans halfway down the block. I guided the Dodge into the empty slot, nestling it between three vans. I took my foot off the brake as quickly as the car stopped.

Then I cut the motor. If this didn't work, I'd have to get out and run.

I ducked down in the front seat and watched the lights of the Cadillac go past behind me. It didn't stop. The street got very still. I sat up, and all I could hear was my heart pounding.

Should I restart the car and dig out? Or wait a minute? What if the Cadillac came around the block again? I sat there, panting.

Then I heard footsteps.

There was no reason on God's green earth for me to think those footsteps belonged to the driver of the Cadillac. But I didn't doubt for a minute that they did.

I sat there frozen. Should I get out and run?

Click, click, click. I could hear those steps. They were behind me.

I realized that the phantom pacer was walking down the middle of the street. And he was coming closer. I'd have to lie down in the seat again, or he'd see me silhouetted against the security lights of the cleaners' drive-through.

I could start the car, back out, and drive off. But what if he'd used the giant Cadillac to block the street? What if I backed out of my parking spot and turned the wrong way and I couldn't get by?

I fingered the door handle. Maybe I'd better get out and make a run for the tavern on the corner.

Then I looked ahead.

I was an idiot! I was sitting in a drive-through! There was nothing ahead of me but a bright yellow rope.

I turned the key, gunned the motor to life. The Dodge shot forward, past the window where I'd dropped off hundreds of garments to be dry-cleaned. The yellow rope popped in two and flew in the air. I whirled around the corner of the building and into the alley, then out onto University, but this time I turned left.

As I passed the intersection, I saw the Cadillac parked in the middle of the street. A figure was running toward it.

My heart leaped into my mouth. The guy was pointing one of his hands at me. The hand was holding something.

I heard a pop, but I didn't stop to investigate. I drove two blocks, turned left, then ducked into an alley. I skidded to a stop, jumped out of the car, and ran to a door.

Yeah! Thank God for fire regulations. The door was unlocked. I yanked it open and ran inside and down a hall.

The music was semi-deafening, and the dance floor was crowded. Crowded with guys. No girls. Only guys.

I swung toward the bar. "Rocky!" I yelled.

A big guy, balding and slightly plump, gaped at me. "Rocky, call the cops!" I yelled again. "Somebody took a shot at me."

Chapter 10

I wouldn't inflict the police on the Blue Flamingo's clientele, although Rocky's customers are a quiet group. Martha, Brenda, and I drop by occasionally, and we've never seen anything more shocking than guys talking to each other—maybe with their arms around each other's shoulders, just like at sports bars.

After Rocky called 911 for me, I waited at the back door. As soon as the patrol car pulled into the alley, I went outside to meet the officer just as a second, unmarked, car arrived. That one held Jim Hammond. I was being honored with the attention of a senior detective.

"Where's your guardian?" he growled.

"If you mean Mike, he's out of town," I answered.

Jim glowered while I talked to a patrolman, who filled out an incident report. The officer was more nervous than I was, thanks to Jim's supervision.

"I guess it was an attempted carjacking," I said. My voice sounded weak even to me.

"Yeah, sure!" Hammond said. "On Wednesday you barely rescue a fellow editor from death by asphyxiation. On Thursday you find the same woman dead after being kicked downstairs. Slightly after midnight Friday you're chased home by a creep in a Cadillac who tries to shoot you. Three completely and totally unrelated incidents. Obviously."

"I know it's weird, Jim! I can't even prove this chase, this shooting, actually happened. I don't see any bullet holes in the car, so I guess he missed me. You can check back by the corner where he fired, but the shots were aimed at the campus. They could have hit a tree or something."

"Oh, I believe the part about the shots, Nell. People leaving that tavern saw the Cadillac. They saw the guy shoot at you. They called 911."

"They saw him? What did he look like?"

"He looked like a normal-sized man wearing dark clothes and a ski mask."

"Oh, nuts!"

"Yeah. Nuts. But don't try to convince me this car chase doesn't have something to do with the murder down at the *Gazette*. Somebody must be out to get you."

"But why?"

"You're more likely to know that than I am."

"If I knew, I'd tell you in a New York minute! I like being alive. I don't like being chased and shot at!"

Jim looked at me narrowly. Then he took my arm and led me over to the other side of his car, away from the patrolman.

"Listen, Nell, I got out the incident report on the asphyxiation accident—so-called. In that report you said that Martina was the only one who used that ladies' lounge down in the basement."

"She was the only person who used it that time of the evening. In the daytime—"

Jim made an impatient gesture. "But in the statement you made today about finding her body, you said you just happened to decide to go down there."

I didn't say anything, so Jim went on. "Why? If you didn't normally go down to that lounge, why did you go that time?"

"Martina asked me to meet her there."

"What for?"

"I don't know, Jim. She was killed before I could ask her."

"Your desks were right together. She could have talked to you any time all day."

"It was obviously something she didn't want to discuss in the newsroom."

"Would it have been about the newspaper?"

"I don't know! Martina was a terrible gossip. She may have wanted to give me a hot item about the city editor, or somebody else who worked within earshot of our desks. She may have wanted to pump me about something."

"What?"

"Jim, if I knew, I'd tell you." We stared at each other. I was the one who spoke. "Do you want me to amend the statement I made, to make my reason for going downstairs clearer?"

"You can do it when you come in to make a statement on this." He turned and called to the patrolman.

"Follow Miss Matthews home and check out her house. If somebody's laying for her, let's make sure they already haven't broken in and hidden under the bed."

He drove off. The motor of his unmarked car had a growl that matched the one in his voice.

A search of our house involved getting Martha and Brenda out of bed, but no one was hiding in the pantry or in a closet or behind the shower curtain or under anybody's bed. The search simply meant we were all up and excited until after two a.m.

After I got in bed, of course, I couldn't fall asleep, so I had plenty of time to worry about Hammond's questions.

Did someone think I knew something about Martina's death? Why did they think that? Did I know something? Was I linked to her death in some way?

The only conceivable link I could think of was the question I had asked her about my father. But Martina had said she didn't know my father. Well, actually, she hadn't said that. She'd said, "I never worked with anyone by that name."

When I examined it closely, it wasn't quite a denial.

And Mike—he had me terribly confused. First he'd said I should include the information about my father in my statement about finding Martina's body. Then he'd told me not to—yet.

Then he'd left town. Late in the evening. Didn't even get a night's sleep first. What was he up to?

And why had he first urged me to ask my aunt about my father, then changed his mind? Why the switch?

But maybe my father was the link between Martina's death and the crazy things that had been happening. Maybe I did have to ask Aunt Billie.

No, that was a nightmare I couldn't face either awake or asleep. I turned on the light and began reading *Auntie Mame*, the book that always takes my mind off my troubles. It was even more soothing than *Treasure Island*. Once again I fell asleep with the light on.

The telephone woke me at ten a.m. I caught the call on my bedside phone just before the answering machine kicked in. It was the dayside switchboard operator from the *Gazette*.

"Sorry to bother you, Nell," she said, "but you've had a telephone call which the caller claimed was an emergency."

"Who called?"

"Mr. Dan Smith."

"Dan Smith?" In my sleep-drugged state, the name meant nothing to me.

"Yes. He's staying at the Downtown Holiday Inn."

"Oh!" It was Martina's boyfriend, the guy with the angora shawl on his head.

"Do you want the number?"

I took it. What the heck did Dan Smith want? Was it really an emergency? Another one? I washed my face, but then my curiosity won out and I called Dan Smith.

He picked up the phone on the first ring. "This is Dan Smith."

"And this is Nell Matthews. What's the emergency?"

"The emergency is in Oklahoma City, Ms. Matthews. I have to go up there for a couple of days." He sounded depressed. "Once they decide about services for Martina, could you let me know?"

"Of course, Mr. Smith." He always made me feel guilty, guilty because I wasn't grieving for Martina. "I'm not sure who'll be handling the arrangements, but I'll find out."

"Well, the only family she had was a brother in California. I don't know if he can come back or not. I told Jake Edwards that I'd handle it if nobody else wanted to."

"You're a good friend, Mr. Smith. Martina was lucky to have you." I hoped that didn't sound too corny.

"We'd known each other a long time." He paused, and I almost said good-bye, but then he spoke again. "I hate to be so much trouble, but can I ask you another favor?"

"Certainly. If it's something I can't do, I'll say no."

"Martina gave me something, something from the *Gazette* library. She asked me to take it away. Said she wanted to get it out of the building."

"From the library? The *Gazette* library? That's odd. Things from the *Gazette* library don't usually leave the building."

"I know. That's why I'd appreciate a friend returning it, just quietly. I don't want to get her in trouble."

It was a little late for Martina to get in more trouble, but it might not be tactful to say so. "I'll be glad to return it," I said. "What is it?"

"I haven't unwrapped it, but it's in a box."

"Do you want me to pick it up?"

"No, I'll leave it at the *Gazette* switchboard for you. Before I leave town tonight."

We said good-bye, and I went back to bed. A box from the *Gazette* library. That could be anything. He hadn't said how large the box was. I decided speculation was a waste of time. I rolled over and looked at the empty side of my double bed. Mike had occupied it a few times, even though Brenda,

Martha, and I—and Rocky—had a rule that boyfriends didn't stay overnight.

The bed looked awfully empty. I missed Mike. And he'd taken my garage door opener away. Did that mean I wasn't going to see him again? The whole episode was weird. I couldn't believe we were breaking up because he wanted me to ask my Aunt Billie about my father and I didn't want to do it. Especially since he'd changed his mind and decided I was right not to approach her.

Now I was wide awake. Aunt Billie would do that to me. There was no rest when she was around, even lurking in the back of my mind.

I lay in bed, staring at the ceiling, and debated. I should ask her about my father. No, I shouldn't. Maybe she didn't know anything. How would I find out if I didn't ask? But if she didn't know about him, who did? Had all knowledge of my father died with my mother? Aunt Billie was the only relative I had left who had known my father.

I should ask her about him.

Then I turned over and buried my head under the pillow. I couldn't face talking to her.

And Mike had told me not to do anything until he got back. But who was he to be telling me what to do? He didn't even want me to have his garage door opener.

I guess I would never have settled the question, but fate—or was it Providence?—intervened.

The telephone rang, and a nasal voice spoke. "Nell? Nell, honey, I'm in Grantham today, and I thought maybe you'd like to go to lunch."

Darned if it wasn't Aunt Billie.

Maybe fate was trying to tell me something.

Aunt Billie comes to Grantham a few times a year to shop. For the ladies of Amity, one hundred and fifty miles away, Grantham's malls and department stores are a magnet. They gladly drive two and a half hours on a Saturday morning, shop their feet off, and drive two and a half hours home that night. They come on Saturdays because they are like most other American women; they all work Monday through Friday.

Aunt Billie works in my uncle's insurance office. Actually, she runs both the office and my uncle, but it's never occurred to her to get her insurance license and become an agent herself.

Her hobby is crafts, which immediately shows that she and I have nothing in common. She likes to do handwork, she says, because it gives her something to do while she watches television. Doing something more interesting than television has never seemed to occur to her.

"I guess you have to work today," she said, sighing.

Aunt Billie can't get over my schedule. Working on Saturday, my goodness! And working nights! She finds it shocking. She's astonished when I point out that if she wants a Sunday paper, someone has to work Saturday night putting it out.

I didn't have to go in to work until four o'clock, so I had no real reason to dodge lunch with her, other than my natural inclination to avoid her whenever possible. We arranged to meet at twelve-thirty in Grantham's biggest craft mall, and I called and made a reservation at the most ladylike restaurant I could think of. I barely had time to shower, blow-dry the hair, and dress in black slacks with a black and tan shirt and my much worn linen jacket. I didn't expect her to like my outfit, but I thought the black and linen was innocuous enough that it wouldn't cause an argument.

I met her in the frame department of the craft shop. She hadn't changed much—same plump face and figure, same professionally curled gray hair, same pastel pants and shirt. We touched cheeks.

"Nell, honey! You haven't been home in months!"

I didn't point out that my home was in Grantham, and I went there every day. She paid for her purchases, and I drove us to the Trellis Room, a standard tea room with an

ambiance that featured fake roses climbing over walls criss-
crossed with dusty white lattices and with a menu that featured chicken salad on croissants and broccoli soup.

Aunt Billie apologized all the way over for the short notice
on her luncheon invitation. It seemed she had discovered
only the day before that one of her friends was driving to
Grantham, and on the spur of the moment Aunt Billie decided to come along.

"But she had to go out to her daughter's house and take
her grandson his birthday gift, and I didn't want to horn in
on a family party," she concluded as we settled ourselves at
our table.

We caught up on my cousin, Carrie, and her husband and
three kids. On Uncle Marshall and on the business. By then
Aunt Billie's chicken salad and my hamburger had arrived.
She took a bite, swallowed, then leaned across the table.

"Nell, I'm just going to come right out and ask. Are you
still seeing this Mike Svenson?"

I shrugged. "As far as I know. He's out of town right
now."

"Do you have any firm plans?"

"Our only firm plan right now is not to make any firm
plans."

She frowned. "I know I'm just a nosy old aunt, Nell, but
we would like to see you settled. Settled and happy."

"Well, I've got one part of your plan accomplished, Aunt
Billie. I am happy. I have friends—Mike, plus others. We do
things that are fun, but I'm not afraid to spend an evening
alone. I'm not getting rich, but I haven't had to get into
Grandmother's money. And I am settled—in a job I love."

"Oh, the job." Aunt Billie dismissed it with a wave of her
croissant. "I mean settled in Life." She gave it a capital L.

I was trying not to let Aunt Billie get me down, so I
laughed. "I spend a third of my life at that job, just the way
you spend a third of your life at your job. I hope neither of

us is spending that much time at something we don't enjoy doing."

Aunt Billie gaped at me. "I never thought about it that way," she said. "I guess I just drifted into working at your Uncle Marshall's office. When he started out, he couldn't afford any office help. I answered the phone at home, and I did some of his typing. As the business grew—well, I did more. After we built our own building—" She quit talking and took a bite of chicken salad.

"And now you're manager for the biggest insurance agency in the southern half of the state."

Aunt Billie laughed. "You make it sound like I should ask for a raise."

"You should think about what it would cost Uncle Marshall to replace you. He doesn't have a realistic business budget if he doesn't take that into account."

She blinked and chewed that thought, along with her chicken salad. I decided it was time to talk about my father. If I could manage to keep it casual.

So I stared at my hamburger, picked up a potato chip, and used my calmest tone of voice. "Your call today was providential, Aunt Billie. I was going to call you. Is there any chance that you know where my father went after my mother died?"

I looked up from my plate in time to see Aunt Billie go into a spasm. Her face contorted, and she dropped her fork. She clutched her napkin to her face. I thought I was going to have to administer the Heimlich maneuver.

Before I could jump to my feet, Aunt Billie dropped the napkin and picked up her iced tea. She gulped several times, then put it down. Her eyes grew round and fearful. "Your father hasn't contacted you, has he?"

"No."

"Oh, thank goodness!"

"What would be so awful about my father giving me a call? Writing me a letter?"

She shook her head, but she didn't answer.

"I'm an adult," I said. "He's not going to sue for custody, try to get me back."

She still didn't say anything. Just sat there, panting.

"I'm just curious, Aunt Billie. I know he and my mother had split up before she died, but I've never understood why he didn't come back after she was gone. Why the split had to include me."

Aunt Billie reached for the giant handbag she'd propped against the table leg. She shook her head.

"I don't want to see him," I said. "I just want to understand why he left. I didn't mean to upset you."

She hoisted her handbag—it was more of a duffel bag—into her lap and dug through it. "I'm all right," she said. "You just caught me by surprise." She pulled out a Kleenex and dabbed her eyes, soaking up the mascara-laden tears that had begun running down her cheeks.

"Aunt Billie—"

"I knew this time would come, Nell. I tried to tell Mother that you needed to know."

"Know what?"

"About your parents. About your father."

I stared at my plate. "Aunt Billie, I don't want to bring up something that is obviously painful for you. But—my father went off and left me. I admit this has always been a problem for me. I've had counseling about it. But it affects my relationships with men. You say you'd like to see me settle down. But I'm afraid—Mike's afraid—I may never be able to do that if I don't dispose of this business with my father, if I don't find out why he deserted me."

"I told Mother you needed to know," Aunt Billie repeated.

"Know what?"

She leaned forward again, her face earnest, the mascara running unimpeded. "Nell, your father didn't want to leave you. He didn't have any real choice. He saw that you'd be better off with Mother and Dad, and he wrote a letter giving them your custody—"

"Yes, I found it among Gran's things."

"—and he told Mother things might be worse if he didn't go."

"Why?"

"Well, things got awfully confused after your mother was murdered."

Chapter 11

"After your mother was murdered."

I have no idea how I reacted to those words.

I had lived twenty years without a mother, and no one had ever so much as hinted to me that my mother's death was anything but an accident. *Stunned* is not a strong enough word to describe how Aunt Billie's statement made me feel. Shocked? Stupefied? Pole-axed?

I do remember that the Trellis Room seemed to turn into a still photo. I must have turned away from Aunt Billie, because when I think of that moment, the memory that pops up is of a delicate spider web covering one of the fabric roses that sprouted out of the individual bower where we were sitting.

Then I realized Aunt Billie was speaking. "Nell! Dear! Did you have no idea your mother was murdered?"

I went into denial. It couldn't be true.

"My mother was killed in an accident," I said. "A car accident."

"She was killed by a car, but it was no accident," Aunt Billie said. Her tears didn't keep her voice from being tart.

"That can't be true."

"I'm afraid it is," Aunt Billie said. She wiped her eyes. Her nose looked drippy. I was glad that the silly bower and its fake roses gave us some cover from the prying eyes of the other lunching ladies. I was glad that I didn't know anybody else in the room. I didn't want to have a scene with Aunt Billie, but she was obviously wrong, and I had to set her straight.

"Gran told me she was killed in a car wreck," I said. "I can't believe she lied to me."

"She didn't lie. She just didn't tell the whole story. And it wasn't a wreck, exactly. Sally was hit by a car."

"Hit by a car?"

"Yes." Aunt Billie gulped. "It was awful! Nobody wanted to tell a little child all the details. I can't talk about it yet."

"Was it a hit-and-run?"

"Only in the sense that whoever hit her didn't stop. It wasn't a hit-and-run accident." She emphasized the word "accident." Then she leaned across the table toward me and made her chin firm. "Whoever did it had chased her down the road, Nell. They followed her into the bushes to hit her. It was definitely done on purpose. It was murder."

The room stood still again. Murder. My mother had been murdered. It didn't seem possible.

"Alan—your father—" Aunt Billie stopped again.

I grabbed at the variation in topic. "Yes, what happened to my father? Why did he go away?"

"He didn't have a lot of choice, I guess."

"Why not?"

"Well, Mother always said . . ." She had to stop and blow her nose. "Mother always said he did it mostly for you, Nell."

"For me? How could deserting me help?"

"Oh, he knew you'd be taken care of! Probably better than he could do it himself." She made a pleading gesture. "Your parents were so young, Nell! They would have grown up—eventually—I guess. But we all worried about them. They didn't seem responsible enough to take care of a baby, of a little girl."

"But he could have come to see me occasionally, Aunt Billie. He didn't have to abandon me completely."

"Oh, I guess he thought it would be worse . . ." Her eyes were swimming again, and her face was screwed up with pain. She stopped talking again.

"Look, Aunt Billie, I'm sorry if I've brought up a subject that's obviously painful for you, but you can see why I need to know. I'm grown up now. I can see that my father might have felt that Gran and Grandpa would be able to take care of me better than he could. But I don't see why he couldn't send a birthday card now and then—why he dropped all contact."

"He didn't want to! I'll give him that much credit. He loved you terribly, Nell. He didn't want to go away. He did it to protect you!"

"To protect me? How could abandoning me—emotionally, even if I was taken care of physically—protect me?"

"Nell, darling—" Aunt Billie gulped twice. Then she spat out words like machine-gun bullets:

"Nell, he was about to be arrested for your mother's murder!"

Then the room did get still. I don't think I even breathed for a long time. Maybe I would have been paralyzed forever if the mundane world hadn't intruded in the form of a middle-aged waitress.

Her voice came from beyond the roses. "More iced tea?"

The question started time moving again. I looked at the plump, gray-haired waitress in her gingham uniform, peeking into the fake rose bower, and I thought, "The world has not ended."

My grandmother had known that her child had been murdered, and she had lived with that knowledge. She had lived a full and happy life. And she had taken me in and loved me and had given me a full and happy life. I knew she had grieved—my mother's picture stood on her dresser always—but she hadn't let grief win. She hadn't let it destroy her. She hadn't let it destroy me.

I'm tough, I thought. I'm her granddaughter. I can do as well as Gran did. I'm strong. It's in my genes.

The waitress was still standing there with her pitcher at the ready. "More tea?" she repeated.

I said, "No, thank you," and I was surprised at how calm

my voice sounded. I waited until the waitress had left, then spoke to Aunt Billie.

"Did he do it? Did my father kill my mother?"

"Yes! I mean, no!" She mopped her eyes again.

I let her get control of herself. I even ate a bite of my hamburger. It tasted like the sawdust special, but putting food in my mouth was another way of reminding myself that life was going to go on.

In a minute Aunt Billie gave a rueful smile. "You can see why none of us ever wanted to talk about all this, Nell. It was the worst thing that ever happened to the family."

"I'm sorry. If I'd known, I wouldn't have brought it up in a public place."

"It seems that's the only place we ever see each other anymore."

Her comment stabbed my conscience. She was right. I didn't have anything in common with her, and I never tried to deal with her on more than a superficial level. Yet she was the closest relative I had. And we saw each other only if she came to Grantham shopping. I'd never invited her to my house because I didn't want to explain Rocky to her. So we only met in restaurants and malls.

"Aunt Billie . . ." I reached across the table, but she waved my gesture aside.

"It's all right, Nell. You've developed other interests. That's natural. But back to your question. Did Alan kill your mother? I always thought so."

"Did he admit it? Confess?"

"No. And Mother always stood up for him. She said she didn't think he had it in him to kill someone."

"But he was going to be arrested?"

"Yes. We were all there, you know. It was four days after Sally's body had been found."

"I remember that part. I remember you and Gran and Grandad coming. I stayed at my friend's house until you came."

"Yes, we drove all night to get there. Straight through. Marshall stayed home with Carrie. She was nine."

"I remember the house on Elm Street. It had a glassed-in front porch."

"Yes, it's the Michigan winters. They use those sun porches to keep the cold out, I guess. I think they're ugly."

"But I don't remember Daddy coming to the house after you all were there."

"No, he was busy, keeping up with the investigation. Since he was managing editor—"

"He was managing editor? I thought he was a reporter."

"He had been city editor in Amity. It was a big promotion, this new job. A real opportunity. That's why they moved so far away. And I think he was doing well. But Sally—she hated it up North."

"I remember that. She wanted to go back to Amity. They were going to make her take a lot of classes to get a Michigan teaching certificate. I remember she was mad about that. She said everybody was unfriendly. And ignorant. They didn't know anything about our part of the country and wouldn't believe we were part of the United States. She had a lot of trouble making friends."

"Yes, she'd call Mother and cry. I never knew how she met—"

Aunt Billie's sentence ended abruptly. She coughed and took a drink of her tea, while I waited for her to go on.

"Sorry," she said. "Anyway, I learned a lesson from Sally's death. I'd always been jealous of her, you know."

"Why?"

"Oh, she was the pretty one. The witty one. The cute one. The one everybody noticed. I was four years older, but she got all the attention."

"Gran always called you 'my good daughter,' " I said. "She never said my mother was the bad one, but—well, I know my parents had to get married, for example. I think Mother embarrassed Gran and Granddad a lot."

Aunt Billie sighed deeply. "Well. Anyway, Nell, I admit I resented Sally. She was always causing a stir in the family, always getting attention. You say your parents 'had to' get married. I always thought Sally had you because she didn't want me getting all the attention by having Carrie six months earlier."

I must have frowned, because she went on. "The jealousy between us was just silly. But we never made it up, never got over being—well, rival siblings. And then she was dead, and it was too late to ever make it up."

She looked at me earnestly. "Don't do that in life, Nell. Settle things. Don't let them fester. And don't learn that lesson the hard way, the way I did."

That pretty well ended our lunch. I drove Aunt Billie to the mall where she was to meet her friend, and I drove myself home, full of crazy emotions.

One moment I was near despair. My mother had been murdered, and my father had been accused of the crime.

The next I was exultant. My father hadn't abandoned me because he didn't want to be bothered with me or even because he didn't think he could manage to raise a little girl by himself. No, it had taken the threat of a prison term to get him to go.

He had loved me. Even Aunt Billie, who thought he was a killer, said so.

My mood bounced back and forth between despair and exultation twenty times between the shopping mall and my house. I went in the back door, and I heard a movie on in the living room TV set. Brenda is devoted to these stupid problem-of-the-week movies. She even tapes them to rerun on her free days.

As I stopped in the hall to check the mail, she saw me. "Hi, Nell. Come sit down. You'll love this. It's about men whose wives are in prison. I don't know how television would survive without dysfunctional families."

Television, huh! I could tell her about dysfunctional families.

But I didn't want to. I didn't want to talk to Brenda about what I'd learned from Aunt Billie. I wanted to talk to Mike about it.

Wherever he was.

I went upstairs, lay down, and stared at the ceiling of my bedroom. I wanted Mike there with me. I wanted him so bad I could hardly bear it. And I didn't even know where he was. He'd left town, left me, hadn't told me where he was going. I didn't know if he'd driven, flown, or hitchhiked.

And he'd taken my garage door opener and my key. I couldn't even go to his house, sniff his clothes, look at his belongings. And our six months wasn't even up.

Maybe I should have married Mike when I had the chance.

The first two weeks Mike and I were lovers were tumultuous. We'd known each other for more than a year, but at that time I was covering the violence beat, and I'd made a rule of not dating cops. Mike claims he'd wanted to ask me out all along, but he knew—or feared—that I'd say no, so he wouldn't.

Then—through factors that included the risk of death, family skeletons, greed, jealousy, and even a lovable orphan—Mike and I were thrown together in both physical danger and emotional crisis. By the time we'd settled the bad guys' hash, found the orphan a home, and come down from our adrenaline high, we were heavily involved, both emotionally and physically. In fact, I'd spent ten nights out of twelve in Mike's king-size bed.

At breakfast on the thirteenth day I'd mentioned that I needed to gather up my clothes and figure out where all my dirty laundry was.

At that time we'd never discussed the future—there'd been too much present going on—so I was somewhat surprised by Mike's reply.

"It might be simpler if you moved in over here," he said, "but there's one catch."

"What's that?"

"You have to marry me."

Mike's reference to moving in had already made my heart bounce halfway up my esophagus, and the word *marry* sent it right to my tonsils. I couldn't say a word because of the fist-sized lump back there.

Mike sipped coffee and looked at me. The silence grew. Finally he spoke.

"Is that a no?"

I choked the lump of heart tissue back into my chest. "Why is marriage a required part of the deal? Lots of people just live together these days. I never have, but—"

"I have." Mike's voice was real firm. "It doesn't work for me."

He drank coffee again. This entire conversation had lots of long pauses in it.

"Annie and I were together for two years," he said. "We even bought a town house together. And just when I decided it was time to get married, she decided she didn't want to live with a guy who has nightmares and gets up in the middle of the night to sit around watching old movies and shake. So she hired a U-Haul and moved to Dallas. I had no warning, no say in the matter." He looked at me directly. "I had no legal rights."

I still didn't know what to say.

"Now—two years later—I think her decision was best for both of us," Mike said. "The nightmares were just the tip of the iceberg for her. She hated my being a cop, and that's all I want to be. So we weren't going to make it in the long run. It was better to make a clean break. But I hated seeing an important part of my life simply drive off in a U-Haul, with no legal complications, no ceremony. Dammit, we didn't even have a big fight! Those two years of my life were important. They shouldn't have ended so . . . casually."

He was glaring at me.

"Mike! I promise. When we break up, I'll holler and scream and throw four hissy fits. I'll get a lawyer and sue you. At least for palimony."

His glare changed to a grin. "I hope you're not planning on a big settlement. That town house in Chicago is still eating me up financially."

"You still own it?"

"We had an offer, but Annie said no. It's rented—most of the time. I can't sell on my own. Which is another problem with having entanglements that aren't settled by simply hiring a U-Haul. Anyway, I found out that living together doesn't work for me. It's marriage or nothing, Nell."

I'd already known about Annie, of course. And I'd known that she'd hurt Mike when they split up. Maybe I hadn't known just how deeply she had hurt him. Maybe I was worried about her—even a couple of hundred miles away, she was my rival, the only other woman who was important in Mike's life.

But right at that moment Mike looked so forlorn that I didn't care how he felt about her. I got up, went around the kitchen table, and sat in his lap.

"I care about you a lot, Mike," I said. "But I think we ought to let our passions come off the white-hot level before we make any permanent decisions."

"I want you with me, Nell, but I'm not sure I can handle our living together. Unless we get married."

"And I want to be with you, Mike, but I don't think I can handle getting married."

We put our arms around each other. He nuzzled my neck, and I licked his ear.

"Maybe we can compromise on great sex," I whispered.

Mike tweaked the belt of the robe I was wearing.

Later that morning we agreed on the six-month plan. I maintained my own address but visited frequently. There was to be no discussion of the future for six months.

And now, after five and a half months, Mike had asked for his garage door opener back.

I could hear the commercial break downstairs, ending Brenda's movie. I got up and slowly combed my hair. Time to go to work.

The thought wasn't enticing. Checking facts, checking grammar, asking reporters why they hadn't included this or that information. Taking out information they shouldn't have included. Tightening the writing. None of it would be as interesting as my personal life.

What had happened to my mother? Had she been killed in the way Aunt Billie said, run down deliberately? Had my father really fled to avoid arrest?

Was he still on the run?

Could I call Michigan law enforcement officials and find out?

I was still looking in the mirror and holding my comb in my hand when that thought finally struck me.

I'm a reporter, I thought. I can call people and find out things. I can get reporters in Michigan to help me. I don't have to stand here, paralyzed, and feel that this is something that happened to me and that I can't do anything about it.

I can do something about this. I may not be able to change any of it. But by golly, I can check it out.

I ran down the stairs and out to the car. I wouldn't be able to do it right away, of course. I'd have to do my regular work. And it was Saturday. Law enforcement officials wouldn't be likely to be in their offices today. I might have to wait until Monday to talk to some of them.

I skidded into a slot in the *Gazette* parking garage, used my electronic card to get in the back door, and ran up the two flights to the newsroom. To my delight, the dayside general reporters hadn't turned in much that morning, and I had read nearly all the Sunday copy on Friday afternoon. The proof file was quickly emptied.

It was less than an hour later when I went to the *Gazette*

library and dug out a road atlas to locate Jessamine, Michigan, the town where we'd been living when my mother died.

Jessamine was a city of twelve thousand in western Michigan, I learned. I wrote down the name of the county, went back to my desk, and pulled out my long-distance credit card. I was borrowing the *Gazette*'s credibility, but I'd pay for the call myself. A quick call to information got me the numbers for the Jessamine Police Department and for the county sheriff's office. If they referred me to the state police, I'd get the number from the Jessamine P.D.

When I called the police department's number, I had a piece of luck. "City-county dispatcher," a voice said. Good, I could contact both city and county at once.

"Hello," I said. "I'm a reporter with the *Grantham Gazette*." I added the name of the state, since Americans are notoriously bad at geography.

The dispatcher's voice was cautious. "Yes?"

"I'm looking into a homicide which supposedly occurred in your county twenty years ago," I said. "Who would have any information about that?"

"What's the case?"

"The victim's name was Sally Matthews," I said. "I believe she was struck by a car."

The dispatcher gave a disgusted snort. "Humph! What's the deal here?"

"What do you mean?"

"That case has been in the dead file for nearly twenty years, and now we have two inquiries about it in one day."

"Someone else called about it?"

"He didn't call. He came by the station. I referred him to the former sheriff."

"Who was it?"

"I'd have to look his name up. It was some big redheaded guy."

Chapter 12

Mike. It had to be Mike.

Mike had left Grantham the night before, flown to Michigan, and gone to the town where my mother was killed.

Why? Why would he do such a thing? Why would he do it without telling me?

Why would he do it without asking my permission?

A flash of anger hit. Mike was manipulating me again, doing things behind my back.

Oh, he'd say he was keeping his eye on the goal, accomplishing what needed to be accomplished by the simplest route, worrying about what needed to be done, not the method he used to do it.

But how could he come by my office to say good-bye and tell me nothing about where he was going? How could he take away my access to his house? How could he leave me emotionally stranded?

And how the hell had he known where to go?

All I'd ever told Mike about my mother's death was that she had been killed in a car wreck. Even when I'd gone into more details, two days earlier, I was sure I'd never mentioned the town or county where the wreck occurred. I had no relatives in Michigan. We'd only lived there for six months. There was no way Mike could even have known where my mother died.

Unless he'd been poking into my background without my knowledge.

That thought made me really angry.

"Nell." Ruth Borah's voice brought me back to the *Gazette* newsroom. I jumped all over.

"Sorry, Ruth. I was a million miles away."

She asked some routine question, and I forced my mind back to the copy for Sunday's paper. It was a half hour before I caught up again. Then I looked at the notepad on my desk and discovered a name and phone number written on it. It was scrawled in my handwriting, using my ballpoint pen. The area code was the one I'd just punched to reach Jessamine, Michigan.

I had no recollection of doing it, but I had apparently written down the name and number of the former sheriff when the Jessamine dispatcher had said it. Thank God for habit. I might have had to call her back. If I wanted to talk to the guy.

I decided I did want to talk to him. But I couldn't do it then. The phone was ringing with the usual assortment of odd calls from the public, the two reporters on duty began to turn stories in, Ruth's husband came by and took her out to dinner, and I didn't have time to do anything but work for forty-five minutes. Then things calmed down a little, Ruth came back to her spot on the desk, and the time for my dinner break arrived.

I decided to call the Michigan sheriff from the library phone. It would be more private than the city desk. I headed back there, taking the note along.

"Ronald Vanderkolk," the note said.

A Dutch name. That jogged my memory. That whole area of Michigan had a lot of people of Dutch descent. I remembered my mother talking to my dad about it. "They don't like me," she'd said. "And I have the feeling it's because I have dark hair, and I don't have a 'van' to my name. You and Nell are blond enough to get along—if you'd just spell Matthews with a double l in it someplace."

I stared at the former sheriff's name, remembering my

mother. She'd been dark and lively, and my father had been much taller than she was. For a moment I could picture her clearly. I could remember my father laughing when she complained about feeling cold-shouldered by the small Michigan town.

"You have to live here ten years before they'll ignore you," she'd said.

I could remember my mother's dark eyes snapping, remember her lips pouting, then smiling. But I couldn't picture my father's face at all.

I stared at the name I'd written on the slip of paper. Ronald Vanderkolk. A good Dutch name in a good Dutch community. I was willing to bet Ronald Vanderkolk had had enough cousins to keep him in office until he had hit retirement age.

I jotted down a few questions for him, then picked up the phone and dialed 9 for an outside line, then 0 for a credit-card call. The phone rang four times before a woman's voice answered.

"May I speak to Sheriff Vanderkolk?"

I heard a sigh. "May I tell him who it is?"

Oh, God! Who was I? I hadn't stopped to figure that out. Was I a reporter for the *Grantham Gazette*? Or was I the daughter of a murdered woman?

I adopted my mother's maiden name on the spot. "This is Nell Lathen," I said. "I'm a reporter for the *Grantham Gazette*."

That brought a sniff. "Just a minute. He's packing."

Packing? Was he going out of town?

"This is Ronald Vanderkolk." The voice sounded vigorous.

"Sheriff, I'm sorry to bother you. I know you're busy."

"Just getting ready for one of my trips."

"Trips?"

"Transporting prisoners. What can I do for you?"

"I'm with the *Grantham Gazette* newspaper. Twenty

years ago a young woman from our area was killed in your county—"

"Is this another call about Sally Matthews?"

Obviously Mike had found him. "Yes," I said. "A local situation has arisen—"

"Yes, and I'd like to know what it is."

His reaction threw me. I had called to get information from him. I wasn't set for him to demand it from me.

"Uh," I said, choking back a stammer.

"Just what's going on down there?" he said gruffly.

"I'm not quite sure," I said. "A relative of Sally Matthews is trying to find out just what happened to her."

"How did the Grantham police get involved?"

"I wasn't aware that they were," I said.

"Then who is this Mike Svenson who showed up here, wanted information?"

"Officer Svenson is chief hostage negotiator for the Grantham Police Department," I said. Vanderkolk could find that out by calling the Grantham P.D., so I wasn't letting any particular cat out of any particular bag. "He's a well-respected officer."

"Big, redheaded guy?"

"With a crooked nose," I answered. And after I got hold of him, his nose might get crookeder.

"Then he's a real Grantham officer?"

"Oh, yes. What did he want to know?"

That brought a long pause in the conversation. Vanderkolk obviously didn't want to tell me, but in a few moments he spoke. "He just wanted to know about this Matthews case. Now, young woman, what is it you want to know?"

"Probably the same things he did," I said. "Was Sally Matthews' death considered a homicide?"

"Murder. Maybe manslaughter if the guy got a good lawyer."

"Did you ever charge anyone?"

"No. We were close to charging the husband." My heart sank. Aunt Billie had been right.

It was an effort to keep my voice steady. "Was he arrested?"

"No. Still at large. And, yes, we'd still like to get him, if you know where he is."

"I assure you that I don't. Can you give me a brief outline of the case?"

Vanderkolk paused again, but he finally went on. "Sally Matthews was a twenty-six-year-old woman, married, with one child. Her husband was the new editor for the *Jessamine Journal*. They were strangers to the area—only been here a few months. She was found dead on a county road north of Jessamine. She'd been hit by a car. Died instantly."

"An accident?" I tried to keep from sounding hopeful.

"We thought it might be at first. Hit-and-run. But we couldn't figure out how she got out there. It was just a farm road. Pretty secluded. Then we found out that her own car had hit her."

"Her own car!"

"Yeah. Car she and her husband owned. They just had the one. Radiator grille was all dented, and we found hair—her hair—on it. Plus some fibers from her coat.

"Then when we found out she and the husband had split up—"

I gulped. It was hard to keep my voice steady. "That left him as suspect in chief?"

"Right. And when we found out the motive, that clinched it."

"Motive? He had a motive in addition to the fact that they had separated?"

"Oh, yes. It was pretty well established that she'd had a boyfriend. Maybe boyfriends. She was a cute little brunette. Husband worked nights, worked long hours. Guess she got lonesome."

I discovered that tears were running down my cheeks. I

tried to say something, but my voice wouldn't work. I grunted some noise out, and that was enough encouragement for Ronald Vanderkolk.

"The husband—I told you he was with the newspaper. He knew several of the Jessamine officers and a couple of my deputies. He had a reporter over at my office all the time. Somehow he got wind that we were about to apply for a warrant. He took off.

"Like I say. He had motive, had access to the car—he'd had enough of the wife's running around, decided to get rid of her. Or maybe they went off to have a talk and the situation got violent. It was a pretty clear case. But we never found him.

"That's the whole story, anyway. Just a domestic disturbance—slutty wife, angry husband."

I don't think I even said good-bye. I just hung up.

My nose was running. I stole a Kleenex from a box on the head librarian's desk. Then I stole another. I stood there and cried through four tissues, angry and grieving.

What a nasty old man, I told myself. He hadn't known my mother. She wasn't a slut. She was a nice person. She read to me. She liked to sew—I remembered the blue and white gingham curtains she'd made for my bedroom in Michigan. She made cookies, for God's sake! And she let me decorate them.

Oh, she was hot-tempered. She and my dad could give each other what-for. But maybe I remembered the bad times because they'd been unusual. There were lots of good times in our lives, too. I remembered wading in Lake Michigan and roasting hot dogs on the beach.

The sheriff was right about my dad working nights. My mom would fix dinner and have it ready to go on the table as soon as he walked in the door. We'd eat together, and he'd have to rush back to the office.

Then I'd help with the dishes, and my mother and I would watch television. She'd liked situation comedies. I remembered lying on the couch, with my head in her lap, watching *M*A*S*H*. She would stroke my hair and rub my back. I got to stay up late as long as I was quiet. Until the ten o'clock news came on.

Wait a minute, I thought. That wouldn't work. The time difference. In Michigan they didn't have ten o'clock news, as we did in the Central time zone. Michigan was in the Eastern zone. Our prime time for television is seven to ten. Theirs is eight to eleven. My mother had let me stay up until the eleven o'clock news. And my daddy had come home from work around midnight.

So when had my mother been seeing other men?

The sheriff was wrong, I realized. My mother hadn't been out running around while my dad worked nights. And no one had come to the house. In a strange town, with no friends, my mother had spent night after lonely night watching sit-coms with an eight-year-old.

I went through two more Kleenex. Then I heard my name. "Nell Matthews!" it boomed.

I jumped all over. It was the building's intercom. The switchboard operator was paging me. "Nell Matthews! Call the switchboard!"

I called. *"Grantham Gazette,"* Kimmie answered.

"This is Nell. Did you page?"

"Oh, yes. You have a caller."

"A caller?" I heard a squeaky voice in the background, and I remembered. Martina's boyfriend had been planning to bring something to me, something she'd given him. "Oh, I guess it's Dan Smith. Tell him to wait for me a few minutes."

I was going to need a few minutes to get myself together. I had to look like a wreck. Thank God I dye my eyelashes. If I'd been using mascara, I would have had it all over my face. As it was, I was puffy-eyed and runny-nosed. I headed for the ladies' room via a back hallway.

Five minutes later, as I walked toward Dan Smith, I saw

that he was holding a cardboard box—a stout corrugated box about the size of a department store shirt box. It had a computer company logo on the side, and I immediately was sure it had come from the *Gazette* computer department. Computers, annoying as they can be, do deserve credit for one thing—their makers ship equipment and parts in solid, well-constructed boxes. I always beg a few discarded boxes from the computer guys for any Christmas mailing I do, and I was willing to bet that Martina had gone to the same source for a container to store whatever she had given Dan Smith.

He leaned across the little railing that defined the reception area and pushed the box toward me almost secretively.

"What is this?" I asked.

Dan looked shocked. "Oh, I haven't looked in it! Martina just asked me to keep it for her. She said it was something from the *Gazette* library that she wanted out of circulation for a few days."

I took the box, and I almost dropped it on my toe. "It's heavy," I said. "Or heavier than I expected."

Dan nodded. "Yes, but she said it wasn't breakable. If you'll just see that it gets back to the right place . . ."

I renewed my promise to let him know about funeral services for Martina and carried the box back to the library. With so few staffers on duty, I wasn't likely to be interrupted if I opened the box there. But what could be in it? I undid the box's tricky cardboard latches warily and folded the top back, almost ready for something to jump out.

But nothing jumped. Inside I saw white fake leather with embossed red letters. TALON, it read, in letters several inches high. Smaller letters said, EASTWICK METHODIST COLLEGE.

"Hell's bells," I said. "It's a yearbook. No wonder the box was so heavy."

The box held a thirty-year-old copy of the Eastwick College yearbook, *The Talon.* Heavy, slick paper and a classy binding make a yearbook heavy for its size.

Looking across the library, I immediately saw where the

book had come from. Thirty years ago the wife of the *Gazette*'s publisher was an active Methodist laywoman. I'd helped with her obituary the first month I worked at the *Gazette*, and I knew she'd served as a regent for Eastwick Methodist College. She must have felt obligated to buy a yearbook every year—or maybe they gave her one—because we had fifteen years' worth of them in our library.

Why had Martina hidden this book?

"Weird," I said. I opened the red and white cover and riffled through a few of the yearbook's pages. There were no handy place marks forcing the book to fall open at key pages. It would take an hour to go through the book, and I still might not know why Martina had thought it should be "out of circulation." I glanced at my watch. My dinner break was almost over. If I hurried, I could run down to the break room and get some crackers out of a machine before I went back.

I stuffed the empty computer packing box into the biggest trash can in the library, then carried the yearbook to the empty spot on the shelf where it belonged. It had been there for thirty years, along with the other Eastwick yearbooks. Occasionally they were handy for finding out background on some person who was an Eastwick alum.

Was that what Martina had used this yearbook for? Had someone's name come up in a story?

By the time I was halfway down the stairs to the break room I'd rejected that theory. No, she wouldn't have been wanting to keep the book "out of circulation for a few days" if the information was to be printed in the newspaper. Few people outside the staff used the *Gazette* library. It was much more likely that she'd wanted to keep some staff member from seeing the book.

Who? What could be in it? Was some staff member in it?

I plugged money into the junk-food dispenser and pocketed a pack of cheese crackers and a candy bar. Glancing around the break room, I saw a white jacket, topped by fluffy blond hair.

It was Martina! I jumped all over, and I must have gasped, because the person turned around, and I saw a young man who works in circulation. His white shirt and curly blond hair had only a superficial resemblance to Martina's jacket and bleach job.

"Now I'm seeing things," I muttered. "And I'm talking to myself."

Martina was still driving me crazy. I angrily tore my crackers open. The woman was as big a pain dead as she had been alive. How had she become a newspaperwoman, anyway?

I stopped and thought about it. Most of us went into newspapers after journalism school. Had Martina done that? Had she gone to Eastwick Methodist and majored in journalism?

I ate my crackers on the way back up the stairs, and I rushed back to the library and snatched the Talon yearbook off the shelf. Flopping it open on a table, I went for the index.

There was no Martina Gilroy listed.

But—had Martina's name been Gilroy when she was in college? I was pretty sure she'd been a divorcee. She might have had a different name in those days. I turned back to the table of contents and found *Eagle Press* listed. Maybe that was the Eastwick newspaper.

I flipped to the *Eagle Press* staff pages and scanned the pictures. There were small groups of editors, and two larger pictures of reporters, photographers, and other staffers. There were no blondes with fluffy hair, of course. The students from this era had long hair—both men and women.

I looked at the women's faces. Nah. Not one of them could be Martina. In fact—logic set in, and I rechecked the date of the yearbook. Thirty years ago. And Martina had been sixty when she died. If she had gone to EMU—and I didn't know that she had—she would probably have been there ten years earlier than this book.

"Dumb," I said aloud. "Wrong era for Martina."

Then a name caught my eye. "Arnie Ashe."

It was under one of the small pictures, a snapshot showing four people around a typewriter. A typewriter, for God's sake! They'd written on typewriters in those days.

I looked at the collegiate Arnie. A short, squat guy with long dark hair.

It wasn't the Arnie I knew.

I kept staring at the photo, mentally removing the hair to match Arnie's present bald state.

But the picture labeled Arnie Ashe simply was not a picture of the Arnie Ashe who had recently joined the staff of the *Grantham Gazette*. The one in the photo had dark hair—Arnie shaved his head, of course—but the young man in the photo also had dark eyelashes. Our Arnie's lashes were light. The man in the photo had a round face. Arnie had a long head. The man in the photo was the shortest one in his group. Arnie wasn't a giant, but he was taller than the Arnie in the picture.

Was the cutline wrong? Had the picture been flopped, so that left was right and right was left? I knew only too well how easily that could happen.

But no, Arnie was pictured with Mary, Sue, and Carolyn. He was the only guy in the picture.

What was the deal here? I looked carefully at all the other aspiring young journalists pictured, mentally aging them, adding pounds, graying their hair, updating hairdos, subtracting hair.

Whoops! Center of the back row of one of the group shots. Take the hair off, and it was Arnie.

Yeah. That was Arnie. I realized I'd been holding my breath. I liked Arnie. Finding him in another picture relieved me. The smaller picture was merely identified wrong. Arnie was among the *Eagle Press* staffers of the era. He'd had a gorgeous head of hair, light-colored in the black-and-white photo, and his eyelashes had been light. He'd been grinning broadly for the photographer.

He was sixth from the left in the back row. I popped the last cheese cracker in my mouth and ran my finger along the list of names to number six.

"Alan Matthews," it said. "News editor, spring semester."

Chapter 13

"No," I said. "That's not right. Alan Matthews was my father's name. And that's Arnie. That's not my dad."

I calmly closed the book. My hand was steady as I put it back on the shelf. I threw out the cracker wrapper, and I opened my candy bar, and I stared out the library's window as I ate it. I looked into the lighted windows of a building a half block away, watching a custodian go from office to office, dumping wastebaskets. Then I went to the ladies' room, combed my hair, washed my hands, and went back to my spot at the copy desk. I opened up the proof file, and I read copy.

I didn't feel anything.

I didn't dare feel anything.

Ruth didn't seem to notice that my life had turned upside down, so I guess I didn't act as if it had.

If the face in the yearbook crossed my memory, I merely pushed it out again and smugly told myself that the *Eastwick Talon* yearbook staff had been a bunch of rank amateurs, not aspiring professionals like the students I'd been in J-school with. They'd simply gotten the names mixed up. No Alan Matthews had been pictured on that page.

I managed to keep telling myself that until about ten, when Ruth's phone buzzed and Kimmie called her up to the reception desk. That was odd. If someone came by the office—with a complaint or to submit a news story—Ruth would usually send a reporter to talk to him, not go herself. So I looked to see who was getting the special treatment.

It was Boone Thompson, the detective who'd searched the newsroom. The one who had found the shoes in Arnie's desk.

Ruth shook his hand, and the two of them talked, leaning on the dividing railing. I could see Ruth frowning. Then she swung the little gate open and motioned Boone inside. The two of them walked toward the city desk.

"Nell," Ruth said, "Arnie Ashe hasn't called in tonight, has he?"

I shook my head. "Haven't heard a word. Last night he said he had to take care of some personal business. I don't think he called tonight."

Ruth turned to Boone. "Guess that's all we know. If we hear from him, we'll tell him you need to talk to him."

"No." Boone's voice was firm. "No, just tell us you've heard from him," he said. "We'll take it from there."

I was longing to ask why the police were looking for Arnie, but my tongue wouldn't work. I was sure they wanted to arrest him for the murder of Martina Gilroy.

They wanted to arrest my dad.

My teeth were clamped so hard they throbbed, and my throat got so tight I could feel it begin to ache. I sat staring at the screen of the VDT until Ruth had escorted Boone back to the reception area and had returned to her desk. Then I swung my chair around.

"Ruth." My voice was a croak. "I'm exhausted, and I have a lot of overtime. Nothing more's coming for tomorrow. Is it okay if I leave early?"

Ruth frowned. "You all right?"

I nodded. "Just tired." That time my voice nearly broke.

"If you don't feel well, I'll get the photog to drive—"

"No!" I shook my head vigorously, gathered up my purse, and left. I managed to keep myself semi-composed while I collected my raincoat from the closet—the closet next to the one where Mike and I had found Martina's white linen jacket. I was halfway down the back stairs before I began to cry.

I kept going, down the stairs, out the back door, across the alley, and into the first floor of the parking garage, and the tears were flooding every step of the way. I unlocked the door of the Dodge and got inside. Then I fell apart completely.

I gripped the steering wheel and sobbed. It hurt so bad that I thought I would die. Death would have been easier than sitting there knowing that twenty years earlier my father had abandoned me to avoid being tried for murder. And now it had happened again.

Disguised as Arnie Ashe, he had slipped back into my life for a few weeks, and then he had slipped out again.

I wept terrible wracking sobs. I screamed hysterically. I beat the dashboard with my fist. I may have even banged my head against the steering wheel. I didn't fight it. I couldn't fight it. For ten minutes I sobbed and muttered and moaned and generally made a spectacle of myself.

"Daddy! Daddy! I hate you! I love you! I'm so angry!"

Yes, angry. The thought gave me enough pause that I stopped my tirade. Yes, I was angry. Furious.

All those years I'd thought that if my daddy came back, I'd be a really good girl this time so he wouldn't want to go away again. And he had come back, and I hadn't done anything naughty, and he still went away again. Because of something I had no control over. Because of Martina's murder.

Had he killed her? Was the man who taught me to play Dirty Eight a killer?

I couldn't believe it. I didn't want to believe it. But I didn't know.

Luckily, there was a box of Kleenex in the backseat of the Dodge. I used half of it. And then I drove home, forgetting all about the crazy guy in the old Caddy who'd chased me the night before. I crept in quietly to keep from waking up

Brenda or Martha and was in bed long before Rocky came in from the Blue Flamingo. I didn't want to talk to anybody.

Except Mike. Maybe. And I couldn't call every motel in western Michigan looking for him.

I was too upset for my usual "sleeping pill," a chapter of *Auntie Mame*. But I must have been truly as exhausted as I'd told Ruth I was, because I fell asleep quickly and didn't budge until the phone rang at eight-thirty Sunday morning.

I picked up the extension by my bed.

"Hello." My voice seemed to be working, but my head was splitting.

"Nell? This is Wilda." It was Mike's mother. "Where's Mike?"

"He left town," I said stupidly.

"Isn't he back yet?"

"Apparently not."

Long silence. I could hear that information clicking through Wilda's brain, and I could tell it had surprised her. I wasn't sure what I should say. Wilda Svenson is one of Grantham's most successful real estate operators. She and Mike are reasonably close, but they're not in each other's pockets. They're both too busy, for one thing. For another, Mike's not sure how to react to her romantic relationship with Mickey O'Sullivan, who had been his father's best friend. Mike likes Mickey, but his relationship with Mike's mother is a little hard for Mike to accept. So the mother and son have reached an accommodation. Wilda doesn't comment on Mike and me, and Mike doesn't comment on his mother and Mickey. Mickey and I try to stay out of it.

So if Mike doesn't tell his mother something, I don't feel that it's up to me to offer the information. On the other hand, maybe she knew something about what he was up to. I decided to give it a try.

"In fact, Wilda, I need to reach him," I said. "And he didn't tell me where he'd be staying. Do you have a phone number?"

"No. I thought you'd know."

"No."

Another silence. I waited until Wilda spoke. "He said he was checking something out for you," she said.

I clenched my jaw. The jerk! Mike was nosing into my life, and he had told his mother he was doing it for me.

I gulped hard and tried to make my voice sound normal. "Well, I guess he left without getting a reservation," I said. "I'm sure he'll call one of us sometime today."

"I wanted to tell him I'm going to Dallas this morning, and I won't be back until Wednesday. If he could check my mail here at the house—or I can ask the office—"

"I'll tell him. If he calls. If I don't hear from him, I'll call your office tomorrow morning."

"Thanks, Nell. Just ask for Shirley. She'll take care of it."

I hung up the phone too mad to go back to sleep, so I got up and headed for the shower. That's when I noticed that the answering machine in the hall was blinking. I'd been too upset to even look at it the night before. I punched the button.

"Hi, Nell." It was Mike. "I'm calling at ten o'clock Saturday. I know you're still at work, but I wanted to ask what's new."

End of call.

I made an angry guttural noise deep in my throat. "What's new?" It was the code Mike and I used to mean "I love you."

The nerve of the guy! To call me and tell me he loved me when he was off in Michigan poking into my business without being asked to do so. To tell his mother he was checking something out for me. To refuse to tell me where he was going, and to fail to leave a phone number where he could be reached.

"Creep!" I said.

I turned the shower's temperature up to steam, but my temper was hotter than the water.

Maybe breaking up with Mike would be the best thing

that ever happened to me. I was an honest person—or I tried to be. And Mike wasn't. I called him every name in the thesaurus. Mike was a liar, a manipulator, a trickster, a charlatan, a fast talker. This had been a problem for us since we began to date, and it wasn't going to improve.

Boiled red by the shower, but with my headache down to a dull throb, I put on a pair of jeans and a sweatshirt and went downstairs. I felt that I'd been abandoned by the two most important men in my life, but I was still hungry.

Rocky, as a professional restaurateur, is the most enthusiastic cook among the four of us who share the big house. He often sleeps late on Sundays, since he doesn't close the Blue Flamingo until way after midnight. But he was coming out of his downstairs suite—he has two rooms—as I came down the stairs.

"Morning," he said. He scratched his pudgy stomach and rubbed his balding head. "I'm hungry for bacon. Bacon and toast foldovers. Catsup optional."

I heard Martha's voice behind me, on the landing. "Cook me a couple of pieces!"

"Sounds good to me, too," I said. I went out to get the *Sunday Gazette*.

Forty-five minutes later, Rocky had fried enough bacon for a small army, and the three of us were sitting at the round table in the kitchen's bay window. Martha, who works as a buyer for a department store and gets a discount on everything, was wearing a gorgeous house coat and was made up as if she'd just stepped out of *Vogue*. Rocky was in T-shirt and sweatpants mode.

He lifted a slice of sourdough bread and held it over the toaster. "More toast?"

"No, thanks. Three's plenty for me," I said. Martha shook her head.

Rocky dropped his fourth slice in, and the doorbell rang.

I tossed down the entertainment section. "I'll get it. You watch your toast."

At the door, I looked through the peephole. "Hell's bells," I said. Then I opened the door.

"Hi, Boone," I said. "Come on in. Are you here to give me the third degree?"

Boone smiled, but his eyes looked worried. "I doubt I could beat any information out of you, Nell. I'm still trying to track down Arnie Ashe."

"Let me get you a cup of coffee."

"I wouldn't say no."

Boone followed me into the kitchen and looked at Rocky warily. His face grew amused when I introduced them. All the cops know who Rocky is, and most of them think his status in the community is funny. Rocky cleared the newspaper off the kitchen table, poured Boone's coffee, and refreshed the cream pitcher.

Boone seemed more impressed by Martha. For a few minutes I thought he was going to give her the third degree, even if I didn't get it. Then she and Rocky both excused themselves.

All the time Rocky was being hospitable and Martha was wowing Boone, I'd been thinking wildly. What should I tell Boone about Arnie? Should I tell him Arnie was really Alan Matthews? Should I tell Boone that Alan-Arnie had fled a murder charge twenty years earlier and had been on the lam all that time?

Should I tell him Arnie was my dad?

It was that last question which decided me. No. I couldn't tell Boone anything about Arnie and who he really was. It wasn't a matter of protecting him. It was simply that I couldn't push the words out from between my lips.

Then I had to face Boone.

"You seem to be the last person who talked to Arnie Ashe," he said. "Did he give you a hint of where he was going?"

"No. Just said he had to leave town for a few days. Or

something like that. I didn't really pay a lot of attention at the time."

"You worked with him for several weeks, Nell. Did he ever tell you anything about his family?"

"No!" My voice was too sharp, I realized. I tried to soften it. "No, Boone, we just talked about the violence beat, about the *Gazette*. We didn't talk about personal matters."

"What about his relationship with Martina Gilroy?"

"They'd worked together someplace in Kentucky."

"Old friends?"

"Not really. Nobody was friends with Martina." I got up and topped off my own coffee, then sat down again. "Martina was one of nature's mistakes, or something. The only person I've run into who seemed to like her is this Dan Smith. Have you talked to him?"

Boone wouldn't let me distract him. "Did Ms. Gilroy and Arnie Ashe fight?"

"A better word would be 'argued.' And if arguing with Martina puts you on the suspect list, I'd go to the top. She and I argued every day."

"Maybe so. But you're still in town."

"Then you think Arnie 'resorted to flight'? Because the shoes were found in his desk?" I leaned forward. "Boone, anybody could have put those shoes there."

"Yeah. But Arnie's the only one we can't find. And we can't find out anything about him. He doesn't seem to have any family. I called the town in Texas where he lived before he moved to Grantham. No wife or ex-wife. No girlfriend. No poker buddies."

"What about the *Gazette*'s personnel records? Didn't he list a next-of-kin?"

Boone nodded. "Oh, sure."

"Who?" The vehemence in my voice caused Boone to look at me sharply, and I tried to go on more casually. "I mean, maybe he's been in touch with relatives."

"Not likely. Since the address he gave lists the next-of-kin's address as Cincinnati, on a street that doesn't seem to exist, with a telephone number for a bar in Chicago. Where they say they never heard of Arnie Ashe."

Boone closed his notebook. "I guess all I'm getting out of this is a cup of coffee, Nell. I'll leave you and your friends to your Sunday morning plans."

"Big deal. I may go back to bed with a book."

"You and Mike aren't planning anything? When I heard he was taking a few days off—"

"No." I'd let my voice get sharp again. "He's out of town."

"Oh? I hope he's back in time for our appointment."

"When's that?"

"Eight a.m. tomorrow morning. When I talked to him, to set up our session, he said he'd be hard to get hold of over the weekend, but he didn't say anything about leaving town."

"Guess he left in a hurry."

I escorted Boone to the door, then put the breakfast dishes in the dishwasher.

Should I have told Boone that Arnie Ashe was really Alan Matthews?

Probably, I decided. But I simply couldn't do it.

Yet that bit of knowledge made a big difference in the investigation into Martina's death.

The night before, when I'd realized that Arnie and Alan were the same person, I'd thought of that fact strictly from my own viewpoint. I'd lost my father twenty years earlier. He'd resurfaced briefly, then left again. Left without a word to me. The realization had been so devastating that I couldn't think beyond that.

Now I was able to be a little more analytical. For one thing, Martina had hidden away the Eastwick College yearbook. That proved she had known who Arnie really was. Or, at least, we could assume she knew.

Why hadn't she gone straight to Jake, the *Gazette*'s executive editor? Why hadn't she told the *Gazette* management what she knew?

There could be several explanations. The office grapevine had already passed the word that Arnie had been hired because he'd known Jake years earlier. So Martina might have figured Jake already knew that Alan Matthews had assumed the identity of Arnie Ashe, a college classmate.

Or Martina might have kept the news to herself because she wanted to use it in some way. As a club against Arnie? But what advantage would that have given her?

In any case, the fact that Martina knew Arnie's real identity gave him an incredibly good motive for killing her.

How could I justify keeping this information from the investigating officer?

But how could I turn in my own father? How could I make him face charges for the murders of two people—my mother and Martina?

But if the man had killed twice, how could I let him run around loose?

But what could I tell Boone anyway? I didn't know where Arnie had gone.

Thank God.

If only I could distract Boone, distract Jim Hammond from Arnie. Plenty of people had disliked, even hated, Martina. If you keep poking your nose into people's lives, you may get the end of it caught in something. Or by someone.

And Martina had poked her nose into other people's lives. We all knew that she checked the legal notices like a hawk, looking for juicy divorces and lawsuits. Arnie wouldn't have been the only person she stabbed with that long, pointed nose.

But what did she do with that information? I'd told Mike I didn't think she blackmailed people—at least not in the sense of asking for money. And she hadn't used the information to climb the professional ladder. No, she'd been head copy editor for eight years, and she'd seemed perfectly content in that slot.

And where did she keep the information she gathered? Had it all been in her head?

I doubted it. Martina surrounded herself with reference books and special little lists of facts, most of them filed in the computer system.

She'd had a file drawer in the newsroom, as most of the staffers did. The detectives had taken everything in it away, Ruth had told me, when they searched for the missing shoes. I assumed the detectives had searched her home, too.

But judging from Boone's questions, I didn't think they had found masses of incriminating information about her fellow staffers in either place.

No, if Martina kept this sort of thing, it was probably in the computer system, I concluded. She very likely had a file of embarrassing information on the citizens of Grantham, with emphasis on the staff of the *Grantham Gazette*.

Did the police know about this? Probably not. As far as I knew, they hadn't gotten into our computer system.

But now I was convinced such a file existed. I resolved to find it.

Chapter 14

Less than six months earlier I'd had a bad experience when a reporter who was temporarily working in the *Gazette* office opened up the computer, got into a story I'd written, and added some unsubstantiated material. Until that time all three police reporters had shared a file. Afterward, I created my own private file for my stories.

Every user can create a file on the computer system the *Gazette* uses. I hadn't had to ask anyone to do it for me. I just did it. And like my assigned file drawer—in the bank of cabinets along the wall—it probably needed cleaning out. I hadn't looked in either my electronic file or my file drawer since I moved to the copy desk.

Had Martina created a personal computer file for herself? I headed for the office. No one would be there on a Sunday morning. I could nose through the computer system all I wanted.

My Dodge was alone when I parked on the first floor of the parking garage, since the one staff member on duty, the security guard, always took a slot on the second floor. I used my electronic card to get in the back door and waved at the security camera. I wanted the guard to know I was in the building.

I admit it—I find the Gazette Building scary when it's closed. The building is four stories high and half a block long. When it's closed there are a lot of empty offices, locked doors, strange nooks and odd crannies, not to mention that spooky basement. Any other staff member—anybody with an electronic card—could be wandering around in there and could appear suddenly and startle me.

But the empty parking lot almost guaranteed that the building was also empty of people that afternoon. Grantham's public transportation system is a joke. If they don't come in a car, they don't get there.

I went to my desk and opened up the computer. Creating a file on our system requires two codes. One can be up to five letters or numbers and the other up to three. Most of us use something fairly obvious. The crime reporters' file is accessed by typing in "crime" and "rpt." "Crime reporters." Easy to remember. My personal file was "Mary" and "Nll." Very few people know my first name, but it's an easy word for me to remember.

But what would Martina Gilroy have used?

If she'd used anything at all, that is. As copy editor, she didn't write stories. She would have had little use for a personal file for storing her own work. So if—big if—she'd had a file, how would she have labeled it?

I typed in "copy" and "dsk," then hit Execute. The screen remained blank. No stories were filed under those code words.

I tried "Marti" and "gil." Nothing. "Gilry" and "mta." "Desk" and "cpy." "Copy" and "mar." None of them worked.

I stared at the screen. Looking for a private file was a long shot. A real waste of time. Martina could have used "abcde" and "xyz." I typed those in. She hadn't. Maybe she'd used her initials. I typed "copy" and "mg," for "Martina Gilroy." Then "desk" and "mg." Neither got any response.

"Mg." Did those initials mean something? Were they the chemical symbol for magnesium? I looked up magnesium in the dictionary and learned its melting point and atomic weight and several other things I didn't intend to remember. None of them seemed helpful.

But "mg" was a familiar set of initials. It was the name of a make of car. A fun, fast little car.

I typed in "sports" and "car," hit Execute, and nearly yelled, "Eureka!" A list of computer files had come up on the screen. Then I told myself to calm down. There was no guarantee that these stories had even been filed by Martina. Any staffer could have created a "sports" "car" file.

The files all seemed to be news stories—some from the wire and some local. The dates at which each entered the system went back three years, which was the approximate date at which the *Gazette* has installed this particular computer system. I started at the top and looked them over.

The first story, slugged "SuperBowl" in the topic line, turned out to be recipes for hors d'oeuvres suitable for eating while watching football. They sounded awful, except maybe the sausage balls. The second story, also an Associated Press story dated several years back, was about an older woman who had sued her employer for sexual discrimination because she hadn't been promoted. Had Martina had a similar lawsuit in mind? Ruth had jumped over Martina to become city editor. Jack had jumped over her to become assistant city editor. Hmmm. I began to hope that I had discovered Martina's file.

The third story was local and about a year old. I had to read it twice before I figured out why Martina would have kept it. Way down in the bottom I found the name of Jake Edwards's wife. She'd resigned from some committee at Grantham State, where she taught math. So what?

A fourth story, eighteen months old and off the wire, was about the merger of two chains of small newspapers. The merger had nothing to do with the *Gazette*, though it did involve several papers in the state. I wondered if Martina had once worked for one of them. The story quoted the president, one Margaret Gordon Jones, as saying that some "staff consolidations" would occur. A crappy word for layoffs.

So it went. There was a national story about the union that

represents our printers. They were having trouble with their pension fund. There was a *New York Times* story on the legalities of assisted suicide.

There were a few local stories with startling errors and odd sentences in them. One of them was on a couple celebrating their seventy-fifth anniversary. "They have loved on a farm in Catlin County since 1940," it read. I grinned.

These convinced me I had found Martina's file. Apparently she collected these funny mistakes. Why? Just for fun? Or did she rag the reporters who wrote them? I had written one of the crime stories, goof and all, but I didn't remember her ever twitting me about it.

And way at the bottom of the file—an item three years old—was a routine story about a disturbance outside a bar. Why on earth had Martina saved that? I read the screen of type twice before the address caught my eye. Then I gasped.

The disturbance had happened outside the Blue Flamingo, the bar Rocky owned. We don't run the name of the establishment where a fight occurs unless the fight happens inside, but it was the right block.

However, I saw with relief, the incident had happened before Rocky bought into the bar. I knew he and the current partners had tried hard to attract a respectable crowd from the gay community. People who got into fights were not welcome.

Then I hit End, just to make sure I'd read all the story, and I discovered that a second story had been merged into it. This one, a follow-up on the first story, gave the names of two men charged with disturbing the peace as a result of the fight.

One of them was named "E.J. Brown."

E.J. Brown? Could that be our Ed? Our building manager and purchasing agent? Mr. Respectable?

I was seized with a great desire to run over to the police station and look up the arrest record. Instead, I walked around to Martina's desk and dug the heavy Grantham City

Directory out of the rack of reference books the copy editors share.

Everybody should know about the city directory. Nearly any city of any size has one, and it can be consulted at the public library and usually at the chamber of commerce. The largest section lists everybody in town by their name, address, phone number, and employer or profession. Another section lists every street address and tells who lives there. A third has all the phone numbers in the city, in numerical order, matched with the subscriber's name.

Of course, a city directory is often out of date. You may find out what ol' Joe's phone number was four years ago. And people can refuse to give the canvassers information. But hardly anybody does. The city directory is a treasure trove for a reporter. Or a bill collector, or a real estate agent, or a salesman, or any other nosy person.

I looked through the dozens of Browns in the city directory until I found one who worked at the *Gazette*. Sure enough, his full name was Edward J. Brown, Initials E.J.

There was a Mrs. Brown, too. Mary.

I closed the book and went back to my desk. I'd found out that Martina had something on Ed Brown, and I didn't like knowing it. I didn't care what Ed Brown's sexual proclivities were. But if he didn't want his wife to know—if he didn't want the tough crew of electricians, carpenters, plumbers, and janitors that he supervised to know—if he didn't want his boss to know—getting arrested outside a gay bar would have been a disaster.

Had using his initials been enough to hide his identity?

If Martina had threatened to reveal his secret, would he have been capable of killing her to make her keep quiet?

Darned if I knew. Ed seemed too neat and buttoned up to do anything as violent as kicking Martina downstairs. But asphyxiating her with blanket wash might fit his personality.

I closed out Martina's secret computer file. I was sorry I'd found the thing.

Then I opened it again. Martina had been murdered. I couldn't take the responsibility for withholding information that might help the police figure out who killed her. Besides, whoever killed her also might have used his Cadillac and a pistol to try to kill me. But I felt like a fink.

I longed to ask Mike's advice. I even called his number, but the machine answered.

I couldn't just pretend I hadn't found Martina's file, I decided. I had to do something with it.

I saved every item in the file to my own personal file. Then I commanded the computer to print out every item.

Printouts made from the newsroom computers appear, seemingly by magic, in a different place. They come out on a printer located in a room at the back of the newsroom floor, a room that is ruled by our computer expert and his lampful of genies. I went there, ready to collect my printouts as they clicked out.

The printout room is at the back of the building, in a secluded spot, and with the entire building empty, it seemed to be way out in the boonies. I was feeling a bit nervous as the dozens of giant green and white sheets headed SPORTS . . . CAR spewed out of the printer. What if the killer tracked me down in the printer room? It was too crowded with electronic gadgets and loops of cable for me to run. That room is kept just above freezing—to keep the computer from overheating—but it wasn't the temperature that made me give a little shiver as I accordion-pleated the sheets as they came out of the printer.

Nobody came in and chased me. I merely took my folded printouts and went back to my desk, ready to collect my purse and go home. I was opening my desk drawer when I heard a noise behind me.

I whirled my chair around and gave a loud gasp as Ed Brown—the very man I'd been reading about in Martina's hidden file—popped up about fifteen feet away.

He'd apparently been kneeling near the bank of filing

cabinets on the wall closest to the city desk. He'd probably stood up when he heard me.

He looked as startled as I felt. We stared at each other, equally horrified.

"Mr. Brown?" I said.

"Miss Matthews?" he said. As usual, he looked young. In fact, he looked like a young kid caught smoking behind the barn. Then he began to walk toward me, and he entered his older mode, aging before my eyes as the deeper lines in his face became visible.

I remembered that Martina had saved blackmail information on Ed Brown. That made him a suspect in her murder. I didn't want to be alone in the newsroom with Ed Brown.

I clutched my bundle of printouts and my purse, jumped to my feet, and moved away, toward the back door. But that door was clear across the building.

Could I outrun him? Not backward, I decided. And since I couldn't make myself turn my back on him, I couldn't run away from him forward. I'd have to outtalk him.

"Oh, Mr. Brown, you startled me," I said. "I didn't expect to see you here on a Sunday."

I could swear he was blushing. "I was trying to locate a file cabinet," he said.

I gave a nervous giggle and waved my hand at the rows of file cabinets that lined the walls. "We have plenty." I backed up a few more steps.

Ed Brown came forward the same number of steps. "I see there are lots of file cabinets, Miss Matthews. But how are they assigned?"

"I don't think they are." I backed up some more.

He looked horrified again. And he followed me. "Not assigned! Who has a list of them?"

"No one that I know of. You could ask Ruth tomorrow. Or Jake."

"But how do the reporters know which drawer is theirs?"

"When I needed one, I just looked until I found an empty

one. I put my name on it, and it was mine." I backed into a desk, then sidestepped until I came to its end. I kept backing in the general direction of the back stairs.

"But who assigned it to you?" Ed Brown kept right up with me.

"Nobody. I just took it."

"That's most unbusinesslike!"

"Well, this isn't the business office, Mr. Brown. Are you looking for some particular drawer?"

He looked startled. He opened his mouth, but no sound came out.

"I might be able to locate some particular reporter's drawer," I said. I didn't ask why he thought he had the authority to look in some particular drawer.

Ed began to look embarrassed. I thought he was blushing. "Well, uh—I was hoping the drawers would be labeled," he said.

"Some of them are," I said, "but the labels aren't always correct." I backed up again, and again I bumped into something. This time it was the partition around the city government reporters' cubicle.

"What do you mean?"

"If we get a new reporter—for city council, for example—then the new reporter may simply appropriate the old reporter's files. And the new reporter may not get around to replacing the label on the drawer."

Ed Brown stepped closer to me and waved his arms wildly, gesturing toward the walls on all sides of the newsroom. "Are you saying that these dozens of file cabinets and drawers are in use by individual reporters—and nobody knows who's using what drawer?"

"That's pretty much the situation. As I said, you can—"

"That's terrible."

Ed went into a real tirade then. He began to talk rapidly and angrily. His face got redder and redder, and any youthful appearance disappeared. He stepped closer again, and I became acutely aware that my back was against the partition. He was rapidly taking over my comfort zone.

Should I scream? It wouldn't do any good. The security guard was two flights down. And Ed Brown was closing in, still raving.

He finally paused for breath, and I heard a wonderful sound.

A door closed.

I recognized the sound. It was the door that led to the back stairs. It was a heavy metal door, as required by fire safety regulations, and it made a loud metallic thud when it fell shut.

It was the most beautiful sound I'd ever heard. It meant that someone else was in the building. Someone else was on the third floor. Ed Brown and I were no longer alone.

Ed evidently heard it, too, and he backed away a few inches.

It was enough. I sidled away from him and headed for the back.

I hollered over my shoulder as I ran. "You'll have to talk to Jake about this!" And I trotted rapidly along until I came to the back door. There, standing in front of it, was J.J. Jones, the advertising department's Mr. Folksy.

"Well, little missy, you're covering territory like a Texas tornado," he said.

I was so relieved to see someone besides Ed Brown that I almost laughed at his cornball remark, and I didn't feel at all put off by his bright red sports shirt.

"I read that most tornadoes never touch ground," I said. "And I'm flyin' out of here."

"What's your hurry?" J.J. grinned his folksiest grin.

I looked at him sharply. What was that about? He wasn't going to make a pass at me, was he?

He stepped in front of me, and I thought he was going to stop me.

"I was just leaving, and I got into a discussion with Mr. Brown," I said.

J.J.'s eyes popped open. "Ed Brown? Is he here?"

I gestured over my shoulder with my thumb. J.J.'s eyes narrowed, and he stepped aside.

"Wonder what he's up to," he said. "You run along, young lady." He opened the door to the stairwell for me, but he didn't say anything more.

I yelled out a quick thank-you, since my grandmother raised me to acknowledge the everyday forms of chivalry. Then I ran down those stairs, out the back door, and across the alley to my car. I was inside with the door locked in a few seconds.

And then I began to feel silly. After all, what had Ed Brown done to scare me? He'd been upset about the way file drawers were assigned in the newsroom. I had to admit our system wasn't very businesslike. But it worked for us. So what was his beef? And why had he taken it out on me?

It was a strange experience, but I had probably overreacted.

At least I had gotten out of there with the printouts from Martina's files. And what should I do with them? Now that I'd found them, I knew I'd feel like a narc if I gave them to the police.

I was going to have to talk to somebody about this. And it would have to be Mike.

I was keeping two categories of information from the police—Arnie's real identity and Martina's electronic files. Could I get in trouble? Mike could tell me what my legal situation was.

But where was Mike?

Judging from what he'd told Boone, he was planning to be home tonight. I'd ring his phone off the wall, I decided. The minute he came in the door, I'd be talking to him.

I went home and called Mike's answering machine.

"Mike, it's absolutely imperative that I speak to you the

moment you walk in the door," I told the gadget. "No matter how late it is. Call me immediately! And I mean right this minute! Pronto! Quick as a bunny!" I took a deep breath, then spoke again. "What's new?"

That ought to get results.

But it didn't. I wore circles in the kitchen floor and the upstairs hall that day, pacing back and forth, willing the phone to ring. But it didn't. I even tried baking cookies and mixing meatballs by hand, on the theory that the phone is certain to ring if it's not convenient to answer it. That didn't work either.

At ten o'clock that night I gave up and drove by Mike's house. There was a light in the living room, but that didn't mean anything. Mike routinely uses an automatic timer to turn a few lights off and on during the evening, particularly if he's working nights.

I parked at the curb. What if Mike was there and simply hadn't wanted to call me? Did I dare to ring the doorbell?

You're being stupid, I told myself. If it was anybody else in the world, you'd go to the door.

I got out of the car, slammed the door vigorously, and walked up on the porch. I punched the doorbell viciously. The bell gonged hollowly inside. The door did not open, but I can't say there was no response.

"Nell?"

The voice came out of the darkness behind me. I'd been concentrating on the house, and the sound of my name nearly gave me a heart attack. I whirled around.

"Nell, honey? Is that you?"

It was Mike's neighbor. Marceline Fuqua.

"Oh, Marceline! You startled me."

"I saw you park your car and go up the walk. I don't think Mike's home. I wondered if there was any problem. I mean, you usually just go in through the garage."

So much for our discreet practice of keeping my car in the garage. Of course, we'd known there was no fooling Marceline. Mike grew up in the house where he now lives, so Marceline has known Mike since the day Wilda and Irish Svenson brought him home from the hospital. He's used to Marceline keeping an eye on everything. And in her defense, Mike sometimes finds Marceline's deep interest in neighborhood happenings useful.

She was still looking at me quizzically.

"Mike needed my garage door opener to leave with a repairman," I said.

"He said something about that to me," Marceline said. "I don't know who he was expecting, but they sure haven't shown up. Where'd Mike go?"

"I don't know, exactly," I said. "He said he had some business to take care of."

"Humph. Well, I guess you know about that girl he was mixed up with in Chicago. He's had a time getting her out of his hair."

"Oh, I don't think it was anything to do with Annie," I said. "Mike called and left a message, but he didn't tell me when he'd be back in town."

Marceline still had Annie on her mind. "If he's gone to Chicago, he always takes that late plane home."

I moved toward the porch steps. "I'm sure he'll call as soon as he gets in. I do need to talk to him, but—"

"I'll give you the key."

"Oh, no! I wouldn't—"

"Don't be silly!" Marceline headed purposefully across the street. "Mike'll get me if he finds out I didn't let you in."

I didn't argue anymore. I'd already concluded that Mike was planning to be home that night—because of his eight a.m. appointment with Boone Thompson. If he was mad at me for going in his house without permission, we'd just have to fight it out. I took Marceline's key and let myself in the front door.

Inside, I called out, "Mike?" But there was no answer.

I turned on the kitchen light and saw a perfectly clean

kitchen. Mike had even put his dishes in the dishwasher before he left town.

I roamed around the living room and Mike's big bedroom
before I finally turned on the television and watched a talk
show. It stunk, and when it ended at midnight, Mike still
hadn't come in. I switched the television set off and tried
reading a book, but I found I was nodding. I considered getting into Mike's bed, but decided that would be too intimate.
Instead, I took a quilt from the bedroom closet and a pillow
from the bed and made myself a cocoon on the couch.

Once I was comfortably tucked in, of course, I felt wide
awake. When would Mike get there? What would he have
found out? Would he share that information with me? What
would he think I should tell the cops bout Arnie?

Who could sleep with questions like these dripping like a
faucet that needed a new washer?

I'd left the light on, so I picked up my book again. No use.
The questions kept splatting into my mental sink. I had no
interest in reading.

Then the house began to haunt me. Floorboards creaked,
windows rattled, doors seemed to move, plumbing groaned,
beams shifted uneasily.

I wasn't alone.

I told myself not to be silly. Of course I was alone. I was
simply having an attack of empty-house syndrome. It's similar to empty Gazette Building syndrome. The last time I'd
been alone in Mike's house, I'd had the same feeling—that
vague sense that someone was moving around in the house,
creeping up on me with a club, drawing nearer with a gar-
rote, slipping knives out of the kitchen drawers, threatening—

"Enough," I said. I got up and put on my shoes. The only
cure for empty-house syndrome is an inspection tour.

I began in the kitchen, turning on all the lights and looking in the broom closet and even the oven. I went into the
big bedroom, which opened off the living room. There was

nothing in the walk-in closet and no one under the bed. Mike's luxurious bathroom was empty—I even checked the little room he calls the "throne room" and I call the "water closet."

I came out and turned the light on in the little hall that led to the back of the house. I checked the second bathroom, the one with the tub. No place to hide there.

That left the back bedroom, which Mike keeps shut off and unheated, with the bed piled high with junk.

Might as well make a thorough check, I told myself, even though I was sure it was empty. I swung open the door and reached inside for the light switch.

But my hand stopped in mid-reach. The light from the hall had already fallen inside.

It hit the frozen face and bald head of Arnie Ashe.

Chapter 15

I nearly wet my pants.

Arnie was probably having problems along that line, too. He was in bed, with the covers pulled up to his chin. His eyes looked big and scared.

I gibbered. "Uh. Oh. Arn— You're here." Intelligent remarks like those.

"Nell?"

Arnie's voice sounded timid, but it made me turn and run.

"Nell! Wait!"

I could hear Arnie coming after me, but I didn't stop until I got to the garage door—the door I nearly always used. When I got there I realized my car was parked at the front curb, and I was at the wrong door. I whirled around. I guess I would have run out through the front door, but Arnie headed me off.

He came into the living room, wearing wrinkled pajamas, and he was between me and my exit. "Nell?" he said timidly.

When he saw me trapped at the sink, he came to the kitchen door and stopped. His eyes were still saucer big. I think that if I'd clapped my hands, he'd have flown up in the air and come down in a hundred pieces.

"The cops are looking for you," I said.

"I was afraid they would be."

"What are you doing here?"

"Mike was looking into something for me. He told me I

could stay here until he got it done." He grinned. "You might say he ordered me to stay here."

"I can believe that."

"What are you doing here? Mike said—"

"Yeah. He took my key away. But the neighbor let me in."

"I nearly had a heart attack when you came in and hollered a while ago."

"I nearly had a heart attack when I opened the door to that back bedroom."

I realized that my nose was running, and I wondered why. I realized that I was crying. I reached for a paper towel and turned my back on Arnie to blow my nose.

"I guess I'd better get some clothes on," Arnie said awkwardly. He turned.

"Why did you leave me?"

The words were out before I knew they were coming.

Arnie swung back. His face was frozen again. "What do you mean?"

"You left me with Gran and Grandpa. Why didn't you come back?"

Hell, I knew the answer to that. He'd been on the lam for twenty years. I wasn't being coherent. Or fair. Or sensible. But I wasn't feeling coherent, fair, or sensible. I was feeling miserable and angry, and I stood there wallowing in self-pity.

Not only had my father deserted me twice, but he'd actually hidden out with my boyfriend. And neither of them had thought I should know about the situation.

"Why didn't you take me with you?"

I watched Arnie struggle with my question for at least thirty seconds before I realized that until that moment he had had no idea that I knew he was my father.

He finally spoke. "When did you figure this out?"

"Last night," I said. "Thanks to Martina."

"Martina! The damn woman haunted me alive. Is she going to haunt me dead? How'd she find out?"

"She had a yearbook. Eastwick College. You and Arnie Ashe were both in the picture of the newspaper staff. What happened to the real Arnie?"

"He was killed in a car wreck a couple of years after college. I wrote off for a birth certificate. Arnie and I graduated in the same class at Eastwick, and I used his credentials to get a newspaper job. The college closed down a couple of years after we graduated. I figured it would be hard to track down anybody who'd known him."

Then he glared and stepped into the kitchen. "But I see Martina managed. She was a digger. You've got to give her credit for that."

"Did you kill her?"

Arnie's eyes glittered with anger. "No, Nell. I didn't kill her. I've never killed anyone."

"Not my mother?"

"No!"

"Then why did you leave the *Gazette*?"

"Because after those shoes were found in my desk—and I didn't put them there!—the cops were bound to look at me. And if they looked too closely at my background, they'd find out I was wanted in Michigan."

"Why did you run away in Michigan after my mother was killed?"

"Because that Jessamine sheriff had his mind made up! He was fitting me for a life sentence. Wouldn't look at any other suspect!" Arnie made a dramatic gesture. "I had only one hope of getting my daughter back! Only one hope of getting my own life back!"

"And just what was that?"

"I had to find the guy who really did it!"

I was still crying, but I laughed, too. "The guy who really did it! Wow! Have I heard that line before? Was it at the first murder trial I ever covered? Yeah, I remember. The defendant admitted he and his wife had been drinking with the victim for two days. But just before he passed out, or so he testified, he—sort of—well, maybe—remembered the victim looking at the door behind him and saying, 'Hi, Bill.' So, obviously, the evidence that the defendant's knife was used and his clothes were covered with blood and his fingerprints were on the murder weapon—all that meant nothing. This 'Bill' that nobody else ever saw was guilty. He wanted the cops to 'find the guy who really did it.'"

I leaned forward. "The jury didn't buy it." Arnie leaned forward, too, and we stood jaw to jaw, glaring.

And at that moment I knew he wasn't a killer. He hadn't killed my mother. And he hadn't killed Martina. And he wasn't going to kill me.

I knew he wasn't a killer, because I could see how angry my sarcastic remarks had made him. Fury was bubbling behind his eyes, seething like boiling oil, ready to be poured onto those Huns who were besieging his castle. But he didn't hit me. He didn't strangle me. He didn't pull the bread knife out of the drawer two feet from his hand and slit my throat.

Violence wasn't part of his personality.

This was the man who had once refused to spank a little girl who had told a lie, a little girl who richly deserved a spanking.

"Arnie," I whispered. "Why didn't you take me with you?"

The anger in his eyes faded. "I thought I'd be right back," he said. "I thought I'd track the guy down in a couple of days."

That's when we heard the garage door going up.

Arnie—I couldn't call him anything else yet—fled, and I was still leaning against the sink, patting my eyes, when Mike came in the back door. He looked grim.

"I broke and entered," I said.

"You were probably abetted by Marceline," Mike said. "She has her nose pressed to her front window."

"Yeah. She let me in."

"Well, did you find what you were looking for?"

"I found something I didn't expect."

At that moment we heard running water in the hall bathroom, and Mike nodded. "Arnie called me and said he was leaving town one step ahead of the cops. I offered to look into an old case—"

"My mother's murder."

Mike didn't even have the grace to look ashamed. "When and what did you find out about that?"

"I talked to Aunt Billie—as you had instructed me to before you instructed me not to. She told me my mother was murdered. And then I found an old yearbook Martina had hidden away. It had a picture of the real Arnie Ashe, and it turned out he was a short, dark guy. A tall blonde was in another picture on the page. And the cutline under that picture read 'Alan Matthews.' "

"And you're upset."

"No, not 'upset.' I can put a more exact word on it. It's 'enraged.' "

"At me?"

"Yes. I'm enraged at you, and I'm enraged at Arnie,"

"Of course, you've been mad at him for twenty years."

"Right. And I may be mad at him for twenty more. So let's talk about my being mad at you."

Mike dropped a small duffel bag, the carry-on type, on the floor. He crossed to the refrigerator and took out a bottle of beer. "Your father came to me, and he needed some help. I tried to help him. Was that so rotten?"

"It was rotten not to tell me what was going on."

Mike was twisting the top off his beer. He tossed the cap into the trash can under the sink. "Arnie didn't want me to tell you."

"You've only known Arnie a few days. How come what he wanted counted so much more than what I wanted?"

"Did you want it? Did you really want to know your father was a fugitive from justice?"

"I want to know the truth! My aunt had been lying to me.

My own grandmother lied to me! Now you're lying to me! No matter how bad the truth had been, it wasn't as bad as that."

"Nell—"

"All my life I thought, somewhere deep inside, that my father went away because I spoke angrily to him, because I said, 'Just go away and leave me alone!' It didn't help to become a grown-up and tell myself that things are more complicated than that. It didn't help to tell myself that he left my mother, not me. Because he did leave me! I was such a bad girl that my daddy went away and wouldn't even take care of me anymore. Now—after I've battled this for twenty years—I find that none of it mattered! He didn't go away because of anything I did. He went away because my mother was murdered."

Mike reached out, tried to put his arm around me, but I shoved him away.

"Mike, my grandmother lied to me because she wanted to protect me. I was a child then! I'm not a child now. What's your excuse for lying?"

"Maybe I'm trying to protect you, too."

"I'm not a child," I repeated.

"Sometimes you seem as fragile as one."

I whammed my fist on the cabinet. "I won't break. Nothing can make me break but lies! I can face anything but having the people I love lie to me."

"Okay, okay! I'll tell you the truth. No matter how hard it is to take. What do you want to know?"

That stopped me. I'd been so angry over Arnie being ready to skip town without telling me he was my father, so mad at Mike for helping him and for nosing into my mother's death without asking my permission—I didn't really have any questions. But on the spot I determined that I'd find some to ask.

"Why did you go to Michigan?"

"To try to help Arnie. After Boone Thompson found the

shoes in Arnie's desk, Arnie got afraid that his background wouldn't stand up to close scrutiny. He decided to leave town."

"Take a third identity?"

Mike shrugged. "Maybe. He didn't tell me all the details. But he didn't want to leave without telling you he was your father. I guess he called you, at the *Gazette*, but he chickened out. Anyway, he finally decided to leave a message with me."

"And you talked him into letting you investigate."

"Hardest talking job I ever had to do. I've talked guys off of ten-story ledges with less effort."

"I'm sure it was a tribute to your skill and sneakiness."

"I'm a hellava negotiator. So I flew to Grand Rapids, rented a car, and went to Jessamine."

"Did you find out anything?"

"I talked to the former sheriff, a guy named Vanderkolk, and I got a photocopy of his original case notes—such as they are. He wasn't real good with his paperwork."

"I called up there and talked to Vanderkolk myself. Arnie told me he had made his mind up—wouldn't consider any other suspect."

Mike grimaced. "That's pretty close to true."

"Was the evidence that damning?"

Mike drank from his beer. "Oh, most of it wasn't real conclusive."

"Can I read it?"

"Let me show it to Arnie first. Get his slant on it."

"You'll have to arrest him."

"Michigan will have to tell me that officially."

"No, Boone—"

Mike held up a hand so firmly it would have stopped a semi. "You're the one who wants the truth here. I, on the other hand, might not want to know everything in the world. Right away."

I gulped my sentence down. Mike didn't want to be told

that the Grantham Police Department—his employer—was looking for Arnie. Even if there wasn't a warrant out for him, Mike would be forced to bring Arnie in.

"You can't keep from knowing very long."

"Maybe we can all get a little sleep first. Anything else you want to know?"

I sighed. The mention of sleep had made me feel exhausted. "Just about the evidence you found in Michigan. Why this sheriff was so determined that Arnie had killed my mother."

"One witness was the most damning. She told Vanderkolk Arnie had called the house and quarreled with your mother. She said that your mother had planned to meet with your dad the night she was killed."

"Who? That neighbor? The one I stayed with until my grandparents came?"

Mike shook his head. "Like I say, maybe I should go over this with Arnie—"

"No! Neither of you is going to keep anything from me! I want to know who told Vanderkolk that!"

"No!" The word from the kitchen door was as vehement as the one I'd yelled. Arnie, now dressed in dark suit pants and a white cotton T-shirt, was standing there.

"She doesn't need to know that, Mike," he said.

"Yes, I do! Maybe it's not important," I said, "but it's simply one more thing you two are keeping from me."

Mike frowned. "We'll have to ask her about it eventually."

Arnie scowled.

"Tell me!" I said. "Who was this witness who made my father go off and leave me?"

Mike took a drink from his beer. His voice was quiet. "It was you, Nell."

"Me!"

"Yes. That's what was so damning about it. It was the evidence of an eight-year-old girl who had no reason to lie, who had no idea she was hurting her father by reporting what she had heard, what her mother had said."

Arnie turned his back and walked away from me.

I didn't swoon.

When I was growing up, my grandmother had a collection of books by Mary Roberts Rinehart, and one summer I started at the left end of the shelf and read straight through them all. Mrs. Rinehart's heroines were usually spunky, but occasionally they swooned. If they received a shock too great, they simply said something such as, "The next two days are a blur in my memory," or "The world went black then, and when I awoke Dr. Diddly was at my side." There have been times in my life when I envied those heroines their ability to clear the emotional decks and simply retire from life for a few days.

At that moment—when Arnie turned away from me—I felt that way. As I took in the implications of what Mike had told me, I wished that the floor could simply open beneath my feet, that I could disappear down the hole, and that the world would go away.

But I didn't collapse or become hysterical. I stood there. Mike put his beer bottle down on the cabinet, and he put his arms around me. I stood stiffly, but I didn't pull away. Neither of us said anything. I had even stopped crying.

Then, looking past Mike's arm, I saw Arnie. He was sitting on the couch in the living room, and he was holding his head in his hands.

God! His whole life had been ruined, and it had been ruined by my testimony. Whatever I had told the sheriff—twenty years earlier, when I was eight years old—it had forced my father to flee. He'd given up his first job as managing editor, a big step up the professional ladder. He'd taken another identity. He'd roamed from city to city as a journeyman reporter, afraid to stay around and build seniority, always afraid that the Martinas of the world would dig out his secret and turn him in. Afraid to marry again. Afraid to contact his daughter, afraid to see old friends.

And I had caused it. I had only the vaguest memory of ever talking to any law enforcement official about my mother's death. I hadn't even known she'd been murdered, and I certainly hadn't thought my father had been involved. But I had condemned him to a footloose and frightened existence.

What had I said? What had I told this Sheriff Vanderkolk?

I really had rejected my father. Perhaps he hadn't gone because I said, "Just go away!" But he had gone because of something I had said.

I moved away from Mike's arms and went into the living room. I sat on the couch beside Arnie. I wasn't quite ready to put my arms around him, but I touched his shoulder.

"Arnie," I said. "I don't know what I told the sheriff—way back then—but I didn't mean to cause trouble. I really don't believe you killed my mother. I'm sorry I made the sheriff believe you did."

He took my hand. "Vanderkolk was ready to believe anything bad about me. We'd been investigating his office—he was blinking at some illegal slots, and I'd encouraged the police reporter to go after the story. Heck, I'd hand-led the kid through the investigation! So there was bad blood between Vanderkolk and me already."

"But what did I tell him?"

Arnie didn't answer, but Mike did. "Your story didn't match Arnie's," he said.

Beer bottle in hand, Mike sat down in a club chair that stood at a right angle to the couch, stretching his legs out full-length and leaning back.

"Apparently everybody in Jessamine knew your parents had split up, Nell. Arnie told the sheriff he had moved out two weeks earlier, and that he hadn't even talked to your mother for three days before she was killed."

"Well," I said. "Only that phone call the night before."

Arnie snapped his head around. "No!"

I stared at him. "What's wrong?"

"I didn't call Sally the night before she was killed. I talked to her on the phone a couple of times, and she met me for lunch one day while you were at school. But I didn't talk to her the night before she was killed."

Now I really was staring. "But I heard you!"

Arnie shook his head, then looked at Mike. Something very like despair filled his face. "See," he said. "See! She still believes it."

Mike didn't change his relaxed position. "Yes, I felt pretty sure that was the situation. Nell, when did your dad call?"

I thought about it. "It would have been after eleven on the night before the evening my mother went out and didn't come back."

"You heard the phone ring?"

"No, I was already in bed. In fact, I think I must have been asleep. I think I woke up when I heard my mother's voice."

"What was she saying?"

"I couldn't tell. I was upstairs in bed. At the front of the house. She was in the kitchen, downstairs and the back of the house."

"How did you know she was talking to your dad?"

I stared at my fingernails. "They were quarreling. She was angry. But I wanted to talk to my daddy. So I went to the upstairs extension and picked the phone up. I heard my dad's voice."

Arnie put his head back in his hands. "It wasn't me," he said.

Mike's face stayed blank. He took a drink of his beer.

"Look," I said. "We hadn't lived there long. My mother was having a hard time making friends. She didn't know anybody. No one ever came to the house. Except that one woman."

Arnie raised his head, but I kept talking.

"I know! I know! Vanderkolk believes she had a boyfriend. He told me that. But I don't believe it. She didn't go out! And I'm sure I would have noticed if anybody came to the house! When I heard a man talking, I thought it was my daddy. Besides, my mother told me it was."

Mike frowned. "She told you? When?"

"That same night. Like I said, when I heard her talking, I picked up the upstairs extension." I stared at the floor. "I wanted to talk to my daddy. But Mother heard the phone, and she shushed my dad. She told me to go back to bed.

"I told her, 'I want to talk to Daddy.' And she said, 'Tomorrow. I'm trying to fix things up so you can see him tomorrow. Hang up now.'"

"How many times did Vanderkolk go over this with you?" Mike said.

"I barely remember the policeman—I guess it was Vanderkolk—coming to the house. But I remember standing there in the hall, talking to my mother on the phone. I was so disappointed."

"Disappointed?"

"Yes, I wanted to tell my dad I was sorry I told him to go away. I always remembered it because I never got another chance. I didn't get to talk to him, and he was right there on the same line."

Arnie shook his head. "Sorry, Nell. I don't know who was on the phone, but it wasn't me."

"But—"

Arnie was still shaking his head, and I shut up. I looked at Mike. "What did Vanderkolk say about it?"

"Same thing both of you say. You thought your dad had been there. Arnie said he hadn't been."

"And Vanderkolk believed me?"

Mike nodded. "Yes. Frankly, I thought he was putting a little too much trust in the word of an eight-year-old girl. He didn't take an official statement. He just asked something like, 'When did your daddy last call your mother, little girl?'

When she said 'Wednesday night,' he didn't go into it any further."

"I didn't call," Arnie said. "Nell was mistaken."

"That's entirely possible," Mike said. "After all, Nell, you were an eight-year-old child who had been upset for a couple of weeks because her parents had split up. Who was blaming herself—the way children do—because her father had gone away. You woke up in the night, and you heard your mother's voice in the kitchen, talking on the phone. You couldn't hear the words—just her quarreling with someone. You jumped to the conclusion that it was your father and went to the phone to try to talk to him.

"But your mother made you hang up, saying she was trying to work things out for you to see your dad."

"If that had been me—" Arnie stopped.

Mike looked at him questioningly, and Arnie went on. "I would have talked to Nell," he said. "I wouldn't have stayed on the line but not said anything. Sulking or something."

Mike was nodding again. "That's what I thought. I think some other man was on the phone, someone who didn't want Nell to hear his voice."

"The supposed boyfriend," I said.

Another long silence. I touched Arnie's arm. "Did you think my mother was seeing someone else?"

"She denied it," he said.

I gulped. "So you were suspicious enough to ask her."

Arnie stared at the rug. "There was a lot of gossip," he said. "We hadn't been getting along. I didn't know what to think."

He stood up suddenly. "But right now I know what I think. I think this situation is small tough, and I don't want to talk about it. Mike, am I still a houseguest?"

"Sure."

"Then I'm going to bed." He walked out of the room.

I stood up, ready to tell the final reason I'd been so sure that my daddy had called the house in Jessamine the night before my mother was killed.

Chapter 16

"**A**rnie!"

I must have sounded anguished, but Arnie didn't look around.

"We need to talk about this!"

He kept walking toward the back of the house, and in a second I heard the bedroom door close. I stared after him. How could I tell him the rest of the story if he wouldn't listen?

Mike was standing up, too. "I have a feeling Arnie's survived twenty years on the run by avoiding confrontation, Nell."

"Well, he's sure avoiding me!"

"When he's trapped, his instinct is to run. When a quarrel arises, he dodges the issue. Odd that he's built a reputation—under whatever name he was using—as a good reporter."

Mike's reaction puzzled me. "Why do you say that?" I asked.

"Because I think of reporters as people who come on strong, who aren't afraid to face facts and ask tough questions."

"There are different styles of news gathering," I said absentmindedly. "Most of the time you accomplish more with cooperation than with confrontation." I was staring after Arnie. Should I go after him, make him listen to the rest of the story?

Or should I tell Mike the really damning part? I turned to find Mike was standing up.

"But maybe Arnie has the right idea this time," he said.

"What do you mean?"

"I'm so tired that I'd just as soon give it a rest. Maybe Arnie has the right idea. Let's just shut up and sleep on it."

That settled my problem. Neither Mike nor Arnie wanted to talk to me.

"I think you should stay here," Mike said. "I'll sleep on the couch."

"On the couch?" I considered laughing. Was Mike afraid of shocking Arnie? Didn't he want my father to know our relationship was intimate?

"Mike, I'm sure Arnie has figured out that we sleep together."

"I thought you were mad at me."

"That's a big bed. You can stay on your side."

"It's better if I'm out here."

He took his beer bottle into the kitchen. I followed him.

"I'll go home. I don't want to put you out of your own bed."

"No. Stay." He lowered his voice. "It'll give me an excuse to sleep in the living room."

"Why do you want to do that?"

Mike leaned closer. "The living room is between Arnie and his car. I want him to be here tomorrow morning."

So I stayed in the bedroom, lonely in the big bed yet not quite sure I wanted Mike on the other side of it. Emotional turmoil doesn't make me feel sexy, and I wasn't sure just where Mike and I stood at the moment. He and Arnie had conspired to keep things from me, things I ought to know. How could I trust either of them?

About four a.m. I heard a noise, and I jumped out of bed and tiptoed to the door. Mike's breathing was regular, but I caught Arnie's bald head sticking into the room from the hall. He pulled it back like a startled turtle taking refuge in its shell.

Maybe Mike had been right. Maybe Arnie wouldn't have stuck around if he hadn't had to pass Mike to get to his car, if he hadn't had to open Mike's noisy motorized garage door to get away. Anyway, Arnie stayed put until the next morning.

The first hint I had that morning had arrived was the soft swish of water in the bathroom sink. I realized that Mike had crept through the bedroom and into the bathroom without waking me. His activities barely disturbed my sleep, but just after the water started, I heard a noise from another direction. Furtive steps in the hall. I sat up. The door to the garage opened, then closed gently. And the noisy motor started lifting the garage door.

My dad was leaving me again!

I wasn't sure how I felt about him just yet. But I knew I didn't want him to go before I could find out.

"Arnie!" I jumped out of bed without worrying about the skimpy T-shirt and underpants I was wearing, and I ran through the kitchen. I threw the door to the garage open, and I yelled. "Arnie! Don't go!"

Arnie cringed guiltily, almost ducking down behind the open door of his Toyota. "Nell! I've got to go! For you as well as for me."

"No! Mike and I will help you! I know you didn't kill anybody! We'll prove it! Please, don't go!"

Arnie leaned on the top of his car. "It's no good, Nell. Things look too bad. If they don't get me for Martina, they'll get me for Sally. My only hope is to keep running."

"Running where? To what? You can't keep living like that!"

A grin crossed Arnie's face. "It's worked so far," he said.

It was exactly what Mike had said the night before. Arnie had stayed free for twenty years because of his well-developed sense of when to run. He had run out of my life when I was eight years old. And he was about to run out again. But I couldn't just stand there and wave good-bye. We hadn't had our confrontation.

I stepped down into the garage and grabbed the edge of the car door, the door he was holding open. I clutched it as if my grip could keep the car from backing out of the garage. "Why did you even come back into my life! Or did you do it on purpose? Did you just come to the *Gazette* for the job? Did you even know I was there?"

"I knew." Arnie looked away, then went on. "When you and Mike talked that nut out of the belfry of the police station, you wrote it up, telling what it was like to be held at gunpoint by a madman. The story moved on the wire. I was working the wire desk in Texas. I nearly fell over at the VDT when a story by my own daughter moved on the natwire.

"Then you and Mike were interviewed on television. I saw the interview." He made an impatient gesture. "I taped the interview, and I played it over and over. That was my little girl. All grown up. And smart! And beautiful! And brave! And a great writer! Everything I'd ever wanted her to be! And I knew—"

His face collapsed.

My defenses went at the same time. "Daddy!" I said. I put my arms around his neck.

Arnie hugged me back. He gulped and went on, talking into my hair. "And I knew, Nell—I knew I'd made the right decision back there in Michigan when I decided to run for it rather than face a trial for killing your mother. I knew that your grandparents could do a better job of raising you than I could ever do. I knew you deserved a better home than anything I could give you! I knew I didn't want you to have to testify against me—even if you had no idea what your testimony meant."

"But you came back! You came to the *Gazette*."

"When I saw that the *Gazette* had an opening, I couldn't

resist seeing you. And, honey, you're just as wonderful as I knew you'd be. That's why—"

"Arnie!"

"That's why I have to go now. I can't mess your life up any more."

He pulled my arms from around his neck, and he gently pushed me away. "Nell, you've got a good life. You're one of the *Gazette*'s best reporters, and you're getting better all the time. You've got Mike, and he's a fine man, and he really cares about you. Enough to risk his career by helping your old man. It's best for both of you if I go on my way."

"Where will you go? This is going to destroy your life as Arnie Ashe."

"I have another plan."

"You won't be able to get a newspaper job."

He shrugged and got into his car. "I know."

"Won't I ever hear from you?"

"Maybe I'll figure out a way. But you don't need me, Nell. You're doing fine."

"No! Not really. At least—" I was desperate. He was leaving. Again. And I couldn't tell him it would be better if he stayed. Staying might mean prison for my mother's murder. And it might mean a separate prison sentence for Martina's death. And I didn't want to believe he had committed either crime. But who had? He'd never be free if we didn't find out.

"You said you ran away from Jessamine looking for the man who killed my mother," I said.

Arnie nodded. "But I never caught up with him."

"Who was it?"

"I don't know. I had a lead, and I thought I could identify him. But the lead didn't pan out."

"You haven't even told us what this 'lead' was."

"It's too late now."

"No! You've got to help us figure out who killed Martina."

"Martina's death had nothing to do with me."

"I think it did. The night she was killed, two things happened. First, I asked her if she'd ever worked with 'Alan Matthews.'"

"Why'd you think of that?"

"Something she'd said the night before, while she was under the influence of blanket wash. Anyway, she denied knowing you. But later she asked me to meet her in that downstairs ladies' room. She said she needed to tell me something and that was the most private place."

Arnie frowned.

"She was killed before I could meet her! But it's too much of a coincidence. She was going to tell me something about you—"

"Maybe."

"—and somebody killed her before she got a chance. Arnie, if Martina was killed because she figured out that you are really Alan Matthews, then someone else is around who knows that, who had some reason to kill her."

"What do you mean?"

"Think about it logically! The only reason you would have to kill Martina would be because she found out you were wanted for murder in Michigan."

"Right."

"But you say you didn't kill her."

"No. For one thing, I didn't know she'd figured it out. For another, I'm too chicken to kill anybody. I'm all set up to run again. Anytime."

"But somebody killed Martina."

"It wasn't me."

"I accept that. But it may have been somebody who knew about the Michigan case—somebody else who was threatened by her knowledge."

"Nell, that's crazy! Life isn't that full of coincidences. Who could be in Grantham who was in Jessamine, Michigan, twenty years ago?"

"The guy in the Cadillac," I said. "The guy who tried to kill me."

Arnie and I stared at each other. The implications of what I was saying hadn't really soaked in until I verbalized them. Suddenly my bare feet were freezing on the cold garage floor, and the cool air of an April morning was blowing through the open garage door and creeping up under the T-shirt, and I began to shiver violently.

"Kill you?" Arnie was scowling. "Someone tried to kill you?"

"I don't know. Maybe not. Maybe it had nothing to do with Martina's death. Maybe it was somebody who wanted to steal my car."

He swung his legs out of the car. "What happened?"

"It was night before last," I said. I sketched out the car chase down Mississippi and the whizzing run through College Hills, ending with my hideaway between the dry-cleaner's vans and with the shots that missed.

"So I have no proof it had anything to do with Martina's death. But Jim Hammond thought . . ." I paused.

"What? What did Hammond think?"

"Well, he used the same word you did. He said it was awfully coincidental—my finding Martina dead one day and somebody chasing me the next. But, Arnie—Dad—we already knew there was a killer hanging out at the *Gazette*."

Arnie got out of the car. "But we didn't know he had his eye on you," he said. "You'd better get back in the house, young lady."

"But—"

"And I'm coming in with you."

Arnie took my arm and pushed me ahead of him into the kitchen.

"Listen," I said. "I don't want you to go, but I can't swear Mike and I can help you—help you stay out of prison, I mean."

"That's doesn't matter."

"Of course it matters! You shouldn't go to prison for something you didn't do."

"And I shouldn't let some geek kill my only daughter because I'm too careful of my own skin to help the police find the real killer."

"But he didn't—maybe it wasn't—"

Arnie was still shoving me ahead of him, up the steps and into the kitchen. Mike was standing in the middle of the room wearing boxer shorts and a T-shirt. I stopped, but Arnie kept going. Right around me. Right up to Mike. And he tapped Mike on the chest with his forefinger.

"Did you know somebody tried to kill Nell?"

Mike frowned. "I've been out of town," he said defensively.

I cracked up.

I laughed all the way into the bedroom and shook all over so hard that I could hardly put my clothes on. Of course, my laughter had an edge that was pretty close to tears.

By the time I had climbed back into my jeans, sweater, and tennis shoes, Mike had put on the coffeepot, and Arnie had had time to repeat my story to him.

Mike came into the bedroom. "You're not making this up, are you? Somebody really chased you?"

"You can check the police report. Jim Hammond came out to supervise my statement. Having a senior detective there nearly scared the kid patrolman to death."

"Weird." Mike went into the walk-in closet where he keeps his clothes.

"What do we do now?" I said.

"I don't have a clue," Mike said. "But maybe Arnie can give us one."

"Will you take him when you go to see Boone Thompson?"

Mike came out taking a blue oxford cloth shirt out of a plastic laundry bag. "It might be better," he said, "if Boone came here."

"What do you mean?"

"It looks as if someone at the *Gazette* is concerned in Martina's death, right?"

I nodded.

"Entirely too much headquarters gossip finds its way to the *Gazette*. Maybe we'd be smarter to keep quiet about Arnie cooperating."

So Mike called Boone Thompson and asked him to come out to the house and to bring Jim Hammond with him. He didn't tell them why, but they came, which was a tribute to their opinion of Mike. Lowly patrolmen rarely suggest actions to detectives, even when the patrolman can do it as tactfully as Mike can. Especially when the patrolman is as cagey about explaining as Mike was.

While we were waiting, Arnie lit cigarette after cigarette and played solitaire. Mike doesn't really like people to smoke in his house, but he didn't say anything. He just found an ashtray in a drawer somewhere.

And after Jim and Boone arrived, he gave Arnie a little pep-talk introduction. "This is the man who's been working at the *Gazette* under the name Arnie Ashe."

Jim Hammond barked, "Under the name Arnie Ashe? You using an alias?"

Arnie did look panicky then, and I reached over and took his hand. "His real name is Alan Matthews," I said. "He's my dad."

Jim and Boone both looked as amazed as if we'd announced Arnie was D. B. Cooper, and Mike used the moment of surprise to speak again.

"Arnie—or Alan—came to me two days ago and told me a strange story," he said. "I thought it might be better if you all heard it unofficially first."

Jim sat back in his chair. He made his voice its gruffest and most intimidating. "Well, let's hear this strange story," he said.

Arnie squeezed my hand. "It all starts twenty years ago,

when Nell's mother was murdered outside a small town in western Michigan," he said.

His prècis of the events that led up to my mother's death was different from the one Ronald Vanderkolk had given me.

He and my mother, Sally, had been married nine years, he said. They'd met in Amity, her hometown, when Alan/Arnie came there as a young reporter just out of college. My mother had been a freshman at Amity Junior College. She was tiny, with dark hair and snapping blue eyes. Volatile and moody.

"Sexy as hell," Arnie said. "I couldn't get enough of her."

Only four months after they met, they eloped. Then Sally began to find out about reality. She was already having morning sickness, and living on the salary of a young reporter is no picnic. Arnie didn't say it in so many words, but she had apparently needed a guardian more than she needed a husband. He had to cut up their one credit card after she maxed it out.

"But Sally's parents were wonderful," he said. Though the "have-to" status of their daughter's marriage had obviously embarrassed them, they had been supportive. They had given me a baby bed and had loaned Alan and Sally money for a car.

"When Nell was about a year old, Sally finally faced the fact that newsmen's wives have to help earn a living," Arnie said. My grandparents paid her tuition and bought her books so she could return to college part-time, first at Amity Junior College and then commuting to a nearby state college. My grandmother had kept me while my mother went to class.

Alan, meanwhile, had done well professionally. He'd begun to have better job offers, but he'd stayed at the Amity paper until Sally finished her degree and got her teaching certificate, moving up to city editor of the small-town daily, supervising a crew of six newsside reporters when he was only twenty-eight.

Then he got his big break. The Amity paper had been acquired by a small chain, Gordon Publications. The new bosses offered him a transfer and a promotion to managing editor of a paper of approximately the same size—in Jessamine, Michigan. It included a major raise.

He eagerly accepted. My grandparents kept me while he and Sally drove to Jessamine to find a house. They rented a U-Haul and drove off, on their way up the ladder.

But things hadn't gone well in Jessamine.

First, the Jessamine newspaper staff had been demoralized by the former editor's failings, and the general manager was a dunce. Alan had to fight his own boss and his own reporters over every change he wanted to make. The job involved long hours and maximum stress.

And Sally had been miserable. Her peppery personality had rubbed the Michigan people wrong. She'd been tactless. She'd never before lived any place where she hadn't had old friends who were willing to overlook her failings. Now, in Jessamine, she was simply known as that rude Mrs. Matthews.

When she tried to get a Michigan teaching certificate, she was told she'd have to take most of her classes over. "Nobody seemed to have heard that we're literate down in this part of the country," Alan said. "They wanted her to duplicate all her work—at colleges that weren't as good as the one she'd graduated from."

Stuck in a strange community, with no way to get a job, with no friends, and with a husband who was forced to work twelve to sixteen hours a day, seven days a week—no wonder my mother had been miserable.

I'd made a friend—I still remember her, Annette Vandyke. Her mother had liked me, but she'd been coldly polite to my mother. Only one neighbor, another outsider—from Chicago—had been friendly. Arnie's lips tightened when he mentioned her.

But the real trouble started on one of the few occasions

when my parents had been able to get out for the evening. They were to be guests of a printing-supply salesman, along with the general manager and his wife. Since my parents had only one car, Arnie had arranged to ride with the salesman from the newspaper offices to the Elks Club—the only good place to eat in Jessamine—and to meet my mother there.

He hadn't been very pleased to learn she'd come a half hour early and had spent the extra time in the bar, having a drink with some of the Elks. One had been a pressman at the *Journal*.

That had led to a quarrel. Angry, Sally and her Chicago friend had gone back to the Elks Club bar the next night. Another quarrel.

And the gossip began.

"There wasn't a lot happening in Jessamine," Arnie said. "People didn't have much to talk about but each other. Sally was a stranger, and she'd made it clear she didn't like the town or the people there. She was perfect gossip bait. And, of course, I had a whole staff of reporters and a town full of news sources who were happy to pass the gossip along."

"But, Arnie," I said. "I'm old enough to remember. My mother let me stay up until the news came on, and she was there every night. She wasn't out running around."

Arnie nodded. "I know, Nell. I really think ninety-five percent of the talk was completely unfounded. I think those two excursions to the Elks Club bar just about ruined her in Jessamine. Anyway, that's when the phone calls began."

Sally began to get crank phone calls—strangers asking her out, heavy breathers, dirty talkers. Always high-strung, now she was frightened and almost crazy.

"I can remember I wasn't allowed to answer the phone," I said. "I never knew why. She must have been frantic."

"She was frantic to get out of Jessamine," Arnie said. "And I could understand that. But I'd been there less than six months. My first job as M.E.! How was it going to look if I couldn't handle it? I just had to make it on that job, and she couldn't seem to see that. I offered to send her home on a visit, but she said I was trying to push her out of my life, was building up to a separation. No matter what I did, it was wrong!"

Just as things got totally cuckoo, Arnie said, "the motel incident" occurred.

Chapter 17

The "motel incident," simply stated, was this. On an evening when my mother had taken the family car to go to a PTA meeting, she said, some Jessamine busybody had spotted the car at a motel in the town of Holland, thirty miles away.

Since I'd grown up in Amity, a town around the same size as Jessamine, I wasn't surprised she'd been caught. People from small towns not only see each other around town; they tend to go to the same out-of-town spots to do their shopping, dining out, and moviegoing. I've been away from Amity several years now, but so far I've never once gone to Grantham's biggest mall on a Saturday without running into someone from my hometown. People from burgs smaller than Amity run into each other at the Amity Wal-Mart. I've even run into people from Grantham in Dallas restaurants.

Apparently people from Jessamine had routinely driven into Holland, a city three or four times the size of Jessamine, for special occasions and shopping. It was not a good place for my mother to have a clandestine meeting.

My parents' car had been easy to identify because its window still held a parking permit from the small state college my mother had attended in her home state. Everybody in Jessamine knew whose car it was. The news flew, Arnie said.

"She should have known someone would see her," I said.

"I don't know what she was thinking of," Arnie said. "But—I was young and stupid. She'd hurt my pride. I couldn't pretend I hadn't heard about it."

That had brought about the final quarrel, Arnie said. That led to the night burned into my memory, the one when my daddy came in to kiss me good-bye. Distraught, I had yelled at him, "Just go away! Go away and leave me alone!"

I hadn't seen him again for twenty years, until the day two months earlier when he'd been introduced around the *Gazette* newsroom as Arnie Ashe, the new police reporter. We'd shaken hands.

The twenty-years-ago quarrel had ended without any explanation of why Sally had gone to the motel.

"Did you find out who she'd met there?" Mike asked. "Or if she'd met anyone?"

"No. All she said was that she 'hadn't done anything wrong.' Since Sally's idea of what was right or wrong depended pretty much on what suited Sally"— Arnie shrugged —"that wasn't a real reassuring report."

He contemplated his cigarette briefly, then spoke again. "But something had frightened her. Or someone. She said something like 'First that terrible evening, and now you act like this!' But she wouldn't tell me what had happened."

Arnie had left the car for my mother and me, taking a room at a "funny old" hotel near the *Jessamine Journal* office. But he'd talked to my mother frequently, Arnie said, either by phone or face to face.

"I was urging her to go back to Amity," he said. "She'd always been dependent on her parents—even when she resented their 'interference.' But I thought getting away from their steadying influence was a lot of her problem. I thought maybe we could work it out if she'd go back, stay with them a while. I'd look for another job, back in the Southwest, where we were more at home. We'd get the hell out of Jessamine."

But Sally had been adamant, he said. "She kept telling me she hadn't done anything wrong and that she was going to prove it."

"Did she say how she was going to do this?" Mike asked.

"She said she'd find the person who could back up her word. She wouldn't give me any details. When Sally was huffy, she could really be bullheaded.

"Anyway, that's where we were two weeks later when Vanderkolk himself came over to tell me she'd been found dead on a back road. She'd been run over by our car."

"Where was the car found?" Jim asked.

"In the parking lot of one of Jessamine's two grocery stores. Nobody noticed who put it there."

"Fingerprints?"

"Mine, of course. Sally's. Sally's Chicago friend. But it was November. Cold weather in Michigan. People would be wearing gloves."

"How about the Chicago friend? Did she know anything?"

"She said she didn't. Said Sally had dropped her like a hot brick after their escapade at the Elks Club." Arnie shrugged. "I was the most logical suspect, of course. The betrayed and angry husband. And Vanderkolk and I had already bumped heads over a story we ran on slot machines. I can't blame him for considering me the prime suspect. But I couldn't get him even to look at anybody else."

"Did you have an alibi?"

"No. I'd left the *Journal* office for several hours during the evening. All I'd done was walk back to the hotel and lie down and watch the ceiling, but I couldn't prove it. That hotel didn't man the desk all the time. I had a key. Just let myself in and went on up. I went back to the office around eleven and stayed until the presses rolled, but the medical examiner thought Sally had died earlier in the evening."

"Still," Jim said, "your lack of an alibi isn't much to go on."

"That's where little Nell came in," I said. "Apparently I was the one who convinced Vanderkolk that my parents had been together the night my mother was killed."

Mike passed Vanderkolk's notes around then, and there it

was in black and white. A man had been talking to my mother on the phone. I had thought it was my daddy. My mother had said she was going to see my father the next day, then shooed me back to bed.

"And I still say, if I'd been the man on the phone, I would have talked to Nell," Arnie said. "I didn't call that night. I did not arrange to meet Sally the next evening."

I listened to all this, and I still kept my mouth shut about the most important reason I had thought Arnie was the man on the phone.

"Three days later, after I decided Vanderkolk wasn't going to do it, I thought I'd try to find out just who had been registered at that motel in Holland," Arnie said. "I was pretty sure Sally had met somebody and that was the guy she was talking about when she said something 'terrible' had happened. I felt sure he was the person who killed her. Of course, Vanderkolk said he had looked at the people registered, and there was nothing unusual about any of them. But I thought I might recognize a name, a license plate—something.

"Since our car was still being held by the sheriff's office, I had to borrow a car from one of the reporters to drive over there. And I was able to talk to the motel manager. He'd had a full house that night, didn't remember much about anybody who'd checked in—except this one rather furtive individual whose name was supposedly Smith. While I was there, the reporter whose car I'd borrowed called. He said Vanderkolk had been in, looking for me. The gossip was that he'd asked for a warrant."

Arnie shook his head. "My situation seemed hopeless. I decided my only chance was to find this Smith. It was obvious Vanderkolk wasn't going to look for him. I got his name and license number—it was an Illinois tag. I walked across the street to a grocery store, and I cashed a check for the few hundred dollars on our account. Then I wrote Sally's parents a note saying they were Nell's guardians, and I wrote the reporter a note telling him where his car was. I got on the next bus for Chicago.

"I really felt that I could track this Smith guy down and be back in a few days. Of course, it turned out to be hopeless." He stubbed out his latest cigarette.

We all took a break then. The April morning had warmed up, so Mike opened the doors and windows and turned on the ceiling fan. Jim called his office and told Peaches to postpone his ten o'clock appointment. Boone used the bathroom.

I worried. I wanted Arnie's explanation for the fact I was leaving out, but I didn't want to ask him about it in front of Jim and Boone. Or even in front of Mike.

When we came back, Jim kicked everything off. "Let's move on to Martina," he said. "I don't suppose she was on the staff at Jessamine."

"No, I first ran into Martina a couple of years later, in Tennessee," Arnie said.

After a week in Chicago, Arnie had been close to broke. He found a casual job as a dishwater. "My skills are pretty limited," he said. "It's write, edit, or sweep up."

He'd found a newsstand that carried the Grand Rapids paper, and he kept an eye on the investigation into my mother's death. Since he was never officially charged or declared "wanted," the official comments were guarded. But as a former cop reporter himself, he knew the code. Vanderkolk had other cops looking for him.

He'd remembered the tragic car accident that had killed his journalism classmate, Arnie Ashe, so he wrote for a copy of Arnie's birth certificate and started over as a reporter, using Arnie's transcript from Eastwick Methodist College as the basis of his credentials. He'd landed a job in Jenkinsville, Tennessee, where he'd picked up the nickname "Red." After he joined the *Gazette* staff, he and Martina had argued when she used that nickname.

In Tennessee Martina had been covering county government and agriculture.

"That's a big beat in Jenkinsville," Arnie said. "And she was a good reporter. Nosy."

In fact, she'd been as nosy about everyone's personal life in those days as she had been when I'd worked with her at the *Gazette*. "She always made me nervous. Full of questions," Arnie said.

She'd scared him worst after the birth of a baby to one of the reporters. In the flurry of congratulations, Arnie had made an unguarded comment about his own experience with fatherhood.

"She was on it like a cat on a june bug," he said. "I'd let the word get around that I'd come to Jenkinsville in the aftermath of a rotten divorce. But I'd never before let out a hint that I had a daughter. After that she was quizzing and probing all the time."

Arnie snubbed her into silence, but it had been unpleasant. When he heard of a job across the state, he grabbed it.

"Martina won a national prize for breaking a big county scandal that year," he said. "I went to the state press meeting, told her congratulations. I knew she was a digger. If she'd spent as much energy on investigative reporting as she did on office gossip, she'd have been a Pulitzer prize winner."

Mike leaned forward. "Would you have come to the *Gazette* if you'd known she was there?"

"Sure," Arnie said. "She was a digger, true, but she'd never given me any reason to think she'd figured out who I was. She just thought that there was something fishy about my personal life. I always had the feeling that if I made up some soap opera story about my supposed divorce, she'd leave me alone."

Jim, Boone, and Arnie went over the time schedule for the night Martina was nearly asphyxiated by blanket wash, and for the next night, the night she was killed. Arnie had no real

alibi for either night. Both attacks had happened just as his
dinner break ended, at a time when he would logically walk
out the back door of the break room, cut through the warehouse, and go over to the fire department for his late check.
Since he didn't clock in or out at the *Gazette* or at the station, there was no way of proving exactly where he was
when the attacks occurred.

As a longtime newsman, Arnie knew enough about
presses to know that blanket wash was dangerous if inhaled,
and he admitted he'd known about Martina's nap habit.

He'd certainly known enough to snitch a pair of shoes
from a pressman's locker, ambush Martina on the stairs, and
kick her onto the concrete floor. But was he cold-blooded
enough to pick her head up by the hair and smash it against
that floor until she had no face?

I couldn't believe it. But I couldn't conceive of anybody
being that cold-blooded. Martina must have been a real danger to someone.

"Threatened," I said. "Martina had made somebody feel
really threatened. The way she was killed—it was truly vicious. That person must have been desperate."

"Or rotten mean." Jim Hammond shrugged. "Let's recap
for a minute. First, Martina apparently found out that you
were really Alan Matthews. Second, she didn't tell you
about it. Third, someone tried to kill her Wednesday night,
making it look like an accident. Fourth, when that didn't
work, he set up another supposed accident Thursday night,
making it look as if she fell downstairs. But he left a footprint on the back of her linen jacket, and Nell and Mike
found the jacket. Fifth, that person took the shoes he'd worn
to kick Martina and hid them in Arnie's—Alan's—desk.
Sixth, the perp may have tried to kill Nell by chasing her
around in a big car. We don't know why he did this.

"Now, the big question is, why kill Martina at all? If Martina found out Arnie was really Alan, why would that
threaten anybody except Arnie?"

"The obvious answer," Mike said, "is that somebody else now at the *Gazette* was connected with the death of Nell's mother twenty years ago."

Jim looked skeptical. "Pretty much of a coincidence."

"Not necessarily," I said. "If you look at the staff of the *Gazette*, you'll find lots of us worked together at other papers. Three of us worked at Amity—and that's just in the newsroom. Some of the makeup people and pressmen may have worked there, too. Four of our staffers are former employees of the *Duncan Banner*. Generally reporters start on a small paper—sort of an apprenticeship—then move to a bigger one. And the back shop people—if they're members of the union, they can move around easily, too."

"Okay! Okay!" Jim gestured me to silence. "Okay. So the first thing we need to do is take a look at the *Gazette* employment records, find out if anybody lists previous employment in Jessamine, Michigan. In the meantime—" He frowned at Arnie. "What are we going to do about you?"

Arnie puffed his cigarette. "You going to arrest me?"

"I sure don't want you to leave town. You willing to make all this a formal statement?"

"After somebody chased Nell, I am. I came to the *Gazette* because I wanted to see her, not because I wanted to endanger her."

He sighed and rubbed his head again. "I ran twenty years ago because I wanted to protect Nell. Or that's what I told myself. But this time running won't do the job. Until you all figure out who really did kill Martina, the murderer is loose. And if there's a chance he thinks Nell knows something, or if he thinks—well, if there's a chance he might hurt her and I could prevent it, I've got to do it."

Mike spoke then. "It seems to me that Arnie's cooperating, and it might be smarter for us to keep him under cover. If he's arrested—"

"Yeah," Jim said. "Since the U.S. Constitution says we have to file charges and so forth, and the *Gazette* checks up on that sort of thing and on who's in the jail, if we hold you, Arnie—Alan—whoever you are—it won't exactly be a secret."

"He can stay here," Mike said. "Of course, with Marceline Fuqua across the street, he practically has to live in the back bedroom with the lights out. He might rather be in jail."

Arnie snorted. "If you don't arrest me, I can go back to my own apartment, for that matter. Most of my stuff is still there. I was going to write, tell the manager to give my stuff to Goodwill, after I was down the road."

"Where do you live?" Jim asked.

"Liberty Square Apartments. Ten hundred block of Liberty Boulevard. Apartment 8204."

The address rang a bell so loud that I almost gasped out loud. "Mike!" I said. "Did you get newspapers while you were out of town?"

"I sneaked them in off the porch while it was still dark," Arnie said. "News junkie that I am. They're in the back bedroom."

"Did you read the agate?" I asked.

Arnie grinned. "You caught me, Ms. Editor. I don't read the agate unless I write it."

"I don't read it unless I edit it," I said. I stood up.

"What's the agate?" Jim sounded puzzled.

Arnie explained that "agate" is routine news normally printed in a small-type size, and I raced down the hall. I came back with the Sunday morning paper and quickly turned to what we call the "Daily Gazette" page. That's where we list the fire reports, deaths, births, and other routine items in small type—agate type. I scanned down the police reports.

"Here," I said. "Liberty Square Apartments. Apartment 8204. Burglary reported."

Chapter 18

"I thought I remembered copy-reading that address," I said.

Jim called the station and got the desk clerk to find the original report on the burglary. It had occurred sometime Friday night. The door to the apartment had been found standing ajar Saturday morning. The neighbor in 8206 had seen the occupant of the apartment, one Arnold T. Ashe, loading up his car for a trip Friday afternoon. So when she saw the open door Saturday morning, she'd known something was fishy and had called the manager. The manager had called police.

Moving as a body, the five of us loaded into two cars and drove over to the Liberty Square Apartments. Arnie and I drove with Jim Hammond, and Mike and Boone went in Mike's truck.

A new lock had been installed on Arnie's apartment, and he had to get a key from the unit marked Manager near the office.

The manager, a tough-looking blonde, wasn't too gracious about issuing the new key. "We've haven't had a burglary here for three years," she said, glaring at Arnie.

"I've never ever had a burglary before anywhere," Arnie answered, glaring back.

The conversation seemed to be a stand-off.

The apartments in the complex, like most in our part of the country, opened off breezeways that ran through each building, with stairs leading to similar second- and third-floor set-ups. They've always reminded me of the "dogtrots" which pioneers built—two cabins held together by an open, roofed area. Arnie's second-floor apartment had two bedrooms, a kitchen, and a living room with a dining area off one end. I was relieved when I saw that it wasn't bad. I think I'd been picturing him "on the run," in furnished rooms or with thrift-shop furniture. The apartment had obviously been tossed, so it was a mess, but the furniture itself was okay. He had a nice stereo, a television set with a medium-sized screen, a VCR, lots of bookshelves, and a couch, chairs, and dining table with simple lines. Nothing fancy. Like most men, he didn't worry about drapes or ornaments. But it looked comfortable. Or it would when the books were back on the shelves and the cushions back on the chairs.

Arnie looked around and shook his head. "I can't tell you right off if anything's missing," he said. "But I see the TV and the VCR are still here."

"That would seem to rule out a casual burglar," Boone said. "A lot of this stuff is hockable."

I'd been walking around. "One of the bedrooms is nearly empty," I said.

"That's the office," Arnie said. "I packed most of it in my car and took it with me. The computer and such. A couple of folding tables. It's in the trunk of my car, in Mike's garage."

"Don't touch anything until the techs go over it," Jim said.

The Grantham police, like those of most cities, don't have enough manpower to give the full technical treatment to routine burglary scenes, and with the apartment's occupant believed to be out of town, not much had been done in the way of investigation. But the possible link to a murder investigation inspired Jim to call for the full treatment, and the lab van arrived within a few minutes. The apartment began to feel crowded. Mike, Arnie, and I stepped out into the stairwell.

Almost immediately the door across the way opened, just a couple of inches, and an eye peeked out over the chain lock. "Oh, good!" a voice said.

The door closed, then opened again, and a young black woman came out. "Oh, Mr. Ashe, you're back! I'm so sorry about the mess in your apartment."

"I understand you told the manager about it," Arnie said. "I sure appreciate that." He gestured toward me. "Mrs. Marsh, this is my daughter, Nell."

He and I stared at each other, and I felt tears sting my eyes. I think that was the first moment the situation really sank in. "My daughter," he'd said. After all these years I'd finally found my father. And it even turned out that I liked him.

But what was going to happen to him? Jim Hammond and Mike were acting as if his story was gospel, but what did they really think? Was he still a suspect? Would he be snatched away again, just when I'd found him? He could still wind up spending the rest of his life in prison. For a moment I almost despaired.

By the time I had my emotions under control, Arnie had introduced Mike to the young woman, and Mike—as usual—had taken over the conversation.

"Did you hear anything over at Arnie's apartment Friday night?"

Mrs. Marsh shook her head. "No, I'm sure sorry to say I didn't. I mean, not to notice. My husband, he works nights, and I had the television on most of the evening Friday. It's company for me after the baby goes to sleep."

Mike nodded. "So the first thing you noticed was the door ajar Saturday morning?"

"That's right. I came out to get the paper, and it was open—just a few inches. But I'd seen Mr. Ashe loading up his car the day before. I knew he was out of town. I called his name, but nobody answered. That's when I called the manager, and she came over to look. She called the police."

She turned to Arnie. "They really made a mess in there. Dwayne and I—we could help you clean it up."

"I'll help him," I said. "But that's awfully nice of you."

"Well, he's been a nice friendly neighbor," Mrs. Marsh said. "Polite. Took in a package for me when UPS just dumped it on the porch and anybody might have taken it."

"Did you see anything odd around the complex Friday night?" Mike said.

"I wasn't outside at all," Mrs. Marsh said. "Never so much as looked out the window. Just fixed supper, then bathed the baby and got Dwayne off to work."

"What time does your husband go to work?"

"He leaves at ten. He works the night shift at the tire plant. They report at eleven, get off at seven. It's a thirty-minute drive, and he likes to change to his work clothes out there."

"Did he mention seeing anything out of the ordinary?"

Mrs. Marsh laughed. "He never notices anything unless it's got four wheels and a carburetor. He's a car nut. You could ask him, but all he talked to me about was an antique Caddy."

Of course, we all jumped to attention at that.

"A Caddy?" I said. "Do you mean a Cadillac?"

She laughed again. "Oh, yes. He said it was a dandy. Silver gray, big as a battleship. Cruising through our parking lot. He said it was in prime condition and was worth a lot of money. He said what year it was—sometime in the sixties."

She turned to Arnie. "You see lots of old cars in this complex, but not too many that might be worth money!"

"Is your husband sleeping?" Mike asked.

"He was." A deep voice echoed from inside the apartment, and a large black man came to the door behind Mrs. Marsh. "Who you talkin' to?"

"I'm sorry!" Mike said. He went into an ingenuous, boyish act. "We woke you up. I work the midnight to eight a.m.

shift myself, so I know what a pain in the rear it is when somebody interrupts your sleep."

"The police are here to look after that burglary," Mrs. Marsh said to her husband. "This is Mr. Ashe's daughter. And this is Mr. Swenson."

Mike reached for his hip pocket and produced his badge. "I'm a patrolman for the Grantham P.D.," he said. "But I'm not working on this case. I'm here as a friend of Arnie and his daughter. Your wife said you saw a strange car cruising the apartment Friday night."

Dwayne Marsh frowned. "You mean that Caddy? Sixty-one, silver gray, with moon hubs. I sure never saw it around here before."

"Did you get a look at the driver?"

"No. The windows had heavy tinting. It was a specialty number. Had a custom paint job and a lot of fancy trim. Be worth having just to let it sit in the driveway. Let everybody drool all over the fenders. Sure wish I had the money to buy it."

Mike grinned. "Cars like that don't come on the market very often."

"Oh, it was for sale. Had a dealer's tag."

I practically did a somersault over the railing I was leaning against. Arnie gasped, and even Mike looked up sharply. Dealer's tags! Whee! That could narrow the search for the old Cadillac quite a bit. And it might narrow the search for the driver.

Dwayne Marsh didn't recall which dealer's tag had adorned the Cadillac's rear bumper, but there couldn't be too many lots in a city of 350,000 that handled reconditioned Cadillacs more than thirty years old. If the tag hadn't been stolen.

As soon as the technical crew was through with Arnie's apartment, he and I started putting books back on the shelves. That was the main damage the intruder had done. He hadn't pulled things out of the kitchen cabinets, hadn't shoved the mattress onto the floor, or ripped the stuffing out of the couch.

"Well, whatever he was looking for wasn't very small," I said.

Arnie grunted. "Looks like he threw a tantrum," he said.

Arnie owned shelf after shelf of science fiction and fantasy, mostly paperbacks, I noticed. Then there was a bookcase full of history and one of biography, featuring a lot of newsmen—Walter Cronkite, Eric Severeid, Edward R. Murrow. All the newspaper people I've ever known own a lot of books. And we also patronize libraries. If we didn't like to read, I guess we wouldn't be in the news biz.

Jim Hammond started talking. "Okay," he said. "I'm getting a warrant so Boone can examine the *Gazette*'s personnel records. Ditto the union records, to check on the printers down there. But how about you? Did you recognize anybody down there? Was there anybody you'd known before?"

"You mean from Michigan?" Arnie asked.

"Right."

Arnie lit another cigarette and shook his head. "Not from Michigan. Some of the *Gazette* people I'd met at press association meetings and such. Jake Edwards, for example. There's one guy I'd worked with in Texas. But as for links with Michigan, no."

"So nobody jumps into your mind right off? Nobody seemed familiar?"

"No." Arnie exhaled smoke. "Nobody I wasn't able to place as having met somewhere else more recently. But Michigan was twenty years ago." He rubbed his head. "And of course, I deliberately changed my appearance. I've got a receding hairline, true, but I'm not this bald. But everybody changes in twenty years. It might be somebody I knew fairly well, but they just look different now."

The plan Jim decided on was this: Arnie, Mike, and I were to go back to Mike's house and hide out. Mike said he'd fix

Marceline somehow so that she wouldn't call the cops if she spotted Arnie.

"And, Mike," Jim said, "you get Arnie to reminisce. Remember who he knew in Michigan. Who worked at the newspaper. Who he knew in the community. Who a young, unhappy housewife might have liked."

We had our instructions. Mike, Arnie, and I drove through the McDonald's drive-through, then went back to Mike's. Mike pulled the truck into the garage and shut the door. He went directly over to Marceline's to enlist her in our effort to keep Arnie under cover.

Arnie and I went into the house, and I unloaded the hamburgers and fries on the kitchen table while I tried to get my nerve up to ask the question that had been bugging me since I first heard Arnie's story. But once again I didn't get a chance. Arnie disappeared into the back bathroom. By the time he came out, Mike had come back from talking to Marceline.

"I enlisted her as a spy," Mike said. "She's going to keep an eye out for strange vehicles. And keep her mouth shut."

"Think she will?"

"We can hope. I'd rather have her spying on somebody besides me."

Mike began to quiz Arnie about his Michigan acquaintances as we ate. Arnie listed off the staff members. Most of them had been women.

"We had a crazy soc editor—it was still called society back then. Her name was Florence something or other. She kept a list of when all the couples got married, then compared it to the birth date of their first child. Nosy gal, but she knew everybody in town. We had a young police reporter who went on to better things. J.P. Sutherland. I saw his name on a wire story a couple of years ago. I think he's head of the A.P. bureau in Nashville now."

There had been only a half dozen editorial staffers at the

Jessamine Journal—one sports, one soc, three reporters, and Arnie.

"How about the back shop?" I asked. "Or advertising?" I'd worked for a smaller paper. I knew that the departmental divisions that mark a paper the size of the *Gazette* wouldn't be evident in a smaller paper. If you have four hundred employees, you'll know only the ones you work with. If you have twenty-five, you'll know all of them.

"The ad manager—he was a piece of work," Arnie said. "His name was 'Google' Bernard. Always wore a snappy hat of some kind. He actually had a straw boater for summer. I always suspected that he drank a lot on his off hours."

"Did Sally ever show any particular interest in anyone who worked there?" Mike said.

"She laughed at Google, I remember. Thought he was ridiculous. He was the company clown."

"Anybody else she didn't like?"

"She didn't know anybody very well. I remember she made fun of one of the back-shop guys. A scrawny kid. He rode a motorcycle with a tag that said 'Put something exciting between your legs.' Stupid. She said he was a walking inferiority complex. But that was before he bought her drinks at the Elks Club." He rolled his eyes derisively and took a long drag from his cigarette. "Bobbie Johnson was his name. Bobbie with an 'i-e.'"

"Bobbie Johnson? That sounds—" I gasped. "Bob Johnson! We have a pressman named Bob Johnson!"

"A little guy?" Arnie said.

"He's short, but I wouldn't call him little. He's the one you had a fight with when he yelled at me in the newsroom. He's muscle-bound. And he does ride a motorcycle."

"Maybe we ought to tell Captain Hammond about the names being the same," Mike said. He went to the phone, and I thought about Bob Johnson. Bob Johnson, who had yelled and snarled at me, angry because I had told the police someone left a box of rags soaked in blanket wash in the hall outside the ladies' room. He'd cleaned the press, Bob had said, and he hadn't left rags in the back hall. And Bob Johnson had been among the group of pressroom guys who'd been taking their dinner break when I went down the circular stairs and found Martina's body.

"This could solve Martina's killing," I said. "Bob Johnson was on duty both nights when she was attacked. And he had been in the basement area both times. He definitely fits the 'where' and the 'when.'"

But Arnie was frowning. "I guess he could have killed Martina," he said. "But even if it's the same guy who worked in Jessamine, I can't believe he killed Sally. First, your mother laughed at Bobbie Johnson. Called him the 'pipsqueak.' She would never have gone to a motel to meet him—for any reason. Second, the *Gazette*'s Bob Johnson may have been on duty when Martina was killed, but he was also on duty the night your mother was killed. I'm sure he didn't sneak out that night. That was the end of the cold-type era. Only the punchers—the girls who set the type—had computers at the *Jessamine Journal*. The type was printed up from film, and Bobbie and one other guy pasted it up on grid sheets. He was back there with his X-Acto knife all evening. Had to have been, or we wouldn't have gotten the paper out on deadline."

Mike said good-bye to Jim Hammond and put the receiver back on its hook. He still had his hand on the phone when it rang.

"Hello," he said. "Oh, hi, Martha."

Martha. One of my roommates.

"Yes, she's here," Mike said. "I'll call—" He broke off and listened, frowning.

"Who is it?" he asked. "Just a minute."

He lowered the receiver and looked at me. "Martha says some guy on a motorcycle threw a fit on your front porch. Demanded to talk to you. Claims you're causing him a bunch of trouble."

"Who?"

Mike looked grim. "Well, he told Martha his name was Bob Johnson."

"Bob?" I was completely astonished. I'd never seen Bob away from the *Gazette*. Why had he come to my house? "What is he doing, reading our minds? His name just came up a minute ago!"

Mike spoke into the phone again. "Thanks for the warning, Martha. We'll look out for him." He hung up.

"Arnie, you'd better be ready to hide in the back room. It seems Bob Johnson is on his way over. Harley hog and all."

His statement seemed to be a cue. Right at that moment I heard a motorcycle revving as it turned the corner onto Mike's block.

Chapter 19

"Oh, Lord! He's already here!"

The last thing I wanted was a face-off with Bob Johnson. I'd already done that.

And now—if he was the same Bob Johnson Arnie had known in Michigan—I knew he might even be a murderer.

"I don't want to talk to him," I said.

Mike put his arm around my shoulders and hugged me against his side protectively. "You don't have to," he said. "You and Arnie go into the back bedroom. I'll run him off."

I felt a rush of relief. If there was anybody who could get rid of an irate pressman, it was Mike. He could use his well-trained persuasive abilities to talk him into leaving. And if that failed, he could use his well-trained muscles to pound him into the porch. Mike could take care of Bob Johnson without breaking into a sweat.

But as the rush of relief ebbed, I realized that turning Bob Johnson over to Mike was not a good idea. I was a grown woman. I was already mad at Mike and Arnie for doing things that affected me without telling me what they were up to. I'd been fighting for the right to take care of my own problems. It wasn't time to back down now.

So I pulled away from Mike. "Thanks," I said. "But if Bob Johnson is coming over here to see me, I'd better talk to him."

"Don't be silly!" Arnie jumped up, nearly knocking his chair over. "You don't need to deal with this jerk! I can—"

"No!" I said. "I grew up while you had your back turned, remember?"

Arnie looked as if I'd kicked him, but I was too busy psyching myself up to care. While we'd been exchanging opinions at the top of our voices, the sound of the motorcycle had grown louder. It sounded as if it was in Mike's driveway. Then it had stopped. Bob Johnson was at that moment walking to Mike's door. Decision time was here.

I gulped, cleared my throat, and headed for the front door. Mike was muttering behind me, "Arnie, go into the garage—" I didn't hear the rest.

Keep calm, I told myself. Calm. Bob rants. Bob raves. You keep calm. That's the scenario.

I swung the wooden front door open and found the burly fist of Bob Johnson right at the end of my nose. He'd been ready to knock when I opened the inside door. Of course, the fist was on the other side of the glass in Mike's storm door.

Startled, Bob stood immobile. I opened the storm door, forcing him to step back. And I went out onto the porch. I certainly wasn't inviting Bob Johnson into Mike's house.

"Hi," I said. "My roommate called and said you were on your way over. What's up?"

"My dander's what's up!" Bob kept his fist raised.

"I can see that. But what do I have to do with your dander?"

"I just spent a whole morning keeping away from the police! And it's all your fault for telling them that crap about the rags."

"Bob, I had no idea the rags had anything to do with you. I simply told the truth."

"Well, now it's time for you to drop that story and for you and your boyfriend to let me off the hook!"

He shook the fist and looked over my shoulder. I realized that Mike was standing in the doorway behind me, holding the door ajar. I admit I was glad to see him. Even cops call for backup when they're in a confrontational situation.

"Look," I said, "I don't know what the detectives are up to. I certainly don't give orders to the Grantham Police Department. And Mike doesn't, either. He's only a patrolman—"

"Huh! Everybody knows his dad was chief! He's in with the top dogs—"

"He may know a lot of them, but he's careful not to mix in cases he has nothing to do with," I said. "Neither of us has any influence on the investigation into Martina's death."

Bob Johnson stepped back a step and put his fists on his hips. He stood there angrily.

It occurred to me that a little flattery might go a long way about now. "I have no idea why they'd want to talk to you," I said. "Except that you are so experienced. You know everything about how the pressroom works. The routine. Maybe they just want some background."

Bob's eyes narrowed.

"They're probably going to want to know who had access to the locker room. Who could have taken those shoes. If any strangers were seen down there Thursday night."

Bob pouted. "They asked all that stuff Friday," he said. "They asked everybody. This time they're looking for me. Only me."

"Well, I can't explain that," I said. "But the best way to get along with detectives is to answer their questions. Stop dodging them! Go down to the station and tell them you've heard that they're looking for you and you'll tell them anything you know. That will make you look innocent."

Bob shuffled from side to side, and I realized he was scared.

"That bitch Martina!" he said. "She's causing more trouble dead than alive! And she caused plenty then."

"What do you mean?"

"She got me fired!"

"Fired? But you're still—"

"Not here! In Missouri!"

"You knew Martina at another paper?"

"I was pressroom foreman. She was on the desk. She told the publisher she'd smelled liquor on my breath." Anger lit his features and beetled his brows. "Nosy bitch!"

He needed calming again.

"I'm sorry that happened, Bob," I said. "I'm sure it was frustrating—her word against yours."

"I got fired the day after Christmas! Over one lousy cup of eggnog. And one stupid joke that she didn't like. It took me months to get on at the *Gazette*, and then she turns up here!"

"I never saw her speak to you," I said. "She may not have even remembered you from Missouri."

"Oh, she remembered. Stupid, giggling bitch. Made some remark about 'holiday cheer' the first time she saw me in the break room."

Now, that was news. I'd had no idea Bob Johnson had any special reason for disliking Martina. She had been at the *Gazette* around ten years, so Bob had been hugging this resentment to himself for a long time.

Making this revelation seemed to have calmed him down a little. He listened as I again urged him to talk to Boone or Jim or whoever the detective was who'd tried to reach him. I even glanced back at Mike, and he backed me up. Told Bob to go down to the Central Station and get it over with.

Bob swaggered out to his Harley, threw a leg across, sneered, and fired one final salvo at me.

"Funny how you and the boyfriend turned up every time something went wrong with Martina," he said.

Was he accusing Mike and me of being involved in Martina's death? I stepped forward, but Bob kicked the starter on the cycle, and its noise drowned out any reply I might have made. He revved the motor and dug out. Mike and I were left standing on the porch, staring after him.

"Jerk!" I said. "Paranoid jerk!"

"As a psychological diagnosis, I'd say you're absolutely

correct," Mike said. "Now let's find out if Arnie recognized him."

Mike led the way to the kitchen, and we met Arnie coming in from the garage.

"Did you get a look?" Mike said.

Arnie nodded. "Yeah, the window worked fine, and I'm sure he didn't see me."

"Was he the same guy you knew in Michigan?"

"It's hard to say. If he spent the past twenty years in the weight room, it could be the same guy. He's a lot bulkier. And his eyebrows are heavier."

"If the guy in Michigan was a complete jerk, I'd say he has the same character flaws," I said. "What was that final crack he made? Funny how the boyfriend and I kept turning up whenever something happened to Martina? Mike wasn't there the night Martina was killed. Not until afterward."

"I didn't catch what he said," Arnie said. "But I thought he was referring to Martina's boyfriend."

His comment clicked on a light bulb inside my head. Was I missing something?

"Martina's boyfriend," I said slowly.

Arnie was frowning. "Did Martina have a boyfriend? It's hard to believe."

"She had a friend. I'm not sure just what their relationship is," I said. "He's a salesman for some printing-supply company. He apparently saw her whenever he was in Grantham. And he happened to be around recently."

I turned to Mike. "And the most suspicious thing is—he actually seemed to like Martina and to be grieved at her death."

"That is . . . singular," Mike said. "Nobody else seems to be sad. Everybody was upset. They were horrified. But no one was grieved."

"Martina apparently trusted him. She had given him the yearbook that had Arnie's and Alan's college pictures in it. Said she wanted to 'keep it out of circulation.'"

I thought about it a moment. "Or that's what he claimed. I guess he could have simply wanted to call the yearbook to my attention. He could have used the whole thing as a ploy to get me to find the picture of Arnie, figure out that he was really Alan. Maybe he was trying to underline Arnie's link to Martina's death. Even more than the shoes."

Mike nodded. "It's certainly worth looking into."

I realized that Arnie had turned away from us and walked over to the sink. He was washing his hands.

"Salesman," I said. "Salesman? Arnie, you said that my mother's reputation began to go downhill in Jessamine the night some salesman took you all out to dinner."

He didn't answer.

"Do you remember that salesman's name?"

He tore two paper towels from a roll under the cabinet. Then he turned around and sighed deeply. "He had an ordinary name," he said. "Smith."

"Smith?" I breathed the words. "Dan Smith is the name of Martina's friend."

I quickly described Dan Smith. Of course, his description meant little to Arnie, thinking of a salesman named Smith twenty years earlier. The salesman Smith in Michigan had been a big guy. He might have had curly hair. Maybe. Arnie stood sullenly and didn't say much.

"If it is the same guy—and Smith is, as we all know, the commonest name in the English-speaking world—he didn't have anything to do with your mother's death," Arnie said.

I opened my mouth to ask how he knew, but Mike was ahead of me.

"Smith?" he said. "Was he the one you followed to Chicago?"

Arnie nodded. "When I got to Chicago, I called his office. Pretended to be a customer. He'd been in Cairo, Illinois, the day Sally was killed. That's maybe four hundred miles from Jessamine. Smith was not in Michigan."

Mike was frowning. "But you had suspected he was?"

"Jessamine is in the middle of the Dutch country. There were more people named Van Something-or-other in Jessamine than there were Smiths. When I knew a Smith had been registered at that motel when our car was spotted—" Arnie shrugged. "He was the only Smith I could think of. But I guess a lot of motels have a bunch of pseudo-Smiths registered most nights."

He walked into the living room and dropped onto Mike's leather couch. "Now, after twenty years—I can't even remember what that Smith guy looked like." He picked up the television's remote control from the coffee table. "Mike, do you mind if I turn on ESPN? I've got to think about something different for a while."

"Sure," Mike said. "There should be a basketball game."

I suddenly felt very sorry for Arnie. His life had been a mess, that's for sure. But I was still angry with him, too. He'd brought it on himself, and he'd given me a lot of misery, too.

I turned and went into the kitchen. I began picking up the debris from our McDonald's lunch.

"Doing the dishes?" Mike had joined me.

"Might as well. Seems as if we've talked the situation into the ground. I've got nothing left to say."

"We've said a lot, true." Mike handed me a plastic garbage bag. He kept his voice low. "But it's all been cow."

"Cow?"

"Yeah. You know, like college classes. For cow class exams you regurgitate lots of facts. For bull class exams, you give 'em opinions."

"My opinions are free, and worth what you pay for them. Which one would you like to have?"

"Mainly the one about how you feel."

"How I feel?"

"Right. All these years you wanted to know why your dad went away, why he left you. Now you know. Has it made things worse?"

I glanced through the kitchen door into the living room. With the television on, Arnie couldn't hear us. But I kept my voice low, too. "I feel sorry for him," I said.

Mike nodded. "He hasn't had much of a life."

"He was less than thirty when my mother was killed. Now he's nearly fifty. He's spent the most productive years of his life dodging the law, living under another man's name. Alone. He's been good at his profession, yet he's been afraid to go for promotions, afraid to join larger newspapers, afraid to stay in one job too long."

Mike nodded. He reached out and took my hand.

I kept whispering. "The life has kept his salary low, his benefits minimal. He probably doesn't have an IRA. He isn't vested in any retirement program. He's never dared marry again."

"Alone. The word really expresses the way he's lived."

"All those years I've been so angry and grieved because he'd left me, but I never realized that when he went, he'd doomed himself to a pretty miserable existence."

I drew back into the corner of the kitchen. I couldn't see Arnie from there.

"Mike, did he really do it for me? To keep me from testifying against my own father, from sending him to prison? Or to the electric chair? Or did he do it for himself? Because the risk of prison was so frightening he'd abandon his child— and his own identity—to avoid it?"

"I can't answer that," Mike said. "Probably Arnie couldn't answer that himself."

"There isn't any answer!" I said. "I always think that if I knew this or that—if some particular event occurred—it would answer all my questions. But it never does. More questions keep coming up."

Mike came back into my corner of the kitchen. "I don't have any answers," he said.

"I could use a hug."

"Those I have plenty of."

A few minutes later, I questioned Mike's shirt pocket. "What about Jim?"

"What do you mean?"

"What's Jim's opinion on all this?"

"He hasn't told me."

"I know, but you two read each other's minds a lot. What do you think he's up to? Does he buy Arnie's story? Does he think he's innocent?"

I looked up at Mike. His face had assumed its blandest expression. That meant he wasn't going to tell me anything.

"Arnie's cooperating. That means a lot," he said. "But, Nell, don't bond with Arnie too quickly. Okay?"

I held my head against Mike's shirt pocket until the tears quit stinging my eyes. When I finally started to pull away, Mike began to whisper urgently in my ear:

"Listen," he said, "I'm sorry I had to fib to you about my trip to Michigan. But when Arnie called me, he made it clear that he was on his way out of town. I couldn't think of any way to keep him here—he wasn't officially wanted in Grantham—except to promise I'd look into the current status of the Michigan case. And I couldn't think of any place to stash him except here. And that meant—"

"You didn't want me dropping over. Sorry your plan didn't work."

"It would have except for Marceline. Durn 'er."

"Well, you nearly had a puddle on your hall carpet when I opened that bedroom door and saw Arnie in that back bedroom."

We began to laugh then. It wasn't funny, but we needed a laugh. So we had one. Then Mike went outside and moved the cars around so that mine was hidden in the garage and his truck was sitting in the drive. He and Arnie pretended to watch the basketball game and then a golf match. I read some book that I don't remember the name of, and we all waited to hear from Jim Hammond.

Jim didn't show up until four and I was wondering if

Mike had anything I could cook for dinner. Boone wasn't with him, but Jim was carrying a file folder full of papers. Arnie leaped to his feet and had the television off before Jim got inside the door. Jim pulled up a straight chair and sat facing Arnie and me on the couch.

"Okay," Jim said. "Here's what we found out. So far. First, that Cadillac drove off the Premium Used Cars lot late Friday night—all by itself—and was found abandoned in the courthouse parking lot Saturday morning. Since the courthouse isn't open on Saturday, it was sitting there in solitary splendor, and some patrolman spotted it almost as soon as it was reported stolen. Dwayne Marsh had ID'd it as the same one he saw in the apartment complex. And since it has a new scratch in one fender and a new dent in the bumper, I think we can assume it's also the vehicle that chased Nell later on Friday."

"Stolen?" I was disgusted. "That leaves us nowhere, then."

"It confirms what we already knew," Jim said. "This guy is smart. The lab is checking the car over—but I expect you're right, Nell. I doubt we'll find a fingerprint or a lock of hair or somebody's driver's license under the seat."

Jim opened his file folder. "As for the personnel records of the *Gazette*—well, they're not real complete. People don't always put down their entire employment history when they sign on the payroll. But we found out a couple of things."

"Did you check on Bob Johnson?" Mike asked that one.

"We checked the union records on him," Jim said. "And it looks as if your surmise is right. He first joined the printers' union as an apprentice in Grand Rapids, Michigan. Place of employment, *Jessamine Journal*."

"All right!" I said.

"What about this salesman? Dan Smith?" Mike asked.

"We called him in to make a routine statement," Jim said. "And he was perfectly open. Said he had handled a territory in the Midwest twenty years ago. It included Illinois, Michigan, Iowa, Wisconsin, and Missouri. He remembered the murder of Sally Matthews very well—thought he remembered Alan Matthews. But that was twenty years ago. He said he probably wouldn't know Alan if he fell over him today. He said he had no idea on the final disposition of the case. We didn't enlighten him."

"Apparently I wouldn't know him, either," Arnie said. "Nell says he's been around the Gazette Building plenty. I never gave him a second glance."

"How long had he known Martina?" I asked.

"We're looking into that," Jim said. "Trying to figure out just what their relationship was. He says they were simply old friends. He first knew her as his wife's college friend. From the University of Missouri." Jim shuffled through some more papers.

"Who else did you find?" I asked. "We'd already figured out both Dan Smith and Bob Johnson."

"Only one more," Jim said. "But we're not through looking."

"Who was the other one?" I asked.

"It's the building manager." He turned to Arnie. "Think back to Michigan. Does the name Ed Brown ring any bells?"

Chapter 20

I gasped so hard my ears popped, but Arnie didn't even blink.

"Not a bell," he said. "The name Ed Brown means nothing to me in connection with Michigan. In fact, it doesn't even mean anything to me in connection with the *Grantham Gazette.*"

"Ed Brown is the building and purchasing manager for the *Gazette*," I said. "He has dark hair, and he's usually walking around officiously, holding a clipboard."

"That guy? A lot older than he looks?"

"He's the one," I said. I turned to Jim. "He looks young; then, when you get up close, he dissolves into an old guy. What does he have to do with Michigan?"

"He went to college at Western Michigan University, in Kalamazoo," Jim said. "He's one of the few *Gazette* employees who has a complete résumé in their personnel files. He majored in business, and he was an older student. He was in his mid-thirties when he graduated. And all through college he worked full-time in Jessamine, Michigan—at the cannery."

"The Triple A Fruit Company," Arnie said. "Jessamine's major employer. But strictly seasonal." He took a drag from his cigarette. "I think I met the manager—owner—one of the bosses. I don't remember meeting anybody else from Triple A."

"Brown says he remembers that the newspaper editor's

wife was killed, but he couldn't come up with a name. Any chance your wife knew him?"

"I guess Sally could have met him someplace," Arnie said. "At that Elks Club, if nowhere else. You didn't have to be a member to go there as long as you stayed in the bar and the dining room. Just the lodge room was off limits to the public. For that matter, there's no reason the membership list couldn't have included Ed Brown."

Ed Brown. I went off into a cloud, remembering my run-in with him the previous afternoon. He'd been searching for something in the newsroom on a Sunday afternoon, when the newsroom would ordinarily have been deserted. And Ed's reaction to my unexpected appearance had certainly indicated that he had thought he'd have the place to himself. He'd been angry about something. He had frightened me. I'd been delighted when J.J. Jones showed up and I was able to get away from Ed.

But Ed Brown had been angry even before that episode. He'd been angry the night Martina was nearly asphyxiated, when he had said he expected her to sue the company.

"Ed Brown hated Martina," I said.

Belatedly, I realized that I'd spoken aloud, interrupting something Jim Hammond was saying.

Jim shifted his body so that he faced me. "Beg pardon?"

"The one time I ever talked to Ed Brown about Martina, I really had the feeling he disliked her a lot," I said.

"Nobody seemed to like her," Jim said.

"This was way beyond eye rolling and 'that Martina,' " I said. "This was into serious loathing."

"He didn't seem to feel that strongly about her when he talked to me," Jim said. He turned to face Arnie again. "By the time you all were in Jessamine, Brown had worked his way up from the fruit-sorting line to payroll clerk. He says he remembers talk about the new newspaper editor because he had a Southern accent."

"But Arnie's from Kansas," I said. "He doesn't have a Southern accent."

"It doesn't sound Southern in Grantham," Arnie said. "But when I moved to Jessamine, I'd been in Amity for nearly ten years. I did sound Southern to those Michigan people. Sally and you and I were real outlanders up there. I was busy at work, getting out in the community and meeting people who wanted to get along with the newspaper. But Sally had a genuine problem. Everybody acted as if we were freaks."

He kept on talking to Jim, but his remarks had once again reminded me of what I wasn't saying. What I was afraid to say.

I was still mentally gnawing my nails when Mike reached over and touched my arm. "Did you say you needed to go over to your house and get some clothes?"

"I do have to go to work tomorrow. And I'll be glad to cook dinner if we pick up something at the grocery store."

"We could go now," he said quietly. "While Jim's here."

That made Arnie's situation obvious. Mike and Jim were not prepared to leave Arnie alone. He might be "cooperating," but they were keeping him on a short leash. As I climbed into Mike's truck and fastened my seat belt, I gnawed another nail—not just mentally this time. Arnie was in real trouble.

I'd finally found my dad, after twenty years, and Mike was going to make sure I didn't lose him again. Even if he had to see that he was locked up for the rest of his natural life.

"Who gets Arnie first?" I said. "This state or Michigan?"

Mike squeezed my hand. "I don't think things look quite that black," he said.

I asked him why not, but his answers were evasive.

When we got to my house, the old two-story near the Grantham State campus, it was deserted. I knew Martha had a seminar on Monday afternoons, and Brenda was probably out with her fiancé. Rocky's bar is closed Monday nights, but he was gone, too. The only signs of life were the kitchen light, left on permanently to guide everybody in the back door, and the blinking light on the answering machine in the upstairs hall.

As I went into my room, I punched the Messages button.

"Nell? Miss Matthews?" The lisping voice was hesitant. I didn't recognize it. "I'm calling on behalf of Rocky Rutledge. He went to a picnic out at Panorama Park, and he's run into a problem." A little throat clearing interrupted the message. "His car won't start—and it seems he's not alone. He's eager not to embarrass the, ahem, person he's with. They're at the Westside picnic area. He said he was sure you'd take care of the situation."

I stared at the gadget. "What the heck?" I said. The answering machine clicked off. I punched Save, then clicked it on again. It said the same thing the second time through. The lisping voice still didn't identify the speaker. But there was something familiar about it.

I called down the stairs. "Mike! Come listen to this."

Mike trotted upstairs and listened, frowning. "You're not going to a place as lonely as Panorama Park just two days after some guy in a stolen Cadillac tries to hijack you."

"It doesn't seem as if it would be a smart idea," I said. "But what if Rocky really is stuck somewhere? I can't refuse to help him out."

Mike knew how much Rocky had done for me in the past. He was a friend.

"We'll call a patrol car," Mike said.

"No!" I gulped. "Rocky hasn't been seeing anybody but Jamie for months now. I assumed he was planning to move Jamie in as soon as he gets Brenda, Martha, and me out. But—"

Mike grinned. "You're afraid he really is with someone he can't afford to get caught with."

"Rocky's been well out of the closet for years. But his pal may not be."

Mike leaned over conspiratorially. "Who do you think it is? The mayor? Or Chief Jameson?"

I whispered back. "It's probably Harley Duke." Harley Duke is a city councilman neither Mike nor I like. "Or the worst-case scenario—Sarah Larkin!" Sarah Larkin, Ph.D., is the president of Grantham State and is widely supposed to be a lesbian.

"My God!" Mike said. "If Sarah got caught out with a man—"

"The heavens might fall," I said. "Maybe we'd better rescue Rocky and his pal."

"Or send a rescue party."

I called Rocky's friend Jamie, but he didn't know where Rocky was. Mike and I argued back and forth before we agreed on a plan. I picked up my clothes for the office the next day. Then we went by the store and bought a couple of pounds of hamburger and some spaghetti sauce. Mike dropped me, the clothes, and the groceries off at his house. He and Jim Hammond conferred briefly in the front yard. Jim left.

Then Mike headed for Panorama Park, on a mission to rescue Rocky. In case he did need rescuing.

I was sure Mike could use tact and diplomacy to handle Rocky and any companion he might have, so I didn't feel I was letting Rocky down. And I may be liberated, but Mike was absolutely right. It would have been totally stupid to go to a lonely spot like Panorama Park only two days after the guy in the Cadillac almost managed to run me off the road. We didn't know who had been driving the Cadillac, but the person who tossed Arnie's apartment seemed to have been driving the same car.

I guess I'm as brave as the next person, but as I began to brown hamburger, I allowed myself a smug thought or two. "I hope I'm not dumb enough to be lured to the wilds of suburban Grantham by an anonymous phone call," I told myself.

Arnie interrupted my self-congratulations by popping his head into the kitchen. "Can I help?"

"Sit down and entertain me," I said. "This is going to be a simple supper."

"I could set the table."

"Fine."

He went to the proper drawer and got out the silverware. I was almost jealous. He'd been there long enough to find things in the kitchen, and I hadn't known Mike was hiding him out. But I pushed the feeling aside. Now, at last, we were alone. This was my opportunity to tell Arnie the real reason I'd always believed he was the one I'd heard my mother talking to the night before she died. If I had the courage.

I got out a piece of waxed paper and started chopping onions. I cut the onion into thick slices, then held each slice in my left hand, using the knife in my right and cutting against my thumb to turn each slice into a bunch of little pie-shaped pieces. Because of the natural rings of an onion, the wedges fall apart, and you come out with chopped onions.

Arnie laughed. "You chop onions just like your mother did," he said. "I never understood why she wouldn't use a chopping board."

"That's the way Grandmother taught me to do it," I said. "If you're chopping just one onion or one carrot, Grandmother never thought it was worth getting the chopping board dirty. Aunt Billie does the same thing. It works fine as long as nobody sharpens your knife while you have your back turned. I guess Grandmother taught all of us to cut up vegetables."

"Is your grandmother gone now, Nell?"

"She died five years ago." He started to ask another question, but I went on. "But before we get into reminiscence, I've got to tell you something—now, while Mike's gone."

"What?"

I had to gulp and clear my throat, but I think it was the onion that made my eyes smart. "About that phone call—the one that made the eight-year-old me think you were talking to my mother. There was a reason I thought so—another reason. Besides the ones you and Mike figured out."

Arnie sat down at the kitchen table and lit a cigarette. I washed onions off my hands and cleared my throat a few more times. We both seemed to dread going on.

Finally, Arnie took a deep drag and looked at me. "Well, it's not going to get any easier," he said. "Spit it out."

"Small," I said.

He looked blank.

"When I was little, I remember you always used the word 'small' to mean the superlative of any word. Everybody has their little pet expressions, and that was one of yours. I can remember hearing you tell my mother that a special section the Amity paper had run was 'small hard' to put together. When you assembled my new bicycle on my seventh birthday, with me hanging over your shoulder every minute, I remember that you said the directions were no help at all. 'They made the job small confusing.' You used it that way."

"I don't doubt it," Arnie said. "When I was growing up in Wichita, there was a time when all the kids used the word that way. I don't know if it was a strictly Wichita thing or if it was nationwide—like kids a few years ago using 'bad' to mean 'good.' I guess I hung on to it. But some time back I quit using it so much."

I nodded. "It's a distinctive expression—or I think of it that way. I don't think anybody in Jessamine said it."

"Probably not."

"But when I picked up the upstairs extension and heard my mother talking to someone, that someone had used the word 'small.' "

Arnie frowned.

"The guy said something that ended with '—small disastrous.' Then Mother cut him off and said, 'Nell! Did you pick up the phone?' And I began to whine about talking to my daddy. Then she came upstairs and took the phone away from me, and she talked into it. She said she'd see the guy the next day. And then she hung up."

"And scolded you."

"No. I expected her to, but she didn't. She put me back to bed and sang me a song."

I gave up and ripped down one of Mike's paper towels to mop my eyes. "Sorry," I said. "It's still not one of my happier memories."

Arnie took a drag from his cigarette. "Have you told Mike about this? Jim Hammond?"

I shook my head. "I wanted to hear your—" I quit talking with the word "explanation" unsaid. "I wanted to tell you first."

I stared at Arnie as he sat smoking. When he finally spoke, he said, "Your hamburger's trying to burn." Then he got up and walked into the living room.

His reaction infuriated me. How could he simply turn his back on me after I'd finally spilled the big secret? I gnashed my teeth, took the skillet full of crumbled hamburger off the fire, and followed him into the living room.

"What is the deal?" I said. "Don't you believe me?"

"Yes, Nell. I believed you twenty years ago. You were a truthful child. I believe you heard exactly what you say you heard." Then he raised his right hand to shoulder height. "But I swear, I was not the person your mother was talking to. I don't have any explanation for the use of the word 'small.' "

"Was there any other person who might have used it in Jessamine? Anybody from Wichita?"

"None that I recall. I'm wracking my brain."

I left him to wrack it by himself and went back to the dinner. I had drained the fat from the hamburger and thrown in a can of mushrooms and the onions when Arnie came to the kitchen door and leaned against the door frame. He spoke casually.

"Do you think I killed her?"

I looked at him. The easy answer would be no. But old blunt Nell—I never come up with the easy answer.

"I don't want to think you did," I said.

He laughed humorlessly. "But you're afraid I'm guilty," he said.

"No!" I angrily stirred my cooking, then turned around. "I don't know you all that well," I said apologetically.

"I know. I'm sorry." Arnie's eyes were wet by then. "Are you going to tell Jim Hammond about the word 'small'?"

"I don't know. I don't want to make things harder for you. But if I don't tell it, and they fail to turn up the one guy from Wichita who passed through western Michigan that year— and it turns out somebody you knew in high school came up there and killed her—"

Arnie nodded. "I know. It's not easy."

"What do you want me to do?"

"I'm not real happy about the prospect of prison—or death by injection. But I don't want you to lie, either." He took a deep breath. "I guess I want you to believe me, but I can't tell you one reason that you should. You'd better tell Hammond."

He patted my hand, turned silently, and went back into the living room.

I finished up the casserole and put it in the oven before I joined him. I sat on the floor, facing him across the coffee table. "We could play some Dirty Eight," I said.

Arnie chuckled, but the sound didn't quite sound sincere. He pulled his cards out of his pocket and shuffled them on the coffee table.

"Listen, Arnie. If you think it would be smarter to run—"

"No! I ran away twenty years ago and let you down. I told myself it was the best thing for you. But this time—if someone's out to kill you—and it's linked to your mother's death in some way—"

The telephone cut off his speech. I got it.

"Ms. Nell Matthews?"

"Yes."

"This is Speedy Florist. We have a delivery for you. Will you be at that address for a few minutes?"

"Yes."

"We'll bring it right out."

I went back to the Dirty Eight game. "Who's sending me flowers?"

"Mike?"

"Mike's good at sentimental gestures, but they usually involve food. He sends candy or takes me out to dinner."

We played two hands of Dirty Eight before I heard the sound of a van in the street outside. I got to my feet. "You hide," I said. "Remember, nobody is supposed to know you're here."

Arnie nodded. "Sure. They'll think you're sitting here smoking and playing a two-handed card game all by yourself." But he stood up and pulled a dollar out of his pocket. "Here. In case you want to tip." Then he went into the kitchen.

I got to the door before the bell rang, so I was facing the delivery driver when the door swung open. Again, I had to push the storm door open, forcing a tall, skinny kid to step backward. I stepped onto the porch.

That's when all hell broke loose.

A motor gunned, then brakes squealed. I looked up, and the tall, skinny florist's kid turned around at the sound. We both stared at the heavy dark blue van that was skidding to a stop at the curb, the two of us standing there motionless. Then we began to jump and dodge around.

If we hadn't jumped, we would have made perfect targets for the guy in the ski mask as he leaned out the driver's-side window and fired a large silver-colored pistol at us.

Chapter 21

I roared and shoved the kid, and he dropped a dozen red roses in a green glass vase. The vase hit the concrete porch and shattered like a bomb at the same moment the safety glass in the storm door developed a hole the size of my head and became checkered all over, like a street map of a medieval city.

I grabbed the kid and yanked him into the living room. Then we got all tangled up trying to slam the inside, wooden door. Arnie ran in from the kitchen with cries of "I heard a shot!" and "Get out of the way!"

Two more shots rang out, but we were all jumping back and forth so much that the gunman would have had to be Wyatt Earp to hit any of us. Arnie was yanking my arm, and I was yanking the kid's, and the kid was yanking both of us this way and that.

Escaping from a gunman is an awkward business, but we got the door slammed shut without anybody getting a wound worse than a sprained elbow, and I turned the key in the dead bolt. A dead bolt is so much help in deflecting bullets.

Then I heard the squealing of tires, and I deduced that the van was taking off.

"Call 911!" My voice was shrill.

"Get down on the floor!" That was Arnie.

"It's a drive-by!" That was the kid.

We'd barely gotten the words out when we heard sirens.

"Guess that's our guard," Arnie said. "Where was he when we needed him?"

I ran to the living room window, dropped to my knees, stuck my head between the draperies, and peeked out over the sill. A GPD patrol car sped by, and I belatedly realized that Mike and Jim Hammond wouldn't have left Arnie and me alone.

Somebody had been keeping an eye on us. They didn't want to arrest Arnie, maybe out of kindness to me, but they didn't want him taking off, either. Since they wouldn't have expected me to lie down in the driveway to keep him from driving his car out of the garage, they'd stationed a patrol car down the block.

The tall, skinny kid called in to tell Speedy Florist that he'd have to stick around for a while. Arnie lit a cigarette with a trembling hand and began to write something in a notebook he brought from his bedroom. I went to Mike's computer, opened his word-processing program, and wrote out a brief statement of what had happened. I made a lot of typos. After I was through, Arnie took my place and typed out the statement he'd been making notes for.

Arnie and I had reacted in the same way. Both of us had wanted to write out what had happened before we talked about it. Was it genetic? Or therapeutic? Or just because we'd both been crime reporters long enough that we knew the cops would want a statement and it would save time to have one ready? Did it prove that we were related? Wondering about this gave me something beside gunshots to mull over while we sat there, waiting.

Ten minutes later, Mike and Jim Hammond arrived, almost simultaneously. Through the window I saw Jim come up the walk and stand with his hands on his hips, glaring at the mess on the porch. Mike came in through the garage, and I met him in the kitchen. He put his arms around me and held me so tightly I nearly fainted from lack of oxygen. Then he backed off and looked at me, shaking his head and grinning weakly.

"Can't I leave you alone for a minute?"

I think I would have fallen into a dramatic fit if he hadn't joked. As it was, I managed to stay calm—well, reasonably calm—until we'd all told Jim Hammond what happened, Arnie and I handed over our typed statements, and the tall, skinny kid was released to go back to work. He looked at us strangely as he left. He probably thought he'd fallen in with the mob.

Somehow I wasn't too surprised to learn that Mike had not found Rocky, with or without a companion, in Panorama Park. The lisping message on my answering machine had obviously been a ploy to separate me from my boyfriend-bodyguard. If I had gone to Panorama Park, I was sure the gunman would have followed me there. Since the message lured Mike away, leaving me at his house, the killer had fallen back on the flower-delivery scheme, sure that I would be the one to answer the door.

The scariest part may have been realizing that the killer had been watching us. He must have followed us from my house to Mike's and must have known that I stayed there and Mike went out.

I also wasn't surprised to learn that the van and its masked driver had disappeared, even with a patrol car in hot pursuit. The patrol car had been facing the wrong way, of course, so it had to flip a U-turn before it could begin the chase. It would have been easy for the van driver to arrange that.

The patrol car wasn't there to stop killers from breaking in. It had been there to stop Arnie from taking off. The patrolman hadn't been led to expect an attack.

The patrolman had followed the van, siren blaring, but he hadn't been able to catch up before it pulled up to a gas pump at a busy convenience store and service station three blocks away. A man had gotten out, carrying a small duffel bag and wearing a baggy raincoat and a knit cap—maybe the ski mask, rolled up—that covered his hair completely. He strode into the store, headed toward the rest rooms in a back hall, then disappeared. The assumption was that he'd yanked the hat and coat off, stuffed them into the duffel bag, and walked out the back door. He had probably had another vehicle stashed on the next street. Anyway, he was gone.

And the van was empty of clues. And, naturally, it had been stolen from a used-car lot the night before.

"Well," I said, "the guy is developing a recognizable M.O. He steals a car from a used-car lot, then abandons it."

"There are a couple of other things I've noticed," Mike said. "He acts quickly. We're not talking about an introspective person who sulks before he does something. He comes up with a plan and carries it out. Maybe too quickly, since he hasn't managed to kill you yet.

"And I'm happy to say, he's not a great shot—can't hit a moving target. Also, he's familiar with the Grantham business community."

"How can you tell that?" I asked.

"The car lots. Both of them keep the keys to cars on boards in the back room. Somebody had to slip in there and take them. In the case of the Cadillac, he apparently took the key and had it copied, then returned the original. The van—he just took the key. Or at least the lot manager says it's still gone.

"Also, the guy knew which florist to call."

"What about the florist?"

"Speedy is the one my mom's agency uses. They run an account. It's common for someone from her office to call and order flowers by phone. She gets a discount because she buys a lot of flowers. She makes sure clients are greeted with a bouquet when they move into their new houses."

"Are you telling me that those roses were sent by your mom's business?"

"No, I'm telling you somebody called Speedy Florist and said they wanted the flowers delivered here and to put them on the Svenson Agency account. No other florist in Grantham would have accepted a telephone order for that particular account—with no credit card number or name."

"Didn't the guy tell the florist anything?"

"He told him the client—he called you the client—was leaving her home, so the flowers had to be delivered immediately. For a fairly expensive order, like a dozen roses, they were willing to do that."

"What did he sound like?"

"The office clerk says he lisped."

"Like the guy on my answering machine!"

Mike nodded. "Which means we can be pretty sure he doesn't lisp in real life."

We talked the whole thing inside out, the lab came and dug bullets out of the walls, and Mike punched the rest of the safety glass out of the storm door.

In our climate storm doors are as valuable in summer, when they help keep cool air in, as in winter, when they keep cool air out. Most people leave them up year-round.

"I'm glad I decided to get a new storm door when I moved in here and remodeled," Mike said. "The old one wasn't safety glass. It might have cut an artery for somebody."

I touched a hole in the wooden door. "I owe you a new door," I said.

"I've got insurance," Mike said.

He swept the glass and roses off the front porch, and I vacuumed up debris inside.

By then the casserole was practically dry. I poured water over it, opened a can of green beans, and rescued enough casserole for dinner for Mike, Arnie, and me. No one was hungry, but we went through the motions.

At the end of the meal, Arnie's hand was still shaking, and my upper lip felt as stiff as granny's cooked starch. Mike got up and gestured for Arnie and me to keep our seats.

"I'll do the dishes," he said. "Nell, you and Arnie try to figure out what it is that you know that this guy is afraid you'll tell. Because he is definitely out to get you, and I can't think of any other reason."

I glanced at Arnie. "Tell him about 'small,' " he said. Then he got up and left the room.

I told Mike about my complete recollection of the phone call made to my mother the night before she died.

He frowned as he scraped the leftover casserole into a plastic dish. "That's interesting, Nell, and we'll pass it along to Jim. But I doubt the guy is worried about you remembering anything to do with your mother's death. After twenty years, and with Martina out of the way, he probably feels as if he's pretty much in the clear on that. It's much more likely to be something to do with Martina's death. Think back to the night she was killed. Try to remember every little thing that happened, starting at the beginning. When did you get to work?"

I started with my arrival at the *Gazette*, mentioned the short chat I'd had with Martina, and reported her request that I meet her in the downstairs ladies' room on my break.

"I was so eager to hear what she had to say that I dashed down there the minute my break time got there," I said.

"So far we've identified three guys connected with the *Gazette* who apparently also had some connection with Michigan twenty years ago. Did you see any of them as you dashed down?"

"Mike, I saw all of them. Ed Brown was in the newsroom, looking at a broken chair. He's usually wandering around the building. It's not at all unusual to see him up there at night.

"And Dan Smith came by earlier and had coffee with Martina. She came back to the newsroom alone. The *Gazette* is probably one of his biggest customers, so Dan Smith is probably as familiar with the building as most *Gazette* employees are. If he told Martina something like, 'I'll let myself out the back door,' she would probably have just nodded and come back to the newsroom without checking to see that he really went."

"What about those security cameras?"

"They're only trained on the doors. If he didn't go near the door, if he hid out someplace, the guard would simply think he was still in the building—which would have been the truth. Visitors don't check in and out formally. And if you leave through the warehouse, you can usually slip out behind a truck and not be caught on camera. For that matter, he could leave openly through the back door, then slip back in through the warehouse."

I stared at the surface of the table. "No, the best bet for Martina's killer is Bob Johnson."

"Because he's hot-tempered?"

"That, and because he had the best access to all parts of the basement. Better than Dan or Ed. People might wonder what they were doing if one of them showed up down there. But that's where Bob Johnson is supposed to be. In the pressroom or in the Hellhole."

Mike stuck plates into the dishwasher. "We've identified those three as having Michigan links. But there may be others. Who else was around?"

"The entire night crew! There are a dozen guys in the pressroom. There are a dozen people who work nights building ads on the computers. We have five page designers who work on page building for the newsside. There were even some ad salesmen there that night. I bumped into J.J. Jones on my way downstairs, I remember, and there were lights on in the display advertising department, so he wasn't the only person there. And how about the security guards? Just because they're hired through O'Sullivan Security doesn't mean they couldn't be up to no good."

"Jim's got people checking them," Mike said. "So far he hasn't found any link to Michigan. Jim also took the tapes from the cameras on the doors. That may tell us something."

I put my head in my hands. "It's such a mess. I'm dreading going back to work tomorrow."

Mike whirled around. "You're not going down there!"

"How can I stay away? I don't want to sound self-important,

but with Martina out of the schedule, I may be the only copy editor available on Tuesdays."

"Don't be stupid, Nell! If this guy is so determined to get you that he'll pull that stunt with the flowers, you need to stay away from the *Gazette*."

We argued it back and forth a few minutes, but the disagreement ended when Mike said, "I don't care if they get the damn paper out or not! I could get along without a newspaper for a couple of days! I could not get along without you for as much as an hour and a half!"

My eyes filled. I got up and led Mike back to the corner behind the refrigerator, the one where we couldn't be seen from the living room.

"I love you," I said.

"I love you," Mike said.

Seems as if that's all that needed to be said for a few minutes.

I spoke. "Do you think you have to sleep on the couch again tonight?"

"Not if I've been forgiven," Mike said. "I'll hang some tin cans on the doorknobs in case Arnie decides to leave us." He nuzzled my neck. "Do you think you could scratch my back a little later?"

"Sure. Do you think you could do that thing with your thumbs?"

He slid his hand under my T-shirt. "Is that what you had in mind?"

"Yes, but without the bra."

He took his hand away. "Guess we'd better join Arnie."

"Guess so."

I thought the next hour would never pass, but after the ten o'clock news Arnie went to bed, and then Mike and I did, too. We closed the bedroom door, and I forgot all about Arnie until the headboard began bumping gently against the wall. In a moment of revelation I realized my father was on the other side of that wall.

The thought didn't inhibit me. In fact, it made me feel rather defiant. It was titillating. I made the headboard bump harder. So there, Daddy. I'm having sex. Yah, yah.

Everybody's entitled to a bit of teenage rebellion, even if it comes nearly ten years late. Arnie and I were going through the stages of the parent-child relationship at an accelerated rate.

Afterward, Mike tried again to get me to talk about how I felt about Arnie and about having him pop into my life. Mike is a nice guy, but he's taken far too much psychology. However, I know how to distract him when he begins to get too nosy about my ego, superego, and id. I didn't find it too hard to entice him into showing an interest in my body rather than in my psyche.

I had him completely off the subject when somebody began to pound on the front door.

At the sound, the headboard thumped the wall really loud, and it had nothing to do with sex. Mike rolled over me, and we both started for the walk-in closet. Mike won the race. Standing in the closet door, he snatched a pair of pants off a hanger. I couldn't get past him. The pounding was still going on.

I grabbed up the jeans and T-shirt I'd dropped at the foot of the bed. I pulled them on sans undies, then slammed my tennies on without socks.

"Who the dickens is out there?" I said.

"I don't know," Mike said. "But you're staying here until I find out." He stepped into a pair of loafers, then yanked a sweatshirt off a hanger.

All the time the door banging continued. Minimally dressed, Mike opened the bedroom door and moved out into the living room, which was lighted only by a night light down the hall, outside the hall bathroom. Immediately Mike whirled toward the hall.

"Who's there?" he said.

"It's me!" The voice was Arnie's. "What's going on?"

"That's what I'm trying to find out," Mike said. "You keep Nell in the bedroom."

Arnie came over to the door. He was wearing his striped pajamas, and his hair was tousled. The shenanigans in the next bedroom had apparently failed to keep him awake.

He stood between me and Mike, and Mike went to the door. He turned the porch light on and looked out the peep-hole. "Who's there?"

"Me!" It was a woman's voice, and it sounded scared. "Let me in!"

"It's Martha!" I pushed past Arnie, but he caught my arm. "Let go!" I said. "Martha's out there."

"Who's Martha?" Arnie said.

"One of my roommates!"

He didn't let go of my arm. "Let Mike handle it," he said.

"We can't leave Martha out on the porch! She wouldn't just drop by in the middle of the night! There's some emergency!"

I could hear Mike feeling around on the bookcase nearest the door, and I realized he was getting the key to the dead bolt from the bookshelf. He keeps it in the door in the day-time, but stashes it in a hiding place at night or when he leaves the house. He clicked over both the locks.

Immediately the door swung open, and Martha yelped, then fell inside.

"Let me go!" she said.

She was speaking to a figure who was bending over her. With the bright porch light at their backs, they looked like King Kong and Fay Wray.

"Shut up!" a gruff voice said.

I recognized the sound.

I pushed past Arnie and turned on the lamp at the end of the couch, lighting the living room.

"Bob Johnson!" I said. "What are you doing?"

The light showed Martha, wearing her raincoat, on her hands and knees on the floor. Bob Johnson was holding her coat collar in his left hand, and his right clutched a slim, lethal-looking knife.

He grinned drunkenly.

"Well, if it ain't little Nellie," he said. "Maybe we can talk some sense this time."

He lowered his knife to within inches of Martha's throat.

"Or else!"

Chapter 22

I think I was paralyzed. Arnie may have been paralyzed, too. We stood there, with Martha on her hands and knees—she wasn't moving either—and Bob Johnson standing over her.

Martha had lost her fashion-plate appearance. Her stylish blue coat was pulled out of shape by the grip Bob had on its collar, and her blush looked like war paint against her pallor. Her normally sleek black hair looked as if a bird had been in it.

Bob didn't change his grip, but he wasn't standing still. He was weaving back and forth, and his eyes didn't focus. He was obviously drunk. But he didn't move the knife from Martha's throat.

Mike spoke. "Bob, there's no reason to get yourself all in an uproar. Put the knife down." His calm voice reminded me that he was the person we needed in the current emergency.

Bob was holding the knife in one hand and Martha in the other, and he was threatening her. That's what law enforcement calls a "hostage situation."

And the person the police would call in for a hostage situation is a "hostage negotiator." And that's Mike. Chief hostage negotiator for the Grantham Police Department. Realizing this made me feel a surge of hope. Mike would know what to do.

It's rare, however, for a hostage taker to bring the hostage by the hostage negotiator's house. What was going to happen?

Bob spoke, slurring his words. "I'm not letting her loose until I get what I want!"

"Sure," Mike said. "What do you want?"

"I want somebody to take me sher—sheriously!"

Mike nodded. "I get the message, Bob."

"I want to tell Nell all about the other guys who could have wanted to do Martina in."

"We sure want that information, Bob. But you—you look miserable. You can't talk in that position. You're all bent over with your back in a crook."

Bob pointed his chin at Martha, but he didn't move the hand that held the knife. "She fell down."

"Yeah. There was an incident with the storm door this afternoon," Mike said. "The glass is gone, but the frame is still there. I expect she tripped over the frame when she stepped into the house."

"What happened to the door?" Bob sounded as if he were merely curious.

"We had a little excitement." Mike gestured toward Arnie. "Arnie, push a couple of kitchen chairs over there. Bob must be really uncomfortable."

Arnie went into the kitchen—the door was about six feet from Bob and Martha—and brought out two chairs, carrying them out one at a time. He pushed them toward Bob, and the burly pressman pulled Martha up to her feet.

Bob seemed to forget Arnie, who disappeared back into the kitchen. He came to the kitchen door, standing where Bob couldn't see him, and made a few motions.

"Yes, that's right. That's better," Mike said, still looking at Bob. Arnie disappeared again.

Martha's eyes were incredibly wide, and she was staring at Mike as if he were the chairman of her thesis committee, as if her life hung on his words. It probably did.

Mike ignored her. I knew enough about hostage negotiations to understand why. The negotiator must concentrate on the hostage taker. He never wants to remind the hostage taker that the hostage even exists. He must work only on the bad guy, ignore the person being threatened. This can be hard on the person in danger.

Bob and Martha jockeyed around, with Bob still holding the knife to her throat, until Martha was sitting in one of the chairs. Bob almost sat down in the other. Then he realized that he couldn't do that and also hold the knife in a threatening position. So he stood behind her.

"Now, Bob, I thought you were going to go and talk to Jim Hammond," Mike said. "Explain to him that you're innocent. I thought you agreed."

"That was before I got fired!"

"Gee, Bob! That's rough! What happened?"

"Just one little drink! That's all I had."

"Wow! The *Gazette* must be strict."

"Wes—he said I couldn't be around machinery."

He was talking about Wes McLaird, the pressroom foreman. I thought Mike would figure that out for himself.

"But it was just one drink!" Bob said. "So I thought I'd tell Nell"—he looked at me and nodded—"about the other guys down there."

He leaned toward Mike and lowered his voice. "Everybody hated that bitch Martina, you know."

"I'm not surprised to hear that, Bob."

Bob nodded wisely. "That Ed Brown. She knew something about him, you know."

"No, I didn't know that. Do you know what it was?"

"No, but I think maybe he got arrested once."

Mike whistled.

"Yeah," Bob said sagely. "Ha. Mr. Respectable himself. He was standing right there when Mac fired me. Butter wouldn't melt."

"Gosh, Bob. You've had a terrible time."

"And Wes himself! He got really mad at that woman when she made cracks about the color registration for that damn bridal section! He and J.J. Jones both went for Martina over that one!"

He grinned smugly and gave a hiccup. "Even the boyfriend!"

"Do you mean Dan Smith?"

"Yeah! That jerk salesman." He went into a long yarn about some argument Martina and Dan had had over a cup of coffee in the break room. Of course, he hadn't been close enough to hear what it was about, but they'd looked as if they were quarreling.

Bob rambled on for about ten minutes straight. He enumerated person after person who had disliked Martina. Reporters, ad salesmen, bookkeepers, circulation—she obviously didn't have a friend in any department.

It was the longest ten minutes of my life, and I'm sure Martha thought it lasted an hour. Her eyes never moved from Mike's face. Mike stared directly at Bob Johnson and nodded sympathetically.

"Is that right, Bob? I didn't know that," he said.

Bob kept talking. Mike kept nodding and sympathizing. And I heard a noise. There was someone on the porch. Maybe two people. Whoever it was was quiet, but I could hear them.

I thought Mike could hear them, too, because he raised his voice.

"Listen, Bob," he said. "You have some very valuable information here—the detectives really need to have it."

Bob looked shy in a cross-eyed sort of way. He made a gesture with his left hand, and it nearly threw him off balance. He used that hand to grab Martha's shoulder to steady himself, and he threw his right hand out for balance.

He didn't seem to realize that he'd taken the knife away from Martha's throat.

"Bob, sit down," Mike said. "You're obviously exhausted, and I need to go over this material with you again. Then you can go to sleep."

Bob obediently slumped into the second kitchen chair, but he kept hold of Martha's shoulder, and the knife was still held at the ready. Not near her throat, but close to her side.

"Bob, I need to get a pad so we can write this down," Mike said. "I'm afraid you're so tired you'll forget part of it. Why don't we get Nell and Martha to make us a pot of coffee?"

"Coffee?" Bob's eyes almost closed, but he forced them open.

"Yeah. Strong, black coffee."

Bob nodded slowly. And I expelled the air I'd inhaled when Martha fell in the front door. I think I'd been holding my breath since that moment.

Mike motioned. "Nell, you and Martha go into the kitchen and make us some coffee."

"Sure." I took another deep breath and walked toward Martha. Mike wouldn't want me to get too close, I told myself. After all, I was the one Bob was really mad at. It wouldn't do any good to swap me for Martha. So I stopped three or four feet from her.

"Come on, Martha. You're the coffee expert."

She tore her gaze from Mike and slowly turned to me.

"Coffee?" Her voice was a whisper.

"Yes. Come on." I held my hand out to her.

She looked back at Mike, and he nodded encouragingly. Martha stood up slowly, and Bob's hand fell off her shoulder. She held her hand out to meet mine, and I yanked her into the kitchen.

I didn't know what Mike wanted to do next, but I didn't think it would be to make a list of people who hated Martina.

The door from the kitchen to the garage was standing open. I didn't hesitate. I hustled Martha right out that door into the garage.

"Coffee?" Martha said weakly.

"Forget the coffee! Mike wants us out of there!"

The door to the backyard was also open, so we edged past the front of my car and went outside. Then a figure loomed up out of the dark, and Martha and I both screamed. I screamed again before I realized it was a uniformed officer.

"It's okay, ma'am!" he said. "The gate's open. We'll go out through the front."

Martha was close to collapsing, so he grabbed her other arm, and we almost dragged her through the gate that led to the front yard. As soon as we came around the garage I saw Arnie running toward us. He met me with a big hug.

"You called the cops!" I said.

"Once Mike got me into the kitchen, where the phone is."

Three patrol cars were parked in front of the house, and a fourth one was just pulling up. But there were no sirens, no shouts, no slammed doors.

All the noise was coming from the house. There was a lot of excited talking and yelling. And I could hear Bob Johnson sobbing.

Martha was sobbing, too. I put my arms around her, and Arnie hugged us both.

"Martha, I'm so sorry you got involved in this," I said.

"Nell, I was so scared!"

"Did he hurt you?"

"He just twisted my arm. I'd been to a party and came in late. He was hiding behind Brenda's car, and he ran up on the porch and grabbed me. He wanted you, Nell!"

"Seems as if I'm real popular lately."

"But you weren't there! Nobody was there. Brenda went out with Chuck, and I expect she'll stay over. And Rocky went to see his folks. He won't be back until tomorrow. This guy made me drive him over here. He knew the address and everything! Because I'd told him this afternoon!"

"I know, Martha. He came by here and made trouble earlier," I said. "But Mike and I thought he'd settled down."

"Some time in jail will settle him down," Arnie said. "With related charges."

"Charges?" Martha still sounded dazed.

"Kidnapping. Assault with a deadly weapon. Maybe a few other things," I said.

Three cops led Bob out. He was crying as they stuffed him into a patrol car.

Martha shrank against me. Mike came out of the house. He hugged Martha. "You were great, Martha! I know it was really hard to stay calm while I did all that talking and questioning. You handled it exactly right."

Tears kept running down Martha's face, and her teeth were chattering. I led her back into the house.

As I stepped through the empty frame of the storm door, I heard one of the patrolmen: "Well, Mike, I guess this solves the *Gazette*'s murder," he said.

"Maybe," Mike said.

"Murder?" Martha's voice was more frightened than ever. "You mean, that guy already killed somebody?"

"He's a suspect," I said.

I still had trouble picturing Bob as a killer. I'd interviewed the guy about his motorcycle club, for heaven's sake! He'd convinced the editors that middle-aged, wholesome, hard-working people who rode motorcycles purely for fun were worth a story. I'd thought he was a dull member of a dull group, not far removed from R.V. owners or square dancers or bird watchers or Internet freaks.

How could a person like that go berserk and kill people?

It didn't seem possible, but he had threatened Martha's life. I'd seen him do it. And he obviously did have a drinking problem. Maybe Martina had pushed him over the edge. Maybe he really had kicked her down the iron staircase, then slammed her face against the concrete floor until she died.

But Bob had been drunk when he kidnapped Martha. He hadn't been drunk the night Martina was killed. I'd talked to him that night. He'd come down and offered to help with first aid before he'd seen how serious Martina's injuries were. I'd seen no sign that he'd been drinking.

Besides, he'd been surprised that Mike's storm door had been broken. So maybe he wasn't the guy in the ski mask who had shot it to bits.

I put off any conclusion on Bob's guilt or innocence, and we all tried to comfort Martha. She definitely wasn't ready to go to bed, and taking her home didn't seem to be a good idea, since there was nobody there. I'd read that milky drinks were calming, so I dug through Mike's cupboard and found some lumpy sacks of instant cocoa. I heated some water and made Martha a cup. Arnie made coffee.

Martha got her natural poise back rapidly. As Arnie put a cup of coffee on the kitchen table, she held out her hand. "I'm Martha Henry, one of Nell's roommates," she said. "You helped save my life, but I don't believe we've met."

Arnie looked at me. I looked at Arnie.

"Martha," I said, "this is my dad."

The conversation got crazy after that. For ten minutes we'd try to explain how Arnie and I found each other; then for ten Martha would talk about being kidnapped again. During the next ten we'd talk about the murder at the *Gazette* and how Bob Johnson could fit in. The four of us sat around the kitchen table, drinking coffee and cocoa and talking hysterically. At least, Martha, Arnie, and I talked hysterically. We absolutely babbled. Mike sat by and egged us on, like a good little amateur psychologist.

Martha kept apologizing for giving Mike's address to Bob that afternoon.

"I'm so sorry!" she said. "He said he worked for the *Gazette*, and he seemed perfectly sane."

"It's okay," I said. "He could have found the address in the city directory anyway."

"My phone is unlisted," Mike said, "but that's because I don't want a lot of unscreened calls. My address is no secret."

When Martha finally wound down and was ready for bed, he gave her two choices. She and I could sleep in the king-size bed, and he'd take the couch, or the three of us would go over to the house near the campus.

"You're not going to be alone for a while, Martha," Mike said. "Not a good idea."

She gave a shaky laugh. "I've stopped trembling."

"Trembling is okay. Tremble all you want. But it's good to have company while you do it. We're all going to hang around until you're sick of us."

Martha decided to stay at Mike's, and we all went to bed about three a.m. I didn't sleep much. I heard Arnie moving around, and Mike's couch creaked, so I don't think they did, either.

We were all still in our sleeping places when the phone rang at nine-thirty, but Mike caught it after the first ring.

I got up, washed my face, and put on his robe, then turned the bathroom over to Martha. I found Mike in the kitchen.

"Boone called," he said.

"Oh? Any new crisis?"

Mike frowned. "Not exactly. They got a warrant first thing this morning, and he went over Bob Johnson's house."

"Boone's up early. Did he find anything?"

"Yeah, he did." He was still frowning.

"Are you going to tell me what it was?"

Mike turned and leaned against the kitchen counter.

"He found a set of *Gazette* coveralls, the kind the maintenance workers wear."

"That's an odd thing for a pressman to have. Their uniforms are a blue shirt and pants."

"There was an even odder thing about these particular coveralls. They had some kind of reddish-brown stains all over them. And Bob Johnson claims he doesn't know where they came from."

Chapter 23

I stared at Mike. "Do they think they're bloodstains?"

"Could be. Maybe not."

"How soon will they know?"

"They'll get them to the lab this morning. Should have a preliminary report by noon. Thanks to the *Gazette* connection, they'll go to the top of the list."

The Grantham city-county crime lab, like crime labs all over the world, is always behind. Sometimes detectives wait for weeks for reports on evidence. But because Martina's death had happened in the Gazette Building, because a news medium was involved, because the publisher had called Chief Jameson, the case was getting priority treatment. I felt a twinge of guilt, but I didn't let it bother me. Any prominent citizen—president of a bank, CEO of Grantham's biggest manufacturing company, president of the city's biggest union, college president—they'd all get the same treatment our publisher did. Crimes that involved people like these were high-profile cases, and they were simply going to get more attention, just as cases involving movie stars or politicians get more attention from the national press and television.

By the time I'd absorbed Mike's information on the possible bloodstains, everybody was out. Martha and I decided we'd go home to our own shower and wardrobes, and Arnie began to talk about leaving, too.

"Since all the cops seem to know where I am," he said, "I

guess there's not much point in my cluttering up your house, Mike. I need to get over to my own place and start straightening out the things we left yesterday and moving the stuff in the car back in."

So much had happened in the last twenty-four hours that I had trouble remembering that Arnie's apartment had been ransacked.

Mike nodded. "I'm pretty sure you're off the hook, Arnie. You'd probably better stay in town, but this new development on Bob Johnson—"

Arnie squinted his eyes suspiciously. "Do you think Bob Johnson is guilty?"

"I'm pretty sure he's not. But I think it lets you off the hook with the Grantham P.D. for the moment."

"I can feature Bob Johnson killing Martina real easy," Arnie said. "But we've been figuring that the same person killed Sally."

"You don't think Bob did that?"

Arnie shook his head slowly. "I spent twenty years being afraid my wife had a boyfriend. Maybe it's just ego, but I don't picture Bob Johnson appealing to her."

I thought about it. Bob wasn't particularly attractive, that was true. But it's hard to tell. When Arnie told about the disasters that had fallen on him and my mother in Jessamine, Michigan—well, if my mother had been unfaithful, she might have merely been trying to get even. She might have taken up with the first guy who seemed interested, just because she'd been mad at Arnie and at Jessamine.

Besides, it's hard to tell just who will appeal to the opposite sex. One of the ugliest guys who ever worked at the *Gazette* was a certified lady-killer, a lover with a line that had 'em swooning at his feet. And one of the plainest girls I knew in college always had a lot of guys calling her. None of her girlfriends ever saw what she had that the rest of us didn't. I'd decided it must be her aroma, some hidden attraction that drew men the way female roach hormones attract male roaches. If she bottled it, Estee Lauder would pay millions for the rights.

Did Bob Johnson have "it," whatever "it" is? Or had he had it twenty years earlier? I couldn't even guess.

Arnie cocked his head in my direction. "What are we going to do about Nell?"

Mike frowned. "I don't know what to do about Nell. That guy may still be after her."

I cleared my throat. "Would you all mind including me in this conversation? After all, it's my hide we're talking about here."

"Sure," Mike said. "What's your opinion?"

"I think that I'm in the clear as long as Bob Johnson is the prime suspect, if—big if—if I act as though I'm sure he did it."

Mike frowned, but I went on. "As you said last night, the only reason we can think of that someone might want to kill me is to keep me from telling something the guy thinks I know—whatever the hell it is."

"Right," Mike said.

"If I resume my normal life and tell everybody around me that I'm sure glad they arrested that terrible Bob Johnson who's been trying to kill me . . ."

Arnie nodded, but Mike was still frowning.

"Then the guy ought to realize that I don't know anything, I didn't see anything, I'm not going to tell anything, and he has nothing to fear from me. Which is the truth."

Mike didn't look convinced.

"Mike, I can't live my whole life locked up in your house," I said. "I really think I might be safer if I go back to living my regular life. Provided I spread the right story."

We kicked it around. Mike offered to get me a bodyguard from O'Sullivan Security. Mickey O'Sullivan, who owns the firm, was Mike's dad's best friend and is now his mother's boyfriend. "Mickey would give us a cut rate," Mike said.

"I'm not having a cut-rate bodyguard," I said. "It's the Secret Service or nothing."

"That I can't arrange."

We finally compromised on the first move. Martha and I waited until Mike showered and dressed. Then he followed us over to our house and checked the place—top to bottom—before we entered it. We locked the front door and pulled the curtains and shades on the windows that faced the street. Then Mike headed out the back door, the one we use to reach our parking slots.

"You and Martha keep your doors locked and don't let anybody in," Mike said. "I've got to check in with the sergeant. I may have taken all the leave time I've got."

"Does that mean you'll have to go to work tonight?"

Mike shrugged. "It's likely. I'll call you." He kissed me gently. "Stay put, kid."

I didn't say anything. I just smiled, and I locked the door behind him. Then I took a shower, got dressed, and went to work.

I knew Mike wouldn't like it, but I went anyway. I was more and more convinced that my analysis of the situation was right. If I could spread the word that I'd told the police everything I knew about Martina's death, then I ought to be safe.

And I wouldn't be silly. I would ask the security guard to walk me to my car. Maybe I'd even ask Arnie or Mike to follow me home that night. I wouldn't wander around the building alone. If I left the editorial floor, I'd be sure I was accompanied by some other staffer—somebody I knew hadn't been in that basement the night Martina was killed.

I knew they'd get the newspaper out whether I showed up or not. I'm not that important to the workings of the *Grantham Gazette*. But I had another reason for wanting to go to work. If I was down there, I might learn something. People would ask me about the events of the past couple of days. Talking about it would inspire gossip. I could unobtrusively find out more about the three men we knew were connected with Michigan. So I went to work.

I even went an hour early, so I could talk to anybody who wanted to talk—spread the word that I thought Bob Johnson was guilty. I stopped in the break room and told a couple of people that. Then I went upstairs to my desk. The first thing I did was read the *Gazette*'s coverage of Martina's murder, three days' worth. J.B. and Chuck had done okay. They'd also covered the chase scene with the Cadillac and the shooting that did in Mike's storm door, quite properly pointing out that the same *Gazette* staffer who'd found Martina's body, me, was the one who got shot at.

The previous night's episode with Bob Johnson had happened after deadline. They'd have to write that up for the next day's paper. I might get to copyedit it myself.

My presence during the afternoon shooting was handled tactfully. Arnie and I were described as "two friends" of the police officer who occupied the home. My presence at Mike's house after midnight—which was bound to come out in the story about Martha's kidnapping—was going to be harder to explain to the newspaper-reading public.

I regard myself as liberated. I wasn't ashamed of sleeping with Mike, and I didn't care if my friends, my father, or even my Aunt Billie knew about it. But I didn't want it on the front page of the *Grantham Gazette*. It wasn't public business. I gnashed my teeth. Getting involved in a murder sure can complicate your personal life.

I looked up from that morning's *Gazette* and stared across the newsroom, contemplating my situation. And, unexpectedly, something caught my attention.

Ed Brown was moving along the newsroom wall. He was clutching his clipboard and looking over his shoulder suspiciously. Furtively.

Most of the newsroom desks are in pods, with the people who are assigned to the various areas seated near each other. Within the pods each reporter's space is set off by partitions.

Eye-level moveable walls surround the pods, and short tweed-covered barriers keep each reporter's junk from infringing on other reporters' desks. Good fences make good neighbors, or something like that.

The layout means reporters have to stand up if they want to look across the room. They have to look over the tops of these two-foot-high partitions between the desks and these eye-level walls surrounding their pods.

Editors have no such barriers. The editors who work on local copy work at a pod of four desks. In a tribute to newspaper tradition, this is known as "the rim." That's because old-time editors worked at a circular table—a table shaped like the letter c and named the "rim." The city editor sat at a central place known as "the slot."

I think this layout allowed the copy boys, back in the days when they had copy boys, to walk into the middle and take copy from each editor. The advent of computers did away with this arrangement, just as it did away with copy boys. Now the four of us who work the rim—city editor, assistant city editor, and two copy eds—sit at regular desks, each with a visual display terminal.

The city editor and the assistant city editor supervise reporters. The two copy editors do nothing but read the stories, checking for spelling, punctuation, correct information, complete information, and smooth writing. Then we send the copy on to the city editor and her assistants.

We don't have walls around us. And no partitions separate one desk from another. This lets us talk among ourselves easily, because the editorial team has to work together all evening. And we're not cut off from the newsroom, because the reporters are supposed to approach us with questions and comments.

This layout meant I happened to be the only person in the newsroom right at that moment who could see Ed Brown moving furtively along the west wall, the one that's lined with off-white filing cabinets. He was going from cabinet to cabinet, checking the labels on each drawer. Every now and then he'd pull a drawer open and look inside.

I decided he was continuing the search I'd interrupted Sunday afternoon.

I watched him for a few minutes before I caught on. If the drawer had a label on it, he read the label and went on. If it didn't, he opened the drawer to see what was inside.

What was he looking for? I couldn't imagine.

The drawers belonged to the reporters. Storage space in the reporters' desks is limited. Since a VDT is mounted on one side of each desk, most reporters have only two drawers, one deep and one shallow. So reporters use filing cabinets for extra storage. The city council reporter has several, I'm sure, all full of old council agendas and reports on various city programs and functions. My pal Mitzi Johns, who covers the health beat, has two drawers—one and a half of them full of data on health and hospitals and the remaining half drawer filled with instant coffee, instant soup, instant cocoa, and plastic silverware—emergency rations for the nights she works late. I have two drawers myself, left over from my days as a crime reporter. They're stuffed with crime stats, old law enforcement personnel lists, and other junk. They give me a guilt attack every time I glance at them, because I ought to throw out most of what's in there.

So what was Ed Brown doing? Taking some kind of inventory? If the filing cabinets weren't in use, was he going to take them away? Or was he going to declare a housecleaning day and demand that we all straighten them out before the excess paper made the newsroom so heavy it sank down into the floor below and crushed the display-ad department?

Sunday I'd been too startled to ask him what he was doing. I'd let him ask all the questions. But today I wasn't alone in the building. And I wanted to know what Ed was up to.

He was drawing near a bank of files used by Ruth Borah.

Ruth, who wasn't at work yet, keeps extra boxes of Kleenex in her drawer. I decided I needed a box of Kleenex. My nose definitely felt as if it was about to start running like mad.

I got up and walked over to Ruth's drawer, about six feet down from Ed and his clipboard. "Hi, Mr. Brown," I said brightly. "You're not going to commandeer our filing cabinets for the ad department, are you?" I smiled in a friendly way.

"No!" Ed looked panicky. "It's just—I'm looking—Ms. Gilroy—" Then he pursed his lips tightly. He clutched his clipboard to his chest. "Never mind," he said.

He turned and walked away, his shoulders drooping like a helium balloon a week after the birthday party.

What had all that been about?

I went back to my desk. Ruth came in, and we talked a few minutes. She wanted to know about all the excitement I'd had on my days off. But Ruth's pretty businesslike. Soon she set me to work reading local copy.

I admit I read Mitzi's health department story with half a mind. I was still thinking about Ed Brown. Had he been looking for any files Martina had kept?

At one a.m. this morning Bob Johnson, drunk, had been raving about how many people had disliked Martina. Ed Brown had headed his list. She knew something about him, Bob had said. He'd had no idea what, but he suspected something illegal.

But I thought I knew. It had to do with the fight outside the gay bar. And Ed's arrest.

Had Martina been threatening Ed with that old news story? But surely the *Gazette* bosses knew about that. It had been printed in the *Gazette*, after all. Of course, E.J. Brown wasn't the name we all knew Ed by. Maybe Martina was the only person who had figured it out.

But the police had cleared her desk out the night she was murdered. And I was sure they'd searched her house. If she'd had anything like that in hard copy, the police had it now.

And, I realized, I had her hidden computer files. So much had happened during the past couple of days that I hadn't remembered to tell Mike or Jim Hammond about them.

I might be the only person who knew about those files.

I faced the VDT screen and typed in Martina's code. "Sports" and "Car."

The screen came up perfectly blank.

The list of stories I'd linked to Martina was gone.

Maybe I'd typed the commands in wrong. I typed "sports" and "car" without the capitals, though in theory that doesn't make any difference.

The screen was still blank.

Chapter 24

Martina's file had disappeared from the *Gazette*'s computer system.

The thought gave me the willies. Logically, I had known that Martina was killed by somebody on the *Gazette* staff. But the thought of that person roaming around in the computer system—I shuddered.

Then I quickly checked the "Mary" "Nll" file. Yes, the items I'd copied from "Sports" "Car" were still there. And I knew I had the printouts at home. But that didn't make me feel less scared.

I called Jim Hammond and told him what I'd found. He asked for copies, so I copied Martina's file to disk, then gave each item the printout command and went to the printout room to collect the articles as they came out of the printer. Just as it had the day before, the lonely room made me nervous. The computer terminals, printers, storage cabinets, with thick electronic cables tangled between them—the equipment made me feel trapped.

So I jumped when the door behind me opened. Once again it was only J.J. Jones. I relaxed. He'd saved me from Ed Brown's tirade on Sunday.

"Hi," I said.

"Hello, young lady," he said. "Accordin' to the morning paper and the office grapevine, you had a pretty excitin' day yesterday."

I nodded and remembered to go into my Bob-Johnson-is-a-bad-guy act.

"I'm so glad they arrested that Bob Johnson," I said. "The man is a menace!"

"Then he was the one who shot at you?"

"He must have been! We know for sure he was the one who kidnapped my roommate and dragged her around town in the middle of the night. Surely we don't have two crazy killers at the *Gazette!*"

J.J. laughed. "That would seem to be statistically unlikely." He ripped printouts from a printer I knew was used for advertising proofs. "Do the police know why Mr. Johnson did these threatenin' things?"

"If they do, they're not telling me. Apparently he tried to kill me—twice—and I'd sure like to know why."

"In your position, I would certainly concur with that sentiment," he said. Then he gathered up his printouts and moved in my direction. "May I help you, Miss Matthews?"

I shook my head, but unfortunately the printer picked that precise moment to jump its tracks. It stopped shoving the paper out and began to print line after line in the same space, one on top of the other.

"Darn!" I said.

J.J. Jones came over to my side. "It does that sometimes," he said, "particularly if you're catching the printout and folding it sheet by sheet, the way you were."

"How do you stop it?"

He punched a button and the printer stopped moving. Then he ripped off my printout—it happened to be the one about assisted suicide—and handed it to me. I stood there like a dummy because I don't know anything about the printer. Nor do I care. As long as machines—be they computers, cars, or can openers—obey my commands, I don't care how they work. The problem comes when they don't work.

J.J. Jones opened the back of the printer and readjusted

the tracked paper on its brackets. Then he closed the printer and punched buttons again. The printer resumed its work.

"Thanks," I said.

"You've got a big printin' job," he said.

"Just some old files," I said.

"You'll have to send that one story over, I 'magine." He smiled broadly. "Well, I hope all your personal excitement is over, Miss Nell. And as I came through the newsroom, I saw Arnie Ashe is back at work."

Arnie was back? Why? When? I grabbed up the printouts and rushed out into the newsroom. Arnie was sitting at Martina's desk.

"What are you doing here?" I asked.

"I called in, and Ruth told me she and Jake want me to learn the copy desk."

"Oh!" I thought about it. "That's a good idea."

"I've done mostly desk work for the past five years," Arnie said. "I know the A.P. style book pretty well, but you'll have to help me with the local names and addresses."

"Sure. The ones I know."

Ruth Borah had been talking on the phone. Now she put her hand over the receiver and looked at me. "Nell, will you show Arnie the routine? I've got to take care of one of my kids. I don't know who told me motherhood and a career can mix, but I shouldn't have believed them."

I moved my chair around by Arnie's desk and wrote out a little cheat sheet with the names of the desk files on it. Reporters send their stories to "proof." Copy editors read them, then send them to the proper city desk file. It's not a real tricky system. Stories about Grantham go in "City." Death notices, police reports, and other things that run every day go to "Must." Locally written stories about happenings outside Grantham go into "State." Business-page stories go in "Busns." The wire editors have a set of files for state, national, and international news, but copy editors don't mess

with those, unless we're caught up and simply want some
reading matter.

After the local stories are edited, they go to page builders.
This is another set of editors who worry more about layout
and headline size than they do about exactly what each story
says. Ruth tells them what she wants "played," or emphasized, and they do the actual design, then "build" the pages
on a giant computer, subject to her approval.

"Sports and Lifestyles read their own copy," I told Arnie.
"It's really a simple-minded system."

"I think I can manage it," he said. "Where's the dictionary?"

Of course, the reporters are supposed to run a spell-check
program on every story before we see it, but no mechanical
program can take the place of an English-speaking and reading editor with a dictionary at his or her elbow. I was glad to
see that Arnie knew that.

Each copy editor is provided with a dictionary and an *Associated Press Stylebook*. I showed him the rack of additional reference books we share, pointing out the local items
he might not be familiar with, such as our lists of Grantham
organizations and of the membership of the county medical
association.

He and I had agreed that morning that we wouldn't spread
the word about our relationship until matters were more settled. But I did feel I could say a few personal words.

"Welcome aboard," I said. "I hope the desk was what you
wanted."

Arnie smiled sardonically. "It's the bosses' idea," he said.
"Or maybe Jim Hammond's. I don't think they want me out
roaming the city unsupervised."

I went back to my own desk. His last words had made my
stomach knot up. I knew he was right. Arnie was still under
suspicion.

As long as Martina's murder was unsolved, Arnie would
never be free of suspicion. And an arrest in Martina's death

wouldn't put him in the clear. He might have to go back to Michigan, face the gruff-voiced former Sheriff Ronald Vanderkolk and a jury of Jessamine folks. For a minute I felt something very close to despair. I'd found my father, but he might be snatched away before we could get acquainted.

Then my phone rang, and I looked at the switchboard. Kimmie was on telephone duty, and Mike was in the reception area, leaning on the little rail. "Mike's here," Kimmie said.

"Be right there." I gathered up the printouts and the disk on which I'd saved the stories from Martina's files, then went up to the front.

"Everything going all right?" Mike asked.

I nodded. "I don't know if this stuff will be any help."

"I'll take it over to Jim." Mike leaned closer. "I don't suppose that Dan Smith has been around."

"The boyfriend? I haven't seen him."

"Neither has Jim."

"Of course, Dan has clients all over the state. He could be anywhere, making calls. You'd better ask Ed Brown. He deals with Dan more often than anybody in the newsroom does. He could ask him to call."

Mike shook his head. "We don't want to alert Smith. But if he shows up, give Jim a call. Okay?"

I went back to my desk, mystified. Dan Smith was a traveling salesman. If he was out of touch, so what? He was supposed to be on the road, not sitting around a telephone. Though I would have expected him to carry a cell phone or a pager.

I opened the Proof file and actually earned my salary for at least an hour. I read three stories from the violence beat—a house fire, an armed robbery, and a smash and grab. Then I read about the mental health board, the out-of-town kick-off speaker for the Grantham Library Association's fund-raiser, and the county commissioner's meeting.

Stories I hadn't read were disappearing from the Copy

file, and twice I saw Arnie consult the staff phone list and call some reporter to check on something. So between the two of us, we were moving the copy right along. Ruth, who had long since settled her teenage problem at home, was handing stories on to Layout, and the whole system seemed to be working efficiently.

I should have known it wouldn't last.

The first sign of trouble was the reappearance of Ed Brown. He bustled in with his usual officious air, and dragging behind him was a tall guy with funny hair. Dan Smith.

Ed looked like a Volkswagen towing a two-ton truck on a slack rope. When he stopped, I thought Dan was going to whack right into him in a short of human fender-bender.

They had come up the back stairway, and they stopped right in the middle of the newsroom. Ed gestured widely, then spoke demandingly. "Where?"

"Over there on the west wall."

Ed headed for the west side of the newsroom, the one he'd been examining earlier when I asked him what he was doing. He walked along the filing cabinets, tapping each with a pen.

"This is a disgrace," he said. "I'm going to speak to Jake Edwards about this. There's no organization at all."

"It was somewhere toward the other end," Dan said.

I was staring at them, and I realized that several other people were, too. Ruth was looking quizzical, Arnie was frowning slightly, and one reporter had stood up and was looking over the top of her cubicle, frankly curious.

Dan and Ed didn't seem to notice their audience. They moved along the wall to the other end of the rank of file cabinets, and began to work back. Ed was still tapping each with his pen.

"Marie," he said. "Who in the world is Marie? Doesn't she have a surname? Then Ted Johannson. At least that one's got a name on it. Then Ruth Borah. That's all right. Harry Carter!" He tapped the pen so hard it almost flew out of his hand. "Harry Carter quit two years ago!" He yanked the drawer open. "And here's a whole drawer full of old city council agendas. I'll bet no one even knows they're here!"

At that Ruth stood up, jabbed her pencil into her bun, and grasped her pica pole as if it were a sword. She walked toward the two men. "Ed, just what is the problem?"

"It's these drawers! How do you know whose drawer is whose?"

"I don't know whose is whose, Ed. And, frankly, I don't care. As long as the reporters have the storage they need, they can organize it any way they want. But why does this concern you?"

Ed's mouth snapped shut. I thought I could hear his teeth click together.

Ruth gestured with the pica pole. "Are you looking for something in particular?"

She had spoken to Ed, but he still didn't say anything. So Dan Smith stepped forward with his friendly salesman's grin.

"We didn't mean to disturb you, Mrs. Borah, but Ed's trying to help the family of Martina Gilroy locate all her personal effects. Ed wondered if she'd had a file drawer for extra storage, and I told him I thought I'd seen her use one." He gestured. "I'm not sure which, but I think it was along here. I was here last January, and we went out to dinner. It was a cold night, and it seems as how she got a woolly hat and some warm gloves out of a drawer before we left."

Ruth remained perfectly calm. "Certainly," she said. She backed up to the end cabinet and tapped the top drawer. "It's this one."

"But it's marked Marie, not Martina!" Ed sounded outraged.

"Marie Bloodworth had the drawer at one time," Ruth said. "When she left, Martina moved from the one she'd had to this one."

Trust Martina, I thought. She'd nabbed the drawer easiest to find and closest to her desk.

Ed almost lunged at the drawer, and Ruth pulled it open at the same moment. Ed nearly fell in it.

"As you see," Ruth said, "it's empty. The police took the entire contents of Martina's desk and of this drawer the night she was killed."

Ed looked crushed.

Dan was speaking again. "I am sorry to hear that. I had lent her a book, and of course I'd neglected to put my name in it. I guess it's just gone now."

"There were several books. What was it?"

"It was that wonderful autobiography by Katherine Graham," Dan said. "The last time I saw her, Martina said she'd read it. She promised to get it back to me while I was in town."

"You'll have to ask the police," Ruth said. "I'm sure they'll release her belongings to the family." She turned to Ed. "I'm sorry I'm not more help."

"She had . . . she had . . . a clipping . . ." Ed stammered the words out, then drew himself up and spoke firmly. "Martina had a clipping about my son. I wanted it. As . . . as a souvenir. I'll see about getting it from her family."

He started across the newsroom, leaving Dan behind. Dan gave Ruth another ingratiating smile. "I'm sorry we're such a bother," he said. "What about Martina's computer files?"

Ed stopped and turned so quickly he looked like a Volkswagen popping a wheelie. "Computer files!" His voice squeaked.

"I don't know if Martina even had a computer file," Ruth said.

"Can we look? Where would it be?" Ed almost panted.

Ruth went to her desk. "Reporters use individual files to write and store their stories," she said. "But copy editors don't write much, so they don't have much to store." She looked at me. "Nell, did Martina have a file on the list?"

Her question threw me into a quandary. The simple answer was no. No, Martina did not have a file on the newsroom list. But I had tracked her file down, copied it off to disk, printed it up, and given the whole thing to the cops.

I wasn't sure I wanted to tell Ed and Dan that. I wasn't even sure I wanted to tell Ruth that. But what grounds did I have for refusing?

I decided I'd better tell them, but they didn't need to know all the details. I wanted to protect my fanny.

"I'm afraid it's like the file drawer," I said. "She did have a file, and I was able to locate it. So, it went to the police along with her personal effects."

We nearly had to give Ed Brown CPR. After a moment of gasping and turning blue, however, he revived enough to ask to see the file.

"Actually, I think it's been killed," I said casually. I tried the code words "sports" and "car" again. And again the screen came up blank.

"I don't know who killed it," I said.

"I'm glad it's gone," Ed Brown said. His face was grim. He walked away without a word, defeat in every muscle of his shoulders.

Dan Smith sighed and smiled sadly at Ruth. "Our families, bless 'em," he said. "We can't live with 'em, and we can't live without 'em." He followed Ed Brown out the back door of the newsroom.

"Poor Ed," Ruth said.

"What was all that about?" I asked.

"Ed Brown has a son, Ed Jr., who's been quite a problem. At least Ed's wife lets him be quite a problem."

"I didn't know that."

"The kid is gay. That's not the end of the world for most people today, but it is for Ed's wife. She's sure she's to blame somehow. We all know about it, but she tries to keep the whole situation quiet."

"I see."

"The worst of it is, it's so hard on Ed Jr. She makes him act out some kind of lie. It's no wonder he kicks over the traces sometimes."

"I see," I said again. I turned to my computer screen. And now I did see. The story about "E.J. Brown" being in the fight outside a gay bar was about Ed's son, not Ed himself. Martina had been twitting Ed about his son, the son his wife was ashamed to acknowledge. She'd poked her nose into a family's private business.

For a moment I was so mad at Martina I could have thrown her down the stairs myself.

Belatedly, I remembered that Mike had asked me to call Jim Hammond if Dan Smith showed up at the *Gazette*. I still felt slightly finkish, but I picked up the phone and did it.

I'd barely put the phone down when it rang again. "Ms. Matthews, can you help me out?"

It was Dan Smith.

My stomach jumped. Did he know that the police wanted to talk to him, and that I'd tipped them off, telling Jim Hammond he was in the Gazette Building? I tried not to act guilty.

"Help you out with what, Mr. Smith?"

"You may have to answer quietly."

I covered the receiver with my hand and whispered. "Like this?"

"It's sort of embarrassing. But who is that new fellow sitting at Martina's old desk?"

Chapter 25

If my stomach had jumped before, that question made it do a somersault. "New fellow?" I said stupidly.

"The bald one," Dan Smith said.

There was no getting out of it. "His name is Arnie Ashe," I said.

Dan Smith thought that over before he spoke again. "The name doesn't ring a bell, but his face does. I think he used to have hair."

"I suppose he did," I said. "He's just been here a few weeks."

Dan said thanks, and we hung up. My innards were still jumping around.

Arnie had recognized Dan Smith's name as that of the same salesman who twenty years earlier had visited the *Jessamine Journal*. Smith had taken some of the newspaper's management out to dinner at the Jessamine Elks Club, and my parents had been in the group. My mother had gone to the club early and had flirted with some guys in the bar. The episode had led to her downfall in the small farming community. Within weeks she'd been dead, supposedly murdered by my father in a jealous rage.

But my father said Dan Smith hadn't killed her. In fact, he'd first suspected this particular salesman of being his wife's elusive boyfriend, the "Mr. Smith" she'd apparently met at a motel, the person he believed had run her down with her own car. Then he'd eliminated Dan Smith, because he appeared to have an alibi. But Smith had definitely known my dad twenty years earlier. Would he recognize him now?

I looked up and saw Dan Smith coming into the newsroom. Was he after a closer look at Arnie? What could I do to stop him?

As it turned out, I couldn't do anything, short of having a fainting fit and throwing myself to the floor. Dan headed straight for Arnie. Arnie was looking at his VDT, frowning slightly, and he didn't seem to see Dan coming.

I was tempted to yell a warning. "Look out! Danger! Salesman coming!" But there was nothing I could do. Arnie was on his own.

Dan bustled right up to him, shoving his hand at Arnie over the top of the VDT.

"Hi, there, Arnie. I didn't mean to snub you a few minutes ago, when I was up here with Ed Brown. I know we've met someplace, but you're going to have to tell me where it was."

Arnie froze. Then he thawed enough to shake Dan's outstretched hand. "Sorry," he said. "You've got the best of me. If we've met, it was a long time ago." His voice was wooden.

"Well, I'm sure we've run into each other," Dan said. "You're new to the *Gazette*, aren't you? Where did you work before you came here?"

"Texas."

"No, I've never had a Texas territory. Did you ever work in the Midwest? Missouri?"

"I worked in Tennessee."

"No, that wouldn't be it." Dan gave a throaty chuckle. "Sorry, you probably think I'm crazy. But remembering people is my stock in trade. I don't like to let a familiar face get away without a name. Did you ever work in Illinois?"

Arnie shook his head. I was feeling more and more panicky. When Dan's roll of the states reached Michigan, it was only too likely that the light lashes and pale eyes of Arnie Ashe would remind him of that young, fair-haired managing editor at the *Jessamine Journal*, the one with the nutty wife who got killed. I had to do something.

I got up and rapidly walked to the nearest reporter's cubicle. Luckily, it belonged to my friend Mitzi Johns, who covered health. I ducked down and grabbed Mitzi's phone off the hook.

"Excuse me," I said. "Slight emergency." I punched in the extension for Martina's old desk.

Mitzi turned from her VDT screen, staring at me with wide eyes. "What are you doing?"

"Rescuing Arnie," I said. I could hear the phone ring in both ears, the one nestled into the receiver and the one hanging out in the newsroom.

Arnie answered on the first tinkle. I hoped this meant he was happy to have an interruption. "Copy desk."

"Hi," I said. "Do you need a message that you're wanted in the library?"

"I think it might be a very good idea," he said. "I'll be right there." The line went dead.

I hung up, then stood erect, looking over Mitzi's partition. I could see Arnie and Dan jockeying around, shaking hands again, apparently saying good-bye. Arnie walked away calmly, and we passed as I went back to my desk.

"Whew!" Arnie said.

"Right!" I said.

I was afraid Dan Smith would begin to quiz me about Arnie, but he headed toward the back of the building. I saw him turn into the hall that led to the office of the computer guru who keeps the *Gazette* on line.

I sighed with relief, but I knew the emergency wasn't over. At any moment some unexpected event could jog Dan Smith's memory, and he'd remember who Arnie was. And he might call Michigan and tell them where he was. Arnie was never going to be safe until the real murderer—the killer of my mother and of Martina—was found.

I was relieved to see Ed Brown, Jim Hammond, and Boone Thompson get off the elevator. I hoped they'd come for Dan. If they'd take him away, he wouldn't be an immediate threat to Arnie.

Sure enough, Ed led the group straight back to the computer room. And in a few minutes Boone and Jim came out with Dan. He wasn't handcuffed or anything, but he had lost his professional salesman's cheer.

As they crossed in front of the city desk, he spoke. "This isn't about Springfield, is it?"

"We're investigating the death of Martina Gilroy," Jim answered. "Springfield can take care of its own problems."

They went on through the newsroom and disappeared into the elevator.

I called the library and told Arnie the coast was clear, and he came back to work. I told him what had happened to Dan, and about what Dan had said as he left.

"Springfield?" Arnie frowned. "Wonder what happened there?"

We both went back to work. We barely exchanged a word until time for Arnie's dinner break. Then, instead of leaving his desk, he turned to me. "I might be able to find out something about whatever bugged Dan Smith in Springfield."

"Go for it."

Arnie reached for the rack of reference books and pulled over a copy of the *Editor and Publisher Yearbook*. It is a major trade magazine for the newspaper world, and their yearbook lists the names and phone numbers of every daily and weekly in the United States. We keep a yearbook on the copy desk in case we need to call an out-of-town paper to trade information on a story with Grantham links. Reporters and editors usually cooperate on this sort of thing.

Arnie noted down a phone number from the Illinois section, then punched in a number. In a moment he spoke into the phone. "Copy desk, please." Then, "Joe Phillips, please," and "Hi, Joe. This is Arnie Ashe."

Arnie and Joe had to talk a minute, of course, to catch up on a couple of years in each other's lives. But in a few minutes Arnie got down to business. "Hey, Joe, I'm following up a lead on a murder down here. The lead's sort of nebulous. One of the people being questioned is a salesman for Foster and Company, the printing-supply people. He used to be based in Springfield, Illinois—well, I know he was there twenty years ago. I'm not sure how long ago he left there. Anyway, we got a hint that he was in some kind of trouble while he was in Springfield, and we'd sure like to know what it was. The *Tribune* covers downstate pretty well. You suppose you could find anything?"

I opened my notebook, pulled out the card that Dan Smith had given me, and handed it to Arnie. "Daniel H. Smith," he read aloud. "He's probably close to sixty." He listened. "Sure, Joe, I'll be here all evening. I don't expect you to drop everything, but I'd sure like to know ASAP." He gave Joe the *Gazette*'s number and his own home number. They traded a few more bits of professional gossip, and Arnie hung up.

"Guess I'll go up to Goldman's and get a hamburger," he said. "Do you want me to get you anything?"

"Chili and a side of three-bean salad."

He left, and I went back to reading copy. In less than fifteen minutes, Arnie's phone rang. I hit the magic keys that allow me to answer any phone in our pod, and I picked up my receiver. "Copy desk."

"Arnie Ashe, please."

"Sorry. Arnie's gone to dinner."

"This is Joe Phillips with the *Chicago Tribune*. Arnie called me—"

"Yes. I'm working on the same story. He didn't expect to hear from you this quickly."

"I had a few minutes to do a search, but I'll be busy later on. I found out some very interesting stuff."

I fought the impulse to say, "Tell me about it!" I tried to keep my voice calm. "Arnie will be back in fifteen or twenty minutes. I can have him call you then."

"What's your e-mail?"

"Gazette@Granthamnet.com. But sometimes our local server isn't too fast."

"Can you take a message?"

"Sure." I was dying to.

"Well, about ten years ago this Daniel H. Smith came close to standing trial for murder."

"Murder!"

"Yep. It seems his wife was chronically ill—one of the muscle-wasting diseases—and was also suffering from clinical depression. Luckily for him, she'd been treated for both conditions. Apparently, she saved up her pain pills and used them to commit suicide."

I made a noncommittal grunt.

"The police suspected that Dan had arranged the whole business. Or helped. They thought it might be a case of assisted suicide."

"His wife didn't leave a note?"

"That's what got him off the hook. She hadn't left a note at her bedside, or anything simple like that, but she'd written a letter describing what she planned to do, and she mailed it to an old friend in another city."

"Lucky for Dan!"

"Right, when this Martina Gilroy—"

"Martina!" I yelled so loud that I must have split Joe's eardrum.

Joe was quiet a moment, then he chuckled. "Shall I assume you know her?"

"Right! She's the victim in the murder here, the one Arnie and I are looking into."

Joe whistled. "I remember now," he said. "We ran a story on it. Well, Dan Smith shouldn't have wanted to kill her. She's the one his wife wrote to, and she definitely saved his bacon in Springfield. Without that letter from his wife, Dan could well have been charged. And, by the way, I knew Dan Smith's wife. She covered the courthouse in Effingham when I worked there as a cop reporter. We were both just out of college. She'd gone to the University of Missouri."

He promised to e-mail the complete stories on the death of Dan Smith's wife, and I gushed thanks at him. My heart was pounding as I hung up.

Assisted suicide! Martina had a story on the legal aspects of assisted suicide in her file. This was probably quite a sore topic with Dan. He wouldn't want that episode from his past brought up.

But Martina had saved Dan from possible charges on assisting his wife to commit suicide. He should have been grateful to her. I now recall that Martina had mentioned she'd been in college with Dan Smith's wife. She'd named some other old college friend, too. Acted as if I should know who she was.

Or had Martina come forward with the letter selfishly, to place Dan in her debt? Had she demanded the dinners, the attention Dan had paid her? Was their relationship not friendship but blackmail?

Could Dan have gotten sick and tired of Martina?

In a few minutes, Arnie called to say he and my chili were downstairs. Ruth okayed a slightly early dinner break for me, and I ran down the back stairs. I was in the first-floor hall—the one where I'd once done a little dance with J.J. Jones as he came up from the basement—before I remembered I wasn't supposed to be there alone.

I looked up and down the hall. It was empty, and the doors that led into Classified and Circulation were shut. The coast seemed to be clear. I walked swiftly down the length of the building and into the break room.

Arnie had spread our dinners out on a table on the dividing line between non-smoking and smoking. He looked up when I came in the door. "Do you want to stick your chili in the microwave?"

"I want to tell you about your phone call from Joe Phillips," I said.

We weren't alone in the room. A table full of pressmen occupied the back, and some ad makeup people were between us and the door. So I kept my voice low as I told Arnie about Dan's problems in Springfield.

Arnie whistled, then frowned. "But that's not really much to hold over Smith's head," he said.

I was deflated. "Why not?"

"If his clients and current associates found out about it, it might embarrass him, but he's been cleared by the Springfield authorities. It's not as if he'd wind up in jail."

I could see that Dan Smith's problems looked like nothing to Arnie. If his own past was revealed, he very likely would wind up in jail. It was easy for him to shrug off Dan's troubles. I decided it was best not to say anything. I reached for the styrofoam cup that held my chili.

"Unless . . ." Arnie said. He frowned again.

"Unless what?"

"Unless the letter was a fake."

"Whoa! Surely the police checked the handwriting."

"Didn't Joe say Dan's wife was a reporter?"

"Maybe a former reporter. She had a journalism degree. Why?"

"If you write a letter, do you do it by hand?"

I shook my head. "No, I don't. You've got a good point. Once you learn to compose on the typewriter or computer—"

"On the keyboard—"

"Right. I don't know any reporter who doesn't write letters on the typewriter. So, if Dan's wife followed the pattern, the letter she sent Martina was probably typed."

"So the cops would have had to compare her letter with Dan's wife's signature only. It wouldn't have been as exact as comparing her handwriting for an entire letter. Martina might even have arranged to get hold of the typewriter she would have used."

I stuck my chili in the microwave for thirty seconds, while Arnie spread out his hamburger and fries. We ate silently. It seemed we'd chewed the situation over until there was little left to say. We were gathering up our dinner trash before Arnie spoke.

"Are you going to tell Mike about this? Or Jim Hammond?"

"I'll check with Mike, unless you know some reason I shouldn't. But I'm sure the Grantham P.D. got the straight story from the Springfield police."

We walked upstairs together. I still was frightened about Arnie's safety. I remembered Jim and Boone escorting Dan Smith out of the office. Would they come for Arnie next?

I tried to stick to business for the next half hour. Ruth hadn't said anything, but she must have been thinking both her copy editors had gone crazy. Neither of us seemed to have much interest in local news, which was what we were getting paid for, and we had our heads together all the time. She had no way of knowing why we'd developed this sudden sympathetic mood.

So I conscientiously tried to read copy and not think about murder. Then my phone rang.

"Copy desk," I said.

It was Kimmie's tinkling tones. "Nell, there's someone up here to see you."

Could it be Mike? I looked at the front door, where Kimmie sat beside the night elevator, but Mike wasn't there. A tall man was leaning over the counter, looking at Kimmie. A potbelly made his windbreaker gap, and his head was square and was covered with a shock of hair that was the light gray of natural wool. He turned his head, and his nose inexplicably made me think of the paintings of van Gogh.

Kimmie spoke again. "It's a Ronald Vanderkolk," she said. "He said he just got in from Michigan. He said somebody from the *Gazette* called him."

Chapter 26

As I watched, Kimmie gestured in my direction, and the man at the front turned and looked at the desk.

I felt as if his eyes were boring straight into me. I wanted to run out the back of the office, down the stairs, and out into the night. But I couldn't. I had to act normal, go up to the front and talk to him.

But first I had to warn Arnie.

Dan Smith had thought he recognized Arnie, but he couldn't figure out where or when he'd seen him. Former Sheriff Ronald Vanderkolk was almost certain to know him on sight. He'd probably had a picture of Alan Matthews pinned to his bulletin board for twenty years. A bald head was unlikely to fool him.

He must not get a good look at Arnie.

I started to lean across the desk and talk to Arnie. Then I realized I didn't dare. Vanderkolk was staring at me. He didn't have a clear view of everybody at the city desk, because of the visual display terminals, but I didn't want to call Vanderkolk's attention to Arnie.

I forced myself to smile at Vanderkolk, and I waved two fingers at him. I hoped he'd understand my message. I'd be up front in two minutes. I could see Kimmie talking to him and gesturing toward the couch in the waiting area, but the old sheriff continued to lean across the railing, staring at me.

I created a computer file called "note" and marked it "FYI, Arnie." Then I typed in a few words. "Ronald Vanderkolk is at the front desk asking for me. I'll get rid of him as quickly as possible. I suggest a quick trip to the library."

I saved the note to the proof file, picked up my notebook and ballpoint, then stood up. I was careful to keep my eyes on the notebook, but I spoke aloud. "Arnie, I put a note for you in 'Proof.' Maybe you ought to read it right away."

Then I went up to the front desk. I was scared stiff, but I didn't know if I was more frightened of what Vanderkolk might say or of what he might see—namely, Arnie. Act normal, I told myself. Act normal.

I went through the little gate that tells visitors to stop in the reception area, and I walked around behind Vanderkolk. This made him turn his back on the newsroom. I stuck out my hand.

"Sheriff Vanderkolk? What can I do for you?"

He took my hand, but he squinted his eyes suspiciously as he did it. "Sheriff, huh? Then you are the young lady who called me Saturday," he said.

Belatedly I remembered that I'd used another name when I called. Damn! I could have denied knowing who he was. But it probably wouldn't have done any good. He would have recognized my voice or something.

"Yes, I called." I gestured at the reception area couch. "Won't you sit down?"

Vanderkolk sat, perching on the edge of the cushion and resting his paunch on his lap. "The receptionist said there isn't any Nell Lathen at the newspaper," he said. "She said you're the only Nell on the staff. Why did you use another name when you called?"

I couldn't think of any reason not to tell him the truth. "Because of what my name is," I said.

"She didn't tell me what your name is."

"It's Matthews. Nell Matthews."

Vanderkolk's jaw dropped. "You're little Mary Nell Matthews?"

"Yes." Right at that moment I saw Arnie moving across

the newsroom, headed toward the back door. He was behind Vanderkolk, of course. His progress drew my eye like a magnet. Hurry, Arnie, I told him silently. Hurry.

I forced myself to look at Vanderkolk, to stare into his eyes sincerely. And to speak. "I only recently learned that my mother was murdered," I said. "I wanted to know more about what happened to her. I am a reporter, and I'm used to getting information from law enforcement people. So I simply called you up to ask about the case. I didn't tell you my real name, to be honest, because I thought you might be more forthcoming with a reporter than with a family member."

Vanderkolk was still staring at me. "You're that little girl."

"Right, the scrawny one with the tangled hair and the skinned knees."

Vanderkolk smiled suddenly. "Well, you turned out all right. And you're an editor? Like your dad?"

"Temporarily. I'm filling in as copy editor," I said. "And the city editor's glaring at me because I left the desk, so I can't talk long. I hope you didn't drive all the way from Michigan to see who called you about that old case."

"What about this policeman who came to Jessamine? How did the police get involved? Who's this Mike Svenson?"

I dropped my eyes and tried to look coy. "Mike is my boyfriend," I said. "He didn't tell me he was going up there to try to find out about my family."

"Then he was looking into it on your behalf?"

"I'm afraid so. I'm sure there was nothing official about his trip."

"Are you in contact with your father?"

That question called for a tricky answer. "I was raised by my grandparents," I said. "In twenty years—if my dad made any effort to see me—well, I wasn't aware of it."

Vanderkolk was frowning. I'd evaded any reference to

recent events. Had he noticed? I went on quickly. "Mike got involved—well, because I never knew why my father left me with my grandparents. I guess I don't need to go into my psychological problems, but it was an issue—an emotional issue—I need to settle before I can—before Mike and I . . ."

God! I was stumbling around like the worst liar in the world. But Vanderkolk was nodding in a grandfatherly way. He even reached over and patted my hand. And I blushed. I felt like an awful liar. I was leading him right down the garden path, and he was being kind and understanding.

"I see," he said, "and I think you're a very smart young woman to understand that." He beamed. He almost chucked me under the chin. He showed every tooth he owned. Then he spoke briskly.

"Now, what about this Martina Gilroy? This murder you've had here at the newspaper?"

I could only hope that my guilty start hadn't blown the whole thing. I did stammer then.

"Well . . . naturally . . . we're all upset—"

He snapped his fingers. "You're the one who found the body!"

I gulped and decided to ask a few questions before I answered any more. "How did you find that out?"

I went to the public library, right down the street here, and looked at the back papers."

"But how did you find out about Martina's death in the first place?"

"I read about it in the *Chicago Tribune*." He smiled his grandfatherly smile again. "Of course, a newspaperwoman as a victim—that put me in mind of the newspaper people we'd had involved in a murder right there in Jessamine. You working on the story about this new murder?"

"No. As I said, right now I'm a copy editor. And I'm not a detective. I leave that strictly to the police. Have you talked to them yet?"

"No. I went by the station and asked about your

boyfriend, this Mike Svenson, but they said he wouldn't be on duty until eleven."

"Mike's not working on the investigation into Martina's death," I said. "The detective in charge is Captain Jim Hammond."

"Well, as long as I'm here, maybe I'll talk to Captain Hammond before I go home." Vanderkolk got to his feet a bit stiffly, went to the elevator, and punched the button.

I stood up, but my stomach stayed down. I might evade Vanderkolk's questions, but Jim wouldn't. He might not want Arnie arrested and taken back to Michigan, but he'd work it out on a cop-to-cop level. He'd tell Vanderkolk who Alan Matthews was today, and that he was a suspect in a new murder.

Unless . . . a bit if hope entered my mind. Maybe Vanderkolk's trip to Grantham was as unofficial as Mike's trip to Jessamine had been. "Are you still an active law officer?" I asked.

"Yes and no. I'm no longer sheriff, but my nephew is, and he lets the old man have deputy status. I don't work a regular shift. But, like I mentioned on the phone, I transport prisoners for the county and for several other law enforcement agencies in western Michigan. I had to make a trip to Dallas, so I stopped by to find out what was going on."

Vanderkolk put his hand in his pants pocket and pulled out a set of keys. "You have something of your mother about you, Ms. Matthews."

"My mother's family always said I was like my dad."

"Your coloring, sure. But you've got the same look around the eyes your mother had."

"You knew her?"

"Oh, yes. She went to PTA at Jefferson Elementary School. Volunteered in the school library. My youngest son was in sixth grade that year. He—well, he had a big crush on her."

I wasn't sure if he meant this as a compliment. "I guess

all the boys liked her," I said. "I guess that was her problem."

Vanderkolk frowned. "I never thought there was much harm in her," he said. "She just thought she could get by on personality. Lots of people think that—men as well as women. They think the rules should be bent to accommodate them because they're cute. They're not content to go through channels. Then they're amazed when being cute isn't enough to keep them out of trouble."

The elevator opened, and Vanderkolk stepped into it. Then he put a hand against the edge of the door, holding it open.

"Your mom may have been foolish, but she sure didn't deserve what happened to her," he said. "I'm sorry about your family's troubles, Miss Matthews. But I've been lookin' for your dad for twenty years. I'm too old to stop now."

He smiled his grandfatherly smile again and moved his hand. The door slid smoothly shut.

I stared at the door. Vanderkolk had given me a couple of things to think about. First, as I'd anticipated, just because he was retired, he wasn't about to give up the hunt for Alan Matthews. Second, his view of my mother's personality had jibed almost exactly with Aunt Billie's and with my dad's. Sally Lathen Matthews had been "cute," and she had used that cuteness to get her way, ignoring the rules of life if they didn't suit her purposes. Vanderkolk had barely known her, but he had understood her personality.

There, I thought, is one slick lawman. I understood why Arnie had fled the country when he thought Vanderkolk was after him. The old Dutch sheriff and his gentle smile had scared me to pieces. And the most frightening thing about him was his similarity to Mike. They both had a way of seeming friendly and interested, and before you knew it, you were telling them things you hadn't intended to reveal.

It would have been interesting to see them quiz each other.

But I was too scared to speculate about that. I headed straight for the library, ready to report to Arnie. I glanced at one of the newsroom clocks. Nine o'clock. If Vanderkolk was going to see Jim Hammond, he'd probably have to wait until morning. So Arnie had a little more than twelve hours to decide what to do.

Would he run? Or stand his ground, sure that someone else had killed Martina and that that same someone killed my mother?

Would this be the last time I ever saw him?

I was mentally wringing my hands by the time I got to the library, ready to spill everything in Arnie's lap. So it was a complete let-down when it was empty. Arnie wasn't there.

I walked back to the city desk slowly, checking in the newsroom cubicles and looking over the tops of the partitions. Nothing and no one seemed out of place. Chuck, the night police reporter, was listening to something on the scanner. The city hall reporter was in; I knew he'd covered a speech the mayor made to a chamber of commerce dinner that evening. And the obit kid was frowning at a stack of faxed death notices.

There was no sign of Arnie. Where had he gone?

When I sat down at my terminal, Ruth was glaring at Teensy Ames, the dramatic brunette who was on the education beat. "You can go to Jake if you want to," she told Teensy. "But he doesn't appreciate the reporters going over my head. I don't appreciate it, either."

I looked at Teensy ruefully. Going over Ruth's head? I could tell her that was the dumbest thing a reporter could do in the *Gazette* newsroom. Ruth and Jake worked closely together. Jake rarely overturned one of Ruth's decisions, because if it wasn't cut and dried, Ruth consulted Jake before she made the decision.

I shook my head. Teensy was like my mother. Cute. And

they both used that cuteness to avoid work, to butter up news sources and other people they wanted help from. My mother hadn't seen why the Michigan rules for teachers should apply to her; she'd wanted a special deal.

I stared at my terminal and thought about my mother and my new knowledge of her personality. She'd been facing a real problem in Jessamine. Her unguarded tongue and her impulsive visit to the Elks Club bar had ruined her reputation in the small town. She and my father had agreed that the only recourse they had was to leave. But he hadn't been willing to quit his first job as managing editor when he'd had it less than a year. He had to prove to the small chain he worked for that he could cut the printers' ink there before he asked for a transfer. She'd disagreed. She'd wanted him to quit, if he had to, so she could get out of Jessamine.

So what would she have done?

The answer was plain. She'd have done just what Teensy Ames had threatened to do. She'd have gone over my father's head, tried to pull strings, called his boss and told him her husband needed a transfer immediately. She'd have relied on her cuteness to charm the boss into doing what she asked.

But had she done this? Arnie hadn't mentioned it. It would have humiliated him. I didn't even know who his boss had been. Would it have been the Jessamine business manager? Or would it have been someone from the chain, a district manager of some sort?

"Nell!" Ruth's voice made me jump. "What is going on?" she asked.

"What do you mean?"

"I can't seem to keep a copy editor on duty tonight. First you disappear. Then Arnie. Where is he?"

"I don't know, Ruth. I suppose he could be in the men's room."

"Well, he's got a problem, then." She pulled her phone

over and punched numbers. "He's a smoker. Maybe he went downstairs."

But whoever answered the break room phone denied that Arnie was taking a cigarette break. Ruth almost slammed the receiver into its cradle. "Well, I'm taking a break for a few minutes. Please read the planning-commission story while I'm gone. We can't move 4A until I get it."

I meekly opened the story. Ruth was madder than I'd ever seen her. I didn't blame her. Teensy was pulling an unprofessional stunt, and Arnie and I hadn't been exactly paying attention to business that evening.

Where was Arnie?

I assured myself that he would show up soon, and I began to read the planning-commission story. I forced myself to read it slowly and carefully, to push my personal problems out of my mind. I didn't want Ruth to throw it back at me. I read it three times and ran spell check on it before I sent it on to her file.

As if I didn't have enough problems, the phone rang.

"Hi," Mike's voice said. "I have a question for you."

I didn't answer, because I was debating with myself. Should I tell Mike about Vanderkolk? About Arnie, who might have to hit the road? Who might have already done that? It took me ten or fifteen seconds to decide not to say anything.

It simply wouldn't be fair to Mike to tell him about Vanderkolk. As a law officer, he couldn't advise Arnie to run. But as Arnie's daughter's boyfriend, he might not want to tell him he should give himself up, either. Better leave him out of it.

By then Mike was speaking again. "Nell? Are you there?"

"Yes, I'm here." My voice quavered. "Things are a little crazy right at the moment."

"One quick question. That chain of newspapers your dad worked for—was it Gordon Enterprises?"

"That sounds right. Why?"

"Just checking something out," Mike said. "Listen, kid, what's new?"

I gulped. He was telling me he loved me. "What's new with you?" I said.

"Nothing much. I'll talk to you later."

Mike hung up. At least he still was telling me he loved me. Would he still love me if Arnie ran away again? Could a cop love the daughter of a wanted man? But if Arnie stayed, Mike might develop another problem. Could a cop love the daughter of a convict?

Ruth came back, and I had to make some effort to clear out the Proof file before she clobbered me with her pica pole. She couldn't move her local pages until I did it.

So I read copy. I made myself read even the simplest stories twice, because I was having a terrible time concentrating. It took me more than a half hour, but I finally opened the last story.

Arnie still hadn't showed up when I finished editing that one and sent it on to Ruth. Then I called up the menu for the Proof file. I expected to find it empty, but here was a file named "note."

Was it the one I'd written Arnie? But surely he'd killed that one. Then I saw that instead of being marked "FYI, Arnie," it was marked "FYI, Nell."

Arnie had sent me a note.

I stood up and looked around the newsroom. He could have used any newsroom terminal to send a note to the city desk. So he must have been in the newsroom within the past few minutes. But I didn't see him.

I quickly opened the note. "Meet me in the basement ASAP," it read. "West end. I may have to hit the road. This has turned into a small disastrous situation."

"Small." There was that word again. I was surprised that Arnie would use it.

But the word it modified, disastrous, sure fit the situation. I fought the impulse to bang my head against the VDT screen. What could Arnie do? What could I do? Should I call Mike and tell him about the latest development? Or, as my grandmother used to say, should I cut my suspenders and go straight up?

Anyway, I had to see Arnie, if only to say good-bye. I got up without a word and walked across the newsroom and down the back stairs.

Chapter 27

I was heartsick. I was going to say good-bye to my dad. I'd known him only a few days, and he was leaving again.

I was blinking hard by the time I got to the second-floor landing. So I kept my head ducked as a figure in a blue uniform came up the stairs toward me. But the person called my name.

"Ms. Matthews?"

I looked up and saw a brush of crew-cut gray hair over a square jaw and bulky shoulders. It was Wes McLaird, the pressroom foreman.

"Yes?"

"Listen, I'm awful sorry about all the trouble Bob Johnson caused."

"It wasn't your fault."

"I feel real bad about it. If I hadn't fired him—"

"If he'd been drinking, you really didn't have any choice."

Wes sighed. "I could have handled it better. Told one of the guys to take him home, waited to talk to him the next day when I was calmer."

He shuffled his feet, and I ducked my head again and tried to walk forward. But Wes was still speaking. "I'm just relieved that you weren't hurt. Or your roommate—"

Wes went on talking, but I had quit listening. I was staring at the floor and at the marks on it.

Wes's shoes—steel-toed work shoes straight from the

pressroom—were covered with ink. As he shuffled from
foot to foot, he was leaving footprints. Their pattern looked
as if someone had been dancing. It looked like the ads I'd
seen back when I read teen magazines, ads offering to send
diagrams of maneuvers that could be used to learn the latest
dances.

The pattern looked familiar. This wasn't the first time I'd
seen patterns of inky footprints like those.

On the night when Martina was killed, I'd run into J.J.
Jones on the first-floor landing, one flight down from the
landing where Mac and I stood now. On that night I'd come
running down the stairs, and J.J. had come up, up from the
basement. We'd bumped into each other; then we'd both
jumped back, then jumped sideways, doing a little dance as
we tried to get around each other. The inky footprints had
been all over the floor.

I realized that J.J. had had ink on his shoes, just as Wes
did now.

But J.J. shouldn't have had ink on his shoes.

In the first place, in a modern newspaper the pressroom is
the only place ink is used, and J.J. would have had no reason to go clear to the basement to the pressroom. No reason,
at least, connected with his job. He edited special sections,
true. But they were built on computers on the second and
third floors, and there they were turned into film—into
photo negatives the size of a newspaper page. These were
used to make the aluminum plates that fit on the press and
actually impress a pattern on the newsprint. He would go to
the pressroom only on the occasions when one of his special
sections was being printed, to check it as the press run
began. A special section had run the night Martina was
gassed in the ladies' room—the night before she was kicked
down the stairs. Not on the night we had done our little
dance on the landing.

And in the second place, if J.J. had had some reason to go
the pressroom, he couldn't have gotten so much ink on his

feet that he tracked it clear up the stairs. It would have worn off in ten or twenty feet. Only old shoes like the ones Mac was wearing now would be so soaked with ink that they left inky footprints for that many steps away from its source. If J.J. had merely stepped in a spot of ink, it would have been gone from his foot after a few steps.

No ad man would hang out in the pressroom so much that his shoes were soaked with ink. For one thing, the pressmen wouldn't like him hanging around, getting in their way.

No, if the fastidious and stylish J.J. Jones had been wearing shoes that were thick with ink, they hadn't been his own shoes.

They could have been shoes he'd taken from the pressmen's locker room. They could have been shoes he'd worn to kick Martina downstairs. They could have been shoes he then hid in a newsroom desk, hoping to draw attention to Arnie and to his real identity as Alan Matthews—wanted man.

For a moment I was sure. J.J. Jones! J.J. must be the killer. But then I doubted. Why? What possible motive did J.J. Jones have for killing Martina? The only time Martina had ever mentioned him to me, she'd told me he got a rough deal from his ex-wife. She'd seemed sympathetic to him.

And why would he frame Arnie? He hadn't been in Michigan twenty years earlier, or at least his record didn't show that. He couldn't have had anything to do with my mother's death. Could he?

It was crazy. He couldn't be guilty.

But maybe—maybe the possibility of J.J.'s guilt would convince Arnie that he should stay in Grantham, that he shouldn't run again. Maybe I could ask Arnie to stick around until J.J. had been checked out.

I cut Wes off rudely, and I went on down the stairs toward the door to the basement. West end, Arnie had said. The break room was at the east end. Instead of entering the basement by the crazy metal grate and the circular iron staircase,

I'd go down the stairs at the other end of the building. The ones that connected the circulation and classified departments with the basement and that came out near the ladies' room where Martina was almost asphyxiated.

I clattered down them, my loafers rattling, and came out in the hall that gives access to the ladies' room. I went past it and entered the paper-storage area. Then I stopped and looked around.

Stretching off into the dim reaches of the basement were giant rolls of paper, some standing end on end and piled two and three high, and others lying on their sides like giant rolling pins. The bright industrial lighting blasted some areas, but left other areas in deep shadow. It was coffee-break time for the pressroom crew, and the basement was absolutely quiet.

It also seemed absolutely deserted. Anybody watching should have seen or heard me come out of the hall, but Arnie didn't call to me. He didn't step out of the shadows and beckon. He didn't seem to be there.

"Arnie!" I used a tone that was between a whisper and a shout. "Where are you?"

There was no answer.

I moved forward, down the yellow-outlined path demanded by safety regulations. Dead silence. And no sign of Arnie.

I walked halfway across the building, looking between the rolls of paper. Same deal. No noise, no Arnie, no indication he'd ever been there. I reached the area where the paper to be used that night and the next day was stored. These rolls lay on their sides, ready to be moved onto the elevator that took them down a level, to the sub-basement, where they'd be loaded onto the press.

I leaned against a half roll. It surprised me by rocking back and forth, and I jumped aside. Stupid, I told myself. That half roll weighed around a third of a ton. It wasn't going to roll over my foot unless I pushed it real hard.

I turned away from that area. The diameter of any roll of paper was between three and four feet, and these were lying on their sides, so they were easy to see over. They were in neat rows, lined up and touching each other. There was no way Arnie could be hiding among them.

Where could he be? I was far from the west end of the basement, the end Arnie had specified. But maybe Arnie had been confused. He was new in Grantham. Maybe he didn't know the west end from the east end. So I walked on, still looking down the lanes between the giant rolls of paper, until I was under the circular stairway. I could see a clean spot on the concrete. The place where Martina had fallen had been scrubbed until it was lighter than the rest of the floor.

This was getting too spooky for me. I looked longingly at the metal grate that served as a landing outside the break room, and the heavy soundproof door that separated the break room from the basement. There were always people in the break room.

If I'd heard a noise, I would have been up those stairs and into that room in under three seconds.

But I didn't hear a noise. There was no sound, no movement, no one around.

West end, I repeated to myself. Arnie said the west end. That's probably what he meant. I'll go back that way. I'll even look in the ladies' room. And if he isn't waiting for me this time, I'll go back upstairs.

I belatedly remembered that I'd promised Mike I wouldn't wander around the building alone. The reminder seemed to make the atmosphere grow even spookier.

But I steeled my resolution, and I turned and walked back the way I'd come. This time I looked carefully down every one of the gaps between the paper rolls. If there seemed to be more space hidden back there, I edged between the rolls and looked into it. I explored every corner, every crevice. All were empty.

I was nearly back to the door leading to the hall and the ladies' lounge when I heard a noise.

A groan.

It terrified me. I stopped and listened, but I didn't hear anything else. I looked down an aisle between rolls of paper, and this time I saw something.

Feet.

They wore brown Hush Puppies, and they were lying on their sides. They didn't move. The legs they were attached to disappeared behind one of the rolls of paper.

I tiptoed toward them. Don't ask me why I tiptoed. I'd been calling out and clicking my heels—my own way of whistling in the dark. If there was anybody there, he knew I was walking around, winding among the rolls of paper. But now I tiptoed, barely breathing, as if the feet might disappear if I made a sound.

When I reached the feet and looked around the roll of paper that hid their owner, I got down on my knees.

"Arnie!" I said. "Dad!"

He lay on his stomach, with his arms hidden under his body. His face was turned sideways, and blood was pooling under his bald head.

But he was breathing.

I had never been so grateful in my life as at that moment when I saw Arnie's rib cage move, when I heard him take a rasping breath.

He needed help.

I jumped to my feet, and a terrible noise came from behind me. A blast echoed off the girders and the concrete floor, and a ragged hole appeared in the side of a roll of paper, just even with where my head had been a second earlier.

I had to stare at the hole before I realized the noise had been a shot.

This time there was no heavy wooden door to hide behind, no storm door to shatter. I was standing on a bare floor, with rows of massive rolls of paper in front of me and on both sides. And the shot had come behind me.

I whirled. Behind me, crammed into a niche I had passed without seeing, was J.J. Jones. He was holding a shiny silver revolver.

My God! I thought. He really is guilty.

"What are you doing?" I yelled. Which was the ultimate stupid question. He was obviously trying to kill me and my father.

J.J. didn't answer. His face had lost any trace of his fabled good humor. He looked steely grim and deadly calm as he raised the pistol and aimed again.

I don't know why I didn't scream. True, there was no one to hear me, but that wasn't the reason I kept quiet. The thought that came flashing through from my subconscious was that J.J. Jones couldn't hit a moving target.

If he'd been the man in the van, he'd taken three shots at the flower-delivery boy and me, and he didn't hit anything but the storm door. And now, at a range of no more than fifteen feet, he'd missed me because I jumped to my feet.

I began to leap back and forth, waving my hands wildly. I jumped around like a playful chimp, zigzagging back and forth, moving toward him, trying to get out of the box canyon of paper rolls where I was trapped.

"Damn you!" He muttered the words. His pistol swung back and forth. Another shot went off, but it missed again. And this time I ran straight toward him, trying to get past, out into the main part of the warehouse.

And then a door opened.

It was the door to the break room, far at the other end of the basement. Voices reverberated, and I opened my mouth to scream.

But J.J. got me. He couldn't aim well enough to shoot me with his pistol, but he whacked me upside the head with it. The blow hurt. It also knocked me sideways. By the time I had caught my balance, he had grabbed me.

He had a hand around my jaw, keeping my mouth shut, and he had me shoved up against a roll of paper. His face was inches from mine, and he had the pistol jammed into my side.

He didn't say anything. But if he pulled the trigger, the bullet was definitely not going to miss.

"Don't think I won't shoot," he said in a hoarse whisper. "Just because the pressmen are back. What have I got to lose? If you tell about those footprints, I've had it anyway."

I couldn't believe how strong he was. Or perhaps it was his considerable heft keeping me immobile. He was leaning his whole body against me. I was squashed against the hard, slick paper.

Then I heard a groan.

J.J. moved sideways, keeping his hand over my mouth. But now he aimed the pistol at Arnie.

Arnie was stirring, but he was still unconscious. He couldn't jump up and dodge around to avoid being shot. He was a sitting duck.

J.J. spoke grimly. "Are you ready to keep your mouth shut?"

I tried to nod.

J.J.'s grip on my jaw yanked me forward. He threw me across the little open area. I landed heavily, lying across Arnie's feet.

J.J. moved in close. "Just keep your mouth shut until the presses roll," he said. "Maybe I'll let you go then."

I got up on my knees, and I moved around until I could sit down and lean back against a roll of paper. I tried to turn Arnie over, but he was a dead weight and I couldn't budge him. I lifted his head enough to slide under him, to put his head in my lap. The wound was still oozing blood, but it didn't look like a bullet hole. It looked as if J.J. had hit him, with the pistol or with some other heavy object. The skin was broken, but the wound wasn't deep.

Arnie rolled over onto his side, and I realized his hands

were bound. J.J. had taped his hands together with pieces of masking tape. I'd seen similar tape in the back shop. He'd probably stolen a roll somewhere.

Arnie stirred again. He'd be conscious soon. But that might make the situation worse. If he moved around or groaned loudly as he regained his senses, J.J. might panic and shoot us both.

With the pressmen working in the other end of the basement, J.J. wouldn't want to fire his pistol. The sound would reverberate off the hard rolls of paper, off the concrete ceiling and walls, off the metal girders and plumbing pipes and air-conditioning ductwork that snaked around the ceiling.

But once the press started, once its roaring and clicking began and the pressmen had put on their ear protectors, J.J. could shoot us both dead without worrying about anybody hearing. And he could get out of the building without being seen.

And it was getting close to press time.

Mike should be here, I thought wildly. Arnie and I were hostages. Mike was a hostage negotiator. He would know what to do. I didn't.

I rested my head against the paper roll at my back and took several deep breaths. Mike didn't talk a lot about his law enforcement specialty, but I'd picked up some of the principles—as a reporter and as a girlfriend.

Don't rush the hostage taker. That was one principle. But we didn't have much time. The presses were due to roll soon.

Keep 'em talking. That was another principle. Keep the hostage taker talking.

Maybe I could get J.J. to talk.

"J.J., why are you doing this?" I said.

He showed his teeth, but I can't say he smiled. It was more like the snarl of a cornered animal. He didn't answer me.

I tried again. "What's all this about?"

The teeth flashed again.

I remembered the inky footprints on the landing, the foot-prints J.J. had mentioned. And I lied. "It can't be Martina. You had no reason to kill her."

That time he snarled out loud. "The bitch! Everybody who knew her had a reason to kill her."

"Yes, but she liked you! She told me you'd gotten a rough deal. She had a lot of sympathy for you."

"Yeah, and her sympathy was going to send me right to prison!"

"How?"

"Shut up!"

That ended the conversation pretty effectively. Arnie stirred and opened one eye. I squeezed his hand. "Shhh," I whispered. "Shhh."

The eye stared around dully, and he moved again. "Shhh," I said. "Just lie still."

Arnie closed his eye, then opened it again. This time the eye looked as if it was actually focusing on something; it looked alert and conscious. He squeezed my hand. His body lost its frightening limpness.

"J.J. says we can go after the presses roll," I said. "Just lie still."

A sardonic, unbelieving expression passed over Arnie's face. I was sure he was awake enough to catch on to the situation. He knew we were hostages, that J.J. intended to kill us.

J.J. spoke suddenly, his voice an urgent whisper, "Is he awake?"

"Not really," I said. "How did you get him down here?"

He laughed. "Just like I got you down here. Sent him a message on the computer. Told him to meet you here."

"I didn't know you were that familiar with the newsroom system," I said. I tried to sound admiring.

"It's easy! That bitch Martina showed me how to use it when I started working on special sections."

"Special sections! Oh! That's how you—" I broke off. There was no use telling him I'd figured out how he knew where Mike's mother ordered flowers, and where Grantham's used-car dealers kept their keys. J.J. had edited the New Homes section, and I knew it had included an interview with Wilda Svenson, one of Grantham's leading realtors. He could easily have learned about her custom of sending flowers to clients. He'd edited the Used Car Buying section, too. So he could have visited car lots, figured out easy ways to steal first an old Cadillac and then a van to use in attacking me.

J.J. was reading my mind. "Now you know how I got hold of the Caddy." He laughed. "You're a hotshot driver."

I shook my head. Maybe I could keep him talking. "I guess we had it all wrong," I said. "After the shoes were found in Arnie's desk, I figured somebody was trying to call attention to him, to link him up with my mother's murder twenty years ago."

J.J. looked sharply at me.

"But you had nothing to do with that, did you? It was in Michigan. You've always worked in Texas, right?"

He showed his teeth again. "That's right, little lady. Ah'm a Texan through and through. Born and bred. Ever since the day I turned twenty-five and got the hell out of Wichita."

"Wichita! You're from Kansas?"

Suddenly, like a voice from heaven, my name was shouted through the basement.

"Nell Matthews. Please call extension 1110."

I jumped all over, and I was happy to see J.J. shrink back against the roll of paper behind him.

"They're paging me," I said.

"You're not going to answer," J.J. said.

No more than thirty seconds went by before the intercom system screamed again. "Arnie Ashe. Arnie Ashe. Please call city desk, extension 1110."

"Both the copy editors have disappeared," I said. "Ruth must be furious. She'll send somebody looking for us."

J.J.'s grin looked almost genial. "They won't look down here."

He checked his watch, and I peeked at mine. It was getting very close to press time. My heart pounded. What should I do? I couldn't stand the thought of sitting there, idly talking to J.J., while we waited for the press to roll, waited for the noise that would cover the shots that would kill my father and me.

Arnie's eyes were open now, though he was still lying limply, pretending to be semiconscious. Should I shove Arnie's head off my lap and run for it? If J.J. chased me, Arnie might have a chance.

Down at the other end of the basement, the door to the break room opened and shut.

J.J. lifted the pistol, his face grim. "Quiet!" he said.

I sat rigid. I knew the door wasn't a chance at rescue. People went in and out that door all the time. They used it to cut through to the ground-floor loading docks as well as to reach the basement.

But the noise of the door made me look that way, and for the first time I realized that I could see part of that landing and the stairs. Because of some weird variation in the way the paper rolls were stacked, there was a crack that let me see out into the yellow walkway, and at the end of that walkway was the circular metal staircase that had been a death-trap for Martina.

Ed Brown was standing on the landing, clutching his clipboard.

I looked at J.J. He had gotten to his knees, only a few feet away. The pistol was aimed at Arnie's back, almost touching him. No, I didn't dare move.

J.J. whispered. "Quiet!"

I sat paralyzed. Ed kept looking around the basement. He

didn't go down the stairs, and he didn't go into the warehouse, and he didn't go back into the break room.

J.J. was holding his breath, but he aimed his pistol at Ed.

And Arnie casually rolled over and sat up. He held his hands out in front of him.

"What the hell is going on?" he asked. "My head is killing me. And why are my hands tied like this?"

Chapter 28

I think Arnie's very casualness kept him from being shot. J.J. simply gaped.

Then Arnie pulled his bound wrists up to his chest, almost prayerfully. He reached the fingers of his right hand into his shirt pocket, pulled out a cigarette and a throwaway lighter. And he flicked the lighter into flame.

That got a reaction. J.J. whacked his arm with the pistol, and the lighter went flying.

Arnie clutched his arms against his chest. "Sorry," he said. "Is this the no-smoking section?"

"Shut up!" J.J. hissed it out.

I pressed myself back against the roll of paper. Had Ed Brown seen the lighter's glow? Had he heard our voices across the length of the basement? Could he have heard the click of the lighter? Would he know that someone was hidden in a cubby hole between the massive cylinders of paper? Would he guess that it was Arnie and me?

I looked down the slit between the rolls of paper, and I saw that Ed was still standing on the metal landing, still clutching his clipboard and looking around the basement.

The basement probably looked entirely normal to him. He hadn't seen the lighter's flash, hadn't heard our voices.

Ed turned around and went back into the break room. I was sure he wasn't going for help. My heart sank.

J.J. looked at his watch, and his action made me check mine. The press was going to roll at any minute. We had only seconds before the pressmen put on their earmuffs and punched the proper buttons. The noise from the press would fill the basement. The noise and the ear protectors would provide all the cover J.J. could want for gunshots.

We had only minutes to live.

If only Ed Brown had seen us, if only he'd known we were there. If only he'd realized we were hostages—he could have called Mike.

Hostages were Mike's specialty. He would know what to do. I felt absolutely helpless.

Then Arnie spoke to J.J. "Is it this lousy headache, or do I not know you?"

J.J. sneered and smiled. "I'm sure your daughter won't mind introducing us," he said.

Arnie slowly turned his head toward me. "He knows the big secret, Nell. So who is he?"

"He's one of the *Gazette*'s ad men," I said. "He does all the special sections. His name is J.J Jones."

Arnie's head yanked back in J.J.'s direction. Then he groaned and held it again.

J.J. laughed. "You didn't recognize me? Fair enough. I'd never have recognized you if Martina hadn't figured it out." He carefully aimed the pistol at Arnie. "But you remembered the name, huh?"

"I remember the name Jimmy J. Jones." Arnie frowned. "But what did it matter if I remembered the name? I was the one Martina could send to jail. Not you. You weren't around when Sally was killed."

J.J. laughed.

I couldn't face dying with my curiosity unsatisfied. "Who is he?" I asked Arnie. "Who was he?"

"Jimmy J. Jones was my boss when we were in Michigan," Arnie said. "He worked out of Memphis as area manager for Gordon Enterprises, Inc. They owned the *Jessamine Journal*."

He raised his head and looked at J.J. levelly. "In those

days he was also the son-in-law of the chain's owner. What happened to your soft spot, Jimmy? Did your wife toss you out? And the job went along with the marriage?"

"Thanks to your slutty little wife!"

Arnie's fist clenched.

"I don't understand all this," I said. "Were you involved with my mother? Did you have an affair?"

J.J. turned and glared at me. "No! That's the irony of the whole thing. The little bitch led me on, but she never came through."

I heard Arnie exhale a long breath. It was almost like another groan.

"How did you even know her?" I asked.

"He met her when he came to Amity to interview me for the Jessamine job," Arnie said.

"Yeah," J.J. said. "And she was really interested then! All over me. So what was I supposed to think when she called me, wanted me to meet her in Holland!"

"She called you?" Arnie sounded amazed.

"Sure. When I named a motel for a meeting place, she didn't even hesitate. Said yes right away. Said she'd be there. She was a tease! Just a tease!"

Arnie was clenching his fist again. I put my hand over it, and I spoke. "Yes, I think she probably was a tease, J.J. Everyone agrees that she was cute and flirtatious."

"But she didn't mean anything by it," Arnie said.

"No, she didn't," I said. "She simply thought she could use her cuteness to get what she wanted. And right then she wanted out of Jessamine, Michigan."

J.J. didn't speak.

"That's why she wanted to meet you, wasn't it?" I said. "She wanted to get a transfer for Arnie—for Alan."

J.J. laughed harshly. "I drove all that way, put the motel on the extra credit card—the one my bitch wife wasn't supposed to know about—and all she wanted to do was talk about her husband."

I glanced at Arnie. A tear was rolling down his cheek.

J.J. waved his pistol back and forth, aiming first at Arnie, then at me. "But she still managed to ruin my life!"

"How did she do that?" I had to keep him talking.

"She called my office two days later. Left a message. And when I called back, she threatened me! Said she'd tell her husband about my 'improper proposals,' said she'd make sure my wife and my goddamn father-in-law found out unless I got that transfer for Alan! She had me in small trouble."

There was that expression again! I gasped. "You! You're the one who called the house the night before she was killed. You're the one who said that on the phone! It wasn't my dad!"

J.J. didn't answer, but he looked at his watch again. "I can't wait any longer!" he said. "Why don't they start the press?"

Arnie inhaled, as if he was going to speak, but at that moment we heard footsteps on the back stairs, the ones I'd come down.

"Quiet!" J.J. craned his neck, trying to see between the rolls of paper. I looked through my own crevice. I saw one of the younger pressmen. He came down the back stairs and went past us and toward the pressroom.

"This is the last plate!" he called.

J.J. leaned back against the paper behind him. "It won't be long now." He muttered the words to himself.

It takes only seconds to fit a plate on the press. We had only seconds to live.

I guess I should have folded my hands and made my peace with God. Instead I stretched out my fingers and rebelled. If I was going to die—if Arnie was going to die—I wasn't ready for us to die meekly. If I was going to be shot, I wanted to be shot with my hands around J.J. Jones' throat.

I got to my knees. "Arnie," I said. "It's been nice knowing you."

He seemed to understand immediately. "Right," he said. He got to his knees, too.

"Stay still." J.J. snarled and raised the pistol.

And then everything happened at once.

I heard the final bell that signaled that the press was about to run, followed immediately by the rumbles and the clicks that meant it was starting up.

The break room door opened again, and Mike came through it. He didn't pause on the landing. He started right down the stairs, and he didn't slow down until he was around the first curve. Then he stopped to look around.

J.J. raised his pistol and pointed it at him. I knew Mike was a clear target, an unmoving target, the kind J.J. might be able to hit.

I shrieked. "Mike! Get down!"

J.J.'s pistol went off. Mike did a sommersault over the railing. I couldn't tell if he landed on his feet or in a heap, dead on the concrete floor.

The press began to gather speed. Like a train leaving the station, it grew louder.

And Arnie jumped up and butted his bald and bleeding head into J.J.'s side.

The two of us jumped on him. Arnie's hands were tied, and I'm not the most coordinated person in the world, and J.J. was desperate. It wasn't easy.

Our fight was surreal. I'm sure we were all yelling, and once I saw a blackened hole appear in a roll of paper, so I know J.J. fired at least one shot, but the thunder of the press kept us from hearing anything.

Then J.J. used his pistol to whack Arnie in the head again. Arnie sagged. J.J. rolled him aside, and he whammed me back against a roll of paper. He was on his feet.

I rolled over, and another blackened hole appeared just over my head. I tried to remember how to be a moving target, but J.J. had dashed out of our box canyon and was headed back toward the circular iron stairway.

I was flooded with relief. Then I remembered that Mike was down there. Mike had fallen off the iron stairway and might be lying helpless on the basement floor. He might already be dead.

I tried to follow J.J., but Arnie jumped up, too. He and I tried to get out of the narrow passageway at the same time, and it didn't work. By the time we got out into the yellow walkway, I could see J.J. waving his pistol and looking up at the tops of the rolls of paper.

This section was only one roll high—about four feet. And Mike was on top of it. He was running along, bent over to keep from hitting his head on a plumbing pipe or getting tangled in the wiring that drooped from the ceiling.

J.J. was standing still and raising his pistol—belatedly realizing that he might actually hit something if he took a steady aim. Mike was loping along, dragging his knuckles like a chimpanzee, headed toward J.J.

I started to run at J.J., ready to use any method to disturb his aim at Mike. But Arnie used his bound hands to punch me and shouted, "Come on!"

By a fluke J.J. was near the section of the basement in which the paper for tomorrow's press run had been placed. The rolls were stored on their sides, ready to be maneuvered onto the paper carts and shoved into the pressroom.

It took Arnie and me only a second to get to the giant rolls. As the two of us pushed, we were able to rock the roll of paper, all three-quarters of a ton of it, and move it forward enough to get behind it. Then we ducked down behind it and shoved, rolling it ahead of us like a lawnmower.

Mike could see what we were doing, and his face grew horror-stricken. It must have been his expression that made J.J. turn halfway around.

He fired a shot, but he fired it at the roll of paper. And a bullet is meaningless when it comes to stopping three-quarters of a ton of newsprint wound solidly around a cardboard core.

The giant roll of paper whacked J.J. down like a cartoon character.

But it didn't leave him flattened into a spot of grease. It stopped after it ran over his right leg, like a rolling pin crushing cracker crumbs. It crushed his right leg to the knee.

What followed was extremely confusing. Mike jumped down from the top of the paper rolls.

I yelled at him. "What were you doing up there?"

Mike yelled something back, but of course, I couldn't understand him. He pointed at me, then to the circular staircase. He used his thumbnail to trace "911" on a roll of paper.

As I got to the break room, Jim Hammond came running in, and he and Ed Brown told me to make the ambulance call myself. They rushed to the basement, and when I followed them a few minutes later they were standing on the metal grid, waving their arms and arguing about what to do. Then Ed climbed into the forklift and used its arms to lift the roll of paper off J.J.'s leg.

J.J. had fainted. His pain must have been excruciating, but I can't say I felt very sorry for him.

Arnie put his arms around me, and I sat on a half roll and shook. And still, at the other end of the basement, the pressmen in their earmuffs went about the business of printing the *Gazette*. The first-edition run was nearly over before the ambulance came.

After they'd taken J.J. away, one of the EMT's checked Arnie and ordered him off to the hospital as well. I went with him, and we were waiting for the doctor when Mike put his head in the door to the examining room, then joined us.

"Just how did you come to be galloping in on your cavalry horse just as the presses rolled?" I asked.

"I read the message on your VDT."

"Oh! I guess I was so excited when I saw it that I just got up and left the office without killing it."

Mike nodded. "We were already looking for J.J., and Ruth

told us that J.J. Jones knew enough about the newsroom computers to send such a message."

"You were looking for J.J.? How did you know he was the one?"

"Pure routine. Boone kept checking on those employment records, and he found out that twenty years ago J.J. Jones was district manager for a mid-sized chain of newspapers. His territory would have included Michigan, even though he lived in Memphis."

"That's why you called and double-checked the name of the chain Arnie worked for!"

"Right. Boone called Jones's ex-wife, Margaret Gordon Jones, and she told him she'd gotten a divorce because of his womanizing. And, yes, she'd suspected he'd been involved with your mother."

"He wasn't," I said. "But he wanted to be. My mother threatened to tell his wife and his father-in-law that he'd made a pass at her."

Mike nodded. "Her threat gave him a motive for killing your mother. Then he let your dad take the rap. But two years later, or so his wife says, their taxes were audited, and she found some credit-card records that showed he'd been in Holland, Michigan, the night your mother was killed—when he was supposed to be someplace else."

Mike turned to Arnie. "I don't think she realized he'd killed Nell's mother."

"She probably thought he and Sally were involved—just the way I thought Sally had a boyfriend," Arnie said.

"She says she held him morally accountable for Sally Matthews' death," Mike said. "But she still thought Sally had been killed by Alan, by her own husband. She didn't offer to tell the Michigan authorities the name of Sally's boyfriend because she didn't want to be mixed up in a scandal. She divorced J.J., shoved him out of his job with the newspaper chain, and went on. But eighteen years later, J.J.

turned up on the ad staff of a paper that employed Martina Gilroy."

"And Martina knew everybody's business," I said.

"Well, at least she knew the business of the former Mrs. J.J. Jones," Mike said. "She'd graduated from the University of Missouri with her."

"I remember! Martina and Dan Smith's wife and Margaret Gordon Jones were college classmates."

"So when Martina checked that Eastwick College yearbook and realized that the Alan Matthews of twenty years ago was the Arnie Ashe of today—Martina probably figured out that J.J. had known Alan Matthews, so she might have asked him to take a look at Arnie to confirm her identification."

"But why would that bother J.J.?" Arnie asked. "He wasn't the man who was wanted in Sally's death."

"His wife could easily have told Martina that he'd been involved with Sally Matthews," Mike said. "Martina might not have realized that this made J.J. the missing suspect in Sally Matthews's death. But you, Alan Matthews, always thought the man she'd met at the motel was the one who killed her. If you found out that J.J. had been in Holland at the right time—if you told Ronald Vanderkolk, and he looked into it—"

"It would still have been 'small' trouble for J.J.," I said.

"He had to act fast," Mike said. "First he tried to asphyxiate Martina—and to make it look like an accident. A guy who had spent his whole adult life around newspapers would have known enough about the mechanical department to do that. When that didn't work, he stole the coveralls and shoes from a basement locker, kicked Martina down the stairs, and then beat her head against the concrete floor until she was dead."

I shuddered. Both Mike and Arnie reached out toward me. Then Mike's lips tightened, and he moved away. Arnie took my hand.

"If Martina's death had been passed off as an accident, he would have been in the clear," Mike said. "But Nell and I found the jacket with the footprint. So he hid the stolen shoes in Arnie's desk to call attention to him. Later he hid the bloody coveralls at Bob Johnson's house as another little smoke screen."

"And I did have a motive," Arnie said. "I did not want to go back to Michigan and face trial for a crime I didn't commit. I was still convinced that the man Sally met at the motel had killed her, but I had no idea who he was." He touched his head. "J.J. Jones never crossed my mind. Guess I couldn't picture somebody named Jones registering at a motel as Smith."

The doctor came in then and examined Arnie. He wanted to insist that Arnie stay overnight, but Arnie resisted. He didn't think he'd been unconscious more than a few minutes. The doctor relented when Arnie pointed out that he'd only been at the *Gazette* three weeks and wasn't yet covered by our health insurance. The doctor finally agreed to let him go home, if someone stayed with him.

The doctor turned to me. "You're his daughter? You'll have to wake him up every hour all night. Make sure his pupils are the same size. Make sure he's conscious. Any problems? Call right away."

Since Arnie had moved back into his own apartment, I said I'd sleep on his couch that night.

Mike drove Arnie home, while I went by my house to pick up a toothbrush and some clean underwear. By the time I got there, sometime after two a.m., Arnie was already in bed.

"I checked his pupils fifteen minutes ago," Mike said. He reached for his jacket. "Try to get some sleep. And call me if anything happens."

"Don't go for a minute. I want to talk to you."

"Sure."

I took the jacket from his hand and laid it over the back of a chair. Then I took his hand and led him to Arnie's couch. I kept hold of his hand after we sat down.

"What's the problem?" Mike asked.

"Mike, you're not jealous of Arnie, are you?"

He grinned and put his arm around me. "Maybe I am. Don't tell me it's stupid, because I already know that."

"Arnie and I are just getting acquainted. I suppose I have been sort of obsessed with him lately—"

Mike laughed. "I've always told you I'm a spoiled only child," he said. He leaned back into the corner of the couch, pulling me against him and resting his chin on the top of my head.

"You know, Nell, in addition to your intelligence, charm, beauty, and great body, you've had another attribute of the perfect girlfriend."

"Golly! Something besides intelligence, charm, beauty, and a great body? I'm a paragon!"

"True."

"Not true," I said. "Well, what's my other good quality?"

"In the past you've been an orphan." Mike hugged me. "It wasn't so great for you, but it had its advantages for me. You haven't had a family! I mean, you didn't have one you were close to. There was no problem about going to my mother's house for Thanksgiving, no argument over our quiet Christmas at my house, no required visits to Grandma on Sunday afternoon, no interfering questions from a bossy mom. And you've been patient about putting up with my family—"

"There's just your mother, really. And she has her own life."

"—but now things are going to be different. You need to be obsessed with Arnie for a while, really get to know him." He kissed the top of my head. "I'll get used to that. I'll even get used to him riding me about when we're going to get married."

"Has he done that?"

"You betcha. He's looking out for his little girl's interests. Just the way a daddy's supposed to do."

I had to gulp a few times. "Don't let him push you into anything you don't want to do."

"I won't. Besides, I promised you I wouldn't do it for another nine days."

"And you always keep your promises."

"The important ones. Unless the circumstances change."

"Have our circumstances changed?"

"Maybe. Maybe they've gotten even better." He slid down on the couch, and so did I, so that we were lying side by side. He nuzzled. I caressed. We both snuggled.

"Nine days," I said. "Nine days."

SIGNET (0451)

NATIONAL BESTSELLING AUTHOR

BARBARA PARKER

"Sex and danger...top-drawer suspense."
—*New York Times Book Review*

☐CRIMINAL JUSTICE   184742—$6.99

☐BLOOD RELATIONS   184734—$6.99

☐SUSPICION OF GUILT   177037—$5.99

"Superb...masterful suspense...hot, smoldering, and tangy." —*Boston Herald*

☐SUSPICION OF INNOCENCE   173406—$5.99

Prices slightly higher in Canada

Payable in U.S. funds only. No cash/COD accepted. Postage & handling: U.S./CAN. $2.75 for one book, $1.00 for each additional, not to exceed $6.75; Int'l $5.00 for one book, $1.00 each additional. We accept Visa, Amex, MC ($10.00 min.), checks ($15.00 fee for returned checks) and money orders. Call 800-788-6262 or 201-933-9292, fax 201-896-8569; refer to ad #PKR

Penguin Putnam Inc.   Bill my: ☐Visa ☐MasterCard ☐Amex_____(expires)
P.O. Box 12289, Dept. B   Card#_____
Newark, NJ 07101-5289   Signature_____
Please allow 4-6 weeks for delivery.
Foreign and Canadian delivery 6-8 weeks.

Bill to:
Name_____
Address_____City_____
State/ZIP_____
Daytime Phone #_____

Ship to:
Name_____   Book Total $_____
Address_____   Applicable Sales Tax $_____
City_____   Postage & Handling $_____
State/ZIP_____   Total Amount Due $_____

This offer subject to change without notice.